444

RELVIN GONZALEZ

BIRTHMARK PUBLISHING

For everyone who, against all odds, keeps on fighting.

CONTENTS

BOOK 1
HEFND

BOOK 2
PATH OF THE HYBRIDS

PART 1

PART 2

PART 3

BOOK 3
MESSENGERS RISING

BOOK 4

I AM THE DOOR

THE VOID BEYOND THE WALLS
A PREVIEW

BOOK 1

HEFND

CHAPTER 1

Slaughter brought me to life on the last night of Yule. I was thirteen years of age, but whatever had happened before existed only beyond the fog of that night. The festivities had ended, and the entire settlement reeked of mead. I had tried to tell my father of my visions, of the shadow walkers arriving under the moonlight, but I knew he would not listen. Not that day. My words were lost to the memories attached to the festival, for it also signaled my birth many years ago, when my father gained a son, but lost a wife.

"Why must we do this?" I said, looking for a candidate for the Yule log fifty steps outside our settlement. The muffled sound of drums indicated the farmers had arrived at the temple with their sacrificial animals.

"Because your father asked us to," Bjarke said, a strong man with a serious face whose only job was watching over my every breath. "Now keep quiet and look. I want to be back before nightfall."

I touched every felled trunk, knocking on it, picking it up with Bjarke's help and inspecting it. "Not good enough," I said. "None of these are."

Bjarke stared at me for a long time. "Will you force me to take down a tree in this cold?"

"It is not that cold."

He exhaled. "Very well." And he readied his axe.

"Wait," I said.

"What?"

"Don't you hear it?" I meant the sound of rushing steps on the snow.

Bjarke motioned his hand with a stern look and asked me to stay put without uttering a word. He strengthened his grip and ventured out with his axe, disappearing into the white forest.

"Bjarke?" I said. The drums seemed louder now, and so did the beating in my chest. And in the rhythmic silence, the steps were clearer than ever, coming closer. I reached for a weapon even though I knew there was nothing there and shivered.

I gasped at the whooshing sound that flashed in front of me at a hair's distance, striking a nearby tree.

"That one," Bjarke said, spreading leafless branches with one arm and walking toward me. "We can take that log to the celebration." He pulled the axe from the trunk. "Have you frozen, boy? It is not that cold." He said, his lip slightly rising at the corner.

Bjarke had me carry the log by myself. He said it was about time I began my journey to manhood. And so we headed to the celebration and arrived at the grotesque killing of the animals over the altars—the same animals we would eat at the feast later on.

I carried the log as close to my father as I could, and let it fall and roll a few inches in front of him. Its rough bark had scratched my hands, but I did not allow the pain or the cold to show.

"He did all the work," Bjarke said and winked when I turned to him.

With the log now burning in the hall, a symbol of the return of light and the lengthening of days, the feast began.

My father sat next to me, following his toast to Odin.

"Eat, boy," he said, his voice slight under the music of the skalds.

I put a piece of meat in my mouth but spit it out under the table when Bjarke spoke in his ear, a routine I repeated until my plate was empty. Once the feast was over, I crept out of the great hall with a stomach full of throbbing hunger.

After an hour in bed, tossing and turning under the wool, I rose and looked at the moon. I found it soothing when it appeared cut in half, its light coming into the longhouse and falling over me. I was mesmerized by the moon's beauty when I heard it once more. The crunching sound of footsteps focused my attention on the snow outside, every nerve in my body thrumming. I rushed to wake my father, but I found him already standing, peaking out the door, his majestic sword in one hand, and the other resting on a timber post to keep himself from falling. He placed a finger on his lips when he saw me.

"Eindride," he whispered and burped, "Go, my boy, quiet into the night. Remember our training. Wake the others, as many as you can—men to fight, the rest to survive—then go to the hiding place and wait for me there."

I always did whatever my father asked for without question, even in the face of death. Especially so. For he always knew what needed to be done and employed the actions necessary to achieve it.

I couldn't see them, but I smelled them, heard them dragging their feet slowly throughout the settlement, waiting to ambush us all at once. And so I moved swiftly behind horses and piles of hay, crawled through tall patches of grass, blending as one under the snowfall, and sneaked into the next longhouse.

With a finger over my lips, I touched the sleeping men of each house on the shoulder, and they nodded. The women and children moved to a subterranean hiding place we had built under the great hall deeper in the village. I had to awaken the family inside the last longhouse. There was a shadow approaching the door, but this was the most important house of all, for my friend Liv was inside. Liv was important to the settlement and had shown promise in knife carving and throwing, though I valued her for reasons that ran deeper than her utility in battle.

I gathered snow, rounded it inside my hands, and threw the compacted, hard snowball at the shadow, and immediately ran toward the back of the house. The provoked shadow walked in the direction the snowball had come from, swearing into the night. I quickened my step. I pushed the door slightly and squeezed into the house. I found the family already huddled in the middle.

"Eindride!" Liv's face was illuminated by the moonlight coming in from the roof, and my efforts were reinvigorated.

"Take them," Liv's father said, a heavyset man with a long, red beard and eyes that had seen death, though not as much as my father. "And Eindride," he said, turning to Liv, then back to me. "Be careful, boy."

I nodded. Liv's father rushed out toward the shadow which had resumed its position at the door of the house. He rammed the shadow to the ground, and I grabbed Liv by the hand and sneaked us out toward the great hall, her mother running behind us, struggling to catch up.

A few steps away from the great hall, I looked back at Liv's mother and said, "Run! We must—"The hiss of an arrow stopped me from finishing, and Liv's mother cried out. She placed her hand over a red burgeoning blot in her chest and dropped to the snow-dusted stones. I saw it clearly. Liv was about to turn around, but I pulled her forward with all my strength and into the great hall.

"Mother!" she said. "We must go back for her." She pushed and pulled away from me, rushing toward the door. I could only grasp at her cloak before she bolted away.

I chased after her until she stopped when she saw the truth lying on the snow.

"She's gone, Liv," I said, covering her with her cloak. What I saw in her eyes was not grief, not sadness, but determination.

We stepped back inside the great hall and folded over a piece of the rug to reveal the entrance to the hiding place. The swords outside clashed.

Keeping the hatch open to whoever might still be outside, I looked out the open door of the great hall and caught a glimpse of a man. I knew it by his stance, the confidence in his every move, the racing in my heart—a Viking warlord.

"Eindride, close it. Close it now," Liv cried, and pulled me down the ladder. But it had been too late. The warlord had parried my father's attack, and in an upswing, thrusted his sword into my father's abdomen. Father crumbled to the ground, his sword buried into the snow away from his body.

I lunged forward, but Liv held me down. "Our moment will come, but not today, Eindride."

We had emerged from our hiding place once the settlement was silent, and I rushed out the great hall to kneel over my father's corpse. My hands were turning blue by the time I found his sword buried in the snow. And when I held it, a woman put a bear coat on my back and pulled me inside. "We need you alive," she said. I understood what she meant twenty years later, for in time I became the Jarl of the settlement. And we lived there, on the land plains of Norway, where I watched my settlement rebuild with the seasons.

Yet, even as a man, my mind never strayed far from the warlord's image. My spirit was born anew each day to the embers of Loki and Angerboda, with a desire to reach for things just beyond my boundaries. The billowing fire of Muspelheim and the frost from Niflheim had met and sparked the unsettling forces within me. The eyes of the warlord that had killed my father had taken me hostage and robbed me of my childhood, my death, and everything in between. According to our ancestors, the elements from which all life began clashed in the gaping abyss and spawned Ymir, the primordial giant of chaos. In time, the gods killed Ymir, and from its remains, created Earth and the nine realms. I was of the gods, and they were in me. Akin to the gods, the unrest would not stop until I killed my giant and restored order. Against the advice of my wife, I journeyed out to find it.

I rose before sunrise to an empty bed and followed the sound of blades embedding into wood.

"When the goal is to find the deepest water, instead of learning how to swim," my wife Liv, the knife-thrower, said, pulling out the knives from her wooden target, "the mind is far from the shade of Yggdrasil." She threw them again, one after another, without missing her mark once. "It is not your place, Eindride, to meddle in the matters of the gods. They have their wars; we have ours. There are some things you cannot fix by the wielding of your axe or the cunning of your mind."

"I have to, Liv," I said. "Do you not remember?"

"I do," she said, and threw a knife with greater effort, almost splitting the trunk in two. "But I will not abandon our people for a selfish pursuit." Then, she turned to me and after some quiet pondering, "I do not understand why you must go after all this time, but if you must, I will not stop you."

The echo of Liv's sobbing over her mother's body still clawed at the insides of my skull, yet the determination in her eyes had softened through the years following the attack. "Our moment will come," she had said. And I clung to that promise, even if the others had found peace by burying the past.

I stood at the entrance of my settlement for a second's worth. I desired their peace, their pure unbridled joy that merely was, with no battles to bring it into existence. For them, a slow life meant a happy life, but for me, stopping meant death. Only Liv knew of my journey, and she was the only one who came to witness my departure. I placed my hands on her face and put my forehead to hers.

"Come back to me," Liv said, helpless against an enemy she could not slay.

The lands ahead beckoned me. I turned around to face destiny, my unquenchable desire to always move and always forward.

As a beast among beasts, I survived from the produce of the Earth, and the flesh of the creatures slain by the sharpness of my axe. The days fell as trees, and the night brought an abundance of longing for the ones I had left behind. In the landscape's serenity I found worry, for never was silence not accompanied by deafening suffering, a suffering I would have to face alone. But just a few more ways ahead, I might find the giant and return to my clan carrying its head, and we would have a great feast to celebrate the new beginning—a world without shadows. Future happiness propelled my next step. Just as I was ready to stow away my axe, a wind swept across the land, a signal from the gods whispered of better offerings to come. Liv's smile pulled me back and pushed me forward, all at once. I pressed on, for I must not return with a heart in the same shape as I had left with.

Frigid winds came from nowhere, penetrating my hide and piercing skin with a battalion of icy arrows. I found a dark cave ahead which I aimed for with fervent ardor. Once inside, I readied my axe and studied the cave for signs of another visitor. I claimed the empty cave as my own and lay down to rest, axe in hand, heart as a storm. The sound of a beast jolted me awake. I clenched my freezing hands around my axe. It was still dark. A glimmer from within the cave called for me, and upon following its trail, I found a piece of armor hidden deep in the hollow rock. I approached the armor, its metal unknown to me, and the reflection of an elder startled me. The heaviness of suns and moons past haunted me, revealing it had all gone to Niflheim. And for the first time, I felt the ache of my aging body. In the armor, I saw them, the unborn children that waited for me to resolve my anguish. I fell to my knees when I heard their laughter. Their specter little footsteps ran toward me, craving my embrace. But my arms held nothing at all, and the images evaporated with the cold.

Three nights I spent inside the cave waiting for the frost to end.

Protected by the cold, but inflicted by hunger, I questioned my destiny and if I was the Viking strong enough to carry it.

I heard the voice of a woman crying out for me, asking for help. She was drowning, she said, yet I remained in the cave's warmth, for I knew the rivers had frozen, and the voice came not from ours, but from the spirit world. It wanted me to crossover, yet it was not my time.

The next morning, I pulled myself out of my borrowed home. The ice storm had subsided. And I saw it. The path led to nowhere but the end of the fjord, and a mile-high drop. It was time. I had found the limit. It was enough. I must bear the turmoil inside of me with painful grace, and I must endure the will of gods and giants, for, in the end, I was nothing but human. The gods had spoken; I had to turn back.

It took me thrice the time and effort to trace my footsteps back to my harbor. The path welcomed me with the stench of suffering, and the premature death that hung in the air clenched its twisted hands around my neck. I white knuckled my axe, and, clearing the hill that overlooked the settlement, streams of smoke took the strength out of my legs. Moving forward was not a battle I wished to win, for I knew its sorrowful reward.

Liv had tried to tell me we were happy. Small and without a reputation, but happy. I walked among the half-burned buildings. Perpetual silence where there was once familial sound could rip the soul out of the strongest warrior. I rejected reality, reconstructing the buildings as they were in my memories, projecting unto them people fishing, kneading bread, and drinking ale to the stringed music of the jesters. The sounds carried me long enough, as far as my longhouse, and as deep as the hidden chest buried under my bed. Inside the chest, my father's battle sword. It was heavier than I remembered, but anger made this insignificant. I lifted it from its resting place, still as sharp as when my Viking ancestors won the battles in which they had taken these lands. My image lay on the blade, the chaos within spiraled, and I feared for whoever would receive the wrath boiling inside this heart. I had set out to kill the giant and restore order to my spirit, but the endeavor had been a selfish one. A Viking needed not to go hunting for giants, for, in time, one was bound to come knocking at his door.

When I had gathered enough strength to face reality, I stepped out of the remnants of my longhouse. Three men dressed in black robes watched over me from high ground. They stood still as stone altars waiting for an offering. I planted my axe on the burnt soil and pulled my father's sword out of its hilt; it hungered for blood, and I screamed, aiming its battle-born blade at them, ramming through the darkened settlement. I rushed through my life now in vapors. The air carried my clan's essence and filled my lungs with their despair, and I let the chaos take over. But as I got closer, the surrounding air turned black, and their bodies ceased to exist. From the hill, I faced the burnt ruins one last time, and imagined the ghosts of the settlement fleeing in the same way as the three robed men. Revenge, my new giant, urged me once more to move forward, always forward. And the scorching blood in my veins was all there was.

CHAPTER 2

"Dane! Dane!" A voice came rushing down the hills, rustling down the mountains, galloping like a wild stallion. "I saw it all," he said. "They came from the darkness, there. They took only but a few and slaughtered the rest."

He did not have the body of a warrior, and no armor protected him. Friend or foe, it did not matter. I seized him and lifted him by the throat. The air still had the stench of murder. "Speak," I said.

"If you could?" he said, motioning at my hands in a muffled voice. "Surely you could. I can't breathe."

I threw his frail body on the ground, and he took a few moments to gather himself.

"They came by boat at night, sire. Quiet as a sea raven, they floated above the waters and stormed into the village. They started on the shores and consumed it all from the edges to the center."

Peace, I thought, *peace has ruined us.* We had discarded most of the night watchmen—peace did not require their vigilance—and allowed them to sleep huddled next to their families. Now the wind mixed the dust from their bones together with that of their belongings. They were one with eðli, they belonged to nature. "What about the women and children?"

He stared in silence, and I knew. "They only took but a few."

Then I grasped my father's sword, its hilt covered in the dried blood of my ancestors. "Where?"

"That way, sire." He pointed to a path and turned to look around the ruins.

I grabbed him by his cloak, and it was not difficult to pull him with me towards the path. "Your life depends on the truthfulness of your tongue."

"I would. Really, I would." He kicked and reached for something to hold on to. "But I have people waiting for me. I cannot leave!" His feet dragged across the sand and grass, and he never ceased his chatter. "Why are you taking me, anyway? It is you who they wanted."

I stopped. "They looked for me?"

"They butchered many, but it is you they turned every rock of this settlement for. I heard as much."

"Despicable liar. Why would they not stay and wait for my arrival?"

"They wanted to hurt you, that I know. And what deeper hurt than allowing you to live with your past drenched in the acrid stench of fire? That is a deeper wound than death. Death is momentary, life is...long."

It would be easier to aim upon an enemy, but our clan had none. It would be plain to attack a known adversary, to infiltrate their barriers and bring upon them the carnage they had released on me. But there was no reason or footprints left on the trail. I turned back. Two ravens circled in the sky in search of their reward. Such was nature, and we must return to it our borrowed bodies in time. I stood tall with life. And I understood it. Nothing had happened to them, the ones who had to return their bodies to nature. They simply sailed downstream on the river, looking for the next shore of the chain that binds us all together. Yet I cannot live without fulfilling my duty as the jarl. Upon failing to protect, I must seek an answer from the gods, a reason for their rapture to Valhalla. And I concurred that our instincts as men, as warriors, have a reason to exist, for they are also a part of nature, or they would not be.

"Sire? Sire? You have been awfully quiet. I am ready to go back to my village now."

Upon rocks balanced my fate, and whichever direction I walked, whatever pebble I collected and placed on top, could tumble the tower and crumble it all down. Still, I marched with eyes pointing forward, dragging the lively body of a talking idiot as a sun compass. I would decipher the riddle once I was close enough to make sense of the message from the gods. Until then, I walked towards the noise, sharp edge aimed at the giant.

CHAPTER 3

The stranger and I had traversed a forest and had reached a mountaintop. By my threatening sword, he swore he knew the way, yet required the higher vantage point overlooking the path to become certain.

"I traveled by night," he said, "and wandered in the dark when I witnessed a group of awful Christians ransacking your village. I will lead you to them if it is the last thing I do."

We made our way toward the summit. I released my hold on his body, and he crumbled to the ground. For a moment, I saw in his eyes a display of something else, a hidden strength dying to be set free, then, upon meeting his eyes with mine, his face released and shifted once more into that of a weakling. I turned my back to him and stared for long upon the rich horizon, gazing over the plains and the shadows descending from Zeus's throne. I closed my eyes in haste, for the freedom I once sought after, I wished for it to be taken away, and me with it. In my dreams, I taught my children to hunt and fish, to wield a sword for a cause, to be a king for the people, and my hair would grow white, and my face wrinkled, and my bones would ache until I could rise no more. And I would see them playing, growing, and learning the lessons I stopped trying to teach, lessons learned only from facing the dangers lurking beyond my protection. And I would quiet the spirits that possessed Liv when she accepted their fate as unknown, and she released her unconditional embrace by the force of time, for they were never ours but of the world and the gods. All of this, I thought in an instant.

"Where to now?" I said and signaled with my sword for him to approach the viewpoint.

"You know you can just speak the words. No need to display your dominance."

He looked for a long time, then pointed ahead with great zeal. "There! The church steeple. It was those awful Christians who set out to kill you. Oh, how much hate they have for heathens."

"Walk."

"I told you everything I know. You can kill them on your own," he said in a higher pitch, and planted his feet on the ground.

"You will come, and if I cannot prove your story to be true, it will be your blood on my blade."

He walked with a spring in his step, this time leading the way on his own accord.

Although pieces of the village caught the eye from such a high viewpoint, it was still a great distance away, and for days, we walked.

At nightfall, we sat around a bonfire with a dead rabbit over the flame. Once cooked, I ripped apart pieces of it and threw them at the idiot, who hesitated, then desperately took a bite.

"As I imagined." He spat out the meat on the ground. "Bland. No wonder you are so angry all the time," he said.

"Careful, idiot. It is a good night to die."

"I am not an idiot, you know? I have intellect." He put his hands up. "All I am saying is life could be better, easier, at least more enjoyable if we just had some spice."

"You are not going anywhere."

"Fine, leave me tied up to a tree if you wish. I will not escape. Look at me. I am sitting with a Viking deep in a forest, a Viking who I am sure has had his share of enemies, knowing how war-driven a Dane's blood is." He turned to the dark forest. "My last meal could come at any time, from any corner, and I at least want it to be a tasteful one."

In his words, I found once again his hidden strength, and not long after, he was tied up to a tree, shouting out names of plants at me. I brought back garlic, thyme, and mustard seeds. I made a pot out of a felled hollow tree trunk, and following his instructions, I stirred the plants with the remaining pieces of rabbit, and we assembled around the fire once more.

"You first," I said.

"Have you ever trusted anyone? Do you even know how to?"

He took a big sip and scooped chunks of meat with a small, hollow piece of wood, then made a mocking motion at me.

Once I saw it was safe, I tasted a mouthful and found in it a piece of life and normalcy, that which I did not deserve. By the third bite, I had set my sword to the side and sat comfortably on a tree log. I had loosened the idiot's knot so he could move his hands and eat with ease.

"Do you believe in more than one god?" He sipped his soup.

"Many more."

"How do they get along?"

"The answers are there for the ones willing to see them. We eat from a rabbit's meat, yet the rabbit did not know his death was coming, nor did he do anything to deserve such fate. In nature, nothing gets along, but things take what they need to survive. Order is maintained by a balance in chaos, not the eradication of it," I said, and I pondered on my conclusion. "Evil is born when one takes more than one needs, thus disrupting the balance."

Beyond the bounds of what my settlement had ever explored, past the mountain the idiot and I had hiked, across many valleys and just after a spring, a path revealed itself. The village was near. A pebbled road slit the green in two, and lead to a building further along the trail. The weakling froze for a second but walked ahead.

"Alright, then. On we go," he said.

As the buildings grew larger, the idiot walked slower. The adobe walls stood tan in the sun, and the towers at either side harbored arrowed soldiers.

"Halt! What business have you at the Monastery?" said one guard pointing his bow at us.

"I am a monk here, sire. I bring with me a guest."

His words pulled at my face.

"Is that a Dane? We do not allow heathens here."

"A Dane it is, yes. But a friend. He wishes to learn about Christianity."

"Are you seeking baptism, heathen?"

"Answer!" whispered the stranger.

I took perhaps way too long of a time, but compelled myself to answer. "Yes. I wish to learn your religion and be reborn a new man under one God."

The guard looked to his side at the other, who made his armor rise and fall with a shrug. "You may come in."

The steel doors opened, and the idiot dawdled towards the entrance. As I walked toward the opening door, I questioned whether I, too, possessed a hidden power.

CHAPTER 4

Lyminge was not only a monastery but also a commerce town sitting on the borders of the North Sea. The monastery stood proudly in the background like an oak tree, its branches nestled deeply within the pockets of its citizens. A boy ran between us, holding a sack made of a folded piece of linen. Behind him, a guard clinked his armor as far as his breath took him, which wasn't far at all, and he leaned against a city wall. I turned around to see the trail of protesting screams the boy had left behind and saw another guard who twisted his spine to his left as soon as he caught my gaze. His legs followed the rest of his body to face a distressed merchant. The merchant had not noticed the guard and was chasing after his apples rolling on the cobblestone floors. "That bushel will pay the tithe. Out of the way!" the merchant said. He meant the guard, and when he realized, he said, "Excuse me, sire." But the guard didn't feel a thing over the thick steel armor boots, and when I turned around, he was walking again.

I grabbed the idiot as soon as the crowd covered our backs and pulled him into an alley.

"What—?"

I covered the weakling's mouth with my hand and heard for the steel clinking softly on the stone. I could see his shadow now, becoming darker and darker, unscrambled, focused.

I pulled the guard into the alley.

"You are following us. Why?" I had lost my sword to the guards at the entrance, but smuggled a small knife which was now at his throat. His armor could not protect him any more than a patch of grass could protect land from the stroke of a pickaxe.

The guard looked at us, and the idiot raised the cloth around his neck to cover his face up to his nose.

"I am to report your whereabouts to the general." There was a shiver in his voice.

I strengthened my grip. "You'll report to your general that we entered the monastery in peace and prayed until our knees were numb, or you will meet your maker now."

"Such a savage," said the idiot, and pushed my hand away. "No one has to die today." He buffed the guard's armor and gave him back his dagger, which had fallen on some grass. "Where can we find the leader of such a splendid charm of a town? I would love to give him my regards."

The guard looked confused for a moment. His hand rose as if guided by some involuntary nerve in his body. Our luck shone upon us; with all the ways and allies around the town, he pointed in the direction we had been going.

The idiot put his hands on the guard's shoulders. "Your service has honored us."

The noise of exchanges in the merchant city swallowed his metallic footsteps, and we carried on walking as soon as the guard disappeared into the crowd.

"To have a way with words," the idiot said. "Is a much stronger weapon to wield than any steel or muscle. If you come to this world bearing such gifts, no sword, dagger, or axe is more powerful, or can cause more damage. Deadly words make bigger shifts than raids, Dane. Life is simple if you practice your walk, sharpen your tongue, and forge your mind. Forget not, Dane"—he poked at his temple, his eyes as wide as a village seer—"Forge your mind." He reminded me of my grandfather, who, with his words and foresight, moved our clan overseas to settle upon the hills of this land. But not even he could have foreseen his grandchild walking in peace into his enemy's home. I shall make him proud by leaving its center with its heart withering away, beating its last splatters of blood in my hands.

In front of us grew the Monastery. A tunic-dressed, fat, bald man walked towards us, covered by the armor of a line of women at either side. The women wore garments up to the neck and looked at the ground while clasping a miniature rendition of their god. They chanted a strange curse in unison. I did not know the language or their reasons. The curse worked. I did not slaughter them. But walked ahead, instead.

CHAPTER 5

More chants echoed inside their place of worship, and I followed the sound to the tall ceiling where paintings of men and their God depicted a great celestial battle. I read it as if the battle was not between angels and demons, but between gods and giants. Ragnarök. Perhaps chaos and order lived in perpetual war within these people, as it had lived within myself. We made it to the front seats of the building, where a man stood at a podium wearing a white tunic.

"Not yet," the weakling fool said, holding out his skinny arm before me. "I need to make sure."

We walked closer toward the director of this strange congregation.

"Welcome to the house of God," the tunic man said, looking only at me.

"Hello, Father. My friend is looking for a place of prayer. Would it be okay if we spoke with God for a time?" The idiot sounded muffled by the garment that covered his mouth.

"Yes, of course. My family built this monastery to accept visitors from all walks of life." He directed us to an empty bench. "Please."

We knelt in front of the bench.

"Yes, it's him. I know it now. He was leading the group that raided your settlement."

"Tunic man?"

"The father, yes."

I pulled a leg up.

The weakling placed a hand on my arm and pulled. "No, not yet," he whispered, his voice traveling easily in the air. "We will get slaughtered. Look."

There were armed guards posted at every corner.

"We shall wait until sundown and walk as one with the shadows. I will take him out then."

"Splendid plan. But he didn't do any of the killing, he merely gave the orders. It was the guards that did the rest."

"Two against an army would be suicide."

"Unless we burn the entire village down."

"What about the innocent people?"

"What about the innocent people in your settlement? Your family..."

I faced the floor and clenched my fist.

"Eye for an eye," he said.

I assented.

"It is settled then."

The tunic man strolled along the pathway between the rows of benches.

"Amen," the weakling said, louder than he had to, and pulled me up with him. "Thank you again, Father. We will return to this fine monastery in the future."

"Our doors will remain open. We shall always welcome you." He looked at me. I did not see death in his eyes, yet one cannot stop a sword hungered for the taste of blood.

We recovered our weapons on our way out of the village and lighted a bonfire not too far away. I let the idiot roam freely to assemble the spices while I hunted a rabbit and carried it toward the fire.

"Exquisite! Now, we shall finish this up and promptly go about setting the village on fire."

"Why do you care?"

"What?"

"Why do you want this to happen so much?"

"I just... I just want your family and friends avenged, that is all. If you could have seen what I saw. Oh, the horror. The screams. The suffering."

I planted my sword on the ground, and his tongue fell silent.

"All I'm saying is that I'm a seeker of justice. I won't be able to continue with my life until I see justice served. If not us, who will care?"

Night had fallen after we finished eating, and we used its dark cover to approach the village from its side carrying torches lit on fire. We hunched against one of its walls.

"Well?" the idiot said.

"That one is too heavy," I heard the voice of a man say on the other side of the brick wall.

A second voice spoke, "But I want to help, Father."

"You are too young, son," he said, chuckling. "Here, take the basket of spices and let us head home. Your mother is going to kill me for having you out this late."

Only I stand between life and death, I thought. *I have sent many souls to Valhalla, the enemy always holding his weapon, their fates in the hands of the push and pull of gods and giants on the battlefield.* And I recalled Liv's words, "It is not your place, Eindride, to meddle in the matters of the gods." This was no battlefield. And at once I knew it. I was now a shadow walker of the night, a bringer of suffering, releasing giants of chaos in the hearts of the survivors. I had let myself become the shadow that had taken everything from me as a child. No. The thought released the torch from my hand and it fell to the ground between the idiot and I.

"Focus, Viking," the idiot said and picked up the torch. "These people have ruined your life." And when I remained still, looking blankly at him, he stood up and lunged the burning torch over the brick wall. It did not take long for the fire to spread across the roof where it had landed. Then, the idiot shared the fire from one torch to light a second one, and a third, and threw them also over the wall.

The people had noticed and rushed out of their homes screaming in fear.

"Come!" The weakling ran towards the entrance and pulled me with him. The finisher. Now that the guards had left their posts and scrambled into the city, he set the front door on fire. They had nowhere to go. The damage was too strong, their resolve too dire, their future too bleak. Some tried to run still, and climbed up the walls, only to fall to their demise at the slip of a hand.

There was a strange feeling in the pit of my stomach that seemed like a curse vested upon me, a curse so terrible it paralyzed me. Evil. When I looked at the idiot, the source of this feeling became clear.

"Look at it go!" the idiot said with a smile on his face, his disguise now ripped open, and from within, his hidden strength showed itself in its full ugliness. "Who's the mockery of the town now?" He released the garment covering his mouth. "Are you proud of me now, Father? Of my strength? Look at me! Am I the warrior you had hoped for? Is this raging heat passionate enough?"

CHAPTER 6

"What did you do, miserable idiot?" I grabbed him by the throat and propped his body against the hot walls of the village.

"Things take what they need to survive," he said, with a wicked smirk on his face.

"I shall kill you right here, and let your rotting corpse lie among your sins," I said, growling, almost.

"Ah, are you a Christian now?"

A storm brewed in the sky, and his body became light as an autumn feather. I held him in the air for a long time, deciding whether to let him go or put my sword through his intestines. I chose something close to the middle, and with a swipe of my blade, took off his right leg.

He had the most awful scream. Loud, high, and piercing. "What have you done?!"

"I should have killed you." I released him next to his cut off limb. "You may survive, or you may not. I will let the gods decide. But your every move will be a struggle, in your every thought there will be pain."

I walked away, hearing the idiot screaming into the night, his voice louder than the fire that consumed the city, and the walls that held both his body and his ripped, bloody limb would soon crumble.

The horse I stole carried me into the forest until I saw the fire no more, heard the screams no more, and I camped for the rest of the night.

The memory of Liv and the phantom specters of my unborn children were my companions through the restless night. The sky drew them out of stars, and I was an insignificant speck lost in the maze of the realms. I pulled away from sadness and aimed at my giants instead, for a man's life was the quiet struggle of slaying giants visible only to himself. My father's killer, the warlord, for whom I have saved this sword, and the raiders of my settlement, upon whom I would unleash the fury gnawing at my flesh, eating me alive from the inside.

I was not sure when I had fallen asleep, but the sun was out now, and in its fire, a new plan was forged. To find my giants, I needed a clan, an army I could use to scout the land. I rode the horse down the path forward, hoping for a Dane settlement to take me in.

After a journey of two days, the sound of running water stopped me in my tracks. *There must be a settlement not too far.* I tied my horse to a nearby tree and cleansed my body and face in the river.

"Do not move," a voice said behind me. I heard the Viking in his tongue. Dane.

I smiled. "I am glad to see you."

"Dane?"

"Flesh and blood," I said, turning around.

He stowed away his sword.

"Is your settlement close by, warrior?" I said.

"It depends. Are you friend or foe?"

"The only option as of this moment is to be a friend, for I lost my settlement and everyone in it."

"My respects. But do not despair, for they now smile upon us from Valhalla." He held his hand to his chest. "Our settlement is just across those trees."

He waited for me to untie my horse, and we rode toward the trees, the horses trotting in the dirt.

"What happened, if I may ask?"

"For a time, I traveled the land. When I came back, it was all gone. Burnt to the ground. Not one survived."

"Do you know who was responsible?"

"I thought I did, but my informant deceived me."

"Informant?"

"A weakling that swore he had seen it all. Turns out he used me for his own evil conjure."

"That is the biggest of dangers, weakness with ambition."

I nodded in silence.

As we entered the settlement, the smells brought me back home. The baking of bread, the fishing docks full of catch, and the sound of swords hitting the thick logs in the training ground. It was a settlement, five hundred people strong. The air smelled of green pastures.

We approached a tall man with a bearskin overcoat. "Jarl Ilkka, may I present you..."

"Eindride."

"What did I tell you about picking up strays, Oddmund? We cannot feed another mouth."

"Forgive me. I will not take your food, not without offering my sword and service in exchange. I can help."

"What can you do?"

"I can train your drengir."

"And what makes you think we need help?"

"We passed by them when we were walking into the settlement. They should train with wooden swords, not with iron. They need to learn technique first."

A man beside the jarl became nervous and interrupted, "I can assure you, we have trained them well."

"Silence," the Jarl Ilkka said. "We are losing men every time we raid. We should accept help wherever it may come from."

The man walked away.

"Welcome, Eindride. Find yourself some food and ale, rest, and you can show us your skill at sunrise."

CHAPTER 7

The first rays of sunlight had invaded the peaceful cliff on which the settlement stood, 200 men strong, and reflected in the jarl's eyes. Ilkka leaned against the half wall facing the training ring. A group of young warriors stood before me, waiting for me to fulfill the promise of victory. Oddmund exchanged words with Jarl Ilkka, words that seemed too loud to be heard by just the jarl.

"Are you sure to trust him, Ilkka?"

Jarl Ilkka looked in silence.

"You and you. Stand forward," I said. "Here."

"But these are wooden," one drengr said. The other kids laughed in the background.

"Prove your technique on wood, and I shall test you on iron."

"I will not put the future of my family on a wooden stick."

"Very well." I threw him a sword, a real one. "Show me how you will defend your village."

The boy galloped towards me, the poison of rage climbing with each step towards my chest. I turned and disarmed him with a hit of my sword. His weapon reverberated on the ground.

"Pick it up. Try again."

The boy lurched towards the sword, rolled on the ground, stood up, and attacked. I moved away. He tried again. I stepped aside once more. The boy panted, sweated, then swung his sword at me. I slammed it out of his hands and pointed my sword at his chest. He raised his hands, his chest rising and falling with each forced breath.

"We start with wood," I said, only for him to hear. And then louder. "We start with wood. If you do not agree, you can leave."

Everyone accepted. The boy retreated through the crowd, and on he marched towards his house.

"You can't deny him of his talents," Ilkka said. "Let's give him time. Hopefully, clan Völsung will not release its wolves a day sooner."

Another boy stepped forward, this time grabbing a wooden sword.

"May Valhalla have a place for us all," Oddmund said, his voice trailing into a shake.

"Don't be so dramatic, my dear Oddmund. We may have a fighting chance after all."

<hr>

Days ahead brought forth the promise of peace, and the drengir were settling into the shape of Vikings. I disarmed them of their swords again and again until they evaded my attacks and in time we stood there, pointing the end of wooden swords at each other's throats, and smiling. Over time, they became fine make-believe warriors. But the blood-red sunset called for iron. I smelled the stench of horror in the air. It was the same air I had arrived to at my settlement. I walked towards my sword and threw it at one of them, the more advanced Fulco, and grabbed another sword.

"Do you really think I'm ready?" he said.

"I do," I said, and then louder, "You all are."

Once they handled the iron with the precision of a seasoned warrior, they had to learn everything all over again while carrying sacks of heavy rocks on their backs. We repeated the exercise daily to failure—their bodies still sore from the day before.

The settlement had been good to me. The jarl had built a house at the edge of the training grounds where I rested my head and thought of my family. And in the day, we ate leftover stew with bread and cloudberries.

It was saddening to say anything about my premonitions. The visions of the shadow walkers had invaded my dreams and filled my heart with worry. The crisp sound of flames. Smoke infesting my lungs. Outside, the screams of savages ripping through doors and skin. Suffering, the only sound. Blood, the only smell. I rose drenched in sweat, eager to sound the horn and get the drengir ready for battle. For I knew it was coming. While the locals drank ale and made anecdotal jokes, I knew the enemy lurked behind the trees upon these hills, studying us, appraising our worth. Determined to protect my new family, I rose to wake the jarl and convince him the settlement was no longer safe. To run far and fast. But I reached for my father's battle sword and found myself in its blade. I was no longer a boy. A long, painful life had gifted me scars and wrinkles. With every scar, a new flavor of victory, with every wrinkle, a new unspoken courage to face the enemy in battle, as fearful as they might be.

CHAPTER 8

As the settlement lay in secure slumber, the sound of horses galloping echoed down the hills. Confident by their calculated element of surprise, they pushed through the settlement, hacking away and burning hay, and, in a burning second, turning generations of growth to ashes and dust.

I had risen by the nightmares before first light; I did not hold the secret any longer. I had woken up the Jarl in haste. There was fever in my eyes, and passion in my words. My blood carried my father's blood, the vengeance my settlement did not avenge, their sour memories, every bit that never was.

A scout returned an hour later with confirmation. A vast army marched towards us carrying torches and swords. Illuminating the way to us, intending to kill.

The jarl had sent the women and children to the forest, to a hideaway I had built inside a cave in secret after the daily trainings, just a few steps from the stream. Then he made men from the drengir, and they rose to the occasion. The weight of armor did not hold them down but propelled them forward as a challenging fish to a lurking raven. They slammed their swords against their helmets. Their teeth clenched in anticipation.

"It is not for you," Jarl Ilkka said, yelling and pacing in front of a line of warriors. "Or you. It is for all of us we fight. For our home. Our place among the beasts. Today your muscles and bones will cry from exhaustion, but you will swing still. For your father and mother. Your siblings and animals. For your will to live. We will give the cowards something to fear."

A line of warriors grunted and pounded at their chests. Some drengir cried tears of angst covered in regret for being alive at all, for they knew what this meant. The risks involved. The probable outcome.

We waited for them to gallop inside the empty settlement and watched from the darkness. A line of archers stood in front, their hunting bows ready.

"Loose!" Ilkka said.

A cluster of projectiles was launched toward the settlement. Horses whined and fell to the ground; the enemy screamed.

"For Glory..." Oddmund said.

"Or Valhalla!" Ilkka finished, and we all rushed down the hills to the sides of the settlement. All our warriors separated into four smaller groups. The Völsung clan readied their swords at one side, and once they saw our next group of raging Vikings coming from the other, wavered their bodies from side to side.

"What now, sir?" one said.

"Don't back down!" their chief said. "Get ready!"

As I ran down the cliffs and toward the burning settlement, the three men in black garments appeared on the mountain ahead, their bodies lit by the raging flames.

"Eindride, why are you stopping?" Oddmund pushed me forward. When I turned to them, they had vanished. But something changed in me. If blind vengeance propelled me before, I now ran with inevitable victory, navigating by the sails of the gods.

The sky turned gray, the shade which darkness could cover, embracing the moon and the stars. A thunderstorm erupted just as our swords met. I had missed the sound of iron in war, letting the chaos within unleash in an explosion of rage. I screamed for no reason at all, other than being unable to hold it in any longer. A thunderstorm had developed over us, Thor witnessing the encounter. I pushed an enemy warrior to the ground with my shield, and planted my sword in his heart, pulled it out, and rotated in front of another, slashing at his legs. Oddmund was beside me, thrusting his sword and ramming it forward. The drengir came in after us, taking lives that were already on the ground begging for salvation, or for a weapon to be placed in their hands once they had given up on life. It was enough taste of death to fill their developing, weak stomachs. Rain had descended upon us, the muddy ground making it harder to stay upright. The enemy's warriors, still substantial but confused, unprepared for our strategy, congregated in the middle, surrounded by our forces. They formed a shield wall. They were protecting something. We pressed on. Jarl Ilkka commanded for more arrows to be shot against the shield wall. We weakened a side of it, and Oddmund rushed the weakened shield wall with his sword. I ran behind him. Oddmund cleared a path, and that is when I saw it. The shape, the shadow walker, the warlord, hunching in the center of the enemy's shield wall. All the hair in my body rose, and my soul burst into flames. I yelled a war cry louder than the thunderstorm, louder than the clash of sword and shield, louder than the gods themselves. The rain was now a downpour, and I rushed into the shield wall, with no fear for my survival. And the shadow walker turned to me. I knew he recognized me. He looked at my sword, and his eyes opened wider, spellbound, and I rushed harder still. His warriors tried to stop me, but every one that touched me fell back to the ground, convulsed for a second, then perished, their eyes white as if they had been awakened from a terrible nightmare. I was a sword length away from the warlord, which now was not a warlord at all, but a weak, scared, old man that trembled alone under the thunder light. I stood before him.

"Do you recognize me, shadow walker?" I screamed into the night.

He nodded.

With the confirmation that I needed, I lifted my sword in the air, the sound of thunder descending upon me, shivering my every bone. And with the force of the revenge—hefnd—of my father, Liv's mother, the giant's burden in my swelled heart, I descended my sword upon his neck, and his lifeless head fell to the ground in an explosion released from the nine realms.

I looked around me. It had gone by in a flash. And everyone had stopped swinging and now stood looking at me. Oddmund's eyes were bright as lightning. A current had enveloped my body, extending to my sword. Looking back on my trail of death, I had created a path sunken as deep as a water canal. My legs were now half-deep in the burning soil. Their bodies formed a twisted line of sliced charcoal. The drengir dropped their swords and removed their helmets.

"You have the favor of the gods," Oddmund said and knelt, leaning against his sword.

The women and children had descended to the battle's aftermath from the hiding place on the mountain.

"Ilkka!" a woman cried. We turned to look.

Jarl Ilkka's body lay on the floor. His hands still covering the splattering hole in his neck. He gasped for air, his eyes fixated on mine. His life energy left him, one breath at a time.

"What will we do now?" A skinny drengr said as he slid his helmet back into place.

A chant broke, first lighter, then as heavy as the scathed battle we had won. "Eindride," they said. "Eindride."

"What shall we do indeed?" Oddmund said. He walked towards the lifeless Ilkka and pressed his sword against his chest. Ilkka's eyes were wide and motionless. Fresh blood flowed out of his cavities.

The chant intensified.

"Enough!" Oddmund said. The chant dialed down to a silence. "Do you not have allegiance? You'd rather give away your clan to nothing more than a stranger?"

"He saved us," one woman said. "If it was not for his visions, we would have all fallen today."

"We knew this attack was coming. The Völsung clan had been raiding the area for months. What he had was nothing more than pure luck."

"He has the favor of the gods, you said so yourself," Fulco, the oldest drengir, said, removing his helmet.

"Even so, I shall lead according to our tradition. The throne is rightfully mine."

"We will not follow you," Fulco said. The other drengir joined him, raising their swords.

"Silence, child!" Oddmund said, launching at Fulco with his sword. I stopped his sword midair. My iron striking his.

"Only a coward attacks a child," I said, my grip charged.

"Very well, Eindride," Oddmund said to me, then turned to the crowd that had assembled around us. "Is this what you really want? Do you want me to prove myself? Let's settle this here and now."

Enough blood had spilled that day, yet once blood ran, it became difficult to set the boundaries of its addictive reach.

"A holmgang, outcast. To the death. I will put you out of your misery."

I wished at once his words were true. Even with the shadow walker's head on the ground, exorcising the memories that had taken over my life was the greatest gift. Yet I knew. My life was not mine from hereafter. The ancient runes had vibrated for me. Odin had called me from his throne, and blessed me with electrifying purpose. Oddmund had no chance.

CHAPTER 9

Above the ashes of a victory, we took our stances. Inside the square, we fantasized about robbing each other's life. Above, the storm had become as angry as the tormented spirits of Hel. I flourished my blade and walked with my eyes fixated on Oddmund. Black piles of ash had formed by the lightning striking around me. The warriors pounded on their iron chests and grunted for death. Hope for blood became the steaming liquid evaporating in the air. Oddmund was sure of himself. He removed his heavy armor and threw it to the side. Lightning descended upon me. Every strike reigniting my rage.

He swung first. I stepped outside the blow, his sword hitting the burnt rocks on the ground. I saw his body sluggish on the field. His movements were slow and predictable. Deflecting his attacks was easier the longer he tried. My body was lit as charged by the gods. I ducked against one of his attempts and turned around when I had reached his back. With a kick on his legs, he fell to the ground with ease. I saw terror in his eyes. I raised the blade of my father and felt Liv's hand holding my grip. My beloved tribe, ethereal spectators of this moment. At the highest point, my blade became white as sunlight. Thunder landed on its sharp edges, my hands vibrating from the great ancient powers. And I swung down with the heaviness of an orphaned heart.

As my sword reached his heart, he yelled his last words. "I know where they are!" he said.

I let go of my sword. "What did you say?" I grabbed his head, my thumbs at his forehead. "Answer me!" His blank stare, a punishment, the blood pouring out of his blood, a reminder. The answer was in my hands, yet I had silenced it for eternity. "Oddmund!" I cried. Lightning lit up the sky as If Odin himself cried with me. I knelt in surrender.

Away on the hill where we had hidden our people, the three men stood again. The demons of death here to take me away to my eternal prison. I didn't care. Either with them or stomping this Earth in the blind search of my family, a painful sentence waited ahead. Yet another giant pulling at my threads of destiny.

I stood up, pulled my sword out of Oddmund and marched toward the hill. Then, the three spirits of the night turned around and walked away into the dark mouth of the trees.

My sword had stopped buzzing. The skies had cleared, and white spots blinked through the dissolving cloud. I had never seen so many stars.

The people cheered. I felt welcome once more. Yet, with every welcoming adulation, I became wary of Oddmund's words. *I know where they are.* Torn between setting off once more or leading my new people in the reconstruction of their settlement, I looked ahead. If there was a lesson in pain, the gods made it clear. Turning your back on fate only prolonged the suffering of life. And as a true warrior, one must face every step on the ladder to Odin's throne head-on, sword in hand, one's body armored, eyes forward.

In the months that followed, I helped the people elevate their homes back with new raw materials. From the ashes, the settlement was reborn—twice as strong. In time, we expanded our territory to that of my previous settlement. Fear of my name became second nature throughout these lands.

I met a kvinna, I am ashamed to admit. Maarit was good to me, and gave me three beautiful children, one of which survived the first winter—his drengr path as charged by the gods as mine. I recognized the fire in his eyes, for I saw it in the waters of my turmoil roam on the earth.

But there was one thing never far from my mind. *I know where they are.* I asked every merchant, every captor, every riding warrior passing through. But got no further than a hopeless promise of Liv, my ghost, anchoring me to life.

We galloped all across the land. The men, they were loyal to my requests. Every sunrise, a chance to keep my eyes open, to search on the horizon just beyond my grasp for all I had lost. And as my hands became old and wrinkled, and my powers from my youth lessened, my name also diminished. My reputation had gone in a lifetime. And as I lay now, my breath escaping me, and the skin sinking into my bones, know this: I never gave up. I never stopped looking for Liv—always. And once my soul made its final trek to Valhalla, if I could not find her there, I would beg Odin for the freedom to roam the stars. For I wish to haunt the planets for eternity. Within the confines of the universe, I shall look for her forever.

CHAPTER 10

After I blinked for the last time, the gods presented me with flashes of my past. I became a spirit raven and soared over our home, as it had been many winters ago, days before I left.

Children ran after each other, and laughter filled the space between the blacksmiths and the fishermen.

I saw myself in flesh and bone, standing at the edge, looking up. My wife, Liv, radiant even at such a distance, walked to my side. Her steps were quiet, as to not disturb my train of thought.

I hovered far above, searching for my settlement's attackers. Away on the invisible side of the horizon, I found the three men dressed in black garments. I dropped closer to them and heard them devising a plan. The leaves of trees had turned from green to the driest black. Time had lost all meaning.

"We must do this just right," one of the hooded men said.

The hooded man in the middle nodded and said, "No matter what, the bloodline must awaken and prevail."

"Brother, are you certain?" the third one said.

"I am."

The three men lurked in the shadows, away from our Viking

settlement. The day had now drifted into the darkest hours. I, Jarl of the settlement, had left the day before.

"Do we agree this to be the right course of action?" A hooded man said to the other two.

They nodded.

"Then we proceed, aware of the celestial consequences, in the descendant's awakening."

"We rewrite history," one said.

"We rewrite history," they all chanted.

The group of three men snuck closer to the village, which now rested in silent slumber, and lit the torches in their hands. Only a few of the village men remained awake, unaware of impending doom.

One hooded man threw his torch on a roof, setting a house on fire. I dropped closer desperately, but trying to knock the second torch off his hand, flew right through them.

"Fire!" a village man said.

"Ok, now," the hooded man who had thrown the first torch said, and the next man swung his torch at the roof of another house.

I rose once more and hovered over the village, unable to intervene, and I tried to move my wings to get me away from this terrible vision. But my wings were useless, and I was forced to watch this tragedy play out.

The villagers scrambled to find water, but by the time they had organized, the fire had grown to monstrous proportions. They gave up on saving their homes and tried to save their lives instead.

The third hooded man threw his torch as far as he could. The villagers, now huddled in the center, turned to the newborn fire.

The three hooded men hurried from their hiding and into the mass of scared and sleepy men, women, and children, who huddled in the settlement's open space, away from the fire that encircled them in this waking nightmare, half-dressed and scared.

"Stay here!" one villager said to his child.

The three hooded men came in. Armorless and weaponless, they took lives, one by one. Killing without touching. Sending the mightiest warriors of the village flying and crashing on the burning structures. It was pointless to fight, for the three invaders brought devastation without moving more than a hand. Their disposition was not of the gambles of battle, but of determined annihilation.

I wanted to come in closer and stop this massacre. But my body hovered over the nightmare, frozen above the flames.

The villager's boy hid behind a barrel of water, shivering in horror as he looked at his parents and friends crying for help. I saw anger on his face. His wooden sword now turned to ashes with everything he had ever known. A corpse laid near him with his hand open, faceless in the dark. The corpse's sword rested on the ground. The boy reached out to the sword and could barely lift it.

"Michael, behind you!" one hooded man said to another, and the one called Michael turned around. The child, now a Viking warrior in spirit, rushed towards him, bloody sword in hand.

Michael turned around and with a motion of his hand sent the boy flying, and his back flat on the ground. Michael suspended his sword, hilt up, point down, and pushed his hand down. Young blood splattered over the earth, and guts of red slid down the blade, devouring its shine inch by piercing inch.

"For the Great Ancestor," one hooded man said.

"For the Great Ancestor," another repeated.

"One step closer," Michael said.

Liv laid on her back, reaching out for her sword, hoping for Valhalla, her half-moon birthmark on her arm facing the sky.

The hooded man named Michael scanned the corpses, and once locating Liv, approached her. I screamed a soundless cry, helplessly hovering frozen above the vision. Blood came out of her mouth as she reached further out, but her weapon was too far from her. In time, she gave up and succumbed to her destiny. Michael stood over her body, knelt, and reached for her neck. He clenched his hand around her throat and witnessed her attempts to breathe. I screamed with all the force I had inside of me. A gust of wind pulled Michael's hood away from his face, and I saw on his face a terrible smirk—he enjoyed this destruction. Liv's eyes followed the wind and looked for its source up in the flashing stars. Somehow, she found me. Our eyes connected, and she smiled. Somewhere across the realms, we held our gaze and danced once more between realities.

In my heart, one giant fell, and at once another one rose in its place. A new chaos sparked within me, a chaos which would not rest until I found the giant, Michael, and bring it to its death.

BOOK 2

PATH OF THE HYBRIDS

PART 1

CHAPTER 1

Across a lake, tall walls and barbed wire appeared in the gaps of the swaying trees. A flock of bluebirds flit from branch to branch, and sang not only for the perfect, earless nature but also for a row of twenty-nine children standing in front of them. A1, A2, A3... to A29, the children waited in front of the birds. Still, like cold statues, they waited for their signal. They lacked patience, not because they were eager, but because it was unnecessary, for the Archangel Lucifer had engineered it off their DNA a long time ago. The drill was not a new one, and the rifles in their right hands felt as comfortable as a pleasant memory. They killed things; that was their purpose.

The last one in the row of children, A29, used his right hand to hold the rifle and his left hand to keep the right one from trembling. Behind them, a black tower that rose like a spire overlooked everything in the Watcher Development Center and the Fields.

"Where is she?" A voice said to Lucifer behind the glass walls of the tower.

"She will be here, Faith." Lucifer stood like a warrior. When he turned around, his skin sparkled like burnished bronze, and his steps fell hard on the floor. Commanding. Yet his face and body had a soft, human likeness. His voice was calm. The calm that would make a non-deity shiver.

"It has been three times this week already. I wonder if we made a mistake, leaving her here for so long."

Lucifer returned to the glass with his hands clasped behind his back.

A30 welcomed the annoying buzz of her alarm clock, which had been buzzing for an hour now, as her own minor rebellion. Harmless with a potential for danger, she thrived in the messy side of the room she shared with A29. *An hour late. A record, surely.* She opened her eyes and slammed her hand on the alarm clock.

The room had exactly two beds with exactly two nightstands on either side, and a big wooden dresser filled the space in the center. The walls were bare. In a school for assassins, mirrors were redundant, a waste, a distraction. A30 pulled on a loose strand of her hair only to see its blackness, and from that blackness, imagined, inch by inch, the features of her face. She had caught a distorted glimpse once over the Blue Field's waters, but the liquid had since lost its reflectiveness.

A30 reached for the dresser's bottom drawers, swirling garments around until she found her uniform. She zipped her black suit over her body. The label A30 stretched over her chest. An assortment of knives, handguns, and rifles hung on the side of the closet wall. She pulled the rifle and swung it over her head and enjoyed the kick of the rifle's muzzle on her back.

Out of the room, she made a quick descent down the stairs to the main entrance. Children the same age as her, organized in groups of 30, filled the main black hallway, a light sage-colored stretch with a dozen rooms on either side. A30 had no interest in the other children's faces. She wiggled her way through, nudging them to the side. The exit door waited at the end.

"How pathetic," she said before stepping out.

A30 walked toward the arced entrance of the Green Fields. She stopped at the base of the tower and stuck her face over its wall. She put her hands around her eyes, trying to block the light from reflecting over the surface.

"I know you're in there," she said, her voice muffled inside the tower.

"Oh, we should take her with us already," Faith said from the other side.

"Patience, Faith. We still do not know what this means for her, for us. We must observe her progress."

After a few seconds of silence, A30 unglued her face from the wall and walked over the grass of the Green Fields.

Even though they could hear her approaching, the other 29 children remained still. She stood next to the last child, A29, and, without hesitating, took the first shot.

"Always late, yet always early. Now that's balance. Your turn, roommate," she said as soon as she saw the dead bluebird fall to the ground. "Come on, 29."

The tremors returned when A29 moved his grip to his rifle. His throat felt like he had swallowed a gallon of powder. He raised his rifle to the sky. With the flapping of the birds' wings now in the rifle's sight, he hesitated.

A30 scoffed and snatched the gun from him.

"No!"

She pushed him aside and shot another bird, almost without taking aim, and threw the gun back into his arms. "This is hunting, not bird watching." She faced the rest of the group. "Anyone else needs help?" Her voice mobilized the others.

Within seconds, all guns pointed up and fired. Like a cloud feeding on vapor, the guns gave fuel to the downpour of birds. It had only been two weeks since the children gazed in awe at the birds hatching from their eggs.

A loud beep announced it was time to lower their guns. The children turned and assembled in the ascending order of their uniforms and started toward the school. Walking in a queue over the brick road, another group approached. They came marching in the opposite direction, undeterred by group A's presence. The labels on their uniforms went from B1 to B30.

Group A pattered up a flight of stairs into the Game Room, where an array of tables stood arranged in a five-row, two-column grid. Over each table lay a set of chess pieces to one side and a bowl of snacks to the other. From choosing the right table to assembling the pieces to perfection, every little detail was important. A test of their character. Each roommate walked straight to their tables. The males assembled the chess pieces over the walnut and maple boards. The females supervised their every move.

While A29 picked up each piece and remembered where it went, A30 glanced at the other tables, crossed eyes with A15, a boy she remembered only by his Blue Field eyes, and faced her table again.

Whereas human kids hung their jackets over their chairs in a chess tournament, in the Watcher Development Center, the children hung their rifles, their muzzles dangling an inch over the floor.

There was no luck involved in a game of chess. When a game was lost, somewhere along the way, mistakes were made. The lesson was to eliminate such inconvenient mistakes. For each player to forge the perfect game by manipulating every variable.

After scratching his head, A29 moved a piece.

"I see you're as bright as ever," A30 said. She turned her eyes from the table where A15 sat, glanced at the board, and moved a piece.

A29 groaned. He scooped some snacks from the bowl, and left

shiny fingerprints over the pieces. After both had made a few moves, A29 disrupted the silence of the room with a loud cough, louder each time. His face had a terrible reddish hue.

"Checkmate!" A30 screamed as she smashed one knight against the chessboard. Noticing that he was still making strange noises, she looked at him. Her eyes widened. "Unbelievable..." She pushed him to the floor and hit him in the pit of his stomach. "Dead by choking on a peanut."

A29 looked around. The children from the other tables looked at him, though only their eyes moved.

"Trust me, this is more embarrassing for me than it is for you. Stand up, idiot."

A30's bracelet vibrated and blinked with an array of bright colors. *Emergency call.*

Without thinking, she stood up, looking for the matching crystal near the ceiling until she found the right door.

Halfway out the door, she turned back to look at the group, which had now resumed their games as if nothing had happened. A29 had pulled himself up to the chair and had organized the pieces by the side. She saw him inserting his hand back into the snack bowl. She scoffed. *This better be good.*

A30 turned left in the hallway outside the Game Room. She navigated the maze, guided by automated crystals that lit as soon as she approached them. With every turn, her boots stomped harder over the empty halls. She made company out of the echo.

After the fifth crystal lighted, she shouted. "Where are you taking me?"

The glass frame of a door lit up in a green emerald glow. Attached to the side of the door was a square artifact with a hole in the middle. A30's wrist vibrated. When she looked at it, a white light came out of the bracelet and the artifact emitted a matching light.

Her hand was almost at the artifact when she pulled it back. *It's either this or giving Heimlich maneuvers for the next hour to an idiot that can't chew.* She placed her hand up to her forearm into the artifact. The six-foot iron door creaked open.

As soon as she was inside, the door slammed shut behind her. *Total darkness. Breathe. What do we know about darkness? Shut off unnecessary senses.* She closed her eyes. *Breathe.* Although faint, she could hear the whirring of a machine in front of her. She took a few blind steps further into the room. The cold enveloped her, and she remembered the book of seasons she had read in the library. *Winter. The last season.* It had to be some kind of ending.

A wall-sized computer monitor loaded in front of her with a cursor blinking at the top left corner. The light from the monitor revealed a small wooden chair in the middle of the room. A30 sat on the chair. She blinked once for every three blinks of the cursor.

With fingers tapping over the edge of the chair, she waited while the cursor blinked away the seconds. At once she stood up in a rage, pulled the chair from the floor, and swung it at the screen. The screen flapped back and forth like a curtain from the force of the chair. When the projector screen stabilized, the cursor appeared again, as if mocking her for trying.

"Why did you call me? What do you want?"

Congratulations, you've won!—the words appeared on the screen —*You can now move on to the next floor. Thank you for playing!* Circus music boomed from all directions at excruciating volumes and A30 covered her ears. The projector screen flickered in solid colors, changing them at the same tempo as the perturbing music. Her skin mirrored the colors of the perverted spectacle.

Eyes watched. Eyes were always watching in the Watcher Development Center.

"Eyesight, perfect. Hearing, perfect. Body, strong. She's as good as it gets," Faith said.

Lucifer let Faith's words trail off into silence, then said, "Regardless, she's reckless. Impatient. She walks a path of her own. Useless for our purpose."

"Oh, do not speak such things. Look at her, she's perfect. How can you not see?"

Against his instinct, Lucifer allowed her access to the next level. "We have not come this far to let everything crumble by the mistake of one Watcher."

The music stopped, and the words vanished on the screen.

Walk up the stairs, the cursor wrote. As soon as it typed the last period, the lights came back on.

A30 followed the crystals back out into the hallway and to a door hidden away around the corner. She stuck her hand inside a scan artifact near the door, and the door opened. A flight of stairs appeared behind the door. There were no invitations, only commands. Halfway up the stairs, a metal plaque with a number two etched into it was attached to the wall. She approached the plaque and brought her face to it. But tried as she could, there was no reflective angle, and the mystery of her face, it seemed, she had to carry forward another five years.

<hr>

From the new, black hallway, a green crystal guided her to her room. Inside, A29 waited sitting on a bed.

"What are you doing here?"

He blurted, as if making sure he got the words out before running out of breath. "We're stuck together again, it seems. At least the rooms are bigger."

A30 scoffed before sitting beside him. Their feet dangled in the air two inches above the surface.

"I'll take this one," she said.

He didn't protest and stood up to sit on the other bed. Like all the other boys, A29 had dark brown hair that reached over his ears. He enjoyed brushing it to the side. He wished it grew longer, so he could cover his entire face with it. His gray pants stretched a bit too short when he sat, revealing his black dress socks. Embarrassed, he tried to hide them by pulling his pants down, which showed off the top of his underpants. He concluded the socks were a better display, and pulled the pants back up.

She tapped her lap while inspecting her new room. Nothing was that much different from before. From the furniture to the linens, everything seemed like an exact copy of what they had in the floor below.

After a few minutes in silence, their bracelets vibrated.

They marveled at the blue light shining over their faces.

"Blue Fields!" she said.

They opened the drawers to pull out their swimsuits, as if they knew exactly where all things were. Green crystals guided them to a metal door, where the other ten-year-old children stood. The group faced the door in single file, waiting for instructions.

A30 saw a screen with red numbers on top of the door and recognized it from the class Basics of Human Technology. "An elevator." She said and walked to the front of the group.

Behind her, A15 followed her movements. His body stood straight inside the confines of the line, but his head leaned and turned to not miss a second of her.

"And if I'm right..." A30 pressed on the arrow down button by the side of the metal door. The numbers on top of the door counted down. "Ten... nine... eight... seven..." She recited while the rest of the group remained in silence.

A29 noticed A15's face, puzzled with interest.

"Get back. We don't know what will happen for sure." A29 tried to pull A30 a step backwards towards the group, but she wiggled her arm free.

"Get back to the group, boy," she said, pushing A29 back into the herd.

Soon enough, the number stopped at 2, and the doors slid to the side. A wide metal room waited for them with a green crystal shining at the top. Their bracelets gave the order, and the children marched into the room.

A30 was the last to enter. She turned to the control panel and pressed on the button labeled Blue Field, which had a strip of green light around it.

The elevator started at once, a sensation the children had never felt before. Startled by the sudden motion, A30 lost her balance, and A15 held her arm. "Are you all right?" A15 said.

"Yes, just didn't expect it to be so fast," she said.

A29 cleared his throat. "Well, we're almost there."

The other boy, A15, fell back in line with the rest, none of which had moved at all since entering the elevator.

After a few minutes, the doors opened to a white sand and water horizon, and a wind-ridden soundtrack of calm. When they stepped out of the elevator, the wind forced them to hold on to their swimsuits.

While the children stood outside the elevator expecting the next instructions, A30 pushed one to the side, pulled off her boots and socks, and sunk her feet into the sand. The warmth of it travelled up her body and formed a smile on her face. She closed her eyes and took in the salty air, and let the waves mute her thoughts, if only for a minute.

A15 was the next one to step out of the group. He unzipped his uniform and threw it next to A30. She turned. His spontaneity made her smile. A15 walked straight to the water wearing only his swim trunks. To show off his fearlessness, he let the water cover his body up to his chest. A30 leaned back with her hands and feet in the sand, and stared at him.

The rest stood in font of the elevator, which had now closed, and glanced at their bracelets every few seconds. A29 watched A30 lying in the sand and followed her head as it tracked A15's movements in the water. He let a foot inch forward, looked at his bracelet, and pushed his body back to the group.

Inside the black spire that towered over everything, Lucifer and Faith observed the children's progress.

"She is a leader, like her father," Faith said.

"A stirrer, you mean. A defiant. We are still cleaning up the mess he left."

"The Ancestor has a plan. He always does. I am sure He will make things right again."

The comment bore a hole in his skin. "Yes. My brother is executing His will as we speak."

"Well?"

Lucifer considered his words, yet remembered it was her idea to take the child. "He commanded Gabriel to cause a civil war between the children of angels and the children of men."

She grimaced. His attack had been successful. "And then?"

"He will restart the humans again, as He always does, to wipe out the lingering remnants. Another millennium confined to this dimension. This time, with his sights aimed at our faults."

Faith's eyes watered. "How will He do it this time?"

"Only He knows. Celestial debris again, or a catastrophic flood." Lucifer pressed a button. "Release them."

The children's bracelets buzzed, and they ran elated towards the ocean. They splattered water, some of them still in their uniforms, while others ran across the sand.

A29 sat next to A30 in silence. He ignored the children's racket and the waves and allowed the image of A30 to come crashing against him, instead. He gazed at the marks on her skin, her eyes, and the feelings they evoked, the freckle in her lower lip, the—

"Stop staring at me." She jolted up and kicked sand at his face, then walked back to the elevator. When he had rubbed the sand off his eyes and turned back, she was already gone.

Most days, A30 seemed to look slightly over A29's shoulder whenever they talked, distracted by a promise far off into the future. Occasionally, she treated him with disdain for an arranged partnership. And sometimes A30 sought him out and invited him to play games after they had completed the day's training. He had connected the type of day they would have by how much she talked in her sleep. If she called out for a parent, he braced himself.

When A30 opened her eyes, she saw A29 sitting in a corner, his eyes like an owl's under his brown, sideways bangs.

"You called for your father again," he said.

She scratched the corner of her eyes and yawned. "No one here has parents, not like the humans. That much we know." She stood up and pulled her pillow from the bed, then threw it again in surrender.

"I want to show you something," he said. His mattress squeaked when he got up.

"Better hurry. You'll be late for knife throwing."

"May I?" He offered the palm of his hand, and she placed hers on top.

He tried to pull up the sleeve, but she withdrew her hand.

"It's okay." His voice quivered.

She placed her hand again, slower this time.

He pulled A30's sleeve up, uncovering a half-moon birthmark. "See this?" He pointed at it.

"Yeah, so?"

"I read about it. It's called a birthmark. Only humans have it. You know, the ones who are born to a mother and a father."

"Stop talking nonsense." She slid the sleeve back down and turned away.

"I don't have any parents. None of us do." She shuffled through the drawers.

"Why else would you have a birthmark?"

"Because I'm the only unlucky one with an imperfection," she said.

"Because all of us were made. But you... You were born."

The A group marched toward the Green Field for knife-throwing practice. A half-cut tree trunk stood in the middle of a caged yard, and the children walked up to it one by one. When it was their turn, they attempted to throw the knife in such a way that it would stay in the trunk.

The first child, A1, threw the first knife. His bracelet was lit yellow. He took two steps back and tried again. This time, the bracelet was lit with a red hue. He took one step forward and tried with his last knife. The knife stuck to the trunk for a second before it fell, tumbling to the ground. He bent down to pick up his knives and went back to the end of the queue.

One by one, the children made their attempts to stick their knives into the wood, and their bracelets lit yellow, red, and green, signaling how close they were to the perfect distance from the trunk. None of them got the knife to stick. None, but A15, who, when he had put his arms up to celebrate, the knife mockingly slid from the trunk and fell edge first to the ground, standing like a sword on a battlefield.

A30 had stayed in her room for an extra hour, pondering about what A29 had told her in the morning. *A Birthmark? How?*, she thought, with her sleeve pulled up, rolling her forearm back and forth under the light. The burden of existence itself glued her to the bed. It was the unanswered question, the unresolved problem which pushed her out of bed and toward the Green Field.

She appeared next to the line of children in the Green Field, where they tried to stab a trunk from three meters away. The children were in their fifth iteration, and the trunk was left, apart from a few scratches and dents, unscathed. A30 walked straight to the front of the line, rolling her knives between her fingers. She pushed the child about to throw his knife, A15, to the side, and swung her arms toward the trunk three times. Green, green, green, lit the bracelet. All three knives wedged into the wood.

In a planet called Colonia, behind the closed doors of a celestial meeting, two archangel brothers, Michael and Gabriel, spoke to an informant they had nestled deep into Lucifer's ranks. The spy had described the female child at length, as he had been working on the top floor of the Watcher Development Center.

"And that is all I know, sir."

"Thank you, Daniel," Gabriel said.

"So they kept a hybrid child." A slight grin had formed over Michael's face. "Yet, maybe this might prove to be our biggest asset."

"How so?" Gabriel said.

"They are unstable, the hybrids. Like a virus, we will leave her to spread inside the belly of our enemy." Then, louder. "Let our fourth brother keep her. Perhaps it will be his undoing."

Raphael walked into the room, his long red hair bouncing with each step, and his green robe almost touching the floor, and turned to Michael. "The water from the Great Flood has receded, and we have continued the experiment."

"Have you planted the seed again?"

"Yes, we have restarted the visitations—"

"What stage are they in?" Gabriel interrupted.

"Idolizing. Building temples."

Gabriel relaxed in his seat.

Michael pressed his knuckle over his lip. "How many years have passed since the flood on Earth?"

"According to gravitational time dilation, over two thousand years."

"Where are we in the experiment?"

"The bloodline is thriving. The earthling boy is healthy."

"Let the plan unfold as it should," Michael said, pleased.

As the first couple that managed a perfect throw, A30 and A29 got extra leisure time, while the others picked up and stowed away the knives.

"What else do you know about birthmarks?" A30 said the second A29 shut the door.

"Not too much. I read about it by mistake. I was looking for birds."

"Tell me."

"Well, some humans are born with them. It stays on their skin their whole lives."

"Does it come from disease?"

"No, nothing like that. It's just a mark. It's an—" He cleaned his throat.

"Say it."

"I wasn't going to say anything."

"It's an imperfection. That much is obvious. There must be some type of record in this place. An account with our date of fabrication."

"I've seen nothing like that. Other than the books in the library, of course."

She rested her face on her hand and frowned. "I have to do some exploring."

"You can't. It's against the rules to wander outside our room and the lessons."

"And you will help."

"Me?"

"That's right."

"I can't. We can't. I've done too much already. I bet they're listening right now, don't you think?"

"That's a good point, boy." She broke off a piece of paper and wrote. After a few seconds, she folded the paper and passed it to A29.

From now on, all top secret conversations must be written.

He looked back at her. "How will—"

She shushed him.

He whispered, "How will I know it's top secret, or even if it's coming from you?"

A30 snatched the paper from his hands, looked at her birthmark, and drew its shape over the fold. She showed it to him and pointed.

He nodded.

She opened the note again and scribbled. *I'll come up with something. Keep your eyes open.*

CHAPTER 2

Group A visited the Blue Field every week. One time, as their feet fidgeted over the building's edge, the Sun had risen in front of them and had made the concrete warm to the touch. They looked at their bracelets, then at A15 and A30, both of which had jolted to the water.

A15 splashed A30's face with the Blue Field's water, and she laughed, laughed like she never did with A29, the unplanned, uncontrollable laugh that felt like little daggers to an outsider. A29 was about to defy the bracelet and hovered a foot forward when he felt the buzz on his wrist. And the children set off like race horses. The group leaped forward, leaving his hesitant body still stuck to the wall. He was the last child to walk off into the sand.

Though all children carried a striking resemblance to one another, not all were as gifted. A2, for example, was a shorter boy than most. He was also the one out of the herd that threw himself belly-first into the water. He made a splash bigger than his body and sunk deep into the Blue Field.

It had been two minutes since anyone saw A2.

A30 put her hand toward A15, asking him to stay still. "Where is he?"

He tried running to her, but only dragged his legs across the water. A15 took a deep breath and sunk his face below the waves. His head popped back up. "He's not moving."

He took another deep breath, and A30 followed him. They tried pulling him up, but he had sunk to the bottom, his knees scratching the sand over the ocean floor.

Standing over the shore's edge, A29 stood ruminating on his options, his chances of survival, and whether his involvement would make matters worse. He looked helplessly from ten feet away as A30 and A15 took turns to breathe and dove back into the water. A noise whirled behind A29, and he turned his back to the elevator. A group of tall people dressed in white came out and ran, silent as shadows, towards the scene. They pulled A2's body out of the seabed and put him on a canvas gurney. A2 lay still as a limestone, and his head bobbed by the movements of the running tall people.

The children had already studied death. They had learned that everything must end, but nothing is without purpose. Beginnings and endings are the designers of life, they had read. It gives importance to everything in the middle. And though they assumed A2 had reached his ending, he appeared the next day, alive and a little stranger, as if something had interrupted the natural flow of things.

Days had come and gone with no secret notes, and A29 was convinced that A30 had already forgotten all about their little world. He should have known that extinction was the only outcome of it.

As they walked in pairs to the Game Room, A29 felt A30's fingers and a folded piece of paper in his left hand. He turned his face down to see her birthmark drawn over it and grinned.

The plan is simple, he read, *you need to create a big enough diversion.*

He asked for the pencil. *Like what?*

She yanked the pencil. *You're the expert at choking.*

But I'll die, he wrote back.

Fake choke. Just long enough for the tall people to come, and for me to sneak out.

"Today," she said.

He swallowed and entered the Game Room.

The children never knew what sort of conditions they would find when they woke up. Sometimes they rose to excruciating heat, other times they trembled with stomach-churning cold. They had to adapt. The morning had welcomed them with a chill worthy of gloves, jackets, and hats. A30 knew she could hide her hair and face under the hat and jacket. It was either today or who knows when.

Everyone had been seated. The only noises were timers ticking away, and chess pieces sliding and capturing over the game board.

"Feeling hungry?" A30 jerked her head toward the bowl.

A29 was sweating and sighing.

She slid the bowl closer to him. "You agreed."

A15's gaze jumped from A30, and back to his game.

A29 fell to the ground, coughing, grabbing at his throat as planned, better than planned. The performance of the century. Only, unbeknownst to A30, it was real. He turned paler and paler. A30 stood up and creeped into a corner. After a few seconds, a group of four tall people dressed in white entered the room. They knelt before A29, and a female put instruments over his chest while a male pressed over his stomach. The other two unfolded a rolling bed before carrying A29's body over it. His ghostly face turned sideways, and in a blinking nightmare he saw A30 sneaking out with her hat pulled down, and A15 chasing after her.

The crystal shone black on the hallway. But A30 had already passed by it. She turned a corner and stuck her back to the wall, leaning over and looking at the Game Room. The commotion was still underway. She leaned farther and heard a noise approaching. A couple of breaths of silence later, she leaned in again. "You? What are you doing here?"

A15 joined her around the corner. "I could ask you the same question."

"Well, I—"

"It doesn't matter. It sure as hell looks more fun than chess."

Her shoulders relaxed. "I'm looking for the archives."

A15 stared at her with a puzzled look on his face. "Archives?"

"Or a records room or anything."

They had drifted away from the wall and were now close enough to another crystal, which had also turned black.

"Come," he said and pulled her into a room, letting the door close behind her. "We don't have much time."

Their bracelets throbbed with an amber light. She looked up at him. "What is this place?"

He turned away. "Come, this way."

They wandered between rows of tall machinery, but the bracelets only illuminated enough to not crash against anything. A15 scanned the wall with one hand while pulling A30 with the other until he touched the undeniable shape of a light switch.

Now visible under the spotlight, they marveled at thirty mechanical wombs connected to transparent tubes at the top and metal ramps at the bottom.

"Look," A30 said. When A15 turned, something slid down the bottom of the womb over the metal ramp that led into a black hole in the middle of the room.

"I don't know what this place is, but it doesn't look like an archive to me." A15 jerked his head toward the door. "We better hurry before they find us."

She stood in front of the wombs, wondering if one should always push forward for answers or, as the earthling Thoreau had written, suck the marrow out of what was already there. The crude imagery of Earth's literature often stayed with her for months. It was the only thing she had found worthwhile about the lessons. Reading. The challenge of a premise she had never considered, and the power of language to make her feel both afraid and excited. But this was different. This was real. She didn't need to imagine a picture from words. It was right there in front of them. It was then she observed the tubes, the wombs, and the things coming out, the red and sticky balls of meat.

She gasped. "It's a factory."

"What? We have to move on."

"This is what makes us." But she remembered her half moon, her question still unanswered. For a moment she envied A15. For as revolting as reality was for him, at least he had a logical reality. All the while, her mere existence still floated in the air like a lost zeppelin.

———

Faith, who was seated, turned to Lucifer. "What are they doing?"

From the Tower, an array of screens followed the children and composed a movie-like picture.

Lucifer reached for a button.

"Do not." Faith protested. "Let them be a little longer."

———

The boy pulled A30 from a trance and out of the room with the mechanical wombs, but a tall person blocked their escape.

"You should not be out here. Hey!"

But not all matadors can handle two bulls charging toward him, and they ran underneath his arm and made his white coat flap in the aftermath.

"Get back here!"

They left the tall man echoing in the hallway and giggled on their way back to the Game Room.

"Where is A29?" she said when they entered the room.

"I'm sure he'll be back in no time, like A2."

But he didn't come back that evening.

Has it always been this quiet? A30 wandered over to A29's side of the room and saw a sketch pad over his nightstand. She took the sketch pad and sat cross-legged on her bed. She folded each page, pinching it to the back with her other hand. The first pages were drawings of the tower, of its black walls that appeared even hollower and more sinister in every composition. As she flipped the pages, the face of a woman replaced the unfinished tower sketches. The woman had jet black hair that hung over her shoulders. A30 pulled her own hair into view. She studied the drawing. The woman's eyes, green, blue, aqua, seemed to change colors according to light. She bent the page, letting the light bounce off the paint and move down her face. The woman was the focus of all the other drawings. Like the keyframes of an animation, slight differences in shadow and light required new renditions. With every rendition, A30 discovered a piece of the woman. But of all the emotions she could find in the woman's face, she never found joy. On the sketchbook's last page, the face had something written over her forehead. *A30,* the text spelled.

She tore the page out and laid over her bed. She held the drawing on top of her, stretching her arms out to gain focus. Details outlined her face. The paper mirror gave her a retelling of her story, a glimpse into a possibility. Something. For a second, she wasn't as hollow as her thoughts.

Her smile only lasted a second before everything went dark.

She jumped off the bed and the page slipped away from her fingers. The only light was a dim glow coming from under the door. She scanned her body but remembered she had stowed away her weapons inside the closet. The door flung open, and a group of people rushed into the room. At a breath's length, they pinned her face down to her bed. She tried to wiggle herself free. A gauze covered her face. It smelled funny. Everything happened too fast for her to scream, let alone move.

She pressed her eyes shut, forcing a tear down her cheek. All she remembered was the piercing of injections. The sting of rupturing veins. The white robes. A glass flask filling with blood.

"Extraction completed," a tall person said. And they all disappeared into the hallway.

The worst nightmares spill from dreams into reality, haunting both life's rebellion and its rendition. Her energy drifted away. Nightmare. Rendition. Slumber. Deep slumber. It was the last time she slept through the night at the school.

CHAPTER 3

"You found my drawings," A29 said the next morning.

A30 blinked until her eyes opened. Her sore body was as heavy as a boulder. She pulled it up, inch by inch, until she was sitting. "Are—"

"I'm fine," he said. "Are you?"

She tried to understand what had happened the night before. *It must have been a nightmare.* The thought was comforting for a second until she saw a red dot over her arm fold.

"I'm not sure," she said and sat on her bed. "Where did they take you anyway, the tall people?"

A29 perched over his nightstand. "It was a place I had never seen before. Full of beds, covered by curtains that rolled on a metal tube. I can still hear the grating sound of the curtain rolling open, waking me up every time I was about to fall asleep. But the beds were not like these." He tapped on his mattress and caught his breath. "They were narrow and elevated. The tall people put me in a sitting position whenever they came to check on my throat. They stuck an awful long stick in my mouth that made me gag. There were a lot of tall people. Human tall people are called adults, but I'm not sure what we call ours."

"I thought you were acting. I didn't know you choked for real."

"We had to give them a good show."

"I suppose," she said.

"Did you find it? The archive?"

"Not really. Found something else, though."

He stared but didn't rush her.

"The factory."

"Factory?"

"Yes. Your factory. What makes all of you. It's right here on the second floor, and it pumps tiny people all day long, and they slide right down to the first floor, and it was so gruesome. Made my stomach twist."

"Slow down. Slow down. How many of us do you think there are?"

"Enough to fill two planets, probably."

There was a long silence, and they stared at nothing at all.

"Did you like them?"

A30 wrinkled her forehead.

"My drawings, I mean."

"Is it me? Is my face really like that?"

"Yes, as close as I can get with my skills."

"I love them. If I never find out where I came from, at least it's good to know who I am now. Is that how I look? Am I an adult?"

"No. At least I don't think you are. But that's how I see you in my dreams. I keep having the same dreams, and you're always there."

She pushed into the headrest. "What are the dreams about?"

"Oh," he stood up. "When the adults were rolling me out of the Game Room, they took me up, up to the very top, in one of those elevators and into a hallway. That's where that room with the beds was. There were adults coming and going. We were so high up, I saw all the Fields, and the Tower didn't look so tall after all. Anyway, outside of the room, there was a door. I caught just a glimpse, but adults were sliding a card and entering. It looked important. Maybe that's your Archive."

"We need to go there."

"Yes, but I'm not choking again. I want to go this time."

***

The secret notes returned with ferocity the next week. It was time for a rifle lesson in the Green Field, and the children celebrated their twelfth birthday lined up before the trees.

Have you thought of a plan yet? A29 wrote.

We must break it down into smaller parts, A30 wrote. *Phase one: getting up there.*

Elevator.

Precisely.

Which meant an extracurricular excursion on a Blue Field day.

But the elevator only works twice, once at the start and once at the end of the lesson, he wrote and aimed. His gunshot shook every leaf in the trees but hit nothing.

What's your point?

What are we doing with the rest of the group?

It was now her time to shoot, which she did with the paper folded against the trigger. The bird had not hit the ground yet when she wrote; *We use them as a shield. Like the Vikings.* She snorted.

A29 unfolded the half-moon paper, read, and groaned. *That's not funny.*

Hitting all his targets, A15 shot and looked at their paper contraband. "I want in."

A29 and A30 turned to him. A29 hid the paper behind his back.

A15 raised an eyebrow. "Whatever it is. I want in," he said.

***

Partners could not fraternize with other rooms. A16, A15's partner, enjoyed keeping an immaculate record of all her observations to the second, including the time she went to bed and the time she opened her eyes. It was obvious the trio couldn't count on her keeping a secret. Fortunately, the way they set the room clusters up in the Watcher Development Center, A29 and A30's room shared a wall with A15's room.

In the past few weeks, they had added A15 to their secret paper conversation, and A30 had brainstormed ideas during their lessons. But the process proved slow, and A15 was not known for his patience. He waited for his partner to use the restroom and carved his knife into the wall.

A scraping sound near the place where the wall connected to the floor startled A30.

"Did you hear that?" she said.

A29 shrugged and went back to his drawing.

The scraping sound was now followed by a thump, and a piece of wall the width of a knife broke off and crumbled on the floor. The sharp edge of a knife came through the hole and retreated at once.

A29 put the sketchpad to the side and stretched his neck to see past his feet. "What is—"

A folded piece of paper shot through the hole and slid across the floor. A half moon covered the face of the white invader.

A30 stepped out of the bed, picked up the paper, and unfolded it.

I hope my assumption was correct. Who is this?

A30 snapped her fingers. "Quick, give me your pencil."

This is A30, she wrote, and sent the paper skidding through the hole.

A few seconds later, it reappeared like a mouse.

Good. Now we can plan this quicker, and underneath, *P.S. You might want to do something about that hole.*

That last line made A30's mouth rise on the edges. She brushed her finger over it. Both things had been an impulse.

"What is it?" A29 said.

"Hurry. Help me slide the dresser in front of the hole."

Through days of wall telegrams, they had crafted the plan as follows: A30 would open the elevator, as always, and wait for everyone to get in. Then, she and A29 would stand in front and cover the control panel from the group's view as she pressed on the button with the highest number—the group would never allow such anarchy as to press an unlit button. While the duo selected the floor, A15's job was to tell a story, any story, and keep the groups' eyes from the ascending numbers at the top. He was the best talker; they had decided. When the elevator doors opened at their destination, the three of them would ready their hidden knives in case they encountered any tall people, who A29 called adults, for simplicity. They didn't have time to plan the rest since that day their bracelets lit up in blue. It was time.

The sense of weightlessness prompted him to start. "There's an entire world out there outside the barbed wire." The others stared at him. "Yes. I saw it once. A world full of people of all sizes and colors. At first, they were small as insects. I saw them through an opening low enough for me to stand on my toes and get a peek. The next week I returned with a telescope from the Human Instruments class and saw that they were not ants, but people like us. I saw their legs, arms, and faces. They were smiling."

A30 looked at him, then jerked her head at what looked like a microphone on the elevator's wall.

"Anyway, that's why I'm so grateful for being protected behind the confines of the school," A15 continued. "That outside world looked dangerous for kids like us. Too many tall people. We're much better off here."

The elevator stopped. The doors opened. Knives out.

Two adults waited for them, gun in hand. They had been caught.

They're just tree trunks. They're just tree trunks. A30 thought, and with a spin of each hand, sent two knives flying in the air and landing on the adults' chests. They dropped to the ground like dead moths, a thumping sound she carried with her forever after.

"Get out!" she said.

While A29 and A15 stepped out into the hallway, A30 pressed on the green lit button and jumped out of the elevator. Behind them, the A group stood still, their bodies disappearing behind closing doors. The elevator shot down toward the Blue Field.

A30 wished the adults weren't wearing those awful white robes; it would have made the killing easier, without the visible red puddle forming around the knives. They weren't just tree trunks. She pulled the knives out of each one and cleaned the blade with the unstained parts of their robes. A29 and A15 were nothing but spectators to the gladiator. And they waited, waited for her to be ready to continue. They were on her time now.

She saw what she had done to her partners in crime and broke the silence first. "Was that true?"

A15 twitched as if woken from a hypnotic trance. "What?"

"What you said. About the outside."

"Yes," he gulped. "I've been trying to get out ever since."

"That's why you're helping us," A29 said. "Always an agenda."

"Yeah? And why are you helping her?"

A29 turned his face down.

Cards hung from a string clipped in the adults' pockets. She cut the string from one adult and took their card. She dared not read the name. "We have to move on. Where did you say the room was?"

A29 pointed, and they marched on, silently.

They were lucky. During lesson times, adults in lab coats would watch the children and take notes from hidden lookouts scattered through the Fields. The top floor of the school was empty.

"Take a left here," A29 said while leading the other two.

At every corner, A30 looked at the ceiling. There were no crystals. She rubbed her bracelet and hung back until A29 noticed.

"Is everything OK?" He said.

A15 turned his head from one side to the other, never keeping still.

"I don't know," she said, and walked.

Finally, after walking down a few empty corridors lit by square lamps stuck to the ceiling, they arrived at the access-controlled door.

A29 extended his open hand. "Here, let me. I saw how they used it."

She allowed him to take charge for once. Something about the entire floor made her less of herself.

A15 kept his eyes peeled for any adults rushing down the corridor while A29 slid the card down the black magnetic strip.

The door whirred and beeped.

Automatic lighting illuminated the room as soon as they walked in. Towers of gray file cabinets that were stacked on top of each other hugged the walls, and shelves with various bagged objects of unknown origin filled the middle of the room.

A15 locked the door behind him and touched the file cabinet closest to him. "Where do we even start?"

"We'll search faster if we separate. You take that wall, I'll take the opposite. And you, 29, can check out those shelves in the middle. Look for our names. Anything. If it's interesting and small enough to take, take it."

The boys nodded. A15 skimmed through open file cabinet drawers while A29 picked up bags of objects, turned them around, then placed them back neatly over the shelves.

She forced herself to not open a single drawer until she had walked into the entire room and scanned its contents.

There was a corner in the back of the room. A corner that remained darkened from the tall shelves that covered the ceiling lights. It called to her. She wandered to it, extending her hands when her eyes couldn't see further.

"Found something!"

The sound of a slamming file cabinet drawer was not the only thing that startled her, but the feeling of a hand and five fingers which now held her wrist.

"You've gotten so big," the voice said. It had the raspiness of an older person, but she couldn't see a thing. She felt another hand higher up her arm. The other hand pulled her sleeve up, and A30 felt the room's cold air fall upon her naked arm. "There it is. I knew it the moment you entered the room. No other child could be capable of this. A rebel. So full of fire. Just like your father."

"Who are you?" A30 said, afraid she might scare the creature away into the darkness.

"Hey 30! Did you hear? Where are you? Come check this out," A15 called for her, flapping papers in the air. "This folder has your birthmark on it."

A30 turned her face to A15's voice, but the creature spoke again, "Your father loved you so much. He did everything he could for you, for us. But the Archangels' war knows no mercy."

"I don't understand."

"You're too young. All in time. Now, go. Go, dear. Go back to your friends. Come and find me when you've grown. Only then will you be strong enough to survive what's coming."

She stood in awe, widening her eyes at the darkness. Every passing second, she became more accustomed to the dark. The creature now was a silhouette hunched behind a row of steel bars, and in time the silhouette grew into a figure. It had arms, legs, and a head. A30 walked closer. "Who are you?"

"Oh. Don't, please. Not like this. You don't know what they've done to me, dear. My dear. My Luna." The hunched creature caressed her hand.

"A30?"

A30 turned back. The boys stood looking at her, the half of her that was still under the reach of the lights. She heard the creature dragging her body and bury itself in the darkness.

"There was... something here. Someone."

But when A15 illuminated the room with his bracelet, all they saw was a large empty cage.

The door's handle clicked.

A15 whispered, "Hurry, we have to hide over here."

The trio crouched behind a shelf as an adult entered.

"Is anybody here?" A white-haired adult called when he saw the lights were on.

When the white-haired adult walked onto the opposite shelf, the children snuck past him and out of the room.

In the hallway's light, A29's forehead shone like a sweaty cold drink. "That was close."

"We're still not home free yet." A15 nodded in front of them. "A long way to the elevator. If it even works, that is."

The dead adults had already been taken away, and the floor was bare in front of them.

"Let's go," she said, sure that they had been discovered and the elevator wouldn't work.

But the doors slid open, and inside it, the number two was encircled in green, inviting light.

"First there was one, then two. Now she has accrued a group of three. She is infecting the group, as we knew she would," Daniel said, projected over a cylinder. "And they have made their way up to the Archives as we speak. I let them in, as you commanded, marked her file, and left it accessible."

Gabriel was calm. "All according to plan. She is a virus, as you had said."

"I want her to know," Michael said. "I want her to feel so much hate. She will stop at nothing to take vengeance on whoever she deems responsible. But she has to discover it herself. All of it. It is the only way it will mean what it is supposed to mean. We will create a fuming gun. But all guns need a target, and we will provide that target," Michael said.

Raphael reclined in his seat and raised his eyesight to the ceiling.

Michael continued, "It is the only way anyone will ever get close enough to Lucifer. It is the only way to kill him and focus on leaving this universe."

"When will she be ready?" Gabriel said.

"Soon. When she reads that paper, something will awaken inside of her. Something that shall never rest for as long as she lives. Daniel, you will help in poisoning her mind further. We shall rewrite history. Her history."

<hr>

A folded piece of paper with a half moon drawn over it slid through the hole.

A30 ran to it, unfolded it, and read it. *Well?*

She had snatched the folder from A15, and with A29 had run to their rooms and locked the door. They still hadn't caught their breath. The file set on her bed and she wondered if all crossroads were meant to be walked over, or if it wasn't too late to turn back around, secrets still buried, and remain blissfully anxious, rather than disturbingly informed. Ignorance seemed like such a sweet temptation.

A29 snatched the secret lunar paper from her and ran to the bed. "We must read it."

She pushed him to the side. "No," her voice quivered. "Wait."

Her heartbeat had accelerated to the speeds of someone who was about to pull out an arrow from a leg. To prepare for a world of pain in one swift motion, she expelled a shuddering breath and opened the folder.

The papers were overflown with complex information, and their eyes scanned for a focal point.

The watcher Samyaza has impregnated a human. And below that, *we have incarcerated the offending watcher. He has hidden the impregnated woman and will not speak, not even under extreme torture. This proves both the efficacy and gaps in our program. Much improvement needed on subjecting to authority.* She flipped the page. *Day 3, Watcher will not talk. Search continues for the female.* Another page went over. *Torture proved too much for the watcher. He did not survive after the fourth day.* She traced her finger to the bottom of the page. *Impregnated human found in a hidden basement of the city of Sundar. All co-conspirators have been eliminated, female human taken to the Watcher Development Center in the city of Nieve.* She gasped and turned the page over. A29 tried to keep up. *Human female gave birth. Child removed for further studying. Female human kept in the Watcher Development Center's repository for observation.* There were scattered tables, notes, and numbers she couldn't understand. Blood panels, exam results, and psychological evaluations filled the pages. She skimmed through those looking for handwritten notes. Finally, on the last page, she read, *The child seems to advance at a higher rate than the others. Abstract: Combining our DNA with that of a human might provide a better mould for the watchers.* And below, *Methods: Use a series of wombs modeled by the human female and create the watchers within them.* In the last paragraph, *Conclusion: We have disposed the faulty batches. After the first four batches, there seems to be much improvement. Reverence for authority improved, aiming average improved, cognition average improved, notable health issues obliterated. In order to prove we have matched or excelled the abilities of the hybrid child, we have placed her as our control in the first successful batch, hereby referred to as Group A. More observations required. We suggest at this moment to cease production of new hybrids until we have observed Group A to maturity. Consequences of failing these measures, unknown.*

A30 had been lying in silence for a long time, the folder open beside her. A29 stared with intent but waited.

"That creature in the dark. It called me something. It's a word I've heard before in my dreams."

Finally, A29 exploded, shooting breathless inquisitions. "A30, the creature you saw. Do you think it was the woman from the files? Do you think you are the child? It did mention group A. I mean, if all of that is true, that thing you saw could've been your—"

"Luna. It called me Luna. I like that. From now on, my name will be Luna."

"Luna?"

"Yes, call me Luna."

"But we don't choose our names."

"I do." She turned away from A29 and didn't speak another word until morning.

PART 2

CHAPTER 4

When Luna opened the door, the children had already assembled in the hallway and stood waiting for the group to be complete. Their bracelets had never blinked red before, and A29 hated the color. Something about it, he said, made him grief-stricken, chapfallen, disconsolate, just depressed enough to hold on to the doorframe and refuse to come out.

"I don't want to go. I have a terrible feeling about it, Luna," he said.

A15 overheard from the line. "Luna? Who is that?"

"It's my name, now."

He nodded. "Luna. I like it."

Luna's smile pushed A29 out of the room. "I like it, too," he said and stood between them.

She showed A15 her crimson bracelet. "What do you think this is all about?"

A15's eyes mirrored the red from the bracelet, and he wiped a drop of saliva coming from his mouth. "A new Field, maybe?" He looked at his wet knuckle and raised an eyebrow.

"This is the truest color I have ever seen." Luna turned her wrist and studied the bracelet.

"It's so—"

"Pure."

"Yes, pure."

The red triggered a revolt, their consciousness vanished, their heartbeats now at their necks. They craved blood—uncontrolled and purposeless blood.

A29 touched on Luna's arm. "Better fall into line." He wanted to pull her away but waited until she followed him on her own accord. They walked over and positioned themselves at the end of the line. Luna was a fighter before entering the ring, with knives as gloves and a red light as the encouraging spotlight.

They walked, guided by the light, hypnotized, with boots on the ground, yet floating. She heard A29's voice as a distant echo. She didn't know where they were. The setting had shifted from the school to a circular room, miles in diameter. Dim lights made the overhanging red lamp more dramatic than it was. In front of her, a wide screen flashed her given name, A30. She walked to it and felt the ground beneath her feet. Dirt. At the other end, she saw A15 step forward from the other half of the group. A29 said something about luck, and she gripped her knives almost to the point of bleeding. She always had to try harder whenever luck was involved. A15 walked toward her with a spear, his favorite weapon. He looked excited. Until now, the spear had been a collectible—a wall decoration he had only read about and fantasized about. He looked hungry and thirsty all at once. Her arm hair stood on end. It wasn't fear, but excitement. It was all a haze, yet she knew exactly what to do. When he swung high, she ducked and grazed the dust. When he aimed for her feet, she jumped and twisted, and cut his knuckles with her shimmering knives. He tried, but his spear was too heavy and her agility too fast. In a matter of seconds, she had rolled and appeared behind him, striking him with serious cuts on the back of his leg. He was now kneeling, holding his spear with both hands and resting his forehead over the handle. He struggled to catch his breath, but he grinned, consumed by joy. She rolled the knives over her knuckles and stowed them away. She smirked and held a helping hand out. He accepted it and limped next to her, back to his group.

He chuckled. "I take it you read the file? What was in it?"

"From now on. Red means training. Be ready. And in time, we will take this whole place down," she said and released him to his group.

"Are they not somewhat... young for this?" Faith said, looking at Luna slicing A15's calves.

"They appear to be doing perfectly adequate. We must push them to their limits, or else we risk never knowing their potential." Lucifer turned. "Our scientists were right. This group was much better than our previous iterations. I am glad we did not stop fabricating."

"May I remind you, love, that our intention was to observe her until she was ready to come to us?"

Lucifer took a few steps and swept his robe over the glossy floor. He would not give up finding a reason to punish Luna for a sin she did not commit. Her father ruined years of careful evolution, and Lucifer could have almost walked over the bridge to the Ancestor, but now must start again building humanity from scratch. "Then we must continue pushing her to extremes from where she cannot return. We shall erase her humanity, her imperfect humanity, and make her one of us, fully. She must earn her place, if she is to be among us."

Red after red, Luna's hatred grew. In her dreams, an unknown face materialized, line by line, inch by inch, into a demon. She recognized the horns, the scattered facial hair, and the wrinkled red skin from the new books that appeared in their history lessons. Nestled in its eyes, there was something more human. It was the unknown face of an adult with a stern look and fire that emanated from his skull and out of its eyes.

The lessons, which had once told a story of an overlord creating all things in the universe, had shifted to the story of a fallen angel named Lucifer, who once dared to defy the Ancestor. There were drawings to accompany the stories—there had never been drawings before.

As the story went, the fallen angel was banned into a realm as punishment for his anarchy. And in this realm, he had created a planet utopia which the book named Arvo. He also had a second vision, a machine world of an industrialized civilization where half the citizens lived their lawless lives in whatever peace they could afford, while the other half built him an army. An army that, in time, would be strong enough to overtake the Ancestor and steal his hold of the universes.

In the book, Lucifer did not have his machine world in Arvo, but would outsource it to a distant planet, away from any Arvonian's consciousness as to not disturb the perfect ecosystem his utopia provided. He had his dirt packed neatly on the other side of the universe, favored by space and time, productive at all hours of the day. And he called this planet Colonia.

But all the creating and managing, the controlling and fear-mongering, grew Lucifer's hunger. He felt God-like. Addicted to power, he created yet another planet he called Earth, which he populated with experiments and beasts. In time, the beasts walked upright and learned to use tools and created explosives. The new beings, he called humans. Lucifer diluted his Colonial army and created natural-born assassins whose sole purpose was population control and course-correcting the evolution of humans. And if the experiment proved too catastrophic, he pulverized the planet from existence with a meteor shower plummeting from the sky in a flashing, burning, and painful death. And from the debris, he started anew. Again and again. A new day, a new Earth.

Luna ripped a drawing of the fallen angel, Lucifer, from the book and folded it into her pocket. On an empty piece of paper, she drew her birthmark, and wrote, *What the hell is this?* And passed it to A29, who looked over his shoulder and opened it.

What?

She took the note. *This book. It's messed up.*

I don't know what you mean; he wrote.

But before she could explain, their bracelets were red again, and she crunched her hand into a fist, salivating.

The way to the Red Field differed from all the other paths. All familiarities ended when the elevator doors opened, and their lungs filled with a sinister wave of musty air. As they walked into the path, they became encircled by a rocky cylinder that reminded Luna of the Lærdal Tunnel in Earth's Norway. Soft blue light made the rocky walls appear as blocks of ice, and the rest of the tunnel's darkness was lit by flaming torches inserted in holes every ten feet.

It was a long walk from the elevator to the arena, but the expectation was part of the excitement. When they passed a torch, Luna glimpsed at the front of the line and saw A15 hitting his head and mumbling gibberish; a coarse sound that became amplified by the vastness of the tunnel and forced her to turn around and make sure they were still alone.

A29 trembled, and he wished he could exchange places with someone in the middle. *From A10 to A20 would be perfect,* he thought, but said out loud, "What's wrong with him?"

"He's getting ready for practice, as should you. Unless you want to stay behind and play decoy again whenever we get the hell out of here."

"No!" He said, and the others had jerk reactions to the reverberation. "Please don't leave me."

"Fine, but you have to fight this time, not just cower behind your little shield."

As they approached the adobe doors, the arena opened in front of them. Half the group walked to the other side and waited for instructions. Most fights ended in a draw, since divine interaction dictated from birth that they must be equally matched. It was now A29's turn to face A14, A15's partner.

"Go easy on him," A15 said in a loud whisper that travelled straight into A29's ears.

Dust floated, remnants of the previous match. A29 walked over the dirt, his face shiny with sweat, and his shield covering all but a fraction of his eyes. A14 walked methodically, as if their encounter was more a matter-of-fact victory than an event governed by strength or talent.

Bow and arrow was A14's strength, which is why A29 had chosen the shield—nothing more than a reaction instead of a decision.

A29 crouch-walked towards A14. If he could just get close enough without getting an arrow stuck in his leg again, he might have a chance. His previous wounds had healed quickly, almost miraculously, but they had hurt like all hell.

Like a mythological creature, A14's stance resembled Elf royalty, her slender figure, straight as a lamppost, rigid, strong, in control. She kept her weapons like she kept everything else in her life, from her notes to her room, organized and maintained to perfection. Her bow was in pristine condition and shimmered under the arena's soft red light, and her arrows were not arrows, but extensions of her arm. She waited patiently for him to be careless. All she needed was an inch of exposed skin. Aim was her talent, but patience her virtue.

A29 crouched. With each step, he felt the burning pain on his thigh muscles. He knew he couldn't keep it up much longer, his form was already suffering. He felt the thud of a charging arrow hit the rim of his shield, and he strengthened his grip to keep the shield from swaying.

"Come on, come on," Luna said to herself. She looked at A15, who seemed entertained by the encounter, and the girl in the ring was nothing but his avatar. Inspired by the thought of her image drawn on a piece of paper, Luna spouted words of encouragement. Their partners' fight was now their own.

Another arrow hit A29's shield.

"Now, you idiot, while she's still reloading."

At once, A29 released his stance and ran towards A14 like a raging Viking, roaring and prepared to die. She was startled, and the arrows in her quiver escaped her fingers. A29 swung his shield back to gain momentum and pushed it forward with the exploding might of repressed anger. A14 felt the sharp blow, and all she heard afterwards was a high-pitched whistle.

The adults appeared within seconds to take her away. Bracelets shone in daylight white as they carried her out: time to return.

Silence fell on their journey back to their rooms, the group incomplete by a pair of footsteps.

Whatever had possessed Luna and A15 weeks ago had now infected A29 as well, who paced the room with the survival rumination of a caged animal.

Every few steps, he turned to Luna and said, "Did you see me out there?"

A14 returned the next day, as perfect as ever. Only her room became messy, her notes scattered, and her bow rotted before the next epoch.

After the confidence that a victory had allowed him, A29 tried to convince Luna to save what, according to the file they had found, was her mother, and escape the school, according to A15, through a hole he had discovered on the perimeter fence. She assured him they weren't ready yet, and for years they practiced combat in the Red Field arena, raised their stamina swimming in the Blue Field, and perfected their aim in the Green Field. Yet, she always said they were not ready, and every conversation ended with A29 asking, "If not now, when?"

And her response was also the same. "Tomorrow, maybe?"

Secret notes kept popping in daily as a newspaper subscription, and A15's messages were always an insatiable begging for action.

"Look," A29 said, unfolding the note and showing her. "He thinks so, too."

"Not yet. There are too many adults, we'll never be able to get through them. They're too strong, too tall."

"Look at us, Luna. We're as tall as they are now."

Her answer was simple enough to not need unpacking. "Draw me," she said.

"We don't have time for this, Luna. Trust me, we're tall enough, trust me."

She gave him a pen. "Draw me."

"I haven't drawn in forever. I don't even know where my sketch pad is." He pushed Luna's books out of the way. Some fell open on the ground to pages of demonic drawings, with headings of its name, Lucifer. He was about to grab it when Luna rushed him again. Finally, at the bottom of the pile, he found his old sketch pad.

She stood up and straightened. And he made a freehand sketch, exaggerating her facial features, and accentuating her body compared to the rest of the room. Then he turned the pad over to her. "See?"

Luna assented. She had been worrying for so long to be good enough, strong enough, so desperate for perfection before action, that now she wondered if perhaps she had waited too long.

"Do you think she's still alive?"

A29 rested the sketch over the nightstand, sat next to Luna, and held her hand. He just held her hand for a long time.

The worry of all the variables necessary for their plan to work came rushing in. Luna feared the hole in the school's fence had been fixed, or whether they had changed the door's security, rendering their stolen card useless.

She glanced over at the open sketch pad and the drawing. Then she looked at A29. Her determination had consumed her, blinded her, but it was true. In the process of growing strong, they had also grown tall; tall enough to be eighteen years of age. If they wanted to do something, anything, they had to act quickly, for, according to the manuals, at the cusp of adulthood, the students would be sent off to their missions. Graduation day was near.

CHAPTER 5

Their metal bracelets illuminated the room in a blue haze.

"Write to A15. Tell him we will do it today."

A29 ripped out the same page he had drawn Luna on just a few moments ago, with a grin the size of a hammock. He flipped the page over, and in it he wrote, *Today.* And sent the folded paper sliding through the slot on the wall. He didn't even have to draw Luna's birthmark over the cover, and in a heartbeat, he got the reply. *I'm ready.*

"The child is planning another endeavor into the Archives today, masters," Daniel said, between bouts of galactic interference.

The three Archangels listened.

"Clear the halls for her," Michael said.

After a long silence, "Repeat that, sir."

"Kill them all."

The other Archangels looked astonished, for they had never seen their brother so bloodthirsty and determined.

"Leave no trace, Daniel. Only the whole truth shall ravage her full of anger. And only vengeance will sharpen her knives enough to break Lucifer's skin."

"Surely he will notice, sir."

"For the Ancestor," Michael said, which was a way to recruit unassuming angels to do their bidding. In truth, the Ancestor did not know of the happenings of this universe unless the humans were at bay of destruction, when He would, with the flick of a finger, restart their evolution.

"For the Ancestor," Daniel whispered.

The signal was lost, and the projection shrunk into the cylinder.

Their process mirrored the actions they had taken years before on their first exploration to the top floor. Everything appeared to go exactly the same as before, except they now had stronger, taller bodies, and were armed with deadlier, sharper weapons. A14 followed their actions while the rest remained still as zombies waiting for a sudden sound.

"What are you doing?" A14 said, when Luna pressed on an unlit button in the elevator.

A29 didn't have to do much else to dissipate her energy than show off the edge of his shield. "Stay back, 14, if you know what's good for you."

With A14 back in line, the doors opened to an empty corridor. Luna had counted on an adult to be waiting for them, one she could easily kill and steal their access card, but they were met with dreadful silence.

"What has he done?" Lucifer said as he saw Daniel dragging the bodies and hiding them behind a door. He turned off the screens.

Faith put her hand over his arm, imploring him to breathe before taking any action. She tried to remind him of the bigger purpose of what had them stuck in this universe.

But when a man surrounds himself with traitors, his ears become deaf to reason. "I will take care of this myself," he said, pushed himself off the control room, and walked out into the light of planet Arvo's two Suns.

Planet Arvo revolved in orbit between two solar systems right next to the edge of the Universe, where Lucifer felt closer to the Ancestor, and from where he could walk right back to Him once his assassins had course-corrected humanity's evolution into a peaceful, yet submissive state, and proved himself the one worthy of His throne.

"What do you think happened?" A29 said.

A15 had already walked a few steps ahead and stretched his neck over a corner. "It's dead empty."

Luna pressed the green lit button on the elevator and jumped out into the hallway. "Ok, let's just pretend our card will work."

"Wait. You can't do this. I will tell them—" A14's voice echoed in the metallic walls of the elevator before the doors closed.

A29 led with his shield protecting the group, and Luna crouch-walked in the middle, sandwiched by A15, who reared in with his spear ready to lunge at anything that moved.

Luna passed her stolen card to A29, who tried it over the Archive's scanner. Three attempts with a red light, each one followed by a beep that irritated Luna. She pushed A29 aside and tried her knives instead.

"Fantastic, now what?" A15 said when he saw the scanner now slashed to bits, with strands of smoke floating out one side.

Luna stuck her face over the small glass window on the door. The light had been left on, as if someone had left in a hurry. She saw the cage at the end of the room. Inside the cage, a shape trudged, slow and painful, but alive. Luna punched the thick glass.

A29 grabbed her wrist. "Luna, stop. It's probably shatter proof. Bulletproof, like in those Earth books. Remember?"

"There has to be another door, something else we can try," Luna said, but the others had already given up. The last time they had noticed only one door, which now stood with its lock smoking from the cracks.

A29 put his shield down. "Maybe we should just go to the Blue Field before we get into any more trouble."

"No, we didn't come all this way for nothing. We won't get another chance."

A15, who had walked a few steps away from the group, returned. "Vents," he said, pointing his spear at the ceiling.

Luna recoiled. "What?"

"Vents. There are always vents in those human spy novels." He went away again and turned the corner around the room. "Vents!"

Luna and A29 rushed to meet him.

A beep which would go unnoticed if it wasn't for the dreadful silence made them turn their heads. They knew what it was, and how much time they had.

A29's words were fast, almost as fast as they had been as a kid. "Hurry it along." The last syllable ended in a soundless swallow.

"Unless you have a screwdriver in your pocket, you're better off quiet," Luna said with the blade of her knife inserted into the screw drive. She turned the knife by the ends and the sharp end was now slathered in red.

"Luna," was all A15 said, looking up at Luna standing on his shoulders. But it seemed to make her grip the knife even tighter, drawing more blood over the blade, his arms, and the floor, so he stopped.

There were four screws, one in each corner. They could now hear footsteps.

From the noise coming from the hall, A15 counted at least two men and begged Luna to hurry.

A29 had reverted to his useless self, shaking like a leaf in the corner and banging his head over the wall. "I don't know if I can do this."

Luna ignored him and told A15 to maybe not tremble so much.

"You're not exactly weightless," he said.

She didn't intend for the vent cover to fall on the ground as hard as it did, but it resonated through the halls like a beacon of light in the gut-wrenching darkness.

"It came from over there." A guard said. The footsteps made their way around the corner, and were loud enough to make A15's hair stand on end.

Luna pulled herself into the vent and turned to look down through the hole.

A15 thought he had never seen a sight so beautiful, and would do anything to never have to lose her. "Go!" was what he said. "Find her." He looked at her, and said, quieter, "Save her."

Luna wondered if he meant the creature who had been her mother, or if it was her own self as a child she would be saving. She shook off the thought. "What about you?"

He held his spear and turned around. A group of adults walked towards them, and in a second, they were at their throats.

As Luna crawled through the vents, she heard sounds of death: screams, slashing, clinking of metal on the ground, then silence. She ignored the moisture that made its way down her cheeks and focused on the cold floor under her hands and knees instead.

A guard had his hand open in front of the boys and A15 couldn't move. Try as he might, invisible cuffs restrained him.

A29 and A15 watched Lucifer as he levitated in front of the air vent, and gasped. They knew. These adults were not like the others.

"Knife to a gunfight," A15 said.

A29 looked to A15, his raised shoulders now level.

Lucifer stuck his hand inside the vent. "Now, where are you? Where have you gone?" He opened his hand and closed his eyes.

On the other side of the room, Luna kicked the vent cover open. The room was almost as she had remembered it, including the steel bars at the back. After a few indecisive inhales, she grabbed the edges of the vent opening and pushed herself forward. Halfway out, her body somehow felt heavier, as if someone had put a weighted blanket over her. She used up all her strength, pushing herself out until her muscles atrophied. And after an eye blink, she couldn't move. Her eyes still pointing forward, she saw a shadow moving inside the cage. From the cage, a pair of hands came through the openings and held on to the bars. Luna could barely move her lips, yet felt the pressure from a soundless scream cramping in her diaphragm, and felt the moisture sliding over her cheek again.

A whisper came from the cage and echoed in the hollow of her skull. "Luna?"

The creature, her mother, a few feet from her, extended her hand between the bars. And Luna imagined herself doing the same, extending out to reach her, only she didn't move at all.

And at once Luna was suctioned back through the vents as if pushed away by high-altitude winds. Her body slammed over the vent corners, and her hands and knees squealed on the sheet metal. Until she came to a halt.

She didn't dare look at the raspy voice that spoke in a voice so low it demanded her attention. "There you are."

Able to move again, she looked at the hand on her foot, the arm that connected to a trunk, and the head over it. The head of the demon in her book. The harbinger of suffering and all that is putrid and obscure. Lucifer.

CHAPTER 6

Her mother's voice never stopped blustering inside her head. "Luna." Every time it hit, it hit stronger, hurt deeper. It was a nail pressing on rubber, the tip ripping its way to the other side.

She was face down against the vent floor, paralyzed. Defeated. Then she noticed something over the metal vent. Something that moved with the rhythm of her breaths.

Luna felt her body loosening and came closer to the metal, and from the blurry shadow came into view what A29's drawing had tried to capture—her reflection. A burning rekindled inside of her, the same one that urged her to take the less walked path and to bend the rules to her favor.

Lucifer's voice came stronger through the vents. "Come on out, child."

Luna's body relaxed. Whatever had constricted her into stillness now lifted away. She had woken.

"Come."

His voice drove Luna to comply—every word, an incontestable command. As she wiggled her fingers and toes inside her boots, she looked at the two ends of the air vents, and two futures lay within reach, but she knew in order to reach the right path, she must now walk the wrong one, and maybe, when she found her way back, it would still wait for her there, in that room, in that cage.

She pushed herself back out of the vent and dropped to the floor. The sound of her boots slamming on the ground made A15 and A29 turn their faces to her, both held to the ground at gunpoint, and the strange beast, half man, half demon, smiled at her. Only his face was not hairy, red, or scary at all. In fact, she found a soothing quality in the confidence that radiated from him as if he knew exactly what he was doing. Hard as she tried to fight it, she couldn't. She felt terrifyingly at home.

Lucifer had taken Luna to the place outside the barrier of the Academy, where A15 had seen the adults swarming the streets. They had hidden the exit right next to the Green Field, through a door that to her had always been nothing more than concrete overflowing with wall creepers. And as they approached the wall, the door slid to the side and disappeared into a tree trunk. A flock of bluebirds flew out of the branches and scattered to the skies.

Lucifer explained the planet was called Arvo, and a lot of information she then learned he had already explained, but she had not listened. It was hard to make sense of his words over the high-pitched ringing that had taken her ears hostage, and the blood pumping in her chest that had risen to her neck, constricting the air with short and forceful breaths. And the grip over her knives had grown so strong, so tight, her mind only had room for its piercing sting.

He felt her repressed rage, yet he had sent his guards away, and now walked beside her with his hands clasped behind his back.

His house was a tall building with sharp edges cut with precision, and every room served only but one purpose. They had made their way to the second floor, something about having time alone to speak, before a person called Faith arrived.

The second floor had a resemblance to the spire tower in the Academy, and a wide and thick glass overlooked what appeared to be the planet in its entirety. The planet's dirt was yellow with an eerie lilac fog, and the sky had a reddish undertone which she did not recall from her time in the Academy. Lucifer explained the Academy was a controlled ecosystem. From dusk to dawn, they manipulated nature at will from a secret control room to prepare the children for their time on Earth.

Luna looked out of the glass with a soft gaze. She recognized the tower and spire on the far left. As Lucifer approached her, she broke the silence. "Will I ever see them again?"

"Worry not. Soon, the past will be not much more than a scar."

She turned around. "Why? Why do people keep taking everything away from me?"

"Law of life. For some to have everything, others must have nothing at all."

"Why can't everyone have something?"

He fleered at the absurdity.

"There must have been hundreds of options for you to pick. Why choose me?"

"You are special."

She had grown an aversion to the word. "Special... I'm so sick of everyone saying that."

"It is true by definition."

"How so?"

"Daughter of a purebred Watcher and a human. You are both a miracle and a sin. Your mere existence puts everything and everyone in jeopardy."

Her eyes took the wide shape of frightened.

"Do not worry; you are safe with us. No one knows about you."

"Doesn't the Great Ancestor know everything?"

"No, not in this universe. We have free will. He only knows when Earth's chaos is incurable. He senses it and takes action."

"Are you alone in this universe? I mean, are there others like you?"

Her question didn't surprise him, as he had watched her curiosity blossom since birth. "My three brothers are also here, somewhere. Last I knew, they had taken shelter on a planet they called Colonia."

She remembered the word from the Origin book, though its meaning was different. "You don't see them much?"

He exhaled. "In here,"—he touched the side of his head—"we are at war, my brothers and I. But my only goal is to find a way back from this universe to The Great Ancestor, not to kill them. Although, if they stand in my way, all laws be damned, I will."

"Who is this Great Ancestor you keep mentioning?"

"The seer of the universes. The tip on which the scales balance. In the Watcher Development Center, did you learn anything about the Origin?"

"We read some books." She remembered now she still had the terrible drawing she had ripped off the Origin book. The drawing of him, an uglier version of him.

He saw her glowering at him and said, "I did fall for deceiving the Great Ancestor, a mistake I regret often, but I implored the writers to leave that in the book. You cannot escape your past. No one should. It is just as important as your future."

She let go of the wrinkled paper and removed her hand from her pocket. "How did you deceive Him?"

"All children think they can do better than their father, but few show them. I took that chance and failed."

"What happened then?"

"He banished all of us here, for my brothers also attempted a revolution. Incarcerated until we see it that humans evolve into a peaceful and united civilization, instead of destroying one another."

"How many times have you tried so far?"

"There is so much they have not uncovered. Mysteries buried deep inside the soil tell the stories of great civilizations. Brilliant, yet barbarian. I am afraid I have lost the count."

"Is there something anyone can do to make them less... barbarian?"

"I do. I always try. That is where the Watchers come into play."

She recognized reading the word in the file they had stolen from the Archive. "Who are they?"

"You. All of you at the Academy. A league of highly skilled assassins who walk among the humans to fulfill specific bounties."

Mere hours ago, the biggest plan she had schemed had been organized over a lined sheet of paper. Now, it seemed her name had been written into a plan of infinite proportions.

Lucifer continued, "I send the Watchers to Earth to eliminate the barriers between war and peace. When they veer, we push them back to the path."

"I want to go."

"It is in your blood. But I prefer you stayed."

"I want to. I don't know how to do anything else."

"The three spinners decided a long time ago, and I feel the end of my thread is near. When the time comes for my life to end, I will need a successor."

"You know, for an angel, you don't have much faith."

It was the first time he had shown his teeth, and there were no fangs or black slurry pouring out of his mouth.

The staircase creaked under their feet as they made their way down to the first floor. He said he had wooden planks put in there to facilitate this sound, because the house felt too artificial without these imperfections.

The first floor had high ceilings, and his voice reverberated across the room. "I believe you will get along just fine with Faith."

Luna turned to Lucifer. "Who?"

"My companion. She has been alongside me watching the humans for civilizations. I saw it in her eyes the last time The Great

Ancestor restarted Earth. A tear. A single tear. I could not stand it. 'Must He end it again?' She said to me, 'I feel so very powerless. Look at them. Look at them smiling at the top of their structures. Look at their infants playing on the roads their fathers and grandfathers built. Running barefoot over the cobblestone. Must He extinguish the flame just when it has lit up?' I tried to explain it to her. As innocent as they look, as bright as their smiles are, they are capable of so much hurt and pain. She put her hand on my arm and said, 'Can we at least send a message? I wish to see them enjoy life at its fullest, even if for a day.' We then saw a mother embracing her child, caressing his face. Mother and son smiled. The air sparked in a joyful wind. Nonsense. When I looked, Faith was smiling. To my surprise, I was smiling too."

"What did you do?"

"We sent a message when we knew of the Ancestor's plans. Then we saw as the meteorites plummeted the Earth. She stopped observing with me. I never considered a deity might feel Vilomah."

"Vilomah?"

"The grief of a parent who has lost their child. It goes against the natural order of life. I did not have a word to describe what I felt every time we had to see the Earth restarted until Faith told me. 'I learned it from the Sanskrit language,' she said once as I watched the impacts hit the Earth. She stopped me from scratching the skin right out of my arm and embraced me."

Luna didn't find an appropriate thing to say. Her frowning lips said enough.

"After that, I obsessed over giving the humans what I believed they needed to aid in their evolution. For her, for myself. In time I learned in all things love, force never works. By forcing humans to evolve alongside our technology, I made the error worse, providing them with bits and pieces of destruction. Blueprints that brought giant leaps in advancement. I believed it might take them out of their barbaric ways. It had the opposite effect. We created nothing more than heightened barbarians, aiming at each other, not with bows and arrows, but nuclear warheads. That is when we began sending our watchers, not to bring them gifts, but death. But again, we have failed. Our last Watchers did an awful thing. They commingled with human females. Which our Ancestor rectified by washing over Earth with a great flood. Once more, we tried. But I feel the dread. Time is approaching again. A restart."

Luna captured Lucifer's attention once more. "Let me try."

"You do not give up easily."

She grabbed his wrist. "Let me try to turn them around."

"They are beyond repair."

"Then you have nothing to lose."

Lucifer had scratched four red lines into his skin.

Lucifer had called Daniel to a briefing the moment he had seen Daniel's spaceship braking the atmosphere, and was now waiting with his legs propped over a yellow wooden desk.

"Tell me, Daniel."

"Your assumptions were correct, Lucifer. Your brothers... they have restarted the experiment."

"And?"

"I am afraid it gets worse, sir. Much worse."

"Well? Do not keep me waiting, boy." Lucifer kept the knowledge of Daniel's treason at bay.

"The rumor is they have perfected the bloodline. They have bred a portal creator."

Lucifer punched the table so hard, a crack formed from the impact and grew in every direction. "Is it awakened?"

"He, sir. The male is still asleep. He knows nothing."

"They must have not found a way of awakening his power yet. Of course. We have seen it. Every link in their chain awakens in a different way. This means we might still have time."

"Sir, I suggest we send someone at once to kill him."

"And risk awakening him in the process? No. We need assurance.

We might only get one chance." Lucifer rose from his seat and towered over Daniel. "It is very unfortunate."

Daniel's voice quivered while recounting his traitorous trek and wondered if somehow Lucifer had known. "What is, sir?"

"That there is only one person fit for such a task."

"A—and who is that, sir?"

"The offspring of angel and man. The only one with humanity and deity at her disposal."

PART 3

CHAPTER 7

News spread about the previous Earth reset, and days fell hard on Arvo. The weight of failure knocked its habitants down just before the night's dark blanket enveloped them. And while Lucifer swore Luna would be all right, Faith tossed and turned well into the night.

"We have other Watchers to do the work," she said. "Why must you gamble with her life?"

He inhaled while stretching his arms. "She is different. You have seen it. She has something others do not."

"She is also frail. Her emotions are. We know not how the human inheritance flowing through her veins will react."

He turned his body to her. "She always finds a way. She is a fighter."

A long silence poured over them. He almost made a sound when Faith spoke. "Do you really think she can do it?"

"I do."

"I cannot bear to lose her. If anything happens to her—"

"You know better than to worry. It is written. Everything is written."

She rose from bed, and he could only see glimpses of movement in the darkness. Noises of porcelain clinking over the countertops told him she was in the kitchen. He stared at the ceiling, imagining the stars on the other side, until self-reproach took the best of him.

He found her rearranging the cups and plates in the kitchen and grabbed her hand—it was the only way he knew how to soften her anxiety. She pushed him away. She coughed until the cough became a bawl. Her fingers scouted the rim of a white ceramic plate until she found his embrace.

He pressed her body into his chest. "I envy you."

"How come?"

"I have all those feelings inside of me, yet they will not come out. I fear of the day they do."

"Come, let us go back to bed." With her anticipating grief extinguished, she guided him back to the bedroom.

The light in the kitchen was still on the next morning.

The gift of losing everything so often was learning the grace to restart —quickly, elegantly. The brain always found the pattern, and attached to it, forcing a person to see, really see, until they have processed it in full. When a knife opened a wound too many times before the scab healed, the brain took notice. It allocated all its resources for speedy recovery before the sharp blade struck again.

As a kid, Luna had always tried to escape the morning cold by waiting for sunrise. *Sol*, she often said to herself when she learned the word, and she extended her naked forearm and placed it next to the Sun for as long as her eyes could withstand it. At the time, she didn't know what it meant, other than the two—her birthmark and the brilliant power of the sun—belonged alongside each other, together.

When she became an adult, she found the solitude of dawn pleasant. Only a few in Arvo, the ones privy to her story, understood the weight of the wounds Luna carried. The rest found her twilight strolls strange. Her pace was slow as she turned her face from one side to the other, stopping every few seconds for no reason at all. The beauty of the world both amazed and destroyed her. The elders and early risers glared through the windows, perhaps waiting for her to burst into flames, or melt altogether.

Scattered lenses in the city made daylight television an anxious endeavor for Faith. She switched channels when Luna walked outside the field of vision.

"Do you think she will be all right? Must we do something?" Faith said.

"Leave her be, Faith."

"What if she never finds her way?"

"We cannot force her to accept the reality we threw her into. We must be patient and earn her trust." Lucifer's black eyes cut through Faith's anxiety.

"I know." Faith scratched pieces of her nails off. "It is a warm day today, is it not?" She flapped a metal folded fan and felt a breeze on her face as she found a place to seat. Then, she put the fan on the table before standing up and walking towards an open window. She reached for a hair band and arranged her hair into a bun.

He said once more the phrase that she loathed in secret. *Everything is written.*

Faith came closer to him, as she detested screaming almost as much as hearing that phrase. "You always say that. It makes me sick. If everything is written, then why try anything?"

"Because even our futile attempts to change things are part of the story."

Unsatisfied with where the conversation was headed, she changed the subject. "She wanders."

"We all wander. That is how we get to places no one has ever been."

Faith contemplated the empty dish still on the countertop.

"Was there anything else?"

Her eyesight aimed at him, but after a blink, it extended past him, out the window and into the horizon.

"You are brooding again. Was it another vision?"

She looked back at the plate.

"The time is approaching."

"I cannot lose you both," she said.

"She will be fine."

Luna didn't remember the last time she woke up feeling fully rested. Days always had the feeling of an uphill battle, like tipping a ten-ton boulder straight by pulling it with a thin yarn wrapped around its faces. But that morning when she opened her eyes, she was shocked at how much energy she felt. Over her nightstand, a folded piece of paper stood like a pyramid. In its face, the symbol of a half-moon made her snatch it in excitement and turn it over.

I hope you slept well. Meet me at the space dock.

- Lucifer

She threw her back over the pillow and exhaled. She wanted to feel anger or disappointment, but the energy she had been given didn't allow it. Sliding into her black uniform, she was unsure of where she was going, happy to have somewhere to go with all that life-force.

"Whenever you're ready." A guard said outside the building's door, pointing at a floating vehicle in front of them.

As they sped past the landscape of lilac and golden yellow, she remembered holding a knife at A15's throat while gripping the edge of her seat. The leather wrinkled from her strength. For her, silence was the most dangerous sound. She rolled down the window, and her hair flapped in the wind. A cold breeze forced her mind to the present, and between the flashes of Arvo's busy adults and buildings, the yellow dirt clouds, and the wind buffeting, she was at peace.

She knew they had arrived when she saw Lucifer's silhouette coming into view. A spacecraft stood in front of him with an open compartment.

"Finally. Come, come." He called Luna over. His face and hands were covered in grease.

Luna tried to see every inch of the immense metallic beast in front of her, for she had never seen a spacecraft in person. "What are you doing here?"

"Fixing this engine. Point that light here."

"Don't you have people to do that for you?" She grabbed the thing he pointed at, and the light came out when she pressed a button on the back of it.

"Yes, sure. Still, I enjoy doing it whenever I can. Pass me that wrench there."

She handed him the next thing he pointed at. He explained it was an eight-inch wrench from a toolbox, and she nodded without knowing what any of it meant. Watchers don't know what they don't need to know.

"It helps me think. Plus, it gets me away from Faith for some time."

"Don't you enjoy her company?"

"Of course. Yet her love... it's almost too much sometimes. Love like that, it is so immense that it always comes with an unbearable amount of anxiety. How can anyone live up to it? This bolt is giving me a headache," he said it with a smile. "Give me the six-inch wrench."

She inserted the eight-inch wrench into its notch in the toolbox before pulling out the one with the six-inch mark. "Maybe she needs you."

"And I her, always. But her type of love needs the kind of light I can only bring her once I have it, really have it. You cannot deceive love, not for millennia. Relationships. One must bring the light so it can get lost in the other's darkness, absorbing its every drop."

"What do you get in return?"

"Oh, when I bring her the light, she converts it into unconditional love. It is a lovely exchange for those up to the trade."

She moved the flashlight closer to his fingers. "What about when she brings the light?"

"Then I come back from the brink of madness, and I am alive for another century. There." He threw the wrench into the toolbox. "You took a while to get here. I was almost done by the time you pulled in. Do you want to give it a try?"

She grabbed the wrench and inserted it into its designated slot. "I'm not a pilot."

"No one is a pilot until they are one. Besides, there is no better place to learn than the mountains of Arvo."

"I don't—"

"I'll be next to you the whole time. Come."

Even though it looked gigantic to her, it was a small four-passenger carrier meant to transport resources; an aircraft young pilots used often to practice their skills.

He let her first into the ship and watched her discover its interior. Once in the control room, Luna paced towards the left chair. Lucifer sat next to her.

The scattered buttons and levers in the cockpit meant nothing to Luna. She put a hand on either side of the yoke in front of her. "What do I do now?"

"Start the takeoff phase."

She waited.

"The takeoff sequence has three stages. First, power up the aircraft. Here." He tapped his hand over a lever by the yoke.

Luna pushed the lever in. The aircraft's engine groaned, then whirled in a light screech.

"Good. Wait until it has reached full power, then slightly pull on the yoke."

"How will I know?"

"You will feel the difference. There. Do you feel it?"

"The vibration, it changed."

"Now, pull."

The craft floated above the ground with the pull of the lever.

"Now, push the craft forward with this," he tapped on another lever. "And pull on the yoke, ascending at an angle."

Her voice went soft. "How does anyone remember all this?"

"When you do it enough times, it is like walking. You never think about putting one foot in front of the other, or taking the next breath, yet we all do it incessantly." They flew at an angle into the Arvo atmosphere. He chuckled, slapping his leg. "Well done! You are flying."

Her hands gripped the yoke, and a smile escaped. For once, she was over everything, feeling as tall as any person, as boundless as any star.

"Fly between these mountains. We shall turn around over there." He pointed at a peak. "I will land it this time. You watch."

To her eyes, it was an orchestra led by the swinging hands of a maestro. His hands, graceful and purposeful, pressed buttons, pulled and pushed levers, and landing gear came out of hiding from the bottom; she felt the vibration in her seat. The metal beast was under his total control. It slowed down, hovered above the table and the toolbox, which had tipped over by the wind and now lay with all the tools scattered on the ground, and descended slowly, with precision. The whirling sounds became a groan, and the groan, silence. After the silence, the soft pat of a proud father on a daughter's shoulder shot a red flare across time; the lost bullet of profound sadness looming its revenge. Anticipatory grief always starts with a bond. And the bullet, once shot at random, always finds its victim.

***

Lucifer walked among rows of assassins. Watchers, he called them, but Luna knew what they were really here for. "Your task is simple," he said. "Travel, kill, transport." He looked at an assassin. "The only weapons you shall use are ones of close combat." His gaze jumped to the next person. "You will walk among the shadows, you will pull them into the dark, and while your knives are taking their lives, you will think of nothing but the grand future in every move, every action, every breath." Now towards the end of the room, at Luna. "You will have it ingrained in your bones: this is greater than me. Then, you will come back, unnoticed, with the body. Do anything else, or leave the body, and do not bother coming back at all unless you wish to suffer a terrible punishment."

Luna sat in a corner facing the group.

As Lucifer continued his speech, he put his hand on their shoulders, one by one. He smiled at them. He approved. A badge of approval was always more powerful than any payment, or so the human wars had proved. When he was done, he walked towards Luna.

She looked at him. With a soft sigh, she said, "I don't like the name Lucifer for you. It sounds... evil."

Somewhere in her sentence, there was a word that made his eyes wrinkle. "I had no say in it. It is the name The Great Ancestor gave me."

"I will call you something else from now on."

He sat next to her, eager to explore the absurd idea. "What will you call me then?"

"Absalon."

"Absalon? What is the meaning of that word?"

"It is Hebrew. We learned it at school in case our mission took us to Israel. It means *father is peace*."

"Is that what I am to you? A father?"

She had spoken on impulse and now had to suffer the consequences. "I—"

Lucifer wrapped his arm around her shoulder. He allowed himself a chuckle. Over a yellow rock, they stared at the sunset, joined by the embrace of a half hug. "Silly name."

"I know she worries. Faith."

"She loves you. She loves everything, everyone. Which just means her heart aches in perpetuity because nothing lasts for eternity."

"I will be all right. I'm ready."

Lucifer said nothing for a long time, smiling at the horizon. He turned to Luna with what he had excavated from the contemplation. "I want you to cremate me."

"What?" She released herself from his embrace.

"When I pass. Cremate me."

"Why are you saying this now?"

"It is inevitable. There is no use in prolonging the inevitable. Cremate me."

"I won't even entertain the idea of this conversation."

"I will not allow you to go to Earth unless you promise to cremate me when I die."

"You won't get rid of me so easily. I won't let you die."

"Luna..."

"All right, all right. When you die, I will see to it."

"You will see to what? I need you to say it."

"I will tell them to burn your body."

Faith considered keeping quiet to push back the hour Luna would have to leave. But Luna had already gotten ready and now walked toward the kitchen. She looked older in her black uniform, and there was beauty in her determined, green eyes.

Two plates waited empty on the table.

Faith had hoped the day would have never come. She believed the less she mentioned it, the greater the chance of the day evaporating into the cosmic calendar—that somehow they might skip it with no one noticing. Still, a calendar hung from the refrigeration box, and the date matched the red X.

"Oh!" was the only sound that came out of Faith's mouth when Luna was in the kitchen. Faith moved the plate from the countertop to the side of the table, and the aroma of protein filled the room. By the time the two had made their way to their seats, she had served the food. She now sat with all her love, at once holding back her worry and making the best out of the moment.

Apart from the clinking of silver and china, and the soft inhales and exhales of despair, it was a silent morning, and Faith regarded the importance of every clink, every breath, every detail she knew in time would become the essential beats of the memory.

Faith pulled a napkin from a box in the center of the table. She pretended to clean off her mouth but only moved to the mouth when she had dried her eyes.

Luna stopped eating. "Are you okay?"

Faith cleared her throat. She took a deep breath before nodding. "Of course, child."

Lucifer said nothing, but his gaze bounced like a tennis ball as he cut up the meat.

Luna recounted her training. A memory of her knife pressed on A15's throat reminded her. Though she had ended a life by throwing her knife from a distance, she had never pressed with enough force to break the flesh in close combat. A glimpse of her mother in a cage fought its way into her mind. Though her attachment was only genetic, she had not forgotten about her. About all of them. A29, A15, her mother, the ones she had left behind. By the time she was done eating, she convinced herself she had to rescue them, somehow. And if he did this for Lucifer, he might release them. It gave her the motivation to press on.

She looked up at Lucifer and Faith and back down at the shiny plate underneath the food. The image looking back at her was not her own, but that of a monster. She didn't dare to think of anything more beyond the task at hand. The next move. Living short-term was the only way to survive.

A voice whispered in her ear, and she saw the monster had made its way out of the plate and into the air. "You see, Luna? You need me." And now her vision was outside of her head, and she saw herself turn sideways. "Worry not. Follow my instructions. We will get through this. That's right. You're under my control now."

Luna pushed her chair back.

"Do not worry. I will take care of it." Faith grabbed both of their plates.

"Thank you. Luna, are you ready?"

"Nod. Stand," the voice said. And she nodded and stood up. The voice controlled her, forced her to do things she had no intention of doing. It was also freeing to let someone, something else to guide her. Maybe if her actions were not her own, her hands, not her own, then she wouldn't have to kill anyone. At least not while being herself.

Faith placed her plate on top of Luna's. "Wait, wait for me. I want to go as well."

The voice preceded every action. "Look at them. Pity them. They will never be as strong as you. Almost there. In time, you will be far away from all this. Free."

A floating vehicle that had been waiting outside took them to a large red building outside the city, and when she saw it, she felt the familiar pressure on her chest. The color of death activated her.

All three stepped out.

"The day has fallen upon us. This is where we leave," Lucifer said.

Faith wrapped her arms around Luna. "Thank you."

The voice pulled the levers. "She's expecting you to say something. Say something."

"Why are you thanking me for?" Luna saw herself say, though all she did was open her mouth for the words to come out.

"For your presence. For allowing us to take care of you and, in return, giving us what we thought was impossible. Parenthood."

And the voice commanded. "Smile. Nod."

"I will see you in a few days. I know I will. I hope I do. You take good care of yourself." Faith's eyes watered, but she left before the tears fell.

"Will she be all right?" Luna said.

The voice floated over her, circling like a vulture, and spoke only for her. "Good."

Although his face was assurance enough, he said it. "Do not worry about us. Pay attention to your mission. Earth is a volatile place. Get in and get out. Now, go. Go before I come to regret it and send someone else."

"Go ahead, do that thing I hate so much. Smile. Good. Let's get this done," the voice whispered.

Lucifer stood there, waiting. Waiting to see her one last time. He knew his fate, though it pained him to accept it. As soon as the doors closed behind her, he longed for her return. Yet he knew her place was not here, but there. That her journey, though a difficult one, had only just begun. And only her mix of human and deity could lower his defenses long enough to kill him—Robert Cohen, the portal creator.

He walked to the car, repeating to himself. *It is written.*

As Luna entered the building, her hands grazed the red jasper walls. The people of Arvo built everything with precision. Everything had to fight for its life, it seemed, and so everything had a reason for being.

"We have been expecting you. Right this way," a woman wearing a white robe and large transparent glasses said, her hand pointing at a large capsule ahead.

Luna walked among the tonal sounds of mystical things she didn't comprehend but somehow had to trust. Around her, liquid gurgled inside large glass capsules, spitting bubbles to the top. "Better not to say anything," the voiced hissed from ear to ear, floating from one shoulder to the other. "Don't mess this up."

"Whenever you're ready," the woman in the lab coat said.

Luna hesitated. Her breath shifted gears from slow to rapid. Her heart reminded her it was still there, pounding at the walls of her chest. Flashes of past and present intertwined. Pounding. Red. Blood. Killing was near.

She wished for everything to stop, to travel back in time to a conversation she had with Lucifer.

"If you're a deity, does that mean you can control things?" she had asked.

"What kinds of things?"

"The weather?"

"Yes. That is simple enough. Each planet has its contained weather system," Lucifer had answered in earnest.

"Time?"

"That one is more complex since it involves manipulating a whole universe. A universe can only move forward, usually."

"Usually?"

"In theory, the rules don't apply to the Ancestor. He has full control of all the universes, all the dimensions. As long as balance is somehow maintained, he is not bound by the Laws we abide to."

"How do you reach the Ancestor?"

"You're an inquisitive one, aren't you?"

She remained silent, to not disturb the unanswered question still hanging in the air.

He smirked. "You need unfathomable power, aimed at a single point in the edge of a universe to break through and create a portal to Him. But even if you attain this power, somehow get to the edge of the universe, and can focus this power into a single point, you'd have to also persuade Him to bend the whole of existence to your will. Now, remember, as powerful as you would have to be to open up a portal between universes, you would have to be infinitely more powerful to force him to comply. It is impossible. I know."

"How do you know?"

He almost didn't answer, but just as she had given up, he said, "I know because I tried."

Then the memory was gone, and all that remained was the noise, the red, and the task at hand.

"I'm ready," Luna said before the raspy voice could utter a word.

BOOK 3

MESSENGERS RISING

PART 1

CURRENT EARTH

POL

There was a hole where the windshield used to be. Wind fluttered strands of his raven black hair in and out of his horizon. The hair attached to him, and he detached from the world. Depersonalized. Reckless. Vibrations throughout his body, blinding noise in his ears—a glass shattering orchestra. His chest throbbed at 140 heartbeats per minute. Blue blinking lights rose on the mirror's line of sight. A chuckling sound from the heavens sliced through the earsplitting siren.

He looked up from behind his sunglasses.

With a turn of the steering wheel, the car kicked up clouds of dust and the blinking blue lights were his audience around a 360-degree concert stage. He hit the brakes to face his predators.

Dead silent.

Amidst the frenzy, he paused and contemplated on the dust. Dust, as it suspended in the scorching air of the New Mexico Prairie. People in his life couldn't hold their attention on a single thing for more than one second, but his weakness was to fixate on everything for far too long. He opened the door of a 1965 Mustang and stepped out into the grass. He knew the grass was called Blue Grama, though he wasn't sure why he knew that, or how. Maybe a teacher had said it while he fantasized of being a rockstar, a dream which he had since fulfilled. His brain had the bad habit of absorbing facts he had no use for. Burned out by the industry, he had left his career behind some odd weeks ago, or at least that's what his publicists went with. The truth was much stranger.

In the New Mexico desert, he tried to forget the truth. The first policeman that got out of the patrol car was a heavyset man with a serious face and a mustache that covered half his mouth. He tried speaking, but his voice was lost in the deafening noise flying overhead. The policeman waved the helicopter away, then slammed twice over the roof of the car. His partner passed him a megaphone.

"Stop, or we will shoot. I repeat. Stop now, or we will shoot," the voice exploded from the megaphone.

"You can come get me," the Mustang driver shouted.

The policeman looked confused and brought the megaphone back to his mouth. "Don't move. Get down on your knees and place your hands behind your back. We will come to you."

The man with the sunglasses complied. The mustached policeman threw the megaphone into the patrol car and signaled his younger partner to go ahead.

Led by their guns, they approached the offender until the labels on their uniforms were clear enough to read. The man with the sunglasses ignored the younger one, as the buttons on his shirt were silver, meaning he was a newer hire, and focused on the one with the golden buttons and a belt wrapped diagonally over his chest with Senior Patrolman initialized over it. A. Ward, the badge read.

"Officer Ward. Do you care for a story?"

Ward had the stern voice of routine. "Save it." Then to his partner, "Cuff him."

While the silver buttoned youngster cuffed him, the man with the sunglasses said, "A policeman, dedicating his life to protect and serve. Do you even know what you're protecting and serving?"

Ward stowed away his gun. "If I were you, I would stop talking until you get a lawyer."

"But this is so much bigger than you and me. We're probably nothing to these creatures. Nothing."

"Yeah, whatever you say. You people get weirder every year. Damn punks have nothing to do but go about ruining a perfect day. Must be heatstroke. Get up." Ward yanked him from his jacket's collar and pushed him toward the patrol car in front of them.

Once inside the car, the man with the sunglasses pleaded, "They're among us."

Ward turned back, gun aimed at the man, and said, "Shut up!"

"You need to hear this. Everyone needs to hear it. Or everyone will die."

The silver buttoned officer looked at the rearview mirror, then at Ward.

Ward faced his partner, then turned toward the road, put the gun away, and looked at every mirror in the car. "Shut the hell up, you're giving me a headache," he said, and covered his face with his hat before the car made it to the highway.

The man stared at the road and watched the lane lines merge together as one. He accelerated against his will toward the next location, the next stage, some place where new people awaited his performance, knives out to feed from a piece of him. His body eased into the car's vibration, and the vibration joined with the lines, and the landscape blinked into eyelid red, and he slept.

The man was falling, slowly. At first he reached up desperately, hoping for salvation, but it wasn't long before he surrendered to his fate. And he relaxed his body. His arms outstretched, he watched the world shrink on top of him, and he sunk down an infinite well. Darkness swallowed him whole.

The car's harsh stop bumped the man's head against the police car's partition, rousing him from his sleep. White, limestone buildings made everything brighter than it really was, and he squinted his eyes to the bite of the stinging daylight. The car swayed when Ward pushed his body out the door. His attention shifted to the front of the car, then to the rearview mirror, where the young driver emerged with a piercing stare latched onto his face.

He didn't know the city, but it couldn't have been far from the last sign he had read a few minutes earlier, before driving a stolen car straight into the fences of private desert acres. Solano, the sign had read. Yet none of it mattered. He wanted to get arrested, to rest protected behind bars and guns, and, opposed to common belief, it was easy to get what anyone wanted if they tried hard enough.

Behind his desk, Ward let out a groan, and an old swivel chair squeaked when he let his body fall on it. He stared at their prisoner and the younger officer locking him inside a cell. With the gate locked in place, he turned to a Police Officer Shield Plaque hanging on the wall, and smiled when his gaze reached the Employee of the Month commemorative text. He then grabbed the remote, and the TV turned on to a picture of an old woman sitting in an armchair. Ward pressed on the remote again, and the woman spoke.

"—*whenever people ask me, well, what can I do?*" the woman on the TV said, "*I tell them to be ready. I say, keep your eyes open, because the question is not whether they're out there. The real question is, when are they coming for you? For all of us. And will you be ready?*" The old lady stared intensely at the camera, her eyes almost bulging from the sockets.

The man with the sunglasses stood up from the corner and grabbed onto the cell bars. "I killed one," he said.

Ward turned to him. "What?"

The man with the sunglasses repeated the sentence as if it would make sense the second time.

"What do you mean, you killed one?"

"An alien. At least it didn't look human after it was dead."

Ward threw a glance at him,—that fishhook eyebrow that screamed "You're crazy" without uttering a word—and turned back to the television.

The documentary had cut to a helicopter hovering over white

mountain peaks that spanned across the terrain as the vertebrae of Earth's spine. The corner of the TV had Cappadocia, Turkey, written on it. "*Cappadocia is well known for its fairy chimneys, but underneath its devastating beauty lies an ancient multi-level underground city. It is located near the town of Derinkuyu, extending to a depth of approximately eighty-five meters, and it is large enough to have housed over 20,000 people.*"

"No, it's true," said the prisoner over the television's speakers. "I don't regret it either. It was self-defense."

Ward told him to shut up and rolled his chair closer to the television.

"But they're not like in the movies," the prisoner continued, louder to match the increase in the television's volume. "They're just like us. Or at least at first, when they're alive. Once they're dead, it's another story. That's when they let the wings come out."

"You look familiar," Ward said, giving up on the documentary and standing up from his squealing chair. "Give me those." He yanked the man's sunglasses off. "Wait, a minute. I saw a news report on you. You're that musician that went crazy, crazy like the rest of them. Just couldn't handle the pressure of fame, huh?" He shouted at the other room, "Daniel, come in here!" Then back at the man in the cell. "What was your name? A Paul, something. They've been looking for you for weeks, haven't they? No wonder they haven't found you yet. They're all turning stones in Hollywood, while you're stealing cars out here in the desert."

Daniel stepped in and confirmed Ward's suspicions.

"I bet someone's got a hefty bounty on your head. Killing someone from your own staff in cold blood like that," Ward scoffed. "I need to make a few phone calls. Today's our lucky day, Danny Boy. Finally, something interesting happening in this boring drought. Daddy's thirsty, let's drink." Pleased with his joke, he sat in his chair and swiveled, phone in hand.

The prisoner shook the cell's door, trying to stop Ward from making the phone call. "You aren't listening. It wasn't human."

Ward ignored him and continued dialing.

Daniel walked closer to Ward without saying a word. Then one step too close, beyond the threshold of social convention.

The prisoner hesitated; he wasn't sure if saying anything was to his advantage. One man was about to turn him in to the judicial sharks, yet the other one might be a psychopathic murderer using the guise of a police officer to fulfill his urges. It was either dying all at once, or by the pain of a thousand bites; sudden death seemed like the lesser of two evils. He stood, gripping the bars, and felt his heartbeat at his hands, beating against the cold steel. He wished he wasn't looking at reality, but at a stereogram version of it, where if he focused on Ward's red telephone, the clear image of what was about to happen would merge into everything else and disappear forever.

Daniel grabbed Ward's plaque from the wall and struck him on the head with a forceful blow. Ward's head fell to the side, and the phone landed on the floor with a thud. Daniel pulled up the phone by its cord. The dial tone seemed to annoy him. He turned the television off and made sure Ward was unconscious before turning around. The man in the cell pulled away from the bars.

"Be not afraid," Daniel said with an open hand in front of him. "I believe you. We must get out of here, Pol. Fast. If there was one, others will come."

Pol had a terror-stricken face. Those had been the exact words the producer that wasn't a producer had said moments before Pol had killed him. *Be not afraid.*

"Where are your things?" was the first thing any of them said. It had been Daniel who broke the silence once he had driven the police car onto the town's main road.

Pol gave him a puzzled look.

"Your things—clothes, money, passport."

"Passport?" Pol said. "Where are we going?"

"We need to lay low for a while, at least until they stop looking for you." Daniel grinned. "I know a place."

Pol regretted his choice and thought it might have been better to warn Ward of the young police officer creeping towards him with murderous intentions. It was too late now, and this was one more event, the same way the rest of his life had been, from one show to the next, nothing more than a blur, a life happening to him as opposed to him choosing his path. He knew better than to go against it. In time, he learned it was best to ask only one question, which he blurted out to Daniel. "Where?"

Daniel's grin turned into a full smile. "Turkey."

Neither spoke another word until they pulled up in front of a dingy motel in the middle of nowhere.

"Go. I will keep the car running," Daniel said.

Curtains in the other rooms closed as Pol walked toward the motel, perhaps to hide any petty crimes from the sudden arrival of a police car. Pol reached into his pocket looking for the keys, only to find the door slightly ajar, his room turned over, mattress on the floor. They took nothing, whoever they were, and Pol found his passports and cash stashed away inside the removable foam drop ceiling tiles. With his passports in hand, he considered fleeing through the bathroom window, until the ugly picture of the one he had killed invaded his mind. Those wretched wings, the dark blood oozing through the bullet holes, the power it possessed. If he wasn't the insecure, paranoid bastard he had always been, and hadn't been carrying a gun, he wouldn't have stood a chance against the creature. The alien, the thing, the whatever being from whatever bizarro world he had entered, had kicked the door to the green room open with the ease with which a kid might kick a basketball, turned over chairs like they weren't there at all, and right before Pol pulled the trigger, objects flew toward him, objects the shapeshifting monster had never touched. No, he knew escaping was not a choice, not if Daniel was somehow connected to that.

He was used to it, being carried, being told what to do. Life on tour had made him used to being nothing more than a pawn, a glorified monkey. But when there was money to be made, tired, sad, or sick, a monkey must always find the will to dance. When he made sure everything was in the bag, he zipped it closed and stepped out of the room.

"What's the matter?" Daniel said when Pol got into the car.

"Someone was in there. Door was open. They were looking for something, but didn't take anything. Druggy looking for cash, probably." He shook his bag. "But I hid it well."

Daniel looked around them and back through the rearview mirror. "No, no," he put the car in reverse. "They were looking for you. I can only hope we were far away enough that they have not found you by triangulating your DNA."

———

Four hours of silent drive through the New Mexico desert took them to the Denver International Airport. Daniel pulled up to the mechanical arms at the entrance to the long-term parking lot. He hovered a black card under a scanner and the arms raised. The number 444 flashed on the scanner's screen.

Pol knew the airport well from his shows at the Red Rock Amphitheater and worried he might get recognized by fans or law enforcement. He also knew how full the parking lot would be during peak travel season, yet Daniel pulled up to an empty parking spot next to the elevators with surprising ease.

Their footsteps echoed through the empty parking lot. Once at the elevator's doors, Daniel pressed on the button, twice for good measure. They had parked on the top floor, which shared the unsettling silence with nothing but the airplanes taking off and landing. When the elevator doors opened, Daniel waited for Pol to get in, then walked in behind him.

"You better wear these again." Daniel handed Pol's glasses over to him after the elevator began its descent to the terminals on the second floor.

A line of cars dropping off eager travelers froze at the hands of a security guard who had cleared the path for them. The guard nodded at Daniel; he nodded back.

Pol sifted through the contents of his bag. "Last minute flight to Turkey will cost a fortune. I don't think I have that much cash on me."

Daniel grinned. "Stay close."

They walked past the check-in counters, past the security lines, over to a burly TSA agent leaning on a metal pole with a rope across it.

"What are you doing?" Pol said.

The tank of a man straightened as they approached. Then relaxed once more when Daniel pulled up his police jacket and showed him his forearm.

"For His will," Daniel said.

The big man repeated the words and stepped out of the way to let the men bypass security.

Pol hurried behind Daniel, but turned his face back to make sure there wasn't a group of TSA agents rushing to pin them down. "What the hell is happening?" he muttered.

When they arrived at gate 44, an outbound flight to Turkey had been delayed. One hostess nodded at Daniel and Pol, while another apologized to the two passengers being pulled away by force.

"You'll be hearing from my lawyer!" echoed the seething voice of one passenger.

A teenage girl next to the passenger walked voluntarily and ashamed. "You're making a scene, Dad."

Inside the airplane, a male passenger was rearranging his luggage in an overhead compartment, then slid into a seat in coach and stewed while his wife tried to calm him down.

A flight attendant directed Daniel and Pol to two empty seats with an open hand, 1A and 1B.

Pol settled into his seat quickly before anyone recognized him. "What the—"

A beep on the airplane's PA system announced an important message from the pilot, and while the pilot delivered his words, Daniel said, "I will only say this once. Do your best to follow. We were originally called the Watchers. We were bred, trained, and sent to Earth by the Archangels throughout all of history—human history—to target and kill influential or destructive people with the purpose of shifting humanity's evolution. But some of us were not satisfied with the destiny vested upon us, so we forged our own. We saw through the Archangels' intentions for the impure and selfish imperfections they were." He perked up. "I am the leader of a rebel group of Watchers called the Messengers. Whenever human evolution has reached a point of no return where destruction is inevitable, the Great Ancestor restarts its evolution back to zero. The Messengers have survived all the Ancestor's restarts of this planet—great floods, impacts, wars, and other cataclysmic events—by forming hidden underground societies throughout the continents. That is where we are headed, to one of those underground societies. We are everywhere, in every industry, in every field of study and profession, and in every corner of the Earth. We use our training as Watchers, not for killing, but for protecting. Our code is 444"—he pulled up his jacket to reveal the numbers scarred into his skin like a white ink tattoo—"We believe not in interfering, but in providing the circumstances in which free will can blossom. We save as many Watcher targets as we can, and I am glad I got to you in time."

The flight attendant stopped by their seats. The pilot's message had ended. "Can I get you guys anything to drink?"

"The strongest thing you have," Pol said.

Since they traveled light, they were the first ones off the plane.

"Thank you. Have a great rest of your day," the flight attendant said, giving Daniel a slight nod.

Pol kept his eyes glued to the pilot. His arms. They were hairier than Daniel's, but it was there, visible, yet hidden in plain sight for someone not expecting it—444, scarred on his forearm. *Who are these people? A Satanic cult?*

With one foot on the airplane and the other on the boarding bridge, the events that had led him there flashed in his mind. He had stopped all contact with his team and had thrown his phone into a lake when his business manager called for the hundredth time. In time, the Objectivists would conclude he gave up on the world and moved to Galt's Gulch. To the rest of the world, he had simply vanished, running away from the law and hidden in the sewers like the filthy criminal he was.

He had disappeared and took great pleasure in his make-believe power of invisibility. The anonymity offered a way to enjoy the inconsequential things that made life special until a waiter at a small-town diner in New Mexico had recognized him under his hat. In that small town America built on trust, folks left their car doors unlocked, and the keys out in the open. He had fled the diner, picked the fastest car outside, and took off into the desert.

Now, a few hours later, he was on the other side of the world, stepping further into a maze he might not find his way back from. It was exactly why he had gone along, the allure of the mystery. As a rockstar, he had explored his mind with an array of substances, and had met with the world's secret people, the power behind the powerful, yet after a few world tours even the esoteric became routine.

Step by step in this otherworldly trip to the heart of Turkey, events rode as easily as a feather surfed the wind. Every time they needed something, or someone, Daniel pressed a button on a cell-phone-like device and in a few minutes, the solution arrived. Not even in Pol's old life did things get done so quickly. And before sundown, they were flying in a helicopter above the same mountains he had seen in the documentary that morning behind bars.

They were connected to communication channels through large headsets and microphones.

Pol was half convinced that all of it was true, but still had to ask, "Everyone knows about this place, don't they? If there were people living in it, wouldn't someone have noticed by now?"

Daniel seemed pleased, his voice sharper when filtered by the microphone's interference. "We show them what we want them to see. They have only excavated a tenth of Derinkuyu; the rest of it, they will never find on their own."

The helicopter swayed to the right, and Pol faced the window again. They descended on the other side of a peak, away from the archeologists and tourists. They jumped out of the helicopter, their shirts swatting against their trunks. When the helicopter flew away, Daniel pointed to a rock formation in front of them, and they approached it.

"With my blood's ink, I swear to carry the secret to my grave. For His will, we are His Messengers," Daniel said, sliced his hand open with a pocket knife, and let the blood drip over a rock on the ground. A few symbols illuminated on the rock, and so did the numbers burned on his skin. Smoke evanesced from his forearm and his numbers sharpened. His mark reinvigorated. Daniel let out a groan and passed the pocket knife to Pol.

Pol had no trouble reciting the words. Remembering dozens of song lyrics and inflicting that sorrow upon himself had been his daily bread, but he didn't enjoy physical pain. Even drunk, he had jolted away from his first tattoo after feeling the first pinch. He brought the knife closer. His throat was numb from all the swallowing. If he waited for a second longer, he would run away from pain, and give himself in to the authorities. *No more waiting, no more letting things happen. I will make things happen.* He sliced through his skin and let the knife fall and bounce on the ground.

"With my blood's ink"—Pol hissed in pain as drops of blood fell on the rock—"I swear to carry the secret to my grave. For His will, we are His Messengers." The rock illuminated, and so did his forearm. He turned away from the pain brewing in his arm.

Daniel put his hand on Pol's shoulder. "No, look at it. Savor it."

Pol turned back to his forearm. The numbers bulged from under his skin, as if bursting out of his blood. One by one they took shape, slowly cutting open his old self and letting the new one seep in through the cracks. Something woke inside of him. Something he wasn't ready for. A darkness, an evil, and at once the numbers became black, and his whole skin lit in a spontaneous combustion. He found the fire beautiful, the pain calming, the anger uplifting. The darkness was mesmerizing. Pol allowed himself to fall inside it.

Like a cave dwelling creature ascending to sunlight with virgin eyes, Pol climbed to consciousness out of the dark zone into the brilliant white. The daylight was blinding.

Daniel hyperventilated with a hand over Pol's chest. "I lost you there for a second," he said, his grin now a frown. He pulled Pol up from the ground and looked at the blackened numbers tattooed over Pol's skin. His face changed for a second's time, but he cleared his throat and turned his attention to the earthquake at their feet.

"What's happening?" Pol said, crouching.

The huge circular stone in front of them rolled across to reveal a black tunnel of nothingness, a portal of no return. Pol walked in first, and Daniel followed.

They descended a stone stairway that spanned a half mile and ended in a wall at the bottom. On the fourth step, the stone behind them covered the last rays of light and Daniel illuminated the way using a strange-looking metal bracelet around his wrist.

At the base of the pathway, Pol put his hands on the wall, convinced it was where the cult member would kill him and leave his body hidden for eternity. "There's nothing here."

"They see what we allow them to see," Daniel said, and repeated the phrase he had said before, "For His will."

The stone blocking their path rolled from the inside. Every turn of the stone was the volume dial that birthed the bustle of the city behind it. It had been two men, Pol saw, that had pushed the stone out of the way. Pol's presence startled them. The two men had the same metal bracelet as Daniel. They curled their arms, and the bracelets lit the numbers burned on their skin. Daniel did the same.

One man nodded towards Pol. "Has he taken the oath?"

Pol pulled up his black leather sleeve; the blackened numbers almost swallowing the light.

The man who had spoken looked at Daniel, the white overtaking his eyes, then the two men bowed.

Daniel whispered, because sound carried with ease through the stone halls ahead. "This way."

They passed chambers with people of all ages who, seeing fresh blood, stopped talking and turned over to look at Pol. One chamber had vaulted ceilings and an adult standing in front of a group of children.

"Now, your turn. Say it out loud, together," the adult said.

Tiny voices chanted, "For His will."

Pol was certain this was some kind of cult, yet that didn't explain the ritual in front of the entrance, the blood over the shining rock, or the new numbers burned on his skin. *Daniel put something in my water, then burned the numbers on my arm while I was out.* But he knew he was lying to himself. He had seen the numbers forming before passing out, he also had felt the accumulated rage of his life, of actions not taken, of letting others walk all over him, and he had felt the fire, every cell of his body turned on, awakened. *No. It was real.* The more they walked among the stone halls, the more he was convinced his whole life had been a training drill for that moment. That he had spent his life collecting anguish and alchemizing it into songs, when all he had to do was to give in to the darkness.

The cheering crowd quieted down as soon as the background string music came beaming through the PA system. It was an intro he often used to prime audiences for the journey ahead. His band came out one at a time, each one producing small explosions of applause. They took their places at their instruments and wiggled their in-ear monitors. The lead guitar and bass players made sure they were in tune. Pol only used standard tuning, but his ears heard any deviation from perfect pitch—he liked his compositions as true to the source as possible. Then, just as the crowd was in mass hypnosis from the strings crescendoing in the background, Pol came out, guitar hanging over his shoulder, and guided only by the sound, played a chord he couldn't name. He saw each face in the crowd come to life, their hands clapping uncontrollably, and generating deafening screams loud enough to mute a war. And he fed on their light, on them singing his lyrics back at him, on every instrument tuned to perfection, on every measure reverberating as if someone had pressed play on their record player. But he never smiled. His microphone stood a few inches lower than it should, so that he sang into it while staring at the floor, and his long, black curled hair covered the rest of his face.

He was embarrassed by what he had to do every night to keep himself alive. His fans said in interviews how his music filled them up and inspired them, but it was Pol who took a bit of their life-force every night. He thought of himself as a stage vampire, sinking his fangs deep into their souls and sucking from them what he couldn't get anywhere else. Therapists had scoffed and yawned at his pain, because he couldn't articulate it into spoken words, and it was impossible to hear it from his songs, unless somehow they felt it too. But it was there, mixed in the slow-burning compositions, welling in the bends, pull-offs, and hammer-ons of his guitar solos, and barely hanging on to the tremors in his vibrato. Every song was a breadcrumb to a nameless feeling.

Two hours later, his energy depleted, the crew packed everything up to do it all over again at the next venue. There was a heaviness in the air when his concerts ended. He had unloaded some of his burden on the crowd, and now they walked back to their cars, heavier than usual, sadder than usual. Pol liked to see them through the cameras as they left. He knew, for them, it would wear off by the morning, yet the heaviness came back to him just before it was time to perform again. Pol found it a fair exchange to give everything in order to have a few hours of lightness.

A voice pulled Pol out of the deep waters. A chattering down the hall.

Pol remembered following Daniel into an empty stone chamber. He remembered lying down over a bed made of stone. He remembered feeling light.

Pol left his chamber and followed the voices. Flickering candlelight illuminated his path. He looked up at the dimming light, at the candles hanging upside down inside glass spheres that were anchored to the stone ceiling by thick, black chains. And he inhaled the air. Somehow, however many miles below the surface, the air tasted cleaner. *Purified by the stones*. He filled his lungs once more before taking another step.

He tiptoed by people in chambers sleeping on stone beds and headed toward the hissing whispers. One chamber remained lit in the darkened stone hall.

"You brought him here, Daniel, here," a woman's voice said.

"Careful with your emotions, Sarah. You sound very... human these days." The voice that sounded like Daniel paused. "He is here now. Let us find a positive way to use this."

Pol slid towards the light with his back pressed against the wall.

"A positive way to use this?" Sarah said. "You brought the enemy into our home."

"I was not sure. None of us were, not until I saw him awaken and witnessed the absence of light. I stared down at the abyss and saw hell. The kind of hell Samyaza described."

Pol held his breath in the silence.

A raspy, older voice spoke, lengthening some of his vowels for emphasis. "No need to worry. As long as someone is keeping an eye out on the portal creator, everything shall go as planned. For His Will." The rest repeated it. "Soon, we shall be reunited with our Ancestor. He will meet His real children."

"Mark," it sounded like Daniel again. "Have you located the portal creator?"

"Yes. Waiting for the order," a man with a low, confident voice, presumably Mark, said.

"You go ahead, Mark. Word is they will send someone, each of the factions. The Lone Archangel wants him dead, and the siblings want to take him away," Daniel said, his voice now distinct from the others. "But proceed with caution. We still do not know what will awaken him. Do not rush him to come back with you, all in due time. You, Sarah, will get close to our guest. Befriend him. Make sure he keeps what he is at bay. At least until we have secured the other one. But Sarah," he paused. "This is of the utmost importance."

There was a long silence. "I know this."

"Meeting adjourned," Daniel said.

The old man said, "Oh, and Sarah? Pain."

Pol heard the rustling sounds of people standing up and rushed back through the stone hall. *What the hell have I gotten myself into?* He tried to remember the location of the stone door that covered the exit. It had taken two strong men to open it, but he was sure his adrenaline would compensate for the missing second man. Every passageway looked the same. Like houses in a master-planned community, every chamber was indistinguishable from the next one. He turned corners and walked up and down stairs carved into the stone. The underground city seemed endless. It dawned on him. He wasn't a guest; he was a prisoner. Pol never felt claustrophobic in the elevators or small green rooms of the world, but in the vast Derinkuyu, his heart fluttered, his breath intake was faster than his exhales, and the dimly lit stone walls were spinning. Chasing freedom had taken him to the ultimate restraint.

On an abrupt turn, he crashed into another person, a paleskinned woman. When she pushed away from him, and her face fell into the delicate touch of the dim candlelight, he noticed her features fell neatly into his definition of beauty, a definition he had convinced himself was a fairytale until that moment.

"Forgive me. Are you hurt? You are the new one, right? It is nice to finally meet you in the flesh. I am Sarah."

Pol blanked out.

"Can you not speak?"

"Sorry, yes. I'm fine. Pol. Name. Pol. That's my name."

"What are you doing all the way over here, Pol Name Pol?" She chuckled. "Were you leaving us so soon?"

Pol denied the accusation, though it was delivered with such sweetness that he thought it had come from a concerned friend.

"Because if you are," Sarah said, "that is not a problem. I can take you to the exit myself. I am strong enough. Together, we can open the door, and you can be halfway to the United States in less than a day. But that is one long trip. You should at least eat something before you go." Her hand offered a way back into the chamber clusters.

Pol scanned the hallway. He was sure he had passed through there on his arrival. The exit was near. He was also sure he could run away from Sarah, defend himself from her if needed, and leave this place behind, forever nothing more than a memory of when a cult tried to recruit him. But the heaviness of unanswered questions kept him anchored to the stone. *Who are these people? What are these painful numbers on my forearm?*

"It is a difficult decision," Sarah said. "I know what you must be thinking. Look to your right."

To his right was another hallway that cut the stone in half under the shadows, easily missed unless a person was looking for it.

"That passageway is a shortcut to the exit. If you want to leave, just say the word."

He approached it.

"But if you stay, I can help you understand it, control it—wield it."

"What?"

"Your power."

Pol turned around. "Power?"

"Does it still hurt, your forearm? I know it does. It hurts because you are resisting it. We were not sure if the gene had passed on to you. Now we know."

"What genes? How do you know?"

"The rebel Watchers—Messengers—created our own mark, 444, to distinguish us from the others, a mark engineered to react with any gene mutation the way yours did. Mutations were never meant to survive."

Pol let the words finish echoing in the dark stone hall and said, "Are you going to kill me to get rid of this error?"

"For His will. It is not our place to end a life. This is the reason we abandoned the Watchers."

He played along, though the image of Ward's neck to the side of a chair lingered in his mind. "If my destiny was to not survive, then there's nothing we can do."

In a city almost 300 feet below Earth's surface, Sarah walked toward him, put a hand over his wrist, and said, "No. That is what the Archangels want you to believe, that everything has been spinning on the threads of fate waiting to happen since the beginning of time. They indoctrinate their Watchers to believe they can only extend their life as far as their life string will allow. But there is a different truth. I know it. No matter how dark things get, there is always a choice to be made, an action to be taken, a glimmer of hope to guide you."

CHAPTER 3

POL

The exit never seemed so far away as it did when Sarah spoke. It wasn't long before Pol wasn't thinking of it at all.

"Three days," she said. "That is all I need."

And with that promise, she took him to a deeper level of the underground compound, a quiet descent into a dark pit, lit only by a torch she had pulled out from a sconce on a stone wall. In the center of the lower level, instead of a vaulted chanting room, there was a large cave. Sarah hunched down to clear the entrance and beckoned Pol in.

Not much was visible, but the lack of stone beds meant that the cavernous chamber was not made for the living. There was a palpable change in the air, colder, and a chilling sense of dread ran down Pol's spine.

"I beg your forgiveness," Sarah said with her hand pressed against a switch.

She flicked the switch.

A haze of red lights revealed the cave's immensity to be not that of a normal cave, but something far more menacing. Before Pol asked why she was sorry, the same pain he had endured at Derinkuyu's door exploded within him and brought him to his knees. His forehead touched the abrasive ground, and when he looked up, dried red splatter lay on the sand in front of him.

"What is this place—"

"Get up," she said. "Get up and fight me."

It took Pol a great effort to push himself off the ground, leaving him no energy to do much else than stand.

Robbing him of a chance to recover, Sarah ran to him in a violent rush and pinned him to the wall. "You awaken by pain," she whispered, an inch away from Pol's face. "I wish there was another way." Sarah pressed him harder into the rock wall. The rock penetrated his shirt and broke the skin on his lower back. The sting tore the veil that held him together. A generator had turned on and sent an endless supply of energy to every cell in his body. Pol swung his arm and pushed Sarah away as easily as pushing a shower curtain open.

Sarah coughed until her cough turned into a pleased chuckle. "Yes. Well done," she said, lying on the ground. "Hold on to the pain. Embrace it. You are in control. You are in control. Be not afraid."

He held his head as if stopping it from cracking. His screams ripped at his chest and left his throat raw, and the sound might have been loud enough, painful enough, to echo against the reddened cave's walls, travel across the stone, up through the underground city, and form a rift into the Earth itself. Fire surrounded his body, melting his sunglasses, clothes, and skin away.

Still, the spectacle wasn't enough for Sarah. "Is that truly all of it?" she said. "I am not impressed. You are neither the son of God, nor made in the Archangels' image. Humanity has rejected you, accepted only within the boundaries of an entertainer."

Pol recounted chapters of his life as slides in a carousel projector. He saw a cheering crowd filtered through polarized sunglasses. Strangers around the world revered him as a pagan god. But no one knew what the words in any of his songs meant, or where they had come from, other than they found the sounds catchy enough to dance. It angered him.

Then the memory shifted farther back into a young father who had taken him out on a drive with the promise of ice cream, now walking away at the other side of a black closed gate. A group of nuns held Pol back while he heard his own voice as a child crying out for him—his father, the junkie with arms full of red dots, and syringes rolling under the car's seats. The restlessness of his past rushed in as if it were happening in the present. All the subsequent years in which he tried to escape, or understand his fate, before he had to accept it. Too old to garner any interest from visiting parents looking to adopt, he learned his life was not meant to be lived but survived. Pol had found refuge in an old guitar that had been donated to the adoption center. Its wood creaked with every chord, and its rusty metal strings hurt as he slid his hand to match the positions in the torn chord book. He hated the pain, but in music he found an accepting parent, one who didn't care about his origin or tendencies and was not only impartial to his dark thoughts but welcoming to them. He returned to its painful embrace daily, leaving punched holes in the wall whenever the pain became unbearable. In time, rumors of his talents traveled wide, and a producer signed all the relevant adoption papers and took him away. The nuns were relieved. The producer had been careful to groom him into an artist capable of performing hundreds of shows' worth of songs in a year without missing a date. He was eager to gain Pol's trust, until one day he snuck into his backstage room after a show when everyone else had moved on to the after party. Pol learned demons fed from loneliness, they thrived in darkness, and now the producer, the real version of him, flashed before his eyes, dead on the ground, hooks spread out, wings twitching, horns bleeding out of his skin. The fuming gun was still warm in Pol's hand.

He forced his mind back to the rusty strings of his first guitar. *Maybe some pains are necessary.* But his mind vaulted forward to the demon put on the ground by the gun in his hand—the closest thing to a father he had. Pol stopped holding the beast down. *Everyone will know where the pain comes from. They will feel it.* He consumed the fire surrounding him, and with the intake, took out the red lights illuminating the cave. He touched his melted sunglasses, and they burned into the air, flashing glimpses of Sarah's face as they pulverized into the ground. He straightened his body, now a powerful vessel unrecognizable to him.

Sarah turned her chrome bracelet on. The flashlight cast a shadow on her face, and she said, "Well done. Welcome to your destiny. I will help you walk this path. For His will."

"For His will," Pol repeated, though the words came out in a short, convulsive utterance from outside of his consciousness.

The second day had arrived.

Sarah touched Pol's arm at the edge of an incomplete sleep cycle and whispered an invitation to the training cavern. He followed her lead, for he thirsted to feel the power once more, the strength to face anyone, anything, and win.

The entire level had been deserted the day before as well, but this day the silence pushed him away, warning him of incoming danger. Yet he pushed through, eager to walk through the gates of pain and clench at his dormant power—this time, he wouldn't release his hold. He had attempted all night to reproduce the flames and failed, falling asleep only when complete exhaustion kept him from trying.

He entered the cave before Sarah, fear and excitement competing for his attention. Sarah stood before him. Never had a person showed him what he might be, could be, and never had he let his walls crumble and allow the wilderness and chaos of life through, but with Sarah, his jaw unclenched.

Sarah's arms slid from her stomach to her sides, and a light emanated from her crown, and in seconds, she had wings like those of a stork that extended from her back. Her disarming face pointed at Pol with a soft gaze. She smiled and placed a hand slightly over Pol's wrists.

"Do you trust me?" she whispered.

He did. His breath gained speed.

Sarah pulled his hands up and interlaced her fingers with his. "Be not afraid," she said with a smile and pulled his hands to his sides and pressed them against the rock wall.

He stood, feet close together and hands extended to his sides. The cold cave formations against his skin made Pol shiver in anticipation. He focused on her, the idea of her, the promise of her, and what may yet come of himself if he made it through to the other side.

She knelt down, covered by the cave's subtle darkness. A sound of metal clinked at his feet. Sarah came back into the light holding two long, thick iron nails in one hand, and a large rock in the other. The sweetness of her smile had evanesced, and in its place, an intense dread, a hesitation.

Pol's breath sharpened, but he maintained his position.

The breaking of skin was so sudden, the shattering of tendons so violent, the exploding of veins so swift, that he only felt pain when the second nail had entered his other wrist.

Pain.

Sarah dropped the rock at his feet and placed her forehead against his, her wings curling around them. "I have seen this work before. You must trust I am doing this to help you. The ritual once unlocked a precursor."

Pain.

"To walk on water, you must first stand near the well of death and drink of its elixir."

Pol convulsed, his eyes rolling into his skull and back around.

Pain.

"And once satiated, you must walk back into the light. I need you to awaken, fully. I need all of you. The universe does."

Fire.

It was white in every direction.

A voice echoed, "She found you."

"Who's there?" Pol said.

"There might still be hope."

Pol turned around. The white seemed infinite.

"A Father has the most difficult of chores. To hope. To watch his children fail, again and again, and yet wait and hope they will still, somehow, find their way back to the Path. To watch and not intervene is the greatest pain. But I know now. I can admit to my errors. Each one of my Wills have broken free of my intention, and they roam about the universe wreaking a havoc I never created them for. They must be stopped."

Pol looked for the voice's source in the vast, blinding white.

"Follow the Path. It will take you where you need to be. Walk into the light."

A pair of hands clenched around his neck and pushed him to the floor, which had turned into a roaring ocean. Pol tried pulling the hands away, swallowing water with air. The waves swayed him, and his gaze shot up. The sky had turned to crimson red, thundering a great storm against the sea. And the sea carried him, his tired resolve had surrendered to the murdering hands around his neck.

"Pol?"

A white ray broke through the red sky.

The hands released and sunk into the ocean, and Pol's body floated out from the water and levitated into the light.

"Pol?" the voice said once more.

The white light enveloped him, and he coughed. He coughed back into life.

He woke up in a pool of green water, in the middle of a room surrounded by decorated stone columns and Sarah standing by his side.

"How do you feel?"

"Wet."

Sarah chuckled, flapped her wings, and flew out of the pool. She offered a helping hand and placed Pol over the pool's edge, and let a warm towel fall over his back. "What did you see?" she said.

"I didn't see much. I heard a lot. Something about stopping the voice's Wills."

Her face seemed relieved. "What else?"

"Then the sky turned red, and I was drowning. I felt so helpless, there was no strength in my body nothing to pull myself out of the water."

"Worry not. I will always pull you out of the water." Her words filled the room.

Pol tightened the towel around him. "So you're one of them." He motioned at her wings.

"I am one of His Wills, yes. Created for the sole purpose of finding you, and guiding you to the Path. Only you know this. Only you must know this."

Pol opened his hand. "Something feels different. Calmer."

"A rebirth," she said. "It worked. It is now the third day."

A small ember formed on his palm and illuminated their faces. Sarah gasped and scooted closer to him, and they warmed their bodies by an extinguishing flame.

PART 2

CURRENT EARTH

CHAPTER 4

ROBERT

I had no reason to believe there was a bigger purpose for me. But ever since I was a child, I knew it. When I failed at anything, I pulled myself up from the handrails of that illusion. When the other kids laughed at me, I looked at everyone and said, "You'll see one day." But the days passed, and there was nothing to see.

I wished my parents had named me Maximilian, Maximus, Odin, or something impressive. But they named me Robert. My dad's last name was Cohen, so my full name became Robert Cohen, naturally. Most people don't know who they are. Robert and Cohen are two words. My parents gave them to me; it's my name. But it's not me. I am no one. There is absolutely nothing interesting about me. Brown hair. Brown eyes. About as plain as a lettuce.

I walked out of every relationship, or I let them die away because no one engaged me the right way, and I flunked college because no study major called out to me. That was about the time I took comfort in the bottle.

I had hopes of becoming a writer. I convinced myself that's why I didn't fit in university, that I was just too advanced, too unique for my own good.

Authors that had changed the course of literature had suffered for their art, and I was smitten by their biographies. I wanted to mimic their paths, go through the pain, and pay my dues. Only I was as cracked and dry as old, rotten timber; I had nothing else left to give.

A few odd jobs later, one where I burned my hands constantly fighting with a fryer, and another one cleaning toilets in a gas station next to a highway, the romanticism evaporated. People who were just passing through a town had no respect for restrooms.

I forced myself to write a page or two a day while working those jobs, staying at an apartment, if anyone can call it that, close to town. But once, I came back from a ten-hour shift of cleaning shit and found water overflowing the bathroom into the living room and my work in progress floating over it—a ship sailing to Nowhereland. I salvaged what I could and hung the pages from clothespins on a thread next to the window. Instead of fixing the problem, or crying myself to sleep, I just drank and watched the damn pages fluttering from the air coming in. If signs were a real thing, then perhaps that was a sign that screamed to be listened to. But I ignored it, naturally.

Eventually, I called the super to get the problem sorted—four days later. I didn't want to call him sooner, as I was three months behind rent. Alcohol wasn't cheap, but it was easier than hanging out alone with my thoughts. So my booze budget was pretty high back then. When the super came in to check the problem out and saw the water damage, he told me I had to be out by the next day. I didn't listen since he had said that many times before, and it never happened, but the next evening when I came home rubbing some terrible fryer burns on my hand, I saw my stuff in the hallway, including my work in progress. The manuscript was now out of order, and some pages had flown down and fallen over the bushes. I thought about leaving the pages behind and moving on with just the clothes on my back and a suitcase, but I assembled my undulated, dried, out-of-order mess of a project, grabbed what I could carry, and moved on.

My employers loved me at first over the next few days, because I slept near their establishments and was the first employee there. That didn't last long, of course, and days later, when my employers saw me wearing the same clothes and smelled my body odor, they fired me. Both on the same day.

That's when I took to the streets.

Someone stole my ID the first night I fell asleep on a city bench, and losing a two by three-inch plastic card was my ticket into the tunnels, and everything else that came with surviving the floodgates. I got lucky. My aimless direction took me to one of the good tunnels. The eight other people living there told me all about the floodgates, how the city opened them without warning. They said it was the city's way of cleansing it of its rats.

"What do you guys do when that happens?" I said.

People were economic with their responses in the tunnels. They never knew who to trust.

"You die," the old man who they called Priest said. "They baptize us, then they kill us. We die Christians."

Priest was usually the loudest one. He loved to rile people up for his pleasure, but where he shone was giving unsolicited sermons in high-traffic areas outside the tunnels. Sometimes he got lucky and people thought of him as some kind of performance artist, and he came back with enough money to feed our needs—or our addictions.

I sometimes emerged from the dark, wet tunnels into daylight in search of unassuming tourists drunk enough to give me some of their gambling earnings. Whatever coin I collected from strangers, I used to ring up my parents to let them know everything was going well. They asked me how my novel was coming along, and to stay with them if I needed to. My stomach growled, and my mouth salivated when I heard my dad mention lasagna in the background. Still, I told them not to worry and returned to scraping off pizza dough and cheese from a discarded box. *Real artists suffer alone.*

I learned restaurants threw away perfectly good food daily. I also learned expiration dates were mostly there to avoid lawsuits. Mostly.

But sometimes the risk forced however little I had eaten that day to shoot out of one end or another.

I had lost a lot of weight and pulling my jeans up every few minutes had become a nuisance. I found some cables lying around outside an office supply store on the good side of the river, as if there was such a thing as a good side, and I used that to wrap my jeans tight to my body.

A screw came loose in my brain the day a new idea for my story popped in my head, and I needed to put it on paper right away. I had never been so desperate, so wild to achieve something. With no pen or pencil, I scurried the bins outside the office supply store, but the trash guys must have passed before me and had left them empty. I kicked the bins down and they rolled a few feet away from the alley. Below them were some cement blocks that had split down the middle by the bin's weight. I scraped my finger over the cement block's sharp edges until I cut across my skin, and I tried to write with the blood. Ridiculous idea. It just made a splotchy mess over the paper. I cried my eyes out for the first time since living on the streets, not because I was homeless, or because I was hungry and alone, but because I had to throw away a perfectly good idea. I sat with a piece of bloody paper, feeling the thought drifting away.

That's when I met Mark. Mark knew how to play to the crowd and had a black pen out in front of him before I said a word. "Here you go, friend," he said. I thought he had one of those voices that must have facilitated him many friendships in his life.

"Oh, oh, oh," was all I said. I pounded on my head. That helped get the idea out some. I had filled in all the pages, but I wrote in whatever space I found in the margins.

Mark was homeless, like me, but his arms didn't look as bony. And his eyes weren't tired. Yet he became my homeless buddy, always helping me to scan the trashcans for food, or collect soda cans to take to the local recycling center for pennies. Once a month we went to a diner not too far from the casinos. The owner took pity on us and let us buy some pancakes with pennies and quarters if we promised to eat them by the dumpsters. They didn't want their plates contaminated, or to waste plastic containers, so they folded the pancakes inside one lone napkin for the both of us with two packets of syrup.

The local pharmacy had a huge digital sign that displayed the day's specials, but during closed hours, it showed the current time. Most people left the pharmacy with pain pills, probably for those nasty Sin City hangovers. Back when I had an address and a way to prove my name, I went on those drinking binges, too. Those hangovers were a pain like no other. A desperate man could waste a life getting lost in that pain. I wished I had the money to endure that pain again.

Sometimes we slept right across the street from the pharmacy, Mark and I. It was just outside one of the many tunnel exits and made us feel a little more normal to use the sign as our soundless alarm clock.

When I didn't have money, it was all I thought about. When I had some, I used to think about it as units of time. Every dollar spent, I gave away pieces of my life I would never get back. Some transactions hurt more than others, though. For example, at the movie theater, I exchanged my money (time) for an opportunity to spend my time (money) watching other people have a better and more interesting life than my own. Even if I found the picture enjoyable, I lost twice. Fantasizing about better lives was all some people ever did, especially the ones that had nothing at all.

Between the underground tunnel world and the city's tourists looking for a controlled going-off-the-rails experience, taking life day by day took a whole new meaning. But as often happened in the forgotten part of town, there was never enough peace to ponder over deep thoughts. Priest was the first one to hear water rushing in. A cold death came for us from the tunnel's pitch-black intestines. We were lucky we had camped only a few meters deep from the entrance and ran quickly enough to survive. Most of us. The floodgates took our sister, Patty, who had fallen asleep coming down from a drug hit. It also took everything we owned.

We busied ourselves over the next week collecting the best of the worst stuff on the city's trash, dirt, and asphalt. Surviving as a family was easier than surviving alone, and whatever we found was for all of us to share. Mark was a big help. He came back with opened pain pill packets that still had a tablet in them, a pair of dry shoes, and a half-eaten burger some little girl had dropped as her executive mother dragged her to their car.

I became skinnier and skinnier while we rebuilt, yet Mark looked healthy as a horse every day. It made me think he knew of a food source he hadn't shared with the rest of the family. For us, paranoia didn't need an invitation. It came as part of the welcome package to oblivion. Mark made me paranoid.

One night, I pretended to be asleep and watched Mark's body lying on some cardboard boxes next to me. Water level was only a couple of inches deep, and we kept near the tunnel's entrance just in case. I only saw the parts of him revealed by the half moon's grace. At 4:44 a.m., he rose and walked away, disappearing into the sunless morning. He came back right before the pharmacy opened, carrying scraps of bacon and eggs he had dug out of some fast food trash bin. I squinted my eyes as if his noisy footsteps had woken me up from a deep slumber. And we sat to eat our breakfast, watching the manager open up the pharmacy. One could only dream.

Back when I had a job, I used to buy value menu items and give them away to homeless people. I always recall one time when I gave a homeless lady two hamburgers. Instead of eating them, she stored them in a bag inside her shopping cart, gave me a huge smile, and carried on. I thought she would have devoured them while they were still nice, fresh, and warm.

It was winter, and while I chewed on a sandwich I had been saving for days, I thought about that lady. A stranger had given me the sandwich after asking me if I wanted it, as if refusing it was a choice. I might have regretted eating that sandwich later, but a homeless life was not a painless one, but one in which you chose the pain of the day; not making a choice meant to suffer through all of them at once. That day deep in November, I didn't want to feel the gnawing pain of hunger; I knew there would be plenty of that in the cold months ahead.

When the roads became slippery and people locked themselves in their warm homes, food was scarce and our resolve primal. Even if my hands weren't numb yet, I couldn't write anything because the pen had dried out from the cold. I kept the manuscript inside a discarded hardshell briefcase Mark had brought once. No matter how miserable it got, Mark was always in a good mood.

Mark sometimes annoyed me, though he had an exceptional ability to maintain his weight. I had followed him on some of his explorations before winter without him knowing, but never saw him do anything out of the ordinary. Whatever scraps he found, he brought back enough for all of us. I did the same. Though during winter, nothing was ever enough for all of us.

Homeless people lived scattered throughout most of the year, but during the long winter nights we grouped together down in those tunnels—family member or not—away from a potential snowfall, but also away from all the potential food sources. There, it became pure savagery. Especially in late December, when we had eaten through whatever we had stocked up on.

While everyone, at least the sane ones, stayed inside to keep warm, Mark disappeared, sometimes for days, and brought all kinds of treasures hidden in his pockets. He was fearless. Every passing day I saw him more as a giant, and I more as an insignificant rodent.

As a part of a group in survival mode, some advantages had to be kept a secret if we wanted to live to see another year.

"We're half-men and half-women, mismanaged by society," Priest said, and some cheered. "Left in the dark to rot and die. But we shall survive. We shall prove to them we are worthy of life."

Everyone agreed, then looked at their belongings to make sure everything was still accounted for.

There, it was every half-man and half-woman for themselves. We saw people die those weeks. With secret food crumbs in our pockets, we saw them die of hunger.

Mark took a half-eaten pizza crust he had picked up a week ago and broke it in half. "Here, eat."

"But it's your last piece," I said.

A woman perked up and leaned toward us. She limped closer to us and when she saw Mark's hands, lunged at him like a Saxon warrior in a shield wall.

I hadn't eaten for days. Sleep time and wake time became intertwined into one messy reality. I didn't know what was a dream and what wasn't. I pressed on, only because January was just around the corner, and that was when people returned to work. Back to work meant back to throwing out most of their food, and that meant back to our daily scraps of bread.

What happened next, I couldn't explain. The lady grabbed one half of the pizza crust, but Mark, without touching her, pushed the old lady back a few meters. I still remember her broken shoes sliding over the snowy dirt, and her awful screams.

The lady's black teeth seeped out from her lips as she screamed, "Demon! Demon!" dividing the crowd in two and running straight out of the tunnel and into an intersection above. There weren't many cars passing through, but luck wasn't on the lady's side, and a green sedan ran her over, stopped for a few seconds, then sped up over the iced road, twisting some at first, then straightening and screeching its tires into the horizon.

Everyone quieted down, looked for a few seconds, then returned to what they had been doing before. I learned two things that day. One was that magic might be real, and the other was that people ran over the homeless all the time.

. . .

Then came the hard times. Days so cold, we wished for fire to burn us alive. And so long, that when we finally slept, we hoped to never wake up again.

The homeless celebrated New Year's Eve differently that year. After nightfall, it was a bloodbath in the underworld. Priest, the loudest person there, had devised a contest for us. People said a lot of things about Priest, but boring wasn't one of them.

"We've been ripped apart from society," Priest chanted, "Treated like insects."

"Tell them, Priest," said a man they called Toothless Jimmy.

"No more, brother, no more," said another.

My heart was thumping hard. I found out later it was a side effect of going too many days without food. But I was also nervous, anxious about what was about to happen. The air had the taste of sulfur and sweat, a stench my nose had now set as the base for my dysfunctional home. A storm was brewing, and I was about to get sucked in.

"But we'll show them what we're made of, won't we?"—everyone else cheered and clinked pipes and whatever they picked up from the ground on to the tunnel's walls—"A brawl. Each person shall prove their worth by knocking his or her opponent down," Priest continued, "and keep knocking him down until they stay down. Last person standing wins."

The prize? A whole rotisserie chicken Priest had one of his followers steal from a local grocery store; the act had prompted the store to double down on security. The chicken had been sitting there since the morning, but everyone salivated over the dream of sinking their teeth into the cold poultry flesh. The thought of it alone kept us warm with anxiety, our blood sugar dropping inside our shivering bodies.

One by one, I watched the skinny men and women scuffle on the cold tunnel water, pulling hair, biting skin, drawing blood with their untrimmed fingernails. Everyone forgot about the cold. Mark and I hung quietly in our little corner. As a spectator, my blood boiled with the fighters differently. It was normal, like Sunday barbecue with friends while watching footballers head-butting each other and fighting over a fumble.

The calm lasted until the last fight ended, and Priest disturbed the peace. "Wait! Silence." The crowd, which had cheered for the last fight's winner, thinking they were applauding for the champion, had quieted down. "We still haven't seen two opponents battle."

My face burned with embarrassment when I saw everyone's eyes on me. I hated the spotlight. Always hated the spotlight.

"What do you say?" Mark said, grinning. "Let's give them a show."

I stood up to follow him into the improvised ring, which was nothing more than cardboard boxes forming a large fence around a circle.

I barely had enough energy to stand up straight, but I knew the victor would go against the previous winner to compete for the chicken in a final bout. And if either Mark or I won, we'd split the food, anyway.

"Do not hold back now, Robert," Mark said and squared off. Compared to my bony body, he looked like a veteran boxing champion.

I nodded.

Priest knocked a pipe on a bent frying pan and yelled, "Fight!" The others followed.

We were close together, walking in a tight circle.

Voices shouted all around us. *Fight. Fight. Fight.*

"Are you afraid?" Mark said.

I found the question odd but answered, "No, what's the plan?"

"There is no plan. We fight."

"Isn't it easier for one of us to pretend to lose?"

Under the noise of the cheering crowd, the conversation was only ours.

"Easier? Sure. But you need to be ready for what will come. You need to awaken somehow."

He wasn't making much sense, and in less than a heartbeat, his fist was at my mouth. My teeth sunk into my lips, the taste of blood on my tongue. A little harder and my skull would have ripped right out of my brittle cervical spine. It riled the crowd. Men slammed their chests with closed fists, and the women yelled as savages. The distraction gave Mark a chance to sneak up on me with a kick. The blow brought me to my knees, and my torso followed. On all fours, I found the fragment of a broken mirror sitting on the floor. I didn't recognize the half face looking back at me. While Mark raised his arms to garner acclamation from the crowd, I grabbed the mirror fragment as a shiv and pushed myself up. Whatever energy I had left in me, I focused it in one deadly attack. I told myself it would all be well. If Mark really had magic, that was as good as any a time for him to use it. He had his back to me while I ran to him, and I knew the moment the sharp mirror shard penetrated his skin. It had been the first match in which someone might die. The loud crowd muted, and everyone turned to me. I always hated the spotlight.

Mark tried to reach the mirror knife still stuck inside him, but the wound was too far for his arm to reach. He fell face-first to the ground. I must have hit an important organ or vein, because it wasn't long before blood came out of his mouth. "Robert," he said. I turned him to his side. He didn't look normal. Blackness had spread from his irises and covered his eyes.

I hesitated to approach him, yet something pulled on me and brought my face right next to his. Magic.

"Listen to me," he said, "there's no time. Don't believe what they tell you. Keep your eyes open. Look for the Messengers. But don't believe everything. Not all of them are—"

"What are you talking about?"

"My backpack. There are keys and an address. I hope you're ready." He coughed more blood, touched it, and smiled. "Maybe you are."

It looked like he wanted to say more, but Priest yanked my hand. "The winner! Robert from the green tent."

The crowd burst into wild acclamation, and Mark moved his lips, his eyes blinking the slow blink of death. I saw him take his last breath.

"Sorry, kid. We have to keep our bodies warm somehow," Priest said to me, then pushed the chicken to my stomach.

The previous victor ran up from behind the ring. "Hey, what about me? Aren't we supposed to fight? That's not fair."

"I think that's enough fighting for one day. Besides, look," Priest pointed at the sky. Fireworks. "It's already after midnight. No. You two will split the chicken."

The other guy pulled the chicken apart like a savage and gave me half, though I'm sure he took the bigger half. I didn't care. Mark's face still shocked me; his open eyes pointed at our green tent.

Backpack, he had said.

I zipped open our tent to find a backpack in his corner. I set whatever was left of the chicken to the side and opened the backpack. An old key lay inside, nothing else. The key had a string attached to it. At the string's end was a piece of paper with *444* written on it. I turned it over. On its other side, I found the address Mark had mentioned. If that was how far I had to go, I needed as much protein as I could get.

I ate the cold chicken, pulling it from the bone with my fingers, eating without looking, without thinking, staring at the night sky from a small slit on the tent's roof. Every once in a while, I saw in the sky sparks with no sound, far away where normal people lived.

CHAPTER 5
ROBERT

For people outside the streets, life went by in a flash but street time flowed to its own current. I didn't know what year it was, and only knew the day and month because of the fireworks the night before. The fireworks, the blood, and the bacteria-riddled chicken. In January first of year whatever, I took my manuscript out of the briefcase, rolled it up, and tied it with a shoestring. I filled Mark's old backpack with any food scraps I found inside the green tent. And holding my aching stomach, headed to the address strung to the key. Or at least I hoped to find it, eventually. The first step was always the hardest.

Everything seemed frightening in my past life, especially that period after getting kicked out of college when I spent an unhealthy amount of time alone. Unexpected little human interactions were the links in the chain that had kept me locked in my apartment. Of course, the streets shook those fears straight out of me. They didn't leave me fearless, though, but replaced old fears with new ones. Simple things like where to find trash cans with good food traffic, finding privacy in public whenever nature called, and what corner to spend the night in without getting arrested or killed.

I dragged my living corpse as far as my legs carried it. When evening fell, I slept with my head over Mark's backpack, which was now my own, the key under my head in case anyone stole my belongings. I did that until one morning I woke up barefoot. Whoever stole the shoes was desperate, or they didn't see my toes sticking out the front. That was the lifestyle, though. Whenever I survived, life threw another stone at me, another way to pull me down, another squeeze to see if I had anything else to give.

Without talking, Mark had taught me that if I was to get out of this, there was no time to wallow in the hardships. And sometimes it got hard. Forget the greener grass on the other side, forget dried up, sun-beaten-crunchy white grass, there was no grass at all in any direction for miles.

It was a rainy day, no food scraps left, and the rocks on the road never looked so sharp, so wet, glistening with painful invitation. There were other homeless people in that area, the kind that knew each other and didn't welcome newcomers. They had picked the trash cans empty already. I had to move on.

One of them appeared out of nowhere. "Hey, pretty boy," he said.

Another made kissing noises and walked to me from the other side. Then a third one, wearing my shoes, was only two meters in front of me.

"Those shoes," I said.

"What about them?"

"They're mine."

"Oh yeah, why don't you come an' take 'em?"

I said nothing.

"That's what I thought, pretty boy."

No one had ever called me that. *Pretty boy.* I didn't know what to think, but as they got into focus, they became more and more menacing. One had a plank with nails, the other took out a rusty pocketknife, and the one wearing my shoes was so ugly his face was fearsome enough on its own. They were after my backpack, which admittedly they had missed in their earlier round.

"Police," I said, pointing behind them. And when they turned around, I bolted under the rain and over the rocks. I knew I was bleeding when the sharp needles sticking into my feet turned into a sting that left me limping. I heard them catching up behind me. A bus was picking up people at a station in front, and I aimed for it. I aimed as focused as I had ever been. The pain shot tears down the corners of my eyes. I was glad it was raining, for at least the water hid one of my shames. I whimpered as I neared the bus. The driver was about to lean over the door to signal me away, but he must have seen my attackers, because he sat back down and waved me over, slowly, then frantically, like a dog scratching at an ear infection.

"In, you poor bastard. In!" the bus driver said and closed the door behind me. People inside the bus gasped when the other homeless slammed their fists on the rear glass window, and the bus drove away. I sat facing the road behind and saw it shrinking in front of me. One homeless guy pushed another, surely blaming him for my escape. I was dripping all over the floor and I had left a trail of blood from the entrance to the seat, but I smiled. I smiled because I still had more to give, and I had lived for the sole purpose of giving it.

***

"You can get off the next stop," the driver said.

Night had fallen. I looked around at an empty bus.

I had forgotten how comfortable a cushioned seat felt, and how calming the vibrations of a moving vehicle were. But it wasn't just that. Outside, the anxieties of the world kept people in fight or flight. By the look of their headphones, most people seemed to prefer to go through life flying. I didn't have a choice; fighting had become my language, my air, my every thought. But inside the bus, protected by fragile glass and weak metal, I let go. I flew.

"D'you hear me?" he said, and woke me again.

In the face of danger, humans lived up to their ideal. With the danger gone, we were back to normal. And they must put me back in my place. Behind a dumpster, under a bridge, somewhere hidden away from the city investors.

"Thank you, sir," I said, because I strived to exceed all expectations. I ripped off a piece of my shirt and used it as a rag to wipe the floor, then my feet.

The street signs where the bus stopped made no difference to me, but I gave thanks and before walking out I said, "Do you know how to get to this address?" I showed him the tag strung to the keys.

"You're in luck. That's not too far from here. In fact, this is the only bus with a route that passes close to there." He pointed at the tag. "Take a left two blocks down and keep walking until you see that number."

"How long was I out?"

"About an hour. You looked like you needed the rest." The words didn't match the stern face.

I didn't recognize the area and wanted to run after the bus when it drove away, like a pet abandoned by its owner. *Don't focus on the hardship.* I inhaled, swallowed, then exhaled. I repositioned my backpack, limped two blocks forward, and made a left.

I fantasized about what the key was for. I imagined an apartment with running water and a hot shower. A full fridge, perhaps. A box of crackers, at least. With my luck, though, the keys opened to the next level of Dante's Inferno.

444. I looked at the number twice to make sure, then at the keys, then back at the door. A bookstore. An abandoned bookstore. Apart from spiderwebs and dust, it looked intact from the outside. No broken glass, no vandalism, no signs of forceful entry. No one cared about books anymore, which was why I had always wanted to become a writer. The same reason some old folks still made furniture with hand tools, and why some painters didn't stop mixing their colors until they got the right shade of life. It was the harder path, but someone had to keep it alive by walking over it. Caring was the essence of everything.

Dots are believed to be a symbol of disturbance in energy flow according to palmistry, or so I had learned from the homeless lady days before she got run over by that green sedan. The key slid into the lock with ease. Two long, lost friends meeting again at last. I turned it and got a sense of my world turning upside down with the doorknob. I looked at the palm of my hand to see if a new dot had formed, and smirked at the naked line. Stepping in, I locked up behind me.

I grazed my fingers on the fabric, running them up the armrests and leaving a clean trail in the dust. The sofa faced the front door in full display. *Why would anyone want to read out in the open like that?* I pulled a long, thin chain hanging from the ceiling, and a dim light illuminated the rest, enough so I didn't bump into a stack of books. And they were everywhere. Hemingway, Woolf, Steinbeck, and even Dostoevsky. Pieces of souls that had lived at different times, in different places, portals set on a shelf waiting to be entered. I ran my fingers over their spines and imagined myself shaking hands with each of them, hoping to gain a piece of their brilliance with every touch. I stood before them, thinking of a time when novels changed a person, not merely entertained them.

A stairway connected to a small loft above the bookstore. The loft formed a roof over a section on the main level, where some books stood almost in complete darkness. The stoics, the cynics, the Taoists, and the existentialists waited, as they must have while living, for people to be brave enough to navigate the shadows within them and learn all of life's secrets. But it was always hard to give in to such a simple answer. As humans, all we have ever wanted to do was to over-complicate our lives.

I walked around the mahogany checkout counter and pressed on the old register. Empty. I wasn't surprised. I let the backpack slide down my arm to the floor. I must have been really holding on tight to that backpack because my hands were as red as the devil. I hadn't felt safe in a long time.

I walked upstairs to the loft. In the far back was a window that overlooked darkness. *Nature, probably,* since there were no lamp-posts. A desk set against the side wall. I turned on a small lamp over the desk and discovered the rest of the loft. A mini fridge buzzed on the floor; the noise made me hopeful. Inside, I found a single red apple with a brown indentation on the side. *Probably old, but fresher than anything in a trash can.* I took a big bite of the apple and let my body crumble in the desk's office chair. It was a sturdy metal frame with fake black leather over it that had peeled off by the armrests. From up there, I swiveled the chair from side to side and saw portions of the book collection downstairs. With the bitter taste of the mushy apple, I smiled like a fool pirate who had found a treasure only valuable to himself.

The unexpected relaxation the bookstore had afforded me had made me aware of my bladder and bowels. I threw away the pecked on apple and walked to a closed door in front of me. I hoped to open the door and find Schrödinger's cat alive. I extinguished all hope of things going either way when I swung the door open. To my surprise, the cat meowed in all its porcelain glory. A toilet, a sink, a small shower. I turned the faucet's handle knowing luck must eventually run its course, but found water coming out the spout. Dirty and in bouts at first, like an old man waking up from decades of hibernation, coughing, then clear and consistent. I stuck my mouth to the water and drank until my stomach was about to explode.

I checked the vanity to confirm there was toilet paper. After emptying my insides, I jumped into the shower before giving it time to warm up. By the time the water's temperature shifted, I had already been to heaven and back. I felt...normal.

Hot water trickled down my face, turning on every sleeping cell in my body. With shoulders relaxed, since God knows when, I let my subconscious take over. *What did Mark mean when he said to not believe what they tell me? Who are they? Who are the Messengers? Was he hallucinating from the loss of blood? Was I from hunger?* I felt something pull me to him in those last moments. Call it magic, call it whatever. No one else noticed, but it was real. I shook my head. My conscious mind took charge again, and I remembered where I was. Wasting resources was a sin. I shut off the water and wrapped a white towel around my waist. There was a closet inside the bathroom, stocked up with pants and shirts. I had stopped caring about whether something fit a long time ago, and cared more about whether they were comfortable to the touch and whether it kept me warm. The clothes fit as if they were my own.

I walked down, looking for my backpack. My manuscript, my faithful companion, was in there. Blood filled, water damaged, but still somehow surviving my every life stage. I pulled it out of my back-pack, brought it upstairs, and set it on the desk. Inside the desk drawer, an assortment of pencils, pens, and loose paper sheets lay with the precision of a clock repairman who left his tools, expecting to come back to work the next morning. I lifted the paper sheets, and the pens and pencils rolled down one side. Beneath the papers, a ten-inch notebook captivated me. I pulled it out and inspected it. Its beauty begged to be written on—it just had that kind of feel to the touch. The notebook was bound in reddish leather and had golden painted edges, just like a Bible my mother used to read to me when I was a child. The front cover had the numbers 444 embossed on the top right corner in a golden color that matched the edges.

I opened the notebook to the first page, grabbed a fountain pen from the drawer, and rewrote the first word from my manuscript. On I went all night, rewriting all I had written, rescuing my words, exhuming them from certain death and plastering them on the lines inside the red notebook. Somehow, as I put down the words, they felt permanent, as if the notebook was history itself, and I was writing each event down, not as I had imagined them, but as they had happened.

. . .

A bell ringing downstairs startled me. I opened my eyes to the clarity of dawn coming in through the small window. I was right; it had the view of the mountains. The bell rang again.

The store looked even older in the haze of bare daylight, antique, stuck somewhere in time where shops had old-fashioned French doorbells. An old lady stood outside the store, pressing the buzzer to the tune of "Shave and a Haircut". The downstairs lights I had left on all night made her think it was an actual store; that I was an actual human who was selling books, and not the Scum of the Earth, not the crumpled piece of garbage that bounced off the trash cans of the world—no. To that lady, I was a person just like her. I welcomed her error in judgment and unlocked the door. I played along.

I ran the charade daily, allowing regular people into the bookstore's borrowed world. I didn't even care if they bought anything. Watching them glance at books they shouldn't be glancing at was payment enough. Old men's eyebrows raised at a new edition of the Kama Sutra, while younger guys pretended to be very interested in non-fiction books on menopause just to find the courage to talk to an attractive young woman in the self-help section. Every once in a while I made a sale, at a loss at first, because the register didn't have any change, but I eventually found my rhythm. As I swept the floors for the third time that day, I looked at the sofa again, now without cobwebs, and sat on it. It faced the outside world, which I had only explored as far as the grocery store and back. No reason to go any further. There was no traffic that night, which made it easy to notice something moving on the other side of the street. I couldn't shake off the feeling of being watched. I got up from the sofa and walked toward the glass. Two homeless people, a man and a woman, sat on lawn chairs looking at the store. As messed up as my life was, to them, I was that pharmacy man Mark and I used to watch. The person who looked like he was on top of things. They were looking in, fantasizing, or maybe remembering, visions of better times.

I grabbed a brown paper bag filled with bread and fruit that was sitting on the floor near the register, opened the door, and walked to them. They looked frightened. It wasn't an interaction they were used to. I knew the feeling.

"You see us?" the man said.

"I do, always. I see all of you," I said.

The woman smiled and nodded to the store. "I like books."

"I'll bring you some tomorrow. In the meantime, here you go." I handed over the bag.

The man scanned the bag's interior and let out an enthusiastic "Hell yeah," then changed it to "heck yeah" when the woman looked at him.

I took a stack of books and a blanket out the next night, and the next, but I never saw them again. I wondered if the two had been the Messengers Mark was talking about in his last breaths. If he had chosen those as his last words, whoever the Messengers were must be important. But they never came back. Some homeless people were like that. I knew it well, the urge to always be on the move, always on the hunt for something. That gut-wrenching feeling of looking for that which has no name.

People usually came into my bookstore as hungry as stray dogs, looking for an answer, or to lose themselves in someone else's adventure. Eager to go somewhere, anywhere but the place they were in life. I felt bad taking their money, but a man must eat.

When I was a kid, everyone around me looked like the people in my bookstore. Lost. None of them ever seemed to have gotten it right, their life stages in complete disarray. Either they were stuck in the past or being pulled into the future like a teacher does a child who doesn't want to be at school. I promised myself I was going to be different, yet there I was behind a cash register with less than a hundred dollars to my name and an unpublished manuscript hidden away in a drawer where dreams went to die. Perhaps life's game was rigged after all, and winning was not a possible outcome for some.

Luna, on the other hand, always looked so damn sure of everything. It was the first time I saw a face like that, carrying as much experience as possibility. She didn't appear to be in a rush or frozen in time, but merely skirting the surface of the cosmic place where she needed to be. For the moment, at least, for she was as fleeting as the edge of an expanding universe.

She was standing outside by the front door. So confident. An arrow waiting to be launched into the ether. God, she deserved it, too, her confidence. I buzzed the door open before her finger reached for the doorbell. Of course, if I had known she carried probably the sharpest knife in the universe aimed at me, I would have thought twice.

She browsed the store for the longest time. Not even the authors' parents would look at the same books over and over again.

"Ma'am, we're about closed here. Can I help you find something?"

The store had been closed for half an hour already. She smiled and said she was almost done.

Luna was dressed funny, but not too strange compared to other people I saw on the streets. She wore a black, skin-tight outfit straight out of that sci-fi movie where they connected to a computer simulation. She knelt down to tie her shoelaces, and I saw she had an empty knife sheath on the side of her pants. Later, I found out she was kneeling to reach for a knife hidden inside her boot. I didn't know, so I walked right next to her.

"This is a good one," I said, holding a copy of *Stranger in a Strange Land*.

She glanced at the cover. It was the 1966 edition, where the main character, Valentine, is standing with planets and stars in the background.

"I have never contemplated the stars."

Like the character in the book, I tried to grok what she meant. I asked if she had a lot of light pollution wherever the hell she had come from, and she nodded, though her face looked as if I was speaking an unknown language.

In other, more normal, circumstances, where the chances of meeting again were high, I might have let this moment pass, and with it, the chance to get to know the strange-looking woman. I didn't take that risk with my customers, who were just passersby, most of whom I never saw again. If I saw someone interesting, I forced myself to say something. The only alternatives were to come up with something, quickly, or live the rest of my life in regret, fantasizing about conversations that never happened.

"Come. I want to show you something," I said.

When there was no money, people had to get creative. I guided her out of the bookstore, through the back door, and up the set of stairs bolted to the wall. I held her hand on the last steps, though I quickly learned she didn't need any help at all.

There were clear skies that night, and we lay down over the cement roof to look up at the stars. I had always wanted to do that with someone, to feel alone but together, lost in the universe's immensity, all the while coming to terms with our insignificance. It depressed me, riddled me with a celestial nostalgia, but I still did it often.

We stayed like that for what felt like hours until she raised an arm and pulled up her sleeve. Our eyes had adjusted to the dark, and I saw the shape of a half moon on her forearm. It matched the one in the sky almost to perfection, and all the hair on my body stood on end. She was radiant. For a minute, it seemed as if she belonged to the stars, and if left alone, she might have floated away in a heartbeat. I grabbed her hand, a jerk reaction to the thought of her drifting away, and interlaced my fingers with hers.

"We shouldn't be bound," she said.

It made me strengthen my grip. I said nothing else.

She pointed up with her free hand. "Look, one of them is moving."

I laughed and asked if she had never seen an airplane before. Looking back on it now, it was obvious something wasn't right. But I played along, because that's what people did when they didn't want to lose someone. They played along, no matter the game.

"They move so fast. Why are they in a rush? Where are they going?"

I wanted to sound profound and remembered the few times I traveled with my parents as a kid. The truth was, I didn't know where people were going with such haste. It didn't really matter, it seemed, because wherever they landed, they were just as unhappy as they were when they took off. "Nobody knows," I said.

She didn't seem satisfied with the answer, so I blabbered some more. "Maybe there's a thing in life that takes a lifetime to understand. And you wake up one day realizing you haven't learned it yet, and the clock is ticking." I shrugged. "Maybe they're trying to beat the clock in an impossible race."

Either I bored her or pleased her, because she stayed in silence for a long time.

"That must be it," she said later.

My eyesight was now fully acclimated to the night. Moonlight fell over her jet-black hair and she turned to me. That was the shift, I think. The thing that moved everything and changed everything. When she looked directly into my eyes, I awakened.

PART 3

PREVIOUS EARTH

CHAPTER 6

SARAH

Samyaza jolted awake.

"There, there," Sarah said, and pulled strands of his silver hair away from his forehead. From his expression, she knew hell had won.

"Hell won; hell won," he cried.

She shushed him and assured him it had been nothing but a dream.

"A vision," he corrected her. "And in this one, hell won. A deep well of darkness from which even light cannot escape. All things in the universe were trapped in an ecosystem of suffering. The universe was brightened only by an eternal burning anguish."

He tried to get up, but Sarah pushed him back to bed. "You are not thinking clearly. You must rest."

"We do not have time to rest. They will awaken soon. The pure bloodline and the mutation will face each other. We have to find them, guide them."

But in time he did rest, falling asleep by Sarah's gentle voice and loving touch.

Once she was sure he had fallen into a peaceful slumber, Sarah stepped outside Samyaza's privy chamber.

"He is losing his mind, Sarah. We must find another leader or everything we fought for, everything we stand for, will be for nothing," Daniel said.

"And who would you suggest? You?" she scoffed. "You do not have what it takes."

"We can ask the Seer."

"You will do no such thing. Samyaza is still our leader for as long as he lives."

"Do not let your feelings impede reason, Sarah."

She didn't allow the conversation to stretch more than what was necessary. "Call for me if he talks in his sleep again."

Sarah was called for again only a few nights later.

Daniel waited for her at the chamber's entrance. "This cannot go any longer. Sarah—"

Sarah walked past Daniel and into Samyaza's chamber.

Samyaza cried with his eyes closed, still captive in a dream. "No, no."

"What is the matter?" Sarah said.

"My daughter, they took my daughter."

Sarah ran her fingers from his forehead down to his cheek, wiping the tears that had made it there thus far. "Samyaza, you do not have a daughter."

He went quiet, then his lips rose by the corners, and tears ran down the sides of his face again. But the tears looked different to Sarah, who let the dream run its course without uttering a word.

At once Samyaza rose, energized. "Heaven won," he said, rotating and lifting his body into a seating position on the edge of his stone bed. "I stood in front of the gates of Heaven next to my wife and carried my daughter in my arms. The gates were open, and from it seeped a blinding light. I have never felt such joy, Sarah."

Sarah smiled and touched his arm. "Do you remember who the woman was?"

"I remember how she looked. I had never seen so much beauty."

Sarah frowned. "It was just a dream."

Daniel burst into the room. "Samyaza."

"Daniel. Good to see you," Samyaza said merrily. "How are things in the firmament?"

"I have information on a high-value target. A female by the name of Istahar, not too far from here. Who shall we send to intervene?"

"Nonsense, I will go myself. I am very much reinvigorated."

Samyaza propped himself up, using Sarah and Daniel as crutches.

Daniel looked at Sarah and her eyes anchored down at Samyaza's feet.

They waited outside his chamber for Samyaza to prepare for his self-appointed task.

"Have you given any more thought to what I mentioned?" Daniel said.

"Stop your heretic ramblings, unless you wish I command your imprisonment with the proof of your betrayal."

"Betrayal? I only want what is best for our city. Samyaza is not fit to lead, the Seer agrees, but we need one more vote for the majority. For His will."

"Careful, Daniel, it is sounding like your will, not His."

"I am ready," Samyaza said.

Daniel held his arm in front of him and read a holographic report projected from his metal bracelet. "The target, Istahar, is a local archeologist with an excavation on the verge of an evolution-shifting discovery."

"Let me accompany you, at least," Sarah said.

Samyaza turned to Sarah. "I appreciate your concern," he said, placing a hand on Sarah's shoulder, "but leaders do not command from safety. They lead by example, their swords ready at the front of an army. I cannot request you, any of you, to go out alone into the darkness if I am not willing to do so myself." His face beamed with pride at Sarah and Daniel. "Hold down the fort until I come back."

CHAPTER 7
ISTAHAR

Istahar knelt and flicked her brush delicately, uncovering a rigid surface under the loose dirt. She delighted with every uncovered inch of history and let herself enjoy the rewards of her hard work for only a few seconds before moving on to another section. It was not a simple task for her family to support her archeological efforts, an endeavor that proved difficult to monetize, especially for a woman. Istahar had escaped a marriage that had pinned her down to the role of a housewife and had since transformed her life into what was once nothing but a bedtime fantasy.

Now an archeologist, she had made several discoveries in the past, but her findings were always shrouded by her male peers who convinced her their names would be better received by the scientific community and promised to include her name in the official reports—they never included her name.

She annotated her every find in a large notepad that she rested on her knees. Each entry filled a row in a columned table that included a complete record of the excavation. She wrote what they did at the site, a description of the object or structure, the exact place where they had found it, and in the last column she wrote her own name preceded by the words "discovered by". The last column was necessary.

The wind flapped her black bangs over her face, and she rearranged her hair under her yellow hat. Her white, long-sleeved shirt protected her upper body from the sun, but her camouflaged cargo shorts left part of her legs exposed. She almost couldn't feel her feet inside her heavily worn, dirty boots that were a size too small. But the pain was a reminder of the people that had made that dream possible, and that there was still more work to be done. Pleased with her records, she headed over to the tent where her crew of two kept the water cold inside a cooler. She opened the cooler and swirled her hand inside the melted ice water.

A crew member sought shelter under the tent and removed his gloves. "I'm sorry, miss. We're out."

She yanked a plastic straw with a water filter from her backpack and drank from the melted ice inside the cooler. Satisfied, she closed the lid and sat on it. She gazed at their work, smiling. "We have something special here."

"How much do you think we'll make?"

She forgot that not all humans shared her motivations. Although she was driven by knowledge and history, she had to persuade others to join her using the promise of riches. "More than enough."

The man smiled, squinting, and walked back into the sun.

"Istahar! Where are you?" her mother had said.

Istahar hid behind a bush, giggling.

Hearing her giggle, with all worry vanished, her mother's voice had turned into a singsong. "Oh, Istahar?"

The giggle was now a full-blown laughter when she heard her mother approaching.

Her mother jumped toward the bush. "There's my girl!"

Istahar yelped and laughed as her mother grabbed her by the

waist and carried her against her chest. "I will never let anyone harm you."

Her mother kissed her and hugged her so tight, Istahar could hear her heartbeat.

"What's all the racket?" her father said, stepping out the patio door.

"She's a ball of energy, this one."

"I'm a ball of energy, Daddy."

"Oh, are you now?" Her mother passed her to her father with a groan. "Look at you, just beaming with life."

Her mother walked toward the house. "I need some water."

"Hold on to that joy, you hear me?" her father said.

"Yes, Daddy."

"Promise me."

"I promise."

"Okay." Her father put her feet on the ground, took off a string necklace with a leather half-moon dangling from his neck, and put it over her head. "This belonged to your grandmother, her mother and grandmother before her. It protected me all my life, and now it will protect you."

Night had fallen on the excavation camp. The crew had been sleeping in the dig site to save time driving to and from hotels. Istahar slept with her sleeping bag far away from the rest. A loud and painful scream woke her from her dream.

"Dave? Eric?" she called to her crew. "Are you guys okay? Did you hear that?"

Her hands were now shaking—all adrenaline, addiction, adventure seeking, and survival skills turned into mush. She fumbled with her backpack until she found the flashlight. A light shot through the dark with a press of a button and she headed to her crew's campgrounds. The bonfire was out, the sleeping bags opened. "Dave?" She pointed the light at the next bed. "Eric?"

Something moved inside the water cooler tent and when she pointed the light, found a set of eyes peering out at her. The creature's eyes caught a red light blasting from somewhere below it.

"Whoever you are, we don't have any money," Istahar said. "So you best leave. I already called the local police." She tried to get a good look at the creature, but the spotlight shone over a trail of blood that ended on her crew's bodies laying flat on the ground next to the tent. She gasped and covered her mouth. The only weapon in the entire camp was a small handgun Eric had convinced her to bring, just in case. It now rested inside the pockets of his dead body.

The creature stepped out from the tent, and her flashlight made it look human. "Stay right there," she said.

But the person didn't listen. It marched toward her holding a bloody knife. With every step he walked quicker, gaining confidence, with a body stained in her crew's blood.

Istahar put her hand on her clavicle and ran it inside her shirt, looked for the string around her neck, and gripped the leather moon charm as tight as she could without breaking it.

When the person was just a few feet from her, another being ran from the shadows and rammed the other one against a rock. They grappled with one another, both struggling to live. The new being had long, silver hair and a pair of feathered wings that extended from his back four feet into the air.

She switched her flashlight from side to side, trying to follow the fight, all the while blinking profusely, trying to wake up from the nightmarish reality.

"Do not stand in my way, traitor," the first man said, scanning the ground, looking for his knife.

The other one pushed the murderer back without touching him. "Surrender. Do not force me to kill."

Istahar dropped her flashlight and ran toward the tent.

"We both know you will not do such a thing," the killer creature said. Her crew's murderer found his knife and lunged at the man with feathered wings. "I am sure they will reward me when I bring him your head."

She searched Eric's pockets, breathing labored breaths and swiping her eyes when her vision became too clouded.

When she found the gun, she pointed and shot without thinking.

The man without wings lay flat on the flashlight's path cast on the ground.

"Be not afraid." The ground crunched beneath his feet. "You must be the one called Istahar."

"Stay where you are."

"My name is Samyaza, and I am here to offer you protection."

"Protection?" she said, her voice quivering in the dark. "Why would I need protection? I have the papers allowing me to dig here."

"Protection for your life. For reasons still unclear to me, someone has deemed your existence too dangerous to be kept alive," Samyaza said, his voice coming from a deformed silhouette.

Istahar followed the beam of light to its source. "Don't move." She grabbed the flashlight from the ground and revealed the silhouette, legs first, his golden armor gleaming in the light. He appeared to be at least six feet tall, his chiseled face stern and topped with strands of long, silver hair. She cocked the gun in his direction and saw him navigate the ten feet between them in less than a finger snap. He was now right in front of her.

"Forgive me. I do not trust you with a gun." He yanked the gun away from her hand, and she uttered a yelp. "You must come with me. You are not safe here."

She pointed the flashlight upward, illuminating both their faces. Samyaza's eyes widened, his hold on her body relaxing. Istahar turned around to the tent only to find it ten feet away from her—it had been she who had moved. "How—how are you doing this? Who are you?"

"I will explain everything once you are safe." He offered a hand. "Please."

When she turned around, she couldn't find a reason to resist; she fell completely under his command. In a brushstroke's time, she forgot all about her sacrifices and the sacrifices of her loved ones. All of her discoveries and potential adulations vanished into an unimportant gust of thin air. And she fell into his arms, as nimble as a feather, as limp as a piece of unused fabric, and Samyaza flew up into the sky, his wings enveloping the surrounding space. Unable to fly, Istahar had lived her life in a rooting discomfort. Istahar belonged not to the grounding earth but to the freedom of the stars. Istahar was finally at home.

"Where are you taking me?"

Samyaza kept his gaze in front of them at an angle. "Not too far now." They soared through the sky, his wings closed and stretched, penetrating the air at blazing speeds, slightly flapping them to control the altitude.

Istahar was enthralled by the vantage point of Turkey at that height. The lights of Konya came alive as they left the excavation site outside the city and hovered over its busy streets. *Indiana Jones would be jealous.* She recognized the Aksaray Museum when the three-story building appeared in their descending path, its unmistakable cupolas drew the nearby fairy chimneys in her mind. Samyaza banked right at a row of mountains outside the city limits and landed softly in the middle of nowhere. She could barely see their peaks pointed at the sky, forming stone forests made by thin spires of rock nestled closely together, but she had breathed that air, felt that cold—she had been here before. The fairy chimneys. The underground city of Derinkuyu. One of Earth's many archeological mysteries she knew had more of a story to tell than what had been accepted by mainstream archeology, and one of the many thoughts she had to keep quiet to survive in her field.

"This place is off limits, you know?"

"We know," he said, and before she had time to react, sliced both their hands using his sharpened fingernail and said, "Repeat after me."

He conjured the strange spell and urged her to repeat it, word by word.

Istahar winced at the sight of blood, though she was so full of excitement she might have allowed him to cut off a limb just to gain entrance to whatever secrets lay ahead. She grabbed her necklace again before reciting the phrase as Samyaza had said it. "His will," she said after finishing, pressing on her bleeding hand, "is not free, now is it?"

Samyaza cleared his throat.

The mountain opened up before them. She released her hand. Pain dissipated, cut forgotten, the mystery more powerful than blood. Istahar entered without waiting for an invitation.

Istahar had been to Derinkuyu before, yet all the halls, tunnels, parabolic arches, and chambers she was seeing were new to her. They differed slightly from what she had seen on the post-graduate student tours. If they were in fact inside Derinkuyu, the part they were in now was more polished, perfected, as if it had been occupied for centuries instead of abandoned at the feet of great peril.

The people she had seen were all dressed in long tunics and wore a metallic bracelet on their wrists that pulsated a dim, white light. They all held Samyaza in great reverence, bowing to his presence as they walked by. Samyaza came to a full stop in front of a woman who appeared to had been expecting them. Istahar mimicked him.

"Sarah," Samyaza said.

"You must be Istahar," Sarah said. "Please follow me this way." Sarah was halfway on her turn to the lower level staircase when Samyaza interrupted her.

"No, Istahar will be accommodated in a chamber next to mine."

"But, sir, there is no space—"

"We shall make the space."

Sarah swallowed. "Very well." She pointed an open hand to a chamber down the hall. Once inside, Sarah removed any personal objects, clothes, and food preserves from all stone surfaces, and set them on a corner. "Please forgive the trouble. Someone shall take these things away soon."

"Oh, it's no trouble," Istahar said in disbelief that she was actually talking to people living in an undiscovered area of the underground city. When she was younger, she enjoyed movies where the main character somehow made an impossible journey to the past and got a first-hand experience of history. Istahar dared not to even sneeze the wrong way and disturb the miracle she was witnessing. "How long have you lived here?"

The question seemed to surprise Sarah. "Me? All my life. But we, as a society, have been here for as long as humans have existed. In fact, some of us are humans, like you, ones we have rescued over the years, across civilizations. They live in the lower levels, and we, the Messengers, reside in the upper levels as the first line of defense, should an intrusion take place."

"Who would invade this place?" Istahar asked without skipping a beat.

"That question," Sarah said, already halfway to the chamber's exit, "has a much more complicated answer. Samyaza will decide when you are ready to hear it." With that, she left Istahar alone in her chamber with a million competing thoughts in her head.

CHAPTER 8

DANIEL

Daniel had a plan.

"Is she in there?" Daniel said.

Sarah nodded. "She has rarely left her room in a month."

"I spoke to Samyaza. He is delusional, Sarah. He believes Istahar is the female in his dreams. Not only that, but he has told a few of the captains. They are... inspired. Some have even brought in human female targets intending to move them to their chambers. They have told me so, and are planning on asking permission from Samyaza."

"I am aware of this." Sarah tried to walk away from Daniel, but his determination wasn't so easily wavered.

"Do you agree then? He is not fit to lead any longer. He is inspiring total chaos and drifting away from our true purpose."

"What do you suppose we do with him? Throw him out?"

"We do have our laws."

She stopped. "You do not think—"

"It is only a matter of time. He spends almost all of his time inside her chamber. It is bound to happen."

She resumed her walk; her face frowning under the candlelight. "He would not dare."

"He would." Daniel hurried to catch up with her. "You know he would. I heard the other night his guards caught him sneaking into her chamber after midnight. They do not know what to do in a situation like that." He stopped talking and nodded to a man passing them by, then resumed, "In the one hand, their purpose is to serve their leader. In the other, their leader must serve the larger purpose. And the rules state it: No angel shall commingle with a human."

But the rumor spread, and one night Daniel caught five captains peeping through the chambers and saw Samyaza and Istahar being intimate—he had never seen such filth. They deemed the human females already living in the city impure, their presence too familiar, and in the coming days Daniel was wakened by them forming a squad with the mission to seek Earth's women with a likeness to Istahar and to lust over them as Samyaza had done.

"Stop!" Daniel said, blocking their path with his arms stretched to the tunnel's width.

He reminded them of the Law, and the Ancestor's will, but none would listen. The group of five captains had grown to the dozens and all Daniel could do was watch them fly away to Mt. Hermon, thirsting for that which their underground home could not provide. They never came back.

Daniel opened the secret entrance to Derinkuyu and stepped out into the beating of torrential rain. Sarah stood below it, the water almost at her ankles.

"Has it not stopped, not even for a second?" Daniel said.

Sarah's wet hair was stuck to her head, and her body was drenched. Still, she maintained her gaze up. "Seven days in a row without stopping."

Daniel pointed at the heavens. "Do you think He knows? He did give us free will."

"Within reason. This goes against all reason."

"You know what will happen."

"I do. I will pray for their mercy," she turned to Daniel, "and ours."

"What we need is not prayer. What we need is action." The Seer's presence startled Daniel and Sarah. He had never left the city. His eyes were closed to protect him from whatever light seeped in through the clouds. "A new leader. It is time. This has gone on far too long. Sarah, are we in agreement?"

Sarah nodded.

Daniel smiled.

When all three entered Samyaza's chamber, they found him kneeling in front of Istahar, with his hands placed on her belly.

Samyaza turned to his visitors. "I can feel it! I can feel it!"

The Seer grunted. "Her."

"What?"

"Not it. Her. It is a daughter."

"Just as I had dreamed."

"A daughter which you will not meet." The Seer squashed the excitement from Samyaza, who now stood in front of him.

"Speak. What do you see?"

"I see two paths, both just as painful. In one, you end this sin now and we rebuild, and in time, all wounds will heal."

"And the other one?"

"The girl is born to no parents, with a soul on the verge of exploding, and an empty heart which will never be filled."

Istahar wept at the thought and held her stomach in pain. "No."

Samyaza slammed his fist on the wall and turned a piece to rubble. "I accept the risk, but I will not sacrifice my daughter." His voice shattered all silence.

"Then we ask you to abandon the premises. Voluntarily," Daniel said, signaling what used to be Samyaza's Royal Guard into the chamber.

"What is this?" Samyaza said, pushing Istahar behind him.

The Seer stood, leaning on his walking stick. His eyes had never looked so determined. "This is farewell."

One guard sneaked up behind him and attempted to grab Istahar, and Samyaza, seeing him, threw an arm in the guard's direction and hurtled his body across the chamber, crashing against the opposite wall. But in the time it took him to take care of the guard, another one had approached from the opposite direction and pulled Istahar away from him.

Samyaza's voice roared with an uncharacteristic rasp. "Do not touch her!"

"It is over," Daniel said and stopped a guard who had approached Samyaza with an electrocuting harness attached to a pole. "No one needs to get hurt."

"You rat!" Samyaza threw his arm, now at Daniel.

Daniel gestured his hand forward and pursed his mouth in a self-satisfied smirk when he pushed Samyaza down to the floor with ease. "You are weak. Love has made you weak. You have put us all at risk, and for what? So you can lay on the ground powerless, begging for mercy. You are not even the shadow of who you once were. Now get out, get out before I change my mind and ask for your execution, and take your filthy sin with you."

The Royal Guard escorted Samyaza and Istahar out of Derinkuyu. Daniel didn't miss a moment of their expulsion; he needed to make sure the eviction was successful.

"They will not last long in that rain," Sarah said, her voice weak.

"Whatever happens is now in the hands of fate." Daniel's tone was arrogant.

"For His will," the Seer said.

CHAPTER 9
SAMYAZA

"This rain," Samyaza said. "Something is wrong."

Water was at their knees.

Istahar moved through the flood, holding her stomach. "It's just rain. A lot of it."

"No. This is not just rain. This is punishment. For my sin and for influencing others to replicate it. I am afraid our bond does not come without consequences. Consequences from which we will never stop running, consequences she will inherit." He placed his hands on Istahar's abdomen.

"We'll make it work."

"For now, we must survive." Samyaza scanned the mountain, then flew her into a cave that was still higher than the water. He placed her on the ground and stood vigilant at the entrance.

She walked to him and held his hand. "The rain will stop. We can still have a life, all three of us."

The dead bodies of Earth's terrestrial beasts floated above the flood, eyes open, tongues out. Samyaza flew out of the cave and returned holding a dead animal. He gestured his hand at a pile of branches that he had left to dry inside the cave and sparked an enormous bonfire. Pieces of the animal's body lay on sticks assembled on top of the fire, and as it cooked, Samyaza walked to the cave's entrance. He looked down at the city he had helped build. He knew they would survive such a cataclysm—it hadn't been the first. He reached into his pocket, pulled out a chrome bracelet, and unfurled his hand. *If all else fails.*

The next morning, Samyaza was awakened by a wet and cold kiss on his cheek. He smiled. "Istahar?" But when he opened his eyes, the kiss turned into a stream of water that had reached their shelter and infiltrated the cave. "Istahar!"

She knelt in front of him, screaming, two-thirds of her body underwater. "I think it's time. I'm scared," she said in between labored breaths.

A tidal wave came crashing in. Samyaza put an arm under her legs and another under her neck and hovered into the last available air, and he flew them out, their bodies grazing the tumultuous sea as they squeezed out of the cave.

Istahar wailed in pain.

"Hold on."

And it rained.

The water had covered most of the mountains, and only scattered peaks broke through the surface.

"She's coming, Sam. She's coming."

Samyaza clenched his teeth, his tears blending with the rain. "When you arrive," he said. "Remain hidden and wait for me."

Before she had time to react, he had reached into his pocket, wrapped a chrome bracelet around her wrist, and activated it.

Istahar disappeared.

He knew he would not see them again.

CHAPTER 10

SAMYAZA AND ISTAHAR

P ain. Darkness. Pain. Hand reaching out into the unknown. Nothing there. Fell to the ground. Istahar cried. Covered her mouth. Darkness. Pain. She felt invisible tears dropping on her cheeks.

Samyaza flew over endless oceans. It had stopped raining. It had cleansed the sin. Humanity would start again.

Istahar found a soft surface. A bed, maybe. She sat on it. On the next contraction, she lay with her legs folded, knees up, and head pressed against a wall. She found a soft square—a pillow—which she put behind her head. Pain. Darkness. Loneliness.

Samyaza's rage traveled through the water. He screamed at nothing, no one, for there was nothing else over the Earth's surface but him. Him and the corpses of every living thing that had ever walked the Earth.

She wanted to scream. Her hand found a cloth. She pulled at it and the floor made a creaking sound. Chair. She pulled at it softer, quieter. Pain. Darkness. Loneliness. Her throat filled with giant inward screams. She clenched the cloth with her mouth, squeezed her leather half-moon necklace, and pushed.

The Archangel Michael appeared in front of Samyaza. "My brother Lucifer's personal traitor. How long do you think I can keep my brother off my back if I were to deliver you to him?"

"What are you doing here?" Samyaza stalled, knowing his power was nothing against Michael's divinity.

"I was tasked by the Ancestor to make sure nothing had survived the flood. I am afraid that includes you."

"What about the humans? Who will repopulate them this time? Everything is under water."

"Worry not. My brothers and I have enough genetic material to start them anew." He closed his eyes and his inhale was loud against the silence of floating corpses. "Can you smell it? The scent of order, cleanliness, we are one step closer to perfection. The Ancestor will be pleased."

"How did you know where to find me?"

Michael chuckled. "You have a rat inside your nest."

Samyaza thought about Istahar and his unborn daughter, and the dream that had become almost a reality, only to turn itself into a nightmare at the journey's end. "Kill me. End it. I have nothing else to live for."

"No. I do not take orders from a low-tiered nothing such as you. I will hand you over to my brother and keep him busy punishing you for your treason." He reached into the air in front of him and his reach extended to Samyaza's neck, then pressed on his bracelet. Samyaza smiled, breathless.

And she pushed again. Pain. Darkness. The cloth ripping in her savaged bite. Her screams hidden under muted groans. She pushed. Excruciating pain. And once again. Over and over, until something moved near her navel. Istahar removed her half-moon necklace and sawed her way through the umbilical cord with its ragged edge. She sat up and reached for the child's screaming face. She placed a hand below her daughter's head and brought it to the left side of her chest so the child could listen to her heartbeat. Istahar rocked her daughter and hushed her desperately. She hushed her and prayed. Begged for silence. Darkness. Loneliness.

Survival.

CHAPTER 11
ISTAHAR

A light made its way through a small window and bounced off an object in the darkness. Istahar stood up, baby in arms, and reached for it. She rubbed the specks of light floating in the dark, and once she recognized its metal links, pulled on the chain. A lightbulb flickered to life, displaying a dim view of the room she had materialized in. It was only in the light that the cold cement floor beneath her bare feet was apparent.

A river of dried blood painted the white bedsheets red. It was a twin-sized mattress inside a rusty metal frame, next to a damaged wooden nightstand. These things had been left sitting here to rot on purpose, waiting to be used. Istahar placed the baby on the bed next to the red, metallic-smelling river, and grabbed the cloth she had been biting from the floor. She rubbed the cloth between her legs as much as her shaking hands would allow.

The baby demanded to be picked up. Istahar wrapped her in a pillowcase and turned to a set of upward stairs that suggested they were in a basement. She approached the first step, swaying her body slightly to comfort her daughter. She counted the steps as far as the basement light allowed, each step a heavy burden on her body. The baby let out a small cry and squirmed in her arms. Istahar pushed her right leg to climb up the first step, and it trembled in the air. When she planted her foot, her lower back screamed as if it had been shattered to pieces. By the time she had climbed up to the last step, her face was drenched in sweat and tears.

Her daughter must have sensed her anxiety and cried in the pillowcase swaddle.

Istahar clenched her grip over the doorknob, only to discover it was locked. *No, not again*, she thought, releasing her grip. A projection of her ex-husband laughed as he closed the door to their basement and tossed the keys on the table. "And be quiet!" the projection said, and echoed from the past, through times and spaces, to fill her up with strength in the now. She gripped the doorknob once more, turning it forcibly, pulling and pushing on it, the door crashing against its frame.

"Samyaza?" a voice said on the other side of the door. "Is that you?"

Footsteps approached the door and whispered, "For His will..."

The sentence was a prompt that begged a resolution. Istahar straightened when it came to her. "We are His Messengers," she murmured. "We are His Messengers," she said. "We are His Messengers," she screamed and pounded on the door. She cried frantically. "Please. We are—"

The door unlocked.

The blinding light seeping in through the ajar door was like an electrical shock that jerked both of Istahar's hands, one to cover her daughter, and the other to pull out her half-moon necklace, edge first, and hang it over her, ready to tear to pieces whatever was about to emerge. But when the door swung open, a blond-haired creature that gripped her wrists with invisible claws paralyzed her.

Istahar cried and felt her daughter's body slipping. "No!"

The pillowcase unfolded, revealing a tiny forearm with a half-moon birthmark.

The claws released their grip, and Istahar repositioned her hands to support her child. "I despise you, I despise all of you. I wish you were all dead!" Her screams ripped her throat apart.

"Do not waste your hate on me. Though I have learned their creed, I am not part of the Messengers," the creature that looked neither male nor female said, pulling up his sleeve to reveal no numbers on its forearm. "The Ancestor's Wills do not belong anywhere, we are not of any time. We simply are. I protect those who seek the truth. And to that end, I have vouched to serve as an entry point, a guardian to the gateway between Arvo and Earth. I believe in His will, and as such, the Messengers and I, we are only allies of chance. But tell me, human, why do you despise that which was established to defend and protect your kind?"

"Protect? Samyaza"—she hid her pain, but judging by the creature's face, not well enough—"was the only one to ever truly protect me. The rest betrayed us. All of them. They expelled us and left us to die in the floods."

"There are only a number of reasons why a Messenger would be expelled—" the creature looked at the child. "No. No. No. What was Samyaza thinking? And why send you here? Come." The creature walked two steps down the basement and pulled Istahar by the arm with it. "You must leave, now. You must leave at once, back to where you came from, before they kill us both."

"Wait," Istahar planted her feet. "Samyaza, he sent us here for a reason. You must help me. Us."

"One thing is to hide a human, another is to harbor a sin," the creature said, at once with a rough, male tone, and a graceful, female poise. "For both our sakes, please."

Istahar held her baby tight. "For both our sakes," she said, and after a tear-eyed moment, "please."

. . .

Istahar stepped into the main level of the house before the androgynous creature.

"My name is Jophiel."

"Istahar," she said. "This place...is this Earth?"

"Far from it. Does she have a name?"

Istahar sat at a square, wooden table and looked around the house. "It all looks so...familiar. And no, not yet."

Jophiel sat on the chair opposite her. "You *were* created in our image. Besides, to become effective at what I do, once must lead a dull life and hold an inconsequential position in the hierarchy. I bide my time collecting things. Information, artifacts of history—celestial or human. I collect and...wait."

"Wait for what?"

Jophiel looked at the basement door. "To be needed."

Istahar pointed her face at a sword hanging on the wall. "Is that part of your collection?"

"Ah, yes." Jophiel stood up and approached the sword. "This sword belonged to a great Viking warrior, recovered from a battlefield in what would be your next Earth."

"My next Earth?"

"Precisely. This sword will take many lives and its wielder endure awful, unspeakable things, none of which have happened yet in your timeline. You see, for my kind, time is not linear."

Istahar had a puzzled face.

"For you, time is like a river. It follows a path, its current pulling you along. For me, it is a spill spreading in all directions."

The baby cried, and Istahar soothed her. "Why have a power like that if all you do is sit around and wait?"

"Ah, quite a conundrum, isn't it? It appears so simple, does it not? We do not do things merely because they are available. We do things because they are necessary. The balance is fragile, very fragile. One wrong intervention—"

The baby cried, louder, unable to draw a breath for seconds at a time, then cried again.

Jophiel pulled the cloth covering a window and glanced. "Feed her, for the Ancestor's sake, feed her before they notice we gamble with destiny itself!"

CHAPTER 12
SAMYAZA

Samyaza tasted Arvo's yellow dirt when Michael threw him at Lucifer's feet.

"There he is, dear brother. Your traitor, in the flesh," Michael said.

"And what do you want in return?" Lucifer said. "Surely this is not a kindness."

Michael chuckled. "You think you know me so well, do you not? No. I want nothing from you. I only ask you to keep your pet Watchers on a leash."

"Speak plainly, brother. I do not have time for your riddles."

"Keep your assassins off the bloodline. One drop of blood, and I will—"

"Ah, yes. The experiment. How is it coming along now?"

"You have your way. We have ours. No reason we cannot coexist."

"Very well," Lucifer said and motioned his hand. Two men grabbed Samyaza from under his arms and lifted him off the ground. "I hope to not see you for at least another thousand years."

Michael laughed. "Next time we meet, you will kiss my feet,

begging to do my bidding." His feet hovered over the ground and his levitating body shot up into the clouds and out of sight.

When Michael's body had disintegrated, Lucifer turned to Samyaza and said, "Put this filth away with the rest of the traitors."

In the city of Nieve, where the real soul of Arvo stood ten stories above and below ground, traitor Watchers rotted away in cages. The guards pulled Samyaza through the corridors of a dark, underground dungeon. He could almost feel the dirt sticking to his skin, the moist drops from the ceilings falling over him and filling his body with disease.

"Help!" a voice said. "Oh, God, please. Help!" A pair of hands appeared in the guards' torchlight and stretched out between the rusty steel bars of a cage. The noise and light rattled the others.

"Food. Please, it does not have to be much. Anything will do, anything at all," a man said from the next cage.

Samyaza stopped.

"Keep walking," one guard said.

"Praise the Lord," a woman's voice said in Samyaza's left ear. When he turned to the sound, a woman with ribs protruding stood in front of him, so thin, he dared not breathe into her in fear he might break every bone in her body. "People. New people. Praise the Lord. It is always nice to see new people."

Samyaza could almost recognize their faces if he imagined fifty more pounds of flesh to cover their bony bodies and saw their faces under the sunlight. But in that state, they were no longer angels, Watchers, or Messengers. They were no longer civilized creatures, but monsters created by absolute depravity. Lucifer had taken away their light, their nourishment, their dignity, and left them here to ponder on the worthiness of their rebellion and slowly dim away into moments of savagery as their stomachs howled with hunger before death set them free. They hoped for death only to find their bodies desperately hanging on to life.

The guards pushed Samyaza forward.

"I know you," a man said in Samyaza's right ear. "How could you? How could you abandon us? We trusted you! We followed you blindly, and look where that took us!" The man pounded on the rusty bars. "Do not ignore me! I know you, Samyaza."

"Samyaza?" the skeletal woman said.

"Samyaza?" Farther down where the guards and Samyaza had come from, now away from the torchlight, and in complete darkness.

"You deserve what is coming to you!" The old man cackled. "Long time coming!"

"Do not stop," a guard said. "Not too far now."

"In your last draw of breath, as your life slowly expires, remember us," the old man said behind them. "Remember your empty promises, your vicarious sacrifices, your failure as a leader. A true leader does not leave their people behind!" the old man's voice echoed in the dungeon.

Samyaza focused on the path ahead.

"Here we are. A special hole in the wall, for a special traitor," one guard said, the other laughed.

The guard pushed Samyaza and his face hit against the cage's wall. A cage that sealed up completely with no view of the dungeon. Sealed to perish in his own filth, to turn into bones as he suffocated slowly and lost his mind while hallucinating about things he should have done, the difficult things he ran away from.

Remember the dream, Samyaza thought. The dream which had him standing at the gates of Heaven next to Istahar and his daughter in his arms. The dream had resumed when Istahar arrived at Derinkuyu, though he did not speak of it. In the dream, the Ancestor had asked for his daughter. "I shall absolve you of your sin," the Ancestor said, "only if you let go of that which is the most precious to you." And in his dreams, he had to prove his words were real, that what he had created as the leader of the Messengers was founded on a true creed. *For His will.* Above *all*, His will. The following night, the dream had taken him on a journey while strapped to a chair in front of a large screen showing flashes of his daughter's life. Samyaza witnessed his daughter's metamorphosis through every beat of her tumultuous story, and with every chapter, he understood she did not belong to him or Istahar, but to the universes, to His will, and her path began by him saying…"I have a daughter!"

The cage's door, which had only an inch left to be completely sealed, swung open.

"What did you say?"

"I had a daughter with a human." Samyaza spit blood on the floor. "She survived the flood."

"You lie."

"Will you risk it? What do you suppose the Ancestor will think of your precious Lucifer once he finds out? What do you think Lucifer will do to you if I die here before you find her?"

A deafening noise reminded Samyaza he was still alive, his body confined to a small coffin-like box. The lid opened, and a guard pulled him out of the box. The screeching, dual-note was even more disturbing without the protection of the wooden walls.

"Are you ready to speak now?" the guard said over the noise.

The guard flogged Samyaza two, three times, the whip cracking on his skin and sending waves of bright noise down the corridors of the dungeon.

Samyaza turned to the open door of his cell. "God will provide the sheep for the burnt offering," he said, his naked body slit apart.

"Where is she?" the first guard said, reeling the whip in.

Samyaza trembled from the pain. "I cannot give her up. I must, but I cannot."

"Try again," the other guard said, and the first one unleashed the whip on Samyaza.

Layers of blood covered Samyaza's body. The four-day-old blood had dried over the skin. Fresh wounds had formed over it and tiny red streets poured down his legs. "By faith Abraham, when put to the test, offered up Isaac,—"the whiplash stroke and Samyaza fell to the ground"—and he who had received the promises was ready to offer his only son."

"Give it up, you fool!" the guard without the whip said and turned the volume on the noise down.

Samyaza crawled to the wall and tried to stand up, only to be struck down by the whip again.

"Are you ready to die for your secret?." He reeled the whip in, gained momentum, and released it with fury upon Samyaza.

"I am sorry, my Lord. I am weak. I have sunk my teeth into the apple, tasted its sweet flesh, and now find that nothing else compares," Samyaza cried. "I am not worthy of absolution. I am not worthy of your blessing. End it now, if you must. End it so I can begin my punishment at once."

"Bring the bucket," the guard with the whip said and tossed the whip to the floor.

The other guard carried a bucket full of water into the cage and placed it in front of Samyaza, who was kneeling down.

Strands of Samyaza's hair tore out of his scalp when the guard pulled him up and pushed his head into the bucket. Samyaza opened his eyes under the cold water, its transparent color now dyed red. He felt gratitude for the torchlight making this moment possible, for the cleanliness the water afforded him, for Istahar, for the life he had created, and for his place in the universe. And as he sensed his body collapsing and his energy retreating, he smiled, for he knew life would endure, with or without him. Nothing—good or evil—could ever derail existence from His Master Plan. He was not much more than a pebble on the path to enlightenment, and now that the cataclysm of fate was passing over him, he must be left behind. He had no more air and his body reacted by opening the drawbridge of his mouth and breathing, filling his lungs with water. His life-force, a ghost ship once dark and without memory, returned to the harbor from where it had sailed.

CHAPTER 13

LUCIFER

Lucifer stood at the tower's pinnacle, overlooking the Watcher Development Center, the border surrounding it, then the cities of Arvo. "The flood on Earth has subsided."

"Yes, sir," one guard who had delivered the news of Samyaza's passing said.

"Which means?"

"We can resume travel to Earth?" the other guard said.

Lucifer stared at him. "No, you useless fool! It means there is no longer sin on Earth."

The first guard straightened. "Of course."

Lucifer turned back to face the cities beyond the border. "It means she must be here," Lucifer whispered. "But...where? Tear the cities apart. Leave no stone unturned. Move heaven and earth if you have to. But find her, find her if you do not want to find yourself among traitors and wither away into oblivion."

CHAPTER 14
JOPHIEL

"How bad is it?" Jophiel said while picking up a fruit at the street market.

"Word is they are ransacking every city in Arvo in search of the sin," the woman next to Jophiel said.

Jophiel returned the vegetable from its basket and picked up a different vegetable. "How far are they from reaching Sundar?"

"My estimate is they shall be here within two sun cycles."

Jophiel nodded and handed the woman her payment. "What about...him?"

The woman shook her head and Jophiel nodded once more, finished picking up the vegetables, then walked away to the house.

Jophiel opened the front door, the house silent as a coffin, the plates cleaned and dried, the floors without a speck of dust.

"It is just me. It is safe," Jophiel said, and placed a sack of vegetables on the table.

The basement door, which hid behind a fake bookcase full of Jophiel's prized possessions, creaked open. Istahar walked out with the baby in her arms.

"They have started the search. You are not safe here any longer." Jophiel took strides around the house, assembling the table with plates and cutlery, turning around, opening cupboards, setting pans on the stove. "It is precisely what I had feared."

"How? How did anyone know we're here?"

Jophiel turned on the stove burner. "It is unclear to me, but my informant tells me they will be in the city by the end of the week."

"There must be something we can do, somewhere we can go."

"I told you to leave. We must not play God, we must not"— Jophiel opened a spice bottle, sprinkled it on boiling water, closed it, then picked another one, shook its head, set it back and picked yet another one. Jophiel froze in front of the vapor coming out of the pan —"I know not what to make of this."

Istahar placed a hand over Jophiel's arm. "Thank you for everything you've done." She handed over her baby to Jophiel. "Here." She set an array of spices and vegetables from Jophiel's haul over the countertop, and began skinning the vegetables and chopping them in pieces.

Jophiel bounced the baby in its arms. "That red one," Jophiel nodded at a vegetable and said, "is close to what earthlings call boniato. The purple one resembles yam." The baby grabbed Jophiel's finger. "Does she have a name yet?"

"God, I hadn't even thought of it. What kind of mother am I?"

After a long silence, Jophiel said, "Luna."

"What?"

"Her name is Luna. It was stamped on her skin from birth. Look." Jophiel showed the baby's forearm. It had the birthmark of a half-moon.

"Oh, the birthmark? It runs in my family. Luna, huh? I like it."

"It is Spanish for moon, according to my books."

Istahar adjusted the stove temperature and finished cutting the rest of the vegetables. A round, yellow one filled the room with a sweet aroma. A blue one, shaped like a bell pepper, smelled earthy, and Istahar smiled when the knife cut it in half.

Jophiel frowned. *I know that smile. Hope. I know the pain that follows once it is extinguished.*

CHAPTER 15

ISTAHAR

Istahar sat listening to Arvo, looking for the clues that recounted its soul. *Every culture has a sound for whoever wants to listen.* She had studied cultures—ancient or living—on her trips as an archeologist, and felt a closeness to the people she interacted with even before they introduced themselves. On every remote cold mattress, by every lonely window, there was always a sound, and she was always there to listen. Arvo, though silent, kept her awake. *Serves me well for expecting a sound,* she thought.

They came at night, swift as a summer breeze, carrying a stifled violence about to burst. *Thump, thump* at the door. "Official business. Open up!"

"Those are not just guards, those are Redeemers," Jophiel whispered. "They only send Redeemers on pursuits of critical importance, matters that must be resolved in haste. No. I thought we had more time. Quick"—Jophiel signaled toward the bookshelf—"hide in the basement and do not come out no matter what happens."

Luna squirmed on the fashioned bassinet Istahar had made of a laundry basket and towels. "Jophiel, what will happen?"

On the other side of the door, a voice said, "Open up this instant. We are here under the great Lord Lucifer's orders. We have the authority to break into your home and complete a thorough search of your premises."

Jophiel smiled. "Istahar, may the tapestry of fate bind our paths together once more, either in the past or future, this timeline, or the next." Jophiel hugged Istahar, then rubbed Luna's head and kissed it. "Half-human, half-angel. Your path I do not envy, little one."

"Why are you talking like that? It will be all right... right?"

"You have one more chance," said the man behind the door.

Jophiel turned to the door, then back to Istahar, and pushed her gently toward the bookcase. "Go."

"My apologies, officer," Jophiel said after opening the door. "You found me half-asleep."

"Evening," the Redeemer said and held Jophiel by the wrist, his index and middle fingers pressing firmly on Jophiel's radial artery. The Redeemer stepped into the house, followed by his partner.

"Just a plain Arvonian home."

"Is this weapon registered?"

"Ah, the sword. Yes, sir. It is registered. A collectible. It has never left the mount on which it hangs."

The first Redeemer grunted and headed for the living room, while the other roamed in the kitchen, opening and closing cabinet doors.

"Any basement or attic?" the Redeemer in the living room said, his footsteps falling heavy over the hardwood floors.

"No. As I said, I live quite a simple life. All my earnings go toward my only vice." Jophiel pointed at the sword.

"Find anything?"

The second Redeemer returned from the kitchen and motioned a "No" with his head. He stopped in front of the bookshelf and put an open hand in front of him. Everyone went silent. The Redeemer approached the bookshelf and inched in with his face. He sniffed books at random and after a long time, said. "I thought I caught a scent. Must be the kitchen."

"If you are pleased with your findings, I shall go back to my sleep. Gentlemen, please. Allow me to escort you to the door," Jophiel said.

The first Redeemer stepped out the open front door.

The second Redeemer was half out the front door.

Behind the bookshelf, down 15 steps, the hunger cries of baby Luna stopped him in his tracks.

CHAPTER 17

ISTAHAR

Istahar wrapped Luna inside a towel and kept her close to her heart. She rested Luna's head between her upper arm and forearm, and her free hand held a butcher knife she had slipped from the kitchen. She figured, if they ever found the door to the basement, there was no point in hiding, so she stood in a dark corner next to the bottommost step.

She often wondered what compelled a human to quicken their breath and lose all control of their nerves. In the dark, she shivered as if pulled out of an ice bath to be executed; in the dark, she understood.

She clenched the knife when the creaking floorboards overhead approached the basement door.

Silence. She held her breath, and only released it when the creaking sound slithering like a serpent in the ceiling neared the front door. Her grip on the knife softened. Her numb hands regained sensation.

"Oh, baby. Not now, love. Shh, shh, shh," she whispered to her restless baby. "Just a few more seconds." She soothed Luna with her knife holding hand, the knife's flat side softly grazing over her cheek.

The baby jerked from the cold metal's touch and burst into an angry wail.

The footsteps were now fast-paced. "There is someone else in here," a voice said, closer to the basement door.

"I assure you, it is just us. Stop!" the voice was unmistakably Jophiel's.

"On your knees, traitor."

Istahar covered her mouth when a loud thud fell over the ceiling.

"Try to see the larger plan, His plan," Jophiel pleaded, his voice close to the door.

"The bookshelf. It is a door, is it not?"

Silence.

"You are sheltering a sin, are you not?" the same voice said. "Open it."

Rays of light descended over the basement steps, and Istahar strengthened her grip on Luna and the knife.

"You go, I will restrain the traitor," the first Redeemer said to the second.

"I know you are here. I can smell you," the second Redeemer said.

Istahar stepped backwards, hoping for a spot that the open door hadn't yet brightened. When the Redeemer had stepped off onto the basement floor, Istahar covered Luna's face and pushed herself into the light. Her scream was a battle cry that sent the Redeemer reeling back. By the time he realized the rage that had been unleashed upon him, the knife had made it through his abdomen. He fell to the ground, his full face now in the light's path and the blood oozing from his stomach and mouth.

"I'm sorry. I'm sorry," Istahar said to Luna, who cried from the sudden jerks of her mother.

The first Redeemer peeked into the basement. "What is going on down there? Answer me!"

"For His will!" Jophiel said while slashing the Redeemer's neck with his sword. "Istahar! The bracelet. Use it. You must escape. Quick!"

The first Redeemer's head fell on the floor and rolled down the steps, leaving a trail of blood splotches, and landed in front of Istahar.

"Istahar! You do not have much—"

Jophiel levitated at the top of the stairs with the arms and legs glued to the body. The sword slid from its hands and fell to the floor. "Very fragile, indeed. It was a pleasure—" Jophiel said, and its neck snapped and its head hung to the side.

"There is only one way to get such an important thing done the right way. How is it you humans say? Ah, yes. If you want something done right, do it yourself. Do not be alarmed. My name is Lucifer. What I will do is not something I want done, but something that needs to be done. You are not supposed to be alive. But, of course, the blame always falls on the person caught red-handed under the spotlight, with no regard to the preceding events that culminated in this moment. I am only carrying out His will. This was decreed by the ancestor Himself."

Lucifer appeared at the top of the stairs like a being from sleep paralysis. He made his way down, a step at a time, relaxed, as if anything that was about to happen was bound to happen and could not be altered.

Istahar covered Luna and tried to get the knife out of the second Redeemer's stomach, but his body flew to the back of the room. She gasped and turned to Lucifer, who had now made it to the basement floor, his hand open in front of him. "There is no way out of this. It is written."

"Get away from me!"

And before Istahar had finished screaming, Luna was out of her arms and with Lucifer. "Let me see it," he said.

Istahar tried to run toward Lucifer and was met by an invisible wall. No matter how hard she tried, her steps took her nowhere.

"Your passion is respectable," he said. "I will grant you one and only one wish. And that is, how would you like me to kill your daughter?"

Istahar pounded at the air, kicking the floor beneath her.

"Asphyxiation?" He put a hand over her face.

Istahar's head throbbed with pain, the top of her eyes stinging from the flood of tears that had covered her face. She screamed at the suffocating helplessness.

"I cannot bear to look at your face. What is that? Is that love?" Lucifer said, and with a motion of his hand, shot Istahar's face up to the ceiling and out of his field of vision.

"What is taking so long, Lucifer?" a female voice said from upstairs.

"I am fascinated, yet undecided about how to end it."

"I have never seen you hesitating about anything." The woman came down the stairs.

"There is something... strange, Faith."

"Let me see it."

Lucifer uncovered Luna's face.

Istahar stood on the tip of her toes with her face still pointing at the ceiling. "Stay... away... from...her."

"How is she still speaking?" Faith said, taken aback.

"You understand now? These two are different, somehow. It is interesting."

"Oh, we must keep her," Faith said, delighted.

"Whatever do you mean?"

"We could keep her. Both of them. Study their bond, track her progression, and make more of her. That strength, that perseverance...imagine it in an entire army?"

"We would be accomplices of a sin," Lucifer said, astonished by the idea.

"Earth has not given us a sin. Perhaps it has given us everything we ever hoped for."

After a long pause, Lucifer handed over Luna to Faith. "No one must know about this. Take her, discretely. I will handle her mother."

Istahar forced her face down and saw her daughter in the arms of Faith, going up the stairs, into the world, and out of her life.

PART 4

CURRENT EARTH

CHAPTER 18

LUNA

Luna inhaled Earth's oxygen—a warm, yet unwelcoming stench that blanketed over the urban night. Her mouth watered; the smell took her to the Watcher Development Center's dungeons where she had once learned that killing was not just acceptable, but encouraged. Luna had materialized in a dark, narrow passage with brick walls that stood at either side. *Alley.* Her target must be inside a two-mile radius. With her wrist in front of her, her chromium bracelet projected a 3D rendering of her subject, Robert Cohen. His face was disturbing, but she focused on his walk, memorizing how his body morphed when he moved, when he breathed, when he fought. When the projection ended, the alley darkened again. Luna clenched her hands in a fist and the cold rubbed against her thumbs. The thrill of arriving had worn off, and all that remained was her, alone, in a strange and savage land full of loud sounds and putrid smells. If she wasn't careful, a savage human might notice the intruder in her, claw at her skin, break her every bone, and bring her back to a cave where they would feast on her remains.

She allowed her training to guide her. She must walk in the shadows away from danger, fulfill her task, and request a transfer back home. *Get in, kill, get out,* Lucifer had said. But more than following his orders, what she wanted more than anything was to see A29 and A15 again, if they were still alive. *They are. They must be. They have to be.*

Luna—humanity's half-sister—must not be seen, but if she was, they must see only the human side of her and accept her as an equal. As much as she wanted to never leave the alley's dark protection, she had to walk among the humans to triangulate her target's position. The only way to rescue her friends was to make herself visible, vulnerable. She removed her knife from its sheath and slid it into a hidden pocket inside her boot. Luna exhaled before walking out into the street.

Night had gotten rid of most of the humans, and the streets, other than the disturbing noise producing vehicles, were scarce. She had read about the humans, how they loathed the night and the nature that surrounded them. It was as if they didn't belong on their own planet and could only live in it if there were barriers to keep nature at bay.

All but one store was closed for the night. Her bracelet turned from black to yellow when she took a step toward the only lit-up store. *Closer.* A bell rang at the top of the open door and a person came out carrying a bag, and he, Robert Cohen, locked the door from the inside. This was different. At the Watcher Development Center, there was always something to stop her right at the cusp of killing. Here she was alone. No flashing lights would guide her away, no tall people would come rushing to her aid. Killing was expected, and they waited for her to execute. *Closer.* Luna's eyes connected with her victim's for a fatal moment, a long enough moment to flash a memory of planet Arvo in her mind. In her memory, she faced the stream of sunlight coming through her open window. She raised her arm next to Arvo's Sun until her birthmark was at its level, and the sun and moon stood side by side, both shining their unique light. For a time, they seemed to belong together, the half-moon cuddled next to the raging sphere of light. The astral body blurred before her burning eyes, but she couldn't look away. Luna moved her forearm over the sun, slowly dimming its ferocious light until both merged into the perfect total eclipse. She now stood in the cold darkness outside the bookstore, unable to look away. She was eclipsed by his presence, yet she had never been so illuminated, so ready for a new dawn. He threw a grin in her direction from the bookstore's cash register. *Closer.*

"You need me again, don't you?" a voice said, clouding over her. "You can't do this alone. Can you? That's what I'm here for."

The voice had hypnotized her. Under her paralyzed gaze, her bracelet had turned green.

Robert looked up at her and grinned again. *No, don't.* He closed the register and walked to the door. *Please.* Her eyes burned with the sting of future blood. *Stop.* The door opened.

***

Where is the danger? Luna thought, lying next to Robert on the bookstore's roof. Whenever she drifted away from her task, the blade poking at the side of her leg was a reminder of why she was there. It could be as easy as leaning for the knife's hilt. She could end it all in one swift motion. But his hand found hers and pulled her back to the fantasy world she had uncovered, a world perhaps not as violent as the one programmed into her brain during her training. His fingers found their way between hers. *How can anyone say so much without speaking?* She searched for an answer in the stars. Her genetic tattoo was projected on the celestial canopy. A half moon, he called it. Perhaps one dot in the sky was Arvo. Alone behind bars, somewhere out there among the flickering lights, waited a mother for her daughter to fulfill her destiny.

"Kill. All you have to do is kill," whispered the voice inside and outside her head. The voice was everywhere. "Do not stray from your task."

But he has done nothing wrong. Maybe he's different. Maybe he's no barbarian.

"Only filthy daughters keep their mothers in cages. Only vile little humans leave their friends to die." The whisper rose into a growl, shifting from ear to ear.

$A29, A15$. Her hidden knife grew heavier.

Luna's bracelet was automated to ping her victim in thirty-minute intervals. The bracelet beeped, slow nautical radar beeps at first. Then louder, faster, the metal detector had struck gold. And at once the bracelet shone the color of death. Red. A token of motivation for a well-trained Watcher. The light was now impossible to ignore, and Robert had noticed it, too.

"If you won't do it yourself, we will do it for you," the voice said in an authoritative tone.

She closed her hands into fists, and they trembled with her strength. Her nails sunk a sixteenth of an inch into her skin. The craving. The craving. The craving for blood. It was near. "You need to leave," she said.

Robert sat up. "Why? What's wrong?"

In seconds, she wouldn't be able to speak, let alone explain. It was only a matter of time before she stopped being herself and turned into the monster they had trained her to be. "I don't have much time. You have to trust that I'm telling you the truth. I'm not from this planet." Her face contorted in pain, holding back the killing machine, the wolf pounding violently at the door. "I was sent here to kill you." She let out a cry.

"You are majestic, Luna. Let it take you in its full glory," the voice cheered.

"Kill me?" Robert had jolted up. "Come on. Let's get out of this cold and back inside the store."

"Red means death. Red wants death," she said with her eyes closed and her mouth watering. She reached for her boot and pulled out a knife.

"Whoa, what are you doing?" Robert's hands were up. "What do you want? Money? There's not a lot in the register, but you can take it all. You don't have to do this."

Luna had now risen as well. She inched forward, a beast cornering her prey, pushing him back toward the edge. A few more steps and he would fall two floors down on solid asphalt. Her bracelet beamed a bloody crimson red. With every pulse, her anger increased. She became less human, and more Watcher, and with the next bloody pulse of her bracelet, her mind was not on Earth, but in the school's dungeon.

Robert was at his last step. He looked down when he lost his footing, then back at Luna. His only two options led to death. "Why are you doing this?" he said. "Stop."

The red light shining from Luna's bracelet illuminated the path in front of her. And the path ended on Robert. She gripped the knife, turning it slightly, projecting some of the red light at her face. Her beauty emerged under the spotlight of death's radiance.

Robert pleaded, but his arms, which had risen halfway to surrender, relaxed at his sides. The red had reached up into his eyes, and when Luna looked into his irises, she scowled, determined to end his life.

Blue light emanated out of Robert Cohen. Luna shivered against the light's coldness, and her face softened, her body heat cooled.

The voice in Luna's head was more animated than ever and multiplied in binaural echoes. "End it. End it now!"

Luna yelled a war cry while swinging a deathblow at his neck. But the attack was weaker than she had intended. He leaned and evaded most of it, though the knife's tip formed a superficial line across his cheek. Her arm, now at his side from her finishing move's aftermath, was defenseless to an attack. He grabbed her wrist. Robert pressed on her bracelet with a powerful force.

The voice's pitch lowered. Its echo was in slow motion inside her mind. "Kill... Kill."

In an exhale's time, the bracelet disintegrated, and the red night darkened again. Luna fell to her knees. And as the knife fell from her hands and rattled on the concrete roof, the phantom voice in her head silenced into oblivion.

A thunderstorm had invaded the night sky.

Luna rubbed her naked wrist. Her training guided her to do only two things: kill and survive. Her arm had never felt light, her resolve had never ceased to be on the offense, but with no bracelet sustaining her urge to kill, she said, "We're not safe here."

Robert's blue aura had dissipated, yet he stood looking at his hands, exploring his limbs, touching his face as if he was putting out a fire. "What the hell just happened?"

"They want you dead. I tried. I failed. They will try again."

"They?"

"I can now see why. There's great power in you."

"Power? I'm not sure you have the right guy. I'm nothing but a broke bookseller, a failed writer. Hell, even a failed burger flipper."

"Clearly, that is not true." She showed him her wrist, slightly paler than the rest of her arm. The weightlessness of her arm shocked her. "They engineered those bracelets to withstand anything. I was supposed to carry it forever, yet you broke it apart with a single touch."

She had seen power once before. She had felt it when Lucifer had pulled her out of that air vent on her rescue mission with her friends. Lucifer possessed some unknown power, too, that much was apparent, but she had never heard of a human doing anything other than things of savagery, the acts of brute animals.

"Something was...different in me for a moment. Everything was possible for a second, I only had to imagine it. Then it turned off like a switch," Robert said.

Luna grabbed her knife from the floor, and Robert stared with a reproachful look. She stowed the knife away. "How far advanced are you?"

His puzzled face urged her for more.

"I mean," she continued, "is your species close to becoming inter-planetary? Is there a viable means of transportation off the planet?"

"I don't know. I'm sure each government has their secret projects, but as far as I know, we can only go to the moon and back."

"Each government? Secret projects? The moon?" She scoffed. "You people really *are* savages, aren't you?"

"Says the person who tried to kill me." He rubbed the scratch on his face.

She mentioned her wrist again, how she was bound to a psycho-pathic possession, though she refrained from explaining her relation-ship with the bracelet in full. He didn't need to know anything about the other kids and their training in the red dungeon, or the artificial wombs modeled from her mother. Human existence seemed so small, ignorant of the celestial chess game looming over their heads. *Focus, Luna. You're on your own now.*

"What do we do now?" he said.

"I'm still working on that." She paced from one edge of the roof to another, staring at the floor, ruminating. "They might send another Watcher for me when they see my signal's been lost." She looked at both sides of the street below them, then came back to Robert. "They will definitely send one for you to finish the job. Lucifer seemed eager to send someone to kill you."

The mention of the name made Robert stand straight. "What did you just say?"

"That we must stick together. They are going to send someone for either of us, and our chances look better if we do."

"No," he said. "The name."

She repeated it. "I'm sure if I call for help, he'll send for me," she said, looking at the night's sky. "But I don't have my bracelet anymore. We will have to wait for another Watcher to come."

"I'm sorry. Lucifer?"

"Yes. He will be furious for not following his orders. Maybe we can make him understand. Maybe he doesn't know the whole truth. But surely the Watcher he will send will not allow for such a conversation. The Watcher will attack us on sight without question. Especially you."

"My choices are staying here and getting killed by one of you, one of these Watchers, or paying a visit to Lucifer?" Robert said.

The pages of the Origin book flipped through Luna's mind, and the drawings came back to her. The horned monster. The underworld vulture that waited for death and pulled dark souls into a pit of lava where it fed on their eternal pain. *He is scared, the same way I was scared.* She had seen firsthand that the book had been a lie. For what purpose, she wasn't sure. Considering that her mother was a prisoner, her friends hostages, and her upbringing a training for murder, perhaps she didn't know the whole truth, either. No. It wasn't time to reach for her knowledge as a Watcher but for her intuition as a human. To escape to safety. For the time being, to survive. "We have to move."

"But go where? I don't have a car, I don't have any money, I barely just got a roof over my head."

"Surely I must not have been the first of my kind to approach you. Not you. Not with all that power. Have you ever seen anything out of the ordinary?"

"Mark!" Then, he said, calmer, "the Messengers."

"What?"

"I had ignored it as the ramblings of a dying man, but with everything that just happened, I have to stop pretending it wasn't real. I met a man once. He moved things without touching them."

"Then we must go to this man."

"We can't. I... he's dead. But he said something before he died. He told me to seek the Messengers."

"And where are these Messengers?"

A beam of light blinded them, and a voice startled them from above. "Here," it said.

CHAPTER 19

FAITH

Faith paced the room, leaning into one window and pulling its curtain away for a moment, before moving on and doing the same on the next. "She should have been here by now."

"If something was the matter, Daniel would have sent for us," Lucifer said. "Come, sit."

She huffed, then pulled the chair over the tiled floor and sat.

After drumming her fingers over the porcelain table, Faith said, "Can you check her signal again?"

"Still there, close to the target."

Lucifer set the tracker between them, its light bouncing off the table's glossy finish. They watched the red dot coming in and out of existence, holding their breath every time it disappeared, and inhaling when it came back.

Until the light went out and didn't brighten again.

Faith pushed the chair back and stood. "I told you she was not ready. I told you she was different." Her voice commanding, she said, "If you do not send someone, I will."

"Patience, dear."

But all patience afforded them was an incoming message. Daniel. Lucifer was now also standing. "Daniel?"

"Yes, sir. I am afraid it is not good news."

"Speak plainly and be wise with your words." Lucifer played a movie in his head. A movie where Daniel killed the entire top floor of the Watcher Development Center. Still, the traitor was the only bridge to Lucifer's adoptive daughter. He pretended along.

"The target. He has... set Luna free."

Faith's eyes morphed from worry to fear.

Lucifer stood in silence, his hands gripping the top of the chair's backrest. His knuckles white. In an explosion of anger, he swept the tracker off the table, and it broke into a dozen pieces across the floor. "All available Watchers," he said, talking into his bracelet, frowning. "Get in. Kill. Get out."

Faith gasped. It wasn't a rescue mission, but a spoliation of evidence.

CHAPTER 20

LUNA

The humanoid shape hovered above before letting its feet soft-land on the roof. Its golden armor glistened under the moonlight and its feathered wings folded behind its back. "God, you look just like him."

Luna unsheathed her knife and pushed Robert behind her. "What are you?"

The creature spoke slowly. It enunciated every word as if it had an infinite amount of time to speak. "Protecting, sacrificing. Leadership flows in your blood. It burns in your spirit like the ancient embers of a genetic flame. I can only imagine what hidden powers you must possess waiting to be awakened. The question is, what will awaken you? What will make you light up the darkest night?"

The creature was the tallest adult-like being Luna had ever seen. Its long hair fell on its shoulders, and its face resembled a younger human male, yet something told her the being was older than it looked. She had gotten the same feeling in the pit of her stomach when she had met Lucifer for the first time, as if they were all part of the same advanced ancient family.

"Are you a Watcher?"

The creature smirked. "I used to be, just like you. The original Watchers. Ones that were still angels."

"What do you mean? I'm a Watcher still," Luna said.

"You are not wearing your bracelet and,"—it pointed at Robert—"he is still breathing. You have broken the oath in full. They will not welcome you back."

Luna didn't say a word. The creature, whatever it was, was right. There was no going back, not if she wanted to live.

"Be not afraid," it continued, "your place is not with them. Your destiny is much bigger than following the orders of capricious Archangels and their games. You are bound to the Messengers by blood. By his blood."

"What are you talking about? Whose blood?"

"Samyaza, your father," he said.

Luna relaxed her stance. *Samyaza.* She had read that name before on the files they had stolen from the Archives as kids. According to the file, her father had a child with a human before being tortured to death in Arvo. "You are lying. Why should I trust you?"

"I am not capable of lying. All the Messengers know about the miracle child. The only one who survived both the Archangels, and the Ancestor's cleansing floods. The girl with the half-moon birth-mark, and rightful heiress of the Messengers' throne."

"Samyaza," Robert muttered, his voice lost in the presence of a flying angel. "Where have I heard that name before?"

"I am afraid we must continue this conversation, as pleasant as it is, at another time. The Archangels do not react well to failure. We must go before their Watchers arrive and—"

"From the Bible my mother used to read me before bed," Robert interrupted, his eyes closed, as if accessing the vault of his mind. "That's it. Samyaza, leader of a band of angels full of lust, who fell to Earth and consummated their desires with human females. Wait, that makes you,"—he turned to Luna—"half angel, half human?"

"Silence," the creature said in disgust. "The Bible, as you call it, is a version, an *inaccurate* version, of the Origin book, planted on Earth and everywhere else by the three Archangels with the sole purpose of undermining God and His Messengers. It is not the book of creation, but the book of destruction. It seeks to destroy our image and God's image with the purpose of introducing the Archangels' law of the land. They want to dominate not only Earth and this universe but every single being in all dimensions of existence with their specific flavor of religion. To them, Earth is nothing more than a sample experiment, a controlled study before they implement the same in the rest of the universes."

"There's more than one Archangel?" Luna said.

"Yes. You know of one, of course. The solitary Archangel Lucifer, who thinks he is capable of all things by his own cleverness. But there are three others, far more powerful, that work together: Michael, Gabriel, and Raphael. In the end, they all want the same thing, control of the Ancestor's throne. To rule over every living thing." The angel-looking creature stopped for a brief moment, contemplating his words and licking his lips, then shook his head and said, "They shall be stopped."

Luna felt a sudden urge to defend Lucifer. He had been the only adult to treat her with any display of kindness. "Not Lucifer," she said. "He wants to leave it to humans to learn for themselves. He wants to prove to the Ancestor that he has changed, and he is worthy of Him once more, that he, too, can oversee life, and that life can thrive on his watch. He has failed, multiple times, by following the rules. And he has suffered greatly for it."

"Letting humans sort it out for themselves by sending his trained assassins to give them a nudge in his direction is the opposite of free will. That is why he fails and will continue to do so. He has not learned his lesson, and the Ancestor will see right through it. If he wishes to redeem himself, he must first carry out His will."

Robert stood in silence, waiting to be addressed.

The angel looked at him and at Luna. "We can continue this conversation once we are safe. Come with me." It offered its hands to them. "There is no time for a slow introduction. I am afraid we must rush to Derinkuyu at once."

"We don't even know who you are," Luna said.

"My name is Daniel. I have been keeping your throne safe, waiting for your arrival. The Messengers are expecting you."

A beam of light descended from the sky, then another, and at once there were more than a dozen beams projected over the roof's surface. "Watchers. They are here. Our time is running out. We must go. You must make a choice," Daniel said, extending his hands out to them.

"Not much of a choice," Robert said, looking back at the armed beings appearing on the roof.

Luna knew she could take one out, maybe two, but didn't stand a chance against this many Watchers. Some of them were already materializing, their bodies taking shape from thin air, while more beams continued to appear. It was now an army.

Daniel extended his wings, and his feet levitated from the floor.

Luna looked back at the battalion of trained assassins. Their bracelets pulsated in a crimson-red hue. Their mouths salivated, their bodies propelled forward by their thirst for blood. *What have I done?* She sheathed her knife, pushed Robert over the building's edge, then leaped after him.

With Robert and Luna in his hands, Daniel shot up into the sky.

CHAPTER 21

LUNA

Luna felt Daniel's pain when he carved into his skin. "With my blood's ink, I swear to carry the secret to my grave. For His will, we are His Messengers," Daniel said at Derinkuyu's entrance. "It is your choice now."

Daniel had flown Robert and Luna across the world to Turkey in the time it took to drive around a city. Robert was still trembling from the adrenaline. While he hesitated, Luna walked up to the rock, pulled out her knife, and sliced it across her hand. She repeated Daniel's words as droplets of her blood splattered on the rock. "What happens now?" she said and grimaced with pain when the numbers burned into her skin. Luna pulled up her sleeve, the fabric rubbing against the fresh scars. *444.*

"Isn't that the—" Robert said, and approached to get a better view — "the mark of the beast?"

"Different numbers," Daniel said. "However, that is another convoluted addition to your version of the Origin book meant to further confuse humanity. It is an effective tool for control; fear, that is. Add confusion to the mix, and you have an entire race that cannot tell up from down, or right from wrong. No. These numbers are not the mark of the beast, but a symbol of hope. A beacon of light to illuminate the better things ahead. Whenever we are lost, it reminds us about our purpose, and guides us home." He turned to Luna, nodded, then back at Robert. " It is not my place to force you either way. Once you have made your peace, follow us. Come."

Daniel took four steps toward a large rock, and Luna followed.

"I can't just abandon what I have known all my life for something that I just discovered,"—Robert pointed at Daniel's wings—"Even though you have compelling evidence of interesting things to come."

Daniel folded his wings until they disappeared in his back. Without his wings, his demeanor was that of a human. "Here." He tossed his pocketknife at Robert.

At once, the stone in front of them rolled to the side, and they walked into an opening beyond the zone of light.

As if there was a green crystal hanging above her head, and her imaginary bracelet urged her to walk, Luna stepped into the pitch black. Rebel as she was, the pull of destiny was the iron grip from which she couldn't break free. Not on her own. Yet one thing might have been powerful enough to tear the bond apart for her—he had done it once before—and set her back on her course toward saving them, her mother, her friends, everyone. She turned to look at Robert, and she looked until the stone almost covered the last rays of light before her. She inched toward the light, but her body grew as heavy as a limestone. *Lucifer?* She turned her face, only to find Daniel. *No. It can't be.*

Once the door was shut, her body was light again, as light as a feather that has absorbed rain, mud, and blood can be. *They are players of the same game. They move us like pawns on a chessboard,* she thought, but said, "Will he be all right?"

Daniel nodded. "Nothing is as costly as free will." His hand fell on Luna's shoulder, and in a roll of a knife, the future became more interesting than the past, for in front of her lay a pathway that descended into complete darkness.

CHAPTER 22

ROBERT

I clasped the knife until I trembled, and moved it closer pointed to the other hand, edge first. I thought about Mark's face, his opened, terrifying, lifeless eyes, the product of my urges. Only now did the knowledge crash on me, and fell heavy on my soul. I had killed a man—a good man—and no one would ever know. How quickly could the tides of fortune turn and spin a man back and forth between who he was, is, or might become, and all that could keep him from spinning into oblivion lay in a single decision? *Silence.* I worked well with silence. I thrived in it. But not when it's the waiting room of a life-altering choice. Silence was a spotlight, and I always hated the spotlight. *Wind blowing, whistling through the cracks in the reddish rocks.* I could always turn back right now and turn myself in, restart. But the hurt the word inmate next to my name would cause my mother? No. No. But if I don't, then what kind of man am I? I could plead insanity, and turning myself in might lower my sentence. Besides, I could say, given the circumstances, that it was self-defense, do a few years in prison, and, in time, return to my bookstore, my manuscript. Normalcy. A real-life story: publishers love that. But one thing pulled me the opposite way. Luna. An unlikely connection. A pleasant surprise. Something pushed the knife into my skin. A blue aura formed around me. I cannot let her go. I cannot—

"I would not do that if I were you," a tall blond man said. I almost cut myself from the shock.

"Why not? Who are you?" I looked around for possible methods of travel. Nothing. Which meant... "Are you one of them?"

"Let go of the knife, Robert." Another man, this one with red hair, said. He looked annoyed when I didn't automatically comply.

Then, a third one flew down in front of me. He had dark brown hair and a confidence that hit like a weakening shockwave. It paralyzed me. Something inside me wanted to fight, my first impulse to bury the knife in his chest, but I couldn't find the strength. All I could do was kneel and bow.

"You will come with us, for you are our creation. We will show you the way to His door. And you will open it," he said, and in a moment we were no longer on Earth.

CHAPTER 23

LUNA

Rows of torches lit up with fire and revealed the sinking path in front of Luna.

"Ah," Daniel said, turning to the illuminated sloped walkway. "An entrance worthy of royalty. The city knows. It feels your energy."

"Knows what?"

"That they are lost no more. That its leader has arrived."

Luna had her hand locked around her knife. Throughout her life, a metal bracelet had made all of her choices for her, but now, it seemed, destiny had taken the baton of her life's race. And she descended into the pit of a mysterious beast; a beast that had been expecting her. "These people," she said, "they are aware of who I am?"

"The Messengers," Daniel said. "Yes, every one of us is aware."

"How did you know I was coming?"

"As His Messengers, we have eyes in every corner of His kingdom."

"And what do these people expect of me? I'm not sure what the person you keep referring to as my father did for them, but I wasn't raised by him. I was raised by bracelets planning every second of my day, grooming me into becoming a killing machine. It's all I am." She rolled her knife around her fingers with great dexterity.

"Your purpose, your true purpose, has been written in your DNA from birth. Now you are where you need to be, to fulfill the destiny of your life lying dormant within. For His will. Be not afraid. When it is time to act, let your instinct and your blood guide you."

They reached the bottom of the stairwell and stopped at the foot of a stone wall. In a breath's time, the stone rolled to their side, and the silhouette of two men appeared from the dark.

"So it is true," one said in astonishment.

"For His will," the other whispered.

The first man bowed down and hit the other one on his leg. The other one bowed. "Lady. Forgive me. We are forever at your service. For His will."

"At ease," Daniel said. "Call upon the others. Everyone. Tell them to meet us at the Great Hall."

"Yes, sir."

The men closed the entrance, and one ran off to carry out Daniel's request.

Daniel prompted Luna to follow him across the secret underground city.

Daniel led Luna through stone passages left exposed by candlelight. The people opened their mouths in astonishment, then fell to the floor, kneeling in her presence.

"This is too much," Luna said when a row of little children stood by her side and bowed their heads.

"Bow," an adult woman told a child that had remained open-mouthed and staring, "keep your head down."

Luna locked the knife inside her hand, ready in case the strange people turned against her.

"We are almost there," Daniel said.

A set of whispers echoed in the dark void ahead. The air had a warm, welcoming feeling. Luna hesitated to approach it.

Daniel stopped walking, and his face reassembled into a smile. "Go ahead. It is you they have been waiting for."

They had been walking for too long, Luna was too deep into uncovering the truth to run back toward any comfortable lie. There was only one path for her, the human and angel hybrid.

The room she walked into was not a chamber, but a large auditorium filled with hundreds, if not thousands of people, looking up at her, waiting for life to be breathed back into them. In the light, the underground city of Derinkuyu revealed itself in full. Tunnels dug out at every corner connected corridors to chambers, stairs led up and down the seemingly never-ending multi-level structure, and in the middle of it all lay a vast hall where the people stood nervous in anticipation.

With each person having an assumption about her, the crowd murmured, their gazes fixed upon Luna. Some assented, others shushed. They settled down into a complete expectant silence. Luna's hands went ice cold at the fingers. Her breath accelerated. She enjoyed the spotlight, but only during her upper hand in battle. This was a different kind of spotlight. She looked down at their faces staring back at her, waiting. *Pull yourself together. Maybe I can use this, this army.* She stared at them blankly, biding her time until the nerves she had felt dissipated, and in its place was power, the power to command, the power to awaken, a power that had been planted in her genetic coding from her father, the leader of the rebel Messengers, a power which she now had access to in its entirety. As much as she wanted to reconcile why Lucifer had sent his Watchers after her when she failed to end her target, she couldn't. *Time for Plan B.* The path had revealed itself in front of her, and at once she needed no other explanation, no other confirmation that she had found her place. She closed her fist and raised it into the air. The shift inside her burned like a moon among the stars.

"Samyaza lives!" one person yelled. "Praise the Lord."

Luna pulled her sleeve down, and from under it appeared her half moon birthmark, and further down, the number *444,* its promise scarred in her skin.

The crowd cheered and chanted, "For His will."

She gazed at them. Their eyes glistened in a brighter sheen, and their faces lit up. Fear had turned into excitement. *Look at these idiots, how happy they are.*

"Like many of you, they trained me to kill without thinking, to accept orders without considering the implications. Today we must prepare to kill, but to kill with intention, by our own accord, with our weapons and might aimed at the Archangels and their reign of terror."

The crowd looked in confusion, terrified by the word. *Kill.* The one thing they vouched to never do again.

They are so pleased to be led to slaughter with no promise of survival. "I saw the cruelty of the Archangels first-hand," Luna continued. "We have seen the truth. Faith in them is faith wasted. For too long, they have been the deciders of life and death. No more. My parents' sacrifice shall not be in vain. The Archangels must be stopped. For there to be peace, there must first be war."

If this is what I have to do, so be it. A15, A29, Mother. They all depend on me.

The people were infected once more and roared in a wave of energy. Luna let the wave crash against her.

A projection of Daniel whispered, "I was too late. It is the rebel Watchers, sir. They call themselves the Messengers, and I saw them take her."

Lucifer pounded on the table.

"I followed them into the mountains, but they disappeared before I saw where they went. I am sending you the last known location." Daniel heard the roaring crowd and spoke louder into his bracelet. "You must make haste."

CHAPTER 25

LUNA

"It seems I was right," Daniel said to Luna, who had now stepped back into the cover of the stone halls.

"About what?" Luna said.

"You are awakened by your fate as a leader. I wonder, do you have a plan to go along with your words?"

"Yes."

"Excellent. Then we shall meet with the other founders."

He guided her to a large stone chamber in one of the lower levels, away from all the commotion she had caused. A round stone door lay horizontally on top of another to form a table, and two other people sat around it.

"So it is true, then," the woman said, rubbing her nails together and focusing on Luna from head to toe. "Our savior is here."

The old man's voice quivered with varying pitch. "Show some respect, Sarah."

"Please," Daniel said, extending a hand toward the round table, "after you."

"I'm fine standing up. About the plan," Luna said, "there's a large army of Watchers pursuing us as we speak,"—Robert flashed in her mind, then she shook the thought away. *Focus.*—"this is our chance to attack. We must find them first."

"Preposterous. That will only prompt the Lone Archangel to send his full army," Sarah said.

"You're wearing their bracelets. It means you have found a way of removing and reprogramming them for your purpose. I propose we steal their bracelets, and send a transport request signal,"—Luna leaned in and looked around the table— "and destroy them from within before they even know what hit them."

The old man shot a blind stare in Luna's direction and a smile formed on his face.

Sarah leaned her back on the stone wall. "Your plan has one flaw. There is more than one Archangel, and the other army is even stronger. How will we get to them, let alone wage a winning war against them?"

A loud thud silenced the room.

"Earthquake?" Daniel said and turned to the old man. "Seer, what do you see?"

Another, louder bang resonated across the hall.

The Seer stared at the ceiling. "That is no earthquake. While we discussed a way to bring war to them, war has knocked on our door, and we shall respond with full force."

"How did they find us so quickly?" Luna said. *Robert.*

"That is a question for another time, perhaps."

Luna nodded in agreement. "Prepare your warriors."

Sarah sneaked out before Luna had given the order.

CHAPTER 26

SARAH

"The Path," Sarah said while she organized knives, small metallic spheres, and other weapons and rations in a haversack, "has called upon us. Its beacon is shining, taking us in another direction. You and me, we must follow it."

Scattered guards ran down the hall outside their chamber and Sarah peeked into it until they were gone, their voices echoing farther away with each resounding step. She came back into the chamber and showed Pol two chrome bracelets, both different from the one wrapped around her wrist. "I have been engineering a copy of it ever since that weasel conspired to dethrone Samyaza, waiting for this day to come. I hoped to have more time to train you and forge a better plan, but I have seen what you can do. You are ready." She froze for a second to appraise Pol's potential. "We must try, at least. There is no other choice."

Pol wrapped a rifle around his torso. "What if they need us here? Didn't we train to fight, not run away?"

She zipped up the bag. "Your purpose is greater than them. Greater than this pointless skirmish."

Pol looked at her in a long silence. "They will die, won't they?" Sarah didn't say a word. "You know."

Sounds of a rushing crowd traveled from the upper levels of Derinkuyu.

Sarah's eyes locked onto the ceiling and followed the blare of the marching army. "We do not have the time to discuss this. We have to leave. Now. For His will." She offered one of the two bracelets. "Make a choice."

Pol looked at the chamber's exit, then back at Sarah's eyes.

CHAPTER 27

THE SEER

The Seer hesitated at the door standing between them and the approaching carnage. He saw with his eyes closed. The floodgates opened. A red sea awaited.

CHAPTER 28
LUNA

Luna stepped outside of Derinkuyu. A soothing breeze flung her hair against her skin, and the vast space she was in reminded her it had not always been that way. The Watcher Development Center, being guided from one room to another, day after day, year after year, then the hunger, a sense of a higher purpose growing within her. Her path had taken her so far away from everything she had known, she might as well have been reborn. No longer was she protected within the boundaries of the school for lab-bred assassins. She gazed upon the army that would follow her into Hell, if necessary. It was obvious now, in broad daylight, that it had been a long time since many of them had wielded a weapon—there was no need. The underground was not a military facility; it was a haven for rebel Watchers seeking asylum. She closed her hand into a fist. *What have I done?* Reality pounded against her chest. Louder. The creeping bloodthirsty Watchers left no time for remorse. She grasped her knives. In the same inner vault where she had stored her past life, she found the echoes of the people she had left behind, and the hope that they were still alive, waiting for her. The urgency of their wellbeing pushed a war cry out of her, louder than the impending doom about to fall on them, and the cry repeated as a wave of energy that traveled throughout the Messengers, their feeble bodies rising to the occasion. The echoes moved forward to a life-or-death collision against the Watchers.

Daniel soared in front of her and pushed a group of Watchers to the ground with a squall, but the Watchers rose quickly and retaliated. A Watcher reached to her side and pointed a gun at Daniel. *Guns? Since when are Watchers allowed to use—*The Watcher opened fire at Daniel from the other side. He banked, evading most of the damage, though a bullet hit one of his wings, but he recovered quickly and sent that Watcher flying and slammed her body against a weather-worn stone.

The Seer shouted from a safe distance away from the battle, predicting incoming attacks. "Left!" he shouted, and a Messenger shot his weapon in that direction and survived what would have been a fatal strike from a Watcher.

In between flashes of death, Luna looked for Robert at Derinkuyu's entrance. Her eyes focused on the battlefield and the arid lands beyond. But with no time to waste on meaningless distractions, she put away the thought and navigated the blood and howls of dying men and women, discerning from friend and foe in the blink of an eye. *Knife to a gunfight,* she thought, thinking of A15, and the memory fueled her. She rolled her knives in her fingers and threw one of them at a Watcher who was about to kill a Messenger. Then she rushed to the falling body and pulled out the knife before it hit the floor.

"Thank you, Lady Luna," a Messenger said, and removed the fallen Watcher's bracelet.

"Keep your eyes open," she said.

A deep crimson light enveloped the battlefield and turned almost vermilion when it crashed against the orange mountains.

Luna yelled at the sky, hoping her warning would cut through. "Brace yourselves!"

The Watchers' bracelets illuminated the path to Luna's next target, but the red light also awakened a terror within her—the soldiers had been turned into killing machines. The shift in the war was sudden. Messenger bodies dropped like flies, no match for the vile, animalistic killer instinct of the activated Watchers. Then, Luna's gaze fixed to a red intensity above the riot. She recognized her poise, her elegance over a rock as a trophy on a pedestal. She was back to her full glory, A14, kneeling and aiming with her bow at a distant target. Luna followed A14's aim and found the Seer fully exposed to the higher vantage point.

The Seer outstretched his arms and closed his eyes. "Right!" he called. "Sword, left!"

"No!" Luna cried, her voice muted among the sounds of enraged victors and ravaged victims.

Luna marched toward the Seer, pushing through against the flow of slaughter. A Messenger, consumed by war, bumped her shoulder when rushing past her. The clash shifted her attention to the Watcher flanking her from the side with a mace, too close for Luna to evade. She covered her head by reflex, and her exposed back took the blow from the mace's spikes. Her jaw clenched on her way down, the roots of her teeth cracking from the pressure, fracturing in her gums. A ringing in her ears deafened the surrounding misery. In the silent isolation, hurt was all there was. A Messenger pushed the Watcher to the ground in Luna's defense. She propped herself up with her right foot, her eyes fixated on the Seer. The Seer fell to his knees with a hand over his chest. His blank stare was aghast, as if even if he had foreseen this, nothing could have prepared him for this pain.

Luna was too slow to compete with the brazen path of a purposeful arrow. The arrow had drilled halfway through the Seer's chest and out his back. "Incoming overhead!" he said, with blood oozing from his mouth. He dropped his hands to the ground and spit a mouthful of blood on the dirt. "Duck." He lay on his side when he couldn't hold his body weight any longer.

"It is all written. Everything you need is in my chamber," he said. He opened his eyes as if receiving a signal from a distant future. "I am sorry, my dear."

Luna held his head up. "What?"

"For the burden you will have to bear." He smiled. "Watch your back."

She grasped her knife and turned around, but there was no-one there. She gazed up at the rock. A14 was gone. When she faced the Seer, his head was limp on her arm. "Wake up," she said, her voice suppressed under the tinnitus. "Come on, old man. Wake up." She shook his frail body. *This is all my fault.* Her eyes burned with sorrow. *No.* She wiped her tears with the back of her hand. *They depend on me. Everyone depends on me. On my strength. I can't afford to be weak.* She laid the Seer's body gently on the ground and stood up.

Luna turned to the madding crowd and forced herself to see the Watchers as nothing more than tree trunks made of flesh. She locked on a target and lunged at him, her knife pointed at his heart. Once the body hit the ground, she pulled the knife out, and the noise from the war unmuted to a cacophony of screams. She scanned the perimeter and saw a Watcher removing a dagger from a fallen Messenger. Next to him, another Watcher broke a Messenger's neck. The Messengers were outnumbered. It was their fallen bodies which occupied the ground and painted it with blood.

Luna followed the red light in the Watchers' wrists and allowed it to bring out the worst in her one last time. *Some fights require a monster.* Her face scowled with wild anger. She hacked her knives through fabric and skin, putting the enemy down with her precise sharpened blows. With every kill, her rage slipped farther out of her control, and in time she wasn't fighting, but murdering.

The knives rolled in her hands with ease and took lives away with no remorse. She swayed sideways to evade an axe aimed at her and sliced the wielder's shins while he tried to pull his weapon out of the ground. His legs broke apart at the cut, and he fell shrieking and begging for mercy. The blood's red only spurred her on. She gave him no mercy.

The Messengers were gaining ground with the killing machine at their helm. Her sight was on finding A14. It no longer mattered to her if she had to do it alone. A path cleared before Luna. At the end, A14.

"You're mine," Luna said.

Before A14 could grasp an arrow from her quiver, Luna was in front of her, gaining momentum for a lethal blow. But as Luna's knife began its life-ending descent into A14's heart, a man stood in her way and knocked her knife away from her hand with a thrust of his spear.

"A15?" Luna said, humanity rushing back to her with no bracelet to stop it.

His eyes were flaming red.

"A15, it's me."

He swung the spear at her with fury. She leaned to stay away from the spear's path.

"Stop!"

He lunged forward, threatening to penetrate her stomach.

She stepped further back.

Back.

Away from her possessed friend.

And into a knife. Her own knife. In the hands of A29.

Luna lay on her back. A15 moved in closer to finish the job and towered above her, spinning the spear over his head. He stopped the spear mid-spin and held its point over her. Luna turned her face to its side. Some Messengers crumbled to the ground, while others withdrew with a Watcher's bracelet in their hands. Members of the Royal Guard held the door to Derinkuyu open. It was a retreat. *Is this how it ends? With my destiny unfulfilled; my whole life a failure?* Her breath was too fast and shallow to make sense of her racing thoughts. Screams. Metal collisions. The clash of deadly resolves detonated around her.

A blurry vision of an angel descended from the sky and crash-landed beside her, a being that stood as a majestic lighthouse in a sea of blood. Its silver hair, resplendent under the sun, was blinding, soothing, and its armored body overshadowed her, immersing her with a sense of relief. For a transient moment of precisely the perfect length, nothing else mattered.

Luna's heart recovered its rhythm. Her breath deepened. The angel unfurled its wings and stretched them to their impressive limits, then draped them over her, blanketing her body in an absolute absence of light. She closed her eyes and surrendered to its warmth. *Darkness. Breathe. What do we know about darkness? Shut off unnecessary senses.* The noise muted, and she felt the leather of the hilt inside her bare hand. She hadn't let go of her remaining knife. She rolled the knife, turned its blade down, and planted it into A15's feet, who wailed a terrible cry and let his spear fall on the dirt. She pulled out the knife to strike again, but before she gained momentum, A15 was pushed away in a sudden wind.

A Messenger rushed in front of Luna, and his Royal Guard emblem—a serpent curled around a sphere—materialized in his armor. "I only need your bracelet. Shall I only take away your hand or your entire arm?"

"No! It's the bracelets. It's doing that to them. Don't kill them. I can save them," Luna said, her voice trailing off. "I can save them," she whispered, and fell back to the ground. "I can save all of them." Her eyes slowly blinked. She scanned the battlefield for the silvered hair angel, but before her last blink, found another angel at the top of a hill, his aura now paling in comparison, his stance not as impressive, deceitful, weak, almost sinful in the secret betrayal that emanated from his every pore, as if its armored body could not contain the imperfect soul it harbored. The angel threw an unsettled stare at her and crossed its arms. She recognized the face before everything turned dark. She had never seen such an ugly face. Daniel.

PART 5

ALTERNATE EARTH

CHAPTER 29

LUNA

"Sinful souls, may the Lord have mercy over all of you."

"Luna!" the voice next to her hissed. But she was in a trance.

"Sinful, terrible souls. We can only hope you learned your lesson. In time, maybe."

A child wailed.

"Shush now. There is no such a thing as a young age for learning the High Concepts of the Comradeship."

"Luna, what the hell is wrong with you?" the voice hissed again. "Pay attention. You're going to get us killed."

Her eyes moved toward the voice.

"And for the great sin of calling this green, luxurious pen the wrongful color blue," a uniformed man, the Commander, held a plain, blue charcoal pencil over a row of crying toddlers, "and mistaking it for a pencil, no less, you are hereby sentenced to one night in the correctional cell, where you shall learn, no, *accept* our Truth as the *only* Truth, as *the* Truth. I have declared. May the Ancestor yet find in you a redeemable spirit. And don't you forget this lesson the next time you consider going against our Truth. Out

Truth is the Truth of all natural beings. Remember that. Take them away!"

"He's coming over, Luna. Snap out of it!"

Two sets of steps approached her. The Commander and his assistant were now in front of them. "And you, what did these criminals do? Let me see here." He snagged a chart from his assistant, a well-dressed, tall, glassy-eyed man. "Uh-huh. Aha!" He twirled his mustache "Yes. Bad, bad, terrible, inexcusable indeed. The greatest offense." He pushed the chart back into his assistant's hands. "For crimes committed against our Lord, the Communal Equity Servicemen declare you unfit, and you must be discharged from the city and all of its protection at once. Off you go. Out!"

"We will die out there!" A15 screamed.

A29 gave A15 a slight nudge. "Let it go, 15, do not make matters worse."

"Listen to your friend, young man," the Commander said, deadpanned, then approached the leashed trio and said in a whisper, as to not allow the bystanders to hear him, "We do not want you here. You do not belong. Now leave on your own accord, unless you want to be electrocuted to death."

A15 lurched his body forward, but large metal chains restrained him. "You might as well."

"Percy. Make sure they are out of the city by sundown."

"Yes, sir," the assistant, Percy, said.

A Journal, that was what they called a day on Earth, was split into three phases. First phase was for resting, in which every citizen of each sector fell into a deep slumber wearing City-appointed headphones with a stream of the Eternal Love lullaby played on a loop. The second phase, which started by an alarm that blared through the sectors at precisely 8:00 a.m.(local time), was for tightening bolts, pressing buttons, or any other task the Machine couldn't(or wouldn't) do, of course most of these tasks were no tasks at all and not much more different from an older brother giving his younger siblings a fake gaming controller that was connected to the air, and third phase, from 5:00 p.m. to 12:00 a.m., was strictly for, as the Communal Equity Servicemen called it, "releasing the bad spirits". At this gloaming hour, people assembled around the town square with rocks, books, knives, anything with a sharp edge, or a hard, blunt side, to lunge at outsiders, the insensitive, the rebels, while they were pushed out of the city.

The Commander's assistant pulled at a rope, and behind him, with their hands cuffed to the rope, were A29, A15, and Luna.

"Scum of the Earth, those ones," a bystander said, then spit at the ground in front of him. "Play nice or stay outside!" he chanted with clenched fists in the air.

The crowd repeated the chant.

Luna, still in a trance, was jolted awake by a limestone that shot from the crowd and crashed against her cheek. It was only then the muted noise of the world came to life and with it, her will and rebellious ferocity. In a sudden motion, she pulled down and took A15, A29, and Percy to the ground with her. She picked up the rock, launched it up on top of her, then kicked it into the crowd, hitting the same bystander who had thrown it, and knocking him unconscious on the safe blades of grass from where the good citizens yelled. The crowd quieted down, the noise dissipated, and after various attempts at waking up the unconscious comrade, left the town square in droves.

Percy's face changed, as if something had breathed life inside of him. He pushed himself off the ground and pulled the rest up. "I shall haste with my task before you get me killed as well." He fumbled with the keys, and a swarm of electric motors whined in the air. "Oh, no. No, no, no." He tried the keys one by one, but the lock wouldn't budge. He looked up between attempts to unlock the door, then coming back to the keys, couldn't remember which one he had already tried, and had to start over. "See what you have done now? We have overstayed our outside privileges. I am so sorry, Lord," Percy cried. "I am so sorry."

Luna looked at the heavens and followed the hum in the sky until the hum turned into spaceships beaming their spotlights downstream.

Percy shouted, "Quick, crouch! Hide under the trees!" Looking up, he let an exhale out that sounded like, "Not a word."

And they watched as the lights scattered out in the distance.

Percy stood up and was about to unlock the gate but stopped. He watched Luna, studied her. "You. What colony are you from, anyway?"

"Colony?"

"Just tell him already," A15 said. "We live in the tenth colony."

A29 shivered. "Can we make a fire? It is freezing out here."

"You said live," Percy continued, "not come. You are not from around here, are you?"

"Who cares what colony we are from? It's the same everywhere. All we did was take down a few of his posters," A15 said. "I cannot stand to see his face everywhere I look."

"Society can only work if everyone agrees to follow the rules," Percy said. "We cannot tolerate petty crimes, or they will escalate and before you know it, everyone will stop working on the Machine."

"Ah, the Machine," A15 fell to his knees. "Everyone, come hail to the Machine," he chuckled, then bowed, sticking his forehead to the wet ground. "The all-powerful Machine we have been building for years, yet no one knows what it's for, or if it even works. Let us all keep busy turning screws, punching buttons, adjusting settings on the Machine, then push buttons at random just so we can busy ourselves re-adjusting them tomorrow. All hail the Machine. Speak to it, read to it, cradle it as you would a baby, so it learns from us, then, in time, let it take life away from us as well. Let us all build our almighty replacement, our race destroyer. And let us all do so with our heads down, afraid to utter a word against it, and let us all be happy doing it."

"Silence!" Percy shouted, yet his face didn't look at all convinced he should be shouting. "You three children are a disgrace to all humans."

"That is the most stupid thing you have said all night," A15 said.

"Seriously, a fire, anyone?" A29 trembled.

"What, you do not enjoy being called a child? That is what you are. When will you accept your responsibility as a member of our society and become an adult? Adults work. That is what we are here for."

"I am not a child. A man, a young adult, at least, but I will let it go. You see, the stupid thing you said was not calling us children, but calling her," he nodded in Luna's direction, "a human. You see, you stupid, stupid, ignorant man. Our friend here is not a human. Not *only* human, I mean. She is also half-angel, half-divine. The actual divine, not the make-believe, created-in-a-lab-divine like the leader with a machine fetish you so blindly follow."

Percy approached Luna. He grabbed her arm forcefully, slid up her sleeve, and released it in shock. "For His will. Why are you here? Not, not why, how?"

"Play nice, or stay outside!" a lone bystander said.

"Away with you!" Percy said. "Go back to your house before I tell the Commander you have overstayed your welcome. Are you ready to suffer the punishment of ungratefulness? Are you not grateful for all Lord Pol has given you? Go back to your house. You are late for the evening lullaby."

Percy took the prisoners away. "No, wait." A spaceship flew overhead, its spotlight missing them by a hair, and correcting its course. "Now."

They made their way through the gate and into the outside of the city, where an unassuming building with cracked, concrete walls, and rebars sticking out from the cinder blocks stood almost blended with the local jungle flora and entered it from a side door made of wooden pallets.

"I haven't slept in years," Percy said and swallowed a pill he took from his jacket, "waiting, hoping for this moment. You must forgive me. It has been so long, I have drifted away from my oath. I just... forgive me, but I had given up hope. All the others passed away, you see. I am the last one." He turned his arm over and let the overhead lamp's light fall over his scars. 444. A terrible growl that rumbled the building made Percy turn around and knock a stack of books to the ground. "No! You must not read the prophecies of the Seer. Never read them. We might not recover from the consequences." He locked the books in a safe, then took a peek into the jungle through scattered holes in the plywood windows. "We do not have long." He opened a drawer in an archive next to a white plastic folding table. "Where is it?" He picked things up, threw them away, then yanked the entire drawer and turned it on its side, and searched for its scattered contents on the floor. "I never thought a time would come for me to use it. I am elated with joy that the time did come."

A15 looked at A29, rolled his eyes, and mouthed the word "elated." A29 snorted out a small laugh.

"Ah, here it is."

"What is it?" Luna said.

"Whatever you do, Luna, do not let hell win. Now go make Samyaza proud, the Universe is in your hands," he said, and clicked on a device.

The growl thundered upon the building once more, louder, closer, and Luna's urge to protect, to save, awakened. She reached for a knife that wasn't there, and her *Self* zoomed out. A life that she had only just discovered was now nothing more than a projection on a screen. A screen that played the movie of her friends and herself, her other Self, being slaughtered by a blackened beast with horns coming out of its head, standing on two large hooves and terrible hairless wings and sharp bones covered in blood protruding out of its legs and arms and wings, and Luna screamed, trying to reach forward, but was flung farther back, and the beast feasting and shrieking was pushed away at great speed and turned into a gleaming star, and now Luna floated in antimatter, still moving backwards, both falling out of and flying toward something, and all surrounding bright dots in front of her concentrated in one dense point, then, escaping the barrier between universes, nothingness.

PART 6

CURRENT EARTH

CHAPTER 30

LUNA

Luna pushed her torso upwards, trying to sit up, but her wounded, frail body sunk back into the stone bed. She was back at Derinkuyu.

"Pitiful," a voice said, though the world was a blurry and spinning mess, and the face was indistinguishable from any other face. "Such a shame they did not finish the job. Watchers are not as dangerous as I recall them." The blurry shape moved across the room, away from her.

Her hands were connected to machines, the machines connected to her through thick, silicone tubes, and syringes that blended into her hands as extensions of her body.

The blurry shape returned in the blink of an eye, leaned into her, and whispered, "Worry not, moon girl. I will find a way. I always do."

She tried to scream for help but only a slight, breathy rasp came out. The attempt depleted her energy. She slept.

The machines beeped next to her, and the warmth of the shape fell upon her. Its long, thin fingers rubbed her head, its sharp nails pressed slightly on her skull. Then its grip tightened, and the cranial pressure became an unbearable pain she could not acknowledge with a scream. The pressure rose once more, threatening to crush her skull, rising, at the edge of death, until it stopped. The creature craned its neck to look behind it, then turned around, its blackened stare paralyzing, and said, "No, not now. Too risky." The shape shushed her.

She slept.

Upon wakening, Luna found she could blink, but not much else. She observed the shape moving through the room, pacing, coming in and out of her peripheral vision. At times, it appeared as though the shape was not moving its legs, but floated, growing wider and narrower, accelerating to great speeds, almost teleporting from one side of the room to the other. It ruminated, its features had sharpened somewhat, and its face was covered by a black robe. "Running out of time," it said, its voice playful. "Running out of time. Running out of time. Running out of time." Now with the guttural cadence of an underworld demon.

Luna slept to the dim brightness of perpetual candlelight.

She coughed, choked, couldn't breathe. Her throat was constricted. Whenever she tried to swallow, her pharyngeal muscles hit against a foreign object. She gagged. She removed the plastic mask that covered her face but air was still an impossibility. Luna scanned the room with her hands. Apart from the paper-thin robe, she was naked. Her violent hands, now reaching out for something, anything, knocked down glass jars, syringes, and metal trays, causing a great disturbance. The machines beeped desperately. She walked over broken glass, but it was hard to focus on any pain other than her lungs collapsing.

The shape entered the room. It stood in front of her, cross armed, and watched her. "Look at you. The powerful daughter. Fragile. Useless. Weak."

Luna clawed at her mouth, searching for whatever was stopping the air from coming in. Her throat spasmed. She knelt down and took off a shard of glass that had cut into her feet. She gripped the glass and felt it sink into her hand. Breathless, she walked toward the shape, but when she was but six inches away, a group of people rushed into the room, grabbed her by the arms, and pushed her back into bed. The shape fled the room.

"She removed her mask. Someone replace it and restart the ventilator, now," one person said.

Luna lurched forward.

"Easy." Daniel said, placing his hand gently over her neck. "You will heal. In time, we hope."

Luna focused her eyes. The room appeared sinister in its peacefulness. "Where am I?"

"We are inside Derinkuyu."

"The battle? What happened? How many did we lose?"

"As it is often the case with war, both sides lost, and both sides won." He offered a Watcher bracelet. "We finished reprogramming the first batch of bracelets, and you have visitors."

A29 and A15 stood at the foot of the stone bed.

"Birthmark girl," A15 said. "We finally meet again."

"I am sorry for what I did. It was not me, I promise. I would never do such a thing. You know I am not the kind." A29 was sweating.

Against Daniel's advice, Luna sprung up to a sitting position and twisted her face in pain, then drew a half smile. "29! 15! Are you really here?"

Each one approached from either side and Luna pulled them together in an embrace she wished to hold for eternity.

A15 spoke first. "She is still alive, Luna."

Luna pushed away.

"Yes, we saw her. We went back to the Archives on our own as soon as they released us. We thought we would find you, but we found her there instead, in that cage. We tried to save her, too." He looked down. "But they caught us again. That time, we had to spend an entire week locked away in a dark room lit only by small bursts of red light. I don't remember much after that."

Luna rose from her bed.

"Luna, you must not—"

But she was already standing. Daniel let out a huff and left the room.

Luna watched Daniel's shape leaving. She watched in his direction long after he wasn't there at all. Then she turned to A15, and said, "We must return. We must rescue her, take down the Archangels."

"I agree. I will stand with you."

"Me too. I agree. I will stand. With you, I mean"—A29 caught his breath—"That Daniel person is excellent, fantastic. So caring, so dedicated. Truly inspiring. You were lucky to have Daniel at your bedside every night. He insisted on taking the night shifts. I offered, but he insisted."

By nightfall, Luna was left alone to rest. She slid out of her bed and aimed at the Seer's chambers. Once inside his chambers, she found bookshelves overflowed with ancient tomes of varying time periods. She craned her neck at the sound of incoming footsteps but turned back when the footsteps trailed off. She meandered among the Seer's belongings. A mix of humanity's secrets and lost civilizations lay scattered as plainly as children's coloring books over a coffee table.

One book stood out among the rest; a thick volume that was half-pulled out of a bookshelf and appeared to be filled with the Seer's scribbled visions. She opened the book to a bookmarked page. She glanced at the prophecy before her and closed the book when she heard a voice.

"Luna. You must return to bed, you need rest," a member of the Royal Guard said.

Luna rose. "No. It's all very clear to me now. The only rest I will ever have, is the one I find in death. Assemble everyone in the Great Hall."

The Royal Guard member assented and walked away.

In time, he returned and said, "They are ready."

He escorted her to the Great Hall, where the surviving Messengers waited.

Not nearly the amount of Messengers necessary to wage a war on the Archangels had survived. Yet she stood in front of them, projecting an imaginary confidence that infected them as well.

She stepped down into the crowd instead of standing at the podium, and signaled two guards to follow her. The guards carried a wooden stick at either end with the re-engineered Watcher bracelets hanging from it.

Luna walked among the surviving Messengers, taking a bracelet from the stick and wrapping it on their wrists, and placed a hand on their shoulders for a moment before moving on to the next person. When she reached the last Messenger, there were dozens of bracelets hanging on the wooden stick.

And it is written, the Seer's vision had read, *the stars will orbit around the half moon, and immerse themselves in its light.*

The sound of heavy tread came echoing from the stairs.

From the lower levels emerged her old friends, A15 and A29. Smiling.

And from the darkness, the true Messengers will rise. Pure. Uncorrupted.

A15 grinned. "We thought you might need some help."

A racket rose from the stairwell behind them. All the Messengers turned to face the incoming sounds. Thousands of humans who had vanished from the face of the Earth—Watcher targets whom the

Messengers had taken into protective imprisonment—now emerged, their hands shielding their eyes from the Great Hall's light.

And the grandchildren of the Ancestor will stand together as the true carriers of his Will. Then, written in the margins, *If time will not open the Archangels' eyes, perhaps blood will.*

BOOK 4

I AM THE DOOR

PART 1

CURRENT DERINKUYU AND ARVO

CHAPTER 1

LUNA

Every second Luna was awake, the thought of her mother imprisoned in the Archive flashed in her mind like bursts of a thunderstorm. And whenever she slept, she dreamed of driving her knife through Lucifer's heart and setting her mother free. This cycle had invaded her mind to an extent where imagining it was almost like living it, and every morning, she would wake up searching her hands for blood.

Luna had awakened, and, after finding her hands clean, she twisted her body and touched the healing wound from A29's stabbing. It hadn't healed completely, but the attack couldn't be delayed any longer. She slid into her black uniform, grimacing when the fabric grazed the wound. She pushed through it, as she always did.

A15 stormed into her room, an event which would have never occurred during their Watcher training in Arvo. After all, isolation made good assassins. But Derinkuyu had no sympathy for guiding crystals or mindless killing. In Derinkuyu, death had purpose. "Moon Girl, they are talking about quitting."

"Who?"

"All the surviving Messengers. They want to quit. We only have humans now. Only humans...against Watchers." His grip on the spear softened.

"I'll speak with them." Luna walked past A15, who stayed behind in her chamber.

She traversed the corridor, illuminated by the soft light of candles, and into the auditorium, where the disagreeing voices of the surviving Messengers echoed.

"Are you ready to leave your children fatherless?" one Messenger said.

The one who had suggested going to Arvo sunk into his seat. "But we agreed—"

"And we fulfilled that agreement and lost dearly. What it is being asked of us now is beyond loyalty. She is using us—"

Luna interrupted the discourse. "I hear you don't want to fight alongside us."

"Tell her," one Messenger said.

Another one nudged the man in the middle.

"All right, all right," the man said. "We do not want to fight a fight that is not ours. We are safe here in Derinkuyu. You are asking us to sacrifice ourselves in a losing battle against an unknown number of Watchers. I must confess that we were infected with the promise of total freedom, of ridding ourselves completely from Lucifer's shackles. But after witnessing what happened in our skirmish against the Watchers, believing we can win against Lucifer in his home is suicide. I have seen what he can do. His power and evil know no limit."

"I know this," Luna said. "We lost men in battle, but we also weakened him gravely. If we allow him to regain strength, he will come back and he will make sure he doesn't lose this time. We have to attack now that he is weakened. It will take him some time to restore his army of Watchers to what it used to be."

The man stood and removed his bracelet, placed it on the table, and said, "We are all here, as Messengers, because we once said no to an order that was not in accordance to the Ancestor's path. Time has come to say no once more. Forgive me, but I will not, in good conscience, put my men in danger when all that is waiting for us is certain death."

The man turned and walked away. The other Messengers followed suit, removing their bracelets without making eye contact with Luna, and left.

"What are we going to do now, Luna?" A15 said, half of his body under the corridor's shadow.

"Give the rest of the bracelets to as many viable humans as you can find." Luna turned to A15. "Nothing changes. We leave today."

All Luna breathed in was a hot air that seemed to disappear before reaching her lungs. She had been inhaling too much, too fast. Her hands were numb, her chest tight. The humans had assembled in front of her. A hundred of them. Each one a needle that pricked a hole in her skin. With stern faces and straight postures, they readied for battle. Although they were of varying ages—some younger than twenty, others nearing their sixties—they seemed in good physical condition, as if they had been bred and preserved, frozen, waiting for this moment.

"On your command," A15 said, gripping his spear. His voice carried through the air as if an underwater sound. Drowning. Like her and everything else, drowning in a sea of guilt and despair, standing afoot the nightmare of a vibrating train track. From the ghost train, the chime was nearing, its smokey engine filling up their lungs, its honk merely an alert of the certain death that awaited, and another ear-piercing honk, "Move!" it meant to say, "Move or die!". This ghost train was set loose by a cannon fired at her birth, an unstoppable trail of pain that must not veer away from its deadly course.

"It will be all right," A29 said, touching her shoulder and pulling her away from the tormentous train in her mind.

Luna shuddered. She wasn't expecting such a human moment

from one of her half-brothers. A15, A29, and the rest of the pilot group were pieces of her. Walking, breathing copies of her DNA created from a clone of her mother's womb.

Luna nodded and neared a hand to her new Messenger bracelet. She took a step toward the imaginary train tracks. The honk from the incoming metal beast, chugging along its path, howled in her skull. "Stop!" it said. "Their blood is in your hands." But she pressed the button on the bracelet she willfully wore for this occasion. One last dance with the steel cuff, one more flirt with the devil himself. The train was loud, but she was louder. "No more hiding underground and waiting while they make a playground of your home. Your life is your own, as is your fate. Let's take back what is yours. Let's let them know you are not to be played with, controlled, or disposed of." She looked at the human army waiting for her order. "See you in Arvo," she said, thinking of her mother, and released the button. The last thing she heard was the rising tide of a roaring crowd, their hunger for battle burning the train down to ashes and melting the tracks into the ground.

The air was quiet in Arvo. They still had time and grasped the upper hand, if only by a slipping finger.

In front of Luna, the Watcher Development Center stood as a monument to her life. Where she had learned to kill, to bleed, to withstand physical and psychological pain must now be the setting of her redemption. Luna took more than a breath to carry her body toward the building. Even though she knew her way inside it, from the Fields to the Archive, this wasn't the same reckless excursion of her past. This type of mission required a finesse she wasn't sure she had. She leaned on the wall, marking its perimeter, and hugged it close with her back. She closed her eyes. *Pull yourself together. Pull yourself together. Pull—*

One by one, the humans appeared across the Arvonian desert. When they emerged, she didn't know which one was more dangerous, their weapons or their spirits on fire. They mimicked Luna and formed a line glued to the wall.

"See the spire?" Luna said, and A15 assented. A29 inched forward. "We need to form two teams. One goes toward the spire—I always knew it in my guts; that's where they were watching us from— the rest must go to the Archive to rescue my mother. If we don't split up, they might move her before we can reach her...or worse."

A29 gulped but said nothing.

A15 nodded. "I will assemble a team and take the spire. A29, you go with Luna and take the rest to the Archive."

Luna's gaze shifted from the spire to the Archive.

"Don't worry, Moon Girl. You've got this," A15 said.

Her eyes blinked back to life and pointed at him. She smiled. "No. *We've* got this."

"All right, listen up," A15 said to the human beside him. "I need fifty men with me. Assemble a team."

"Only fifty?" Luna said.

A15 gripped his spear, looked at the spired tower, then at the building up to the Archive. "It's all I need."

They approached the front gates of the Watcher Development Center. Luna was ready to break the locking mechanism to pieces but stopped. This time, there would be no air ducts to save them if the method failed. She didn't remember it being so silent, so welcoming.

"Keep your eyes open," she said.

A15 stretched his neck toward the door, then nodded.

The door was wide open. An invitation, a dare, a test. Graduation.

CHAPTER 2

A15

A15 led his group of humans toward the spire. The sound of their chain mail armor shifting, grazing steel with steel, and their gauntlets and chausses moving along the march was the same sound that played in the background of a movie he had seen years before. The film played on repeat for days after the tall people had captured him in the Archive for the first time. In the film, cattle marched slowly on a single file. Their bodies swayed side to side, making a similar sound to the humans behind him. The movie always ended with a graphic depiction of the animals slaughtered and the text *"This is what humans are capable of. Therefore, we must guide them away from these barbaric practices"* flashing on the screen. *Am I capable of this?* A15 thought. *Am I a barbarian?* But he stampeded over the thought by concluding this march must be necessary, this slaughter unavoidable. In the end, blood was the lubricant that kept life going. For one species to survive, another must die. That is what he had learned from the moment he gained consciousness. To kill for the greater good. To kill as a means of survival. He looked back at the marching army with the corner of his eye. *Were they evil in that recording or simply surviving?*

"The name's Ambrose, by the way," the first human behind him said.

A15 flinched. "What?"

"I fear you might think of me as a nameless fool. Well, I am not! I am an accomplished journalist, or at least I was. When I began uncovering certain truths about our government, I lost my mind. Everywhere I went, there was someone or some*thing* following me. I swear! I rarely slept, and when I did, I had a rifle on my lap, loaded. They, of course, let me go from my job, which made matters even worse. Now I had nothing to take my mind off the shadows I was seeing. Now, the shadows had become my life. To make matters worse, I thought cheap whiskey might ease the paranoia. Brilliant minds, you know, they make the stupidest choices sometimes. One night, while I finished an article I had begun in the newspaper, I was getting ready to mail it to several publishers. It had everything in there: proof, events, conversations, quotes, you name it. It could have taken down the entire establishment. The shadows were closer that night than ever, so close that I felt their claws digging into my skin. I was sure I was going to die. That's when Sarah rescued me and took me to Derinkuyu. She cleaned me up, trained me, and turned on the lights once more, so bright, in fact, that no shadow could ever live in it. There is something about that Sarah. Even for an angel, she is special." He looked out into the distance, then returned his gaze to A15. "And there you go. My life in a nutshell, as they say. What about you? We have to trust each other if we're to step into war. Figured we might as well know our first names, at least."

A15 aimed away from Ambrose and toward the spire and wished he had his old bracelet shining its bright red light into his eyes. Life was simple in red, and so was death. After a few seconds, he shook his head and whispered, "Silence! I don't want your name or your history, human. Move." *They're only cattle, barbaric cattle.*

Ambrose nodded and gripped his rifle.

"The air is quiet, too quiet. At this hour, all kinds of groups are supposed to be coming in and out of the Green Field. They must know we're here."

"What do we do now?" Ambrose said.

"We need to find a door of some kind, but we have to make sure we don't get trapped inside, either. Tell ten men to keep guard outside and twenty to look for an entrance in that direction,"—he pointed to the left of the tower—"while the rest will search the right side."

Ambrose dispatched the orders, and the humans divided as told. Among the ten outside was a family of four that wanted to remain together. The family comprised two rescued targets who had fallen in love in the underground darkness of Derinkuyu and had grown even closer now in the light of day. Their two children were in their late teens, and even if they had started with a brave face back on Earth, they now looked like scared little children hiding behind their parents' protection. A15 had different people in mind to stand guard outside but allowed it.

Twenty of the humans crouched to the left side of the wide, spired tower, its black walls disappearing into the distance. Now that they were right next to it, there was no telling how wide and tall the majestic peak really was. Each group was to send an informant if they found an entrance. After fifteen minutes of searching, scanning the walls, and touching its black concrete for some kind of control panel, the groups converged at the back of it, empty-handed.

"Nothing?" A15 said, his eyes still scanning the wall.

"Nothing," the other man said.

Ambrose put his hand on the wall. "You know, when I was a journalist, I got assigned the most difficult investigations. There were no easy ones, not once. More often than not, no leads were willing to talk to me. They closed the doors the instant I told them I was a journalist. Do you know what I had to do? I'll tell you." He took something out of his satchel. It had a blinking red light. "I had to threaten to blow the damn thing open and create a door for myself."

"Stand back," A15 said, motioning his arm and pushing everyone back without touching them.

Ambrose removed strips of tape from the device and glued it on the wall. He put his index finger over the red button, but before pressing it, an opening formed on the wall, a murk inside the dark. Brewing in the darkness was a cold, uncertain feeling.

"See?" Ambrose said with a grin on his face.

Before he thought of a response, a smile had formed on A15's face. A smile he promptly erased. "Don't sing your victory song yet, human. This is only the beginning. Now, for sure, they know we're here. Two of you, bring the ones on the other side over to cover this entrance."

A15 lead the pack. "Stay close together. Four of you walk facing backward."

"Should it be this empty?" Ambrose said.

"I've never been here. Not inside."

Ambrose readied his weapon, a small hatchet with an oak handle and blunt edges. "All right, then." He whispered, "Just what I needed to hear."

"Turn on your bracelet lights," A15 said.

Like fireflies, they walked into the darkness, every step forward amplified in the eerie and cold silence. They made their way up the second level, then the third, and fourth, as a weaponized tank of flesh and blood, with aims pointing at every direction, waiting, almost hoping, that an excuse would appear for them to unleash this monster's built-up rage. But nothing did. Every floor as deserted as the previous one. Every silence eerier, with each staircase a slight push backward, as if to say, "There's still time to turn around." A15 pushed through, and his army followed.

"This must be it, the last floor. Ready your weapons."

"Look around, mate. We have been ready for a long time," Ambrose said, scanning the room and the tensed-up humans.

A15 nodded and opened the door.

The steel door swung open to a control room, enough to accommodate the forty humans and A15, but not much else. And when the last human stepped inside the room, the door slammed shut with as terrible a sound as a gunshot.

"Just the door," Ambrose said, and tried opening it. "Locked." He turned to A15. "What is this place?"

A15 relaxed his stance and stowed away his spear. "Looks like a command center. I bet this is where they watched and guided us. Try."

Ambrose shrugged. "Try what?"

"Anything, everything. I have a terrible feeling about this."

They scattered around the control room, pressing, pushing, and pulling every button, control panel, and lever in front of them. The room remained dimly lit by pulsating lights throughout the floor.

"It's no use," Ambrose said. "Did they know we were coming all along? But how? The battle ended with both sides cutting their losses and retreating. There was no sign from our part that we would follow them here. That was the whole plan, wasn't it? The element of surprise and all."

"The how makes no difference now. Everyone," he addressed the group, "forget our mission, forget what we came here to do. I want you to focus all of your energy and mental power on getting us out of here. Luna and the others are in grave danger."

The humans assented and restarted their search. They turned over chairs, desks, pressed buttons, and scanned the walls for a hidden exit. After a few desperate moments, it was clear that the search was futile.

"Bugger." Ambrose kicked a desk. "I already used my bloody explosive outside."

"And here I thought you were going to make another speech and get us out of here with your brilliant journalistic skills."

Ambrose laughed. "A bit of humor. That sounded human, almost. Don't worry, Fifteen, we'll figure something out."

At the tail end of Ambrose's last word, a set of screens dropped from the ceiling. The room was dead silent. After a few moments of static feedback, the screens' displays sharpened to an image.

A15 approached. "Luna?"

CHAPTER 3

LUNA

Luna and her group had entered the Watcher Development Center. The state of abandonment in which they had found the school left her both at ease and unsettled. At ease, because it seemed whatever had happened here had eliminated the Tall People of her past for her. But unsettled, because she remembered the Tall People as strong, and if they had not survived, then it must have been something even stronger, more vile than white robes violating her in the night, taking her blood, covering her face to keep her from screaming.

"Stay together," Luna said.

They walked across the hallway she had traversed so many times as a child to and from the Fields. She almost aimed toward the elevator, thinking about splitting into groups, or perhaps rush to it and close the doors before allowing any of the others in—no more humans should die for her. She let the thought linger long enough for them to reach the stairs at the end. The place didn't look attacked, but left dormant, like one of those Earth's stores overnight. No signs of an attack convinced her the Tall People and their white robes must still be waiting, not for them, but for her. She imagined them smelling the flask filled with the blood they had extracted from her and finding that same scent in the air, approaching them. In her mind, they were ready. They had been ready since then for another opportunity. This time, they would suck her veins dry.

"Wait," she said.

"Is everything all right?" a human said. Luna was not sure which one. They had all identified themselves to her before leaving for Arvo. She only allowed the names to linger in her mind until they crossed the open door to the compound. Not knowing their names would make it easier when it was time for her to watch them die.

She climbed the last step. "Yes. Let's carry on."

Floor after floor was nothing but ghost halls and open doors leading to empty rooms, the soul of the building abducted by an alien force. Every empty floor fed the feeling in the pit of her stomach. *She is not alive.*

The Archive waited at the top level of the building. Luna turned to the air vent near the open door and readied her knives. She motioned her head and went in first. The rest followed. A flickering light illuminated the room in flashes. In a corner at the far end of the room, the cage stood still. "There." She approached it, discovering a small distance around her guided by the light and stopping when it went dark again. The humans behind her copied her pace.

"Luna?" a voice from the cage said.

Luna walked faster, almost not stopping when the room went dark.

"Is that you?" the voice said.

Luna walked desperately into the dark. "I'm here. I'm here. I'm finally here."

Holding the bars were her mother's hands, her face still covered under the dark. The cage had always been the darkest part of the Archive, but even then, it hadn't been this devoid of light. Closer, so close that she could now grab her mother's hands, and now that her eyes had adjusted to the new level of obscurity, her mother's hands appeared larger, stronger than she had remembered. The figure inside the cage was also different, its silhouette malformed. The shape rose taller, and Luna saw the glimmer in its wrist. A bracelet.

The flickering bulb flashed in a dazzling light, so bright that everyone had to cover their eyes from its shine and remained on. While temporarily blinded, Luna heard the door to the Archive slam shut.

"Luna?" A29's voice quivered in the room.

Luna's hands trembled, her fingers loosening their hold. She strengthened her grip by force and raised her knives to eye level. "Stay calm. Everyone, stay still, have your weapons ready."

Now that the eyes had adjusted to the sudden light exposure, the silhouette of her mother inside the cage was not her mother but a Watcher who pushed open the door to the cage while smiling a terrible smile. "We have got you surrounded," the Watcher said. And when Luna turned, she confirmed it. Surrounding her, A29, and the humans were groups of trained Watchers, aged to maturity, impossible to defend from with just the army that she had taken with her.

If A15 was with her, at least, they would have been able to take care of a few, if not most, of them, and they would still have a slim fighting chance. But with A29 the only ex-Watcher with her, it was impossible. This was a trap with no exit. She pushed A29 behind her, toward the center of the circle the humans had formed. "Stay back," she said. "Let them go. It's me who he wants."

The Watcher that was in the cage still had a smile on his face. "I am C16, and this here are the C group and the D group. Lucifer let me into a secret before he sent me to lead the group. We all know about the great A30, how she broke free from programming and ascended all of its restraints. He told me we were modeled after you, the best parts of you, the stronger parts of you, and that he stripped away the humanity, the weakness. We are you, but vastly improved. You are better off lowering your knives in surrender, for even if we are equaled in strength, you possess a weakness we do not, and that puts you at a disadvantage."

"If you're so sure of your strength, why did you have to bring so many with you? Can't you face me one on one?"

C16 laughed and approached her. "Very well." He signaled his Watchers who shepherded the humans back into a corner, away from him and Luna. "You do not need to believe me. I will show you."

She readied her knives. He put a hand behind his back and chuckled.

Luna attempted to charge toward him, but he stepped out of the way with ease and elbowed her back and sent her to the ground. "You get only two more attempts. He is waiting for us."

Luna regained her strength and pushed herself off the ground. She looked for a weak point in him, in his stance. She looked for ways to use his strength to her advantage. Luna rushed toward his left side, which had the hand on his back. He stood still and waited for her to be an inch away before swerving to the left at the last second. She missed her attack, falling to the ground with the momentum. From the ground, she looked at the humans backed into the corner. The look in their eyes no longer had rage or determination, but defeat. She did that to them. The feeling was enough anger to fill her up with energy, and she turned to C16 and attempted to slice her knife across his leg. When the knife was about to touch his uniform and break skin, he floated in the air for a moment, allowing the knife to slice through nothing, then landed back on the ground when she had missed.

He chuckled again. "We possess the best parts of you, unsequestered by human emotions. It makes us the sharpest, strongest warriors to have ever lived." He turned to the humans. "I am now bored. He requested to bring you alive, but he mentioned nothing about the others."

"Leave them alone!"

C16 motioned his head to his Watchers. "Hold her." Four of them pulled her up and held her while he reached the humans. "Now, let us have some fun. We have been throwing knives at trees, shooting at moving, living targets, and even fighting each other. But I have fantasized about this for a long time. Trees are easy. They do not move, they simply stand there waiting for the blade to strike. Birds, even if alive and moving, are too dumb. And when matched against each other, we are too much alike. We think the same thoughts, plan the same strategies. It is like fighting against a mirror image. But the killing of a human, ah." He wiped saliva off his lips. "The rush, the excitement. To hunt an intelligent being but always maintain the upper hand. That is the closest I will get to feeling like a god. I often wonder if that is how Lucifer feels about humans, and how the Ancestor feels about the Archangels, and how whoever the Ancestor's creators are, feels about Him. And it goes on infinitely in a never-ending pyramid of giants and ants. That one," he said.

A Watcher pulled a man from the group, and once the man moved, he uncovered A29 from the center. Luna jerked by reflex.

"Oh. This one is special, is he not? Will he spark a new fire, perhaps? Bring him."

The Watcher released the human and grabbed A29, who tried to shake him off but was too weak.

C16 studied A29, smelled him, touched his hair. "You are not human, are you? But you are also not like us. Not entirely. You smell...different. Almost like A30." He gasped. "You are from her group, are you not? Even better than a human. A trained Watcher who has a different genetic build than us. I could not have asked for more."

"Leave him alone! It's me you want. Fight me."

"Oh, dear. I already did, and you disappointed me greatly. Now it is time for me to have my fun before I take you back to Lucifer. Hold her, firmly."

The Watchers pulled her arms behind her back, and the other two grabbed her biceps.

"I see you are carrying a shield. Is that your weapon of choice?"

A29 said nothing. He looked at Luna and back at C16.

"Very well. Unsheathe it." C16 walked away and waited.

"Give him hell, 29," Luna said. "You can do it. Just remember the training. You took A14 down once, remember? Dig for that feeling."

A29 shook his head. "They did things to me after that day. I think they took something from me. I never felt that strength again."

"Enough reminiscing. Fight me," C16 said.

A29 stood holding his shield. "I don't remember how. Not unless they want me to." He looked at his bracelet.

"Enough of this nonsense. I am bored with you." In a flash, C16 torpedoed toward A29 and kicked A29's leg. He crumbled to the ground. "Fight!" C16 sent a blow flying toward A29's neck, and he wailed in pain. "Fight, you useless creation!"

A29 swung his shield toward C16 but barely touched him.

C16 put an armlock around A29. "What a disgrace," he whispered. "And as a disgrace for our race. You must perish with no honor, no allowance for last words. You shall vanish into the dark, unknown to the universe—inconsequential and small." He looked at Luna, and a blade sprung out of his sleeve. "It will be slow and painful, but use that time to reflect upon your puny existence." He then ran the blade across A29's neck.

"No," Luna said, and a radiance covered her entire body. She squeezed out of the Watchers' hold with ease. To her, it appeared as if she was moving at normal speed, but the entire world had slowed down. She looked at her hand and opened and closed it several times. What was running through her veins was not anger, but assurance. Assurance that nothing would stand in her way. It was as if a door had opened and an infinite wave of power had come pouring through. She inserted her knife in each Watcher and pulled it out. They remained still and emotionless as tree trunks. She moved on to the next, and marked each one with a small, red slit in their abdomen. All of this she did before A29 had fallen to the ground. His face was still in shock from what had happened. She approached him, and knowing there would be enough time, walked past him and toward C16. "You were right. We're not the same," Luna whispered. "Allow me to show you the difference." She pulled her hand back and in a swift motion inserted a knife to the side of his neck and left it there, then, with the other knife, stabbed him several times in his back, swiveled in front of him, then pierced his abdomen. Every rip of the flesh released a fresh wave of tears, the sting of which recreated a wet painting in her mind, a replica of what she had just witnessed—the last moment in A29's life. She forced her eyes shut, and A29 and she were running across the sands of the Blue Field. Luna inserted the knife into the darkness. They were now throwing knives at a tree trunk. She speared the blade in front of her. A29 was now on the floor, choking on a chess piece while she snuck out of the room. Then he was with her in the Archive. Luna held an image of herself on top of her, a paper mirror, and with all her might, pushed the knife into C16, creating the gash that cemented his death. Luna opened her eyes and faced C16. She watched C16's open-mouthed face, his constricted throat desperate for air, the strength he had displayed just moments before now depleted into total shock. She pulled the knife from his neck when he was on his knees and turned around before he finished his fall.

The paused world caught up to her and her radiance vanished. All the Watchers fell to the ground simultaneously, and A29 landed in her arms. He tried to breathe, tried to reach Luna and speak, but nothing came out but the horrid sounds of certain death.

"I know. Stay quiet. Thank you for drawing me when I felt invisible. For your patience, for staying by my side even when I treated you as awfully as I did. Thank you for showing me a part of me I never knew existed. You did your best. You always did your best by me."

The humans looked around at the wake of dead bodies scattered on the floor. Once they knew they were safe, they cheered on. The commotion distracted Luna, who, returning her sight to A29, confirmed he had passed. It wasn't long after, with no time left for celebration or grief, when a set of screens came down from the ceiling. They broadcasted a control room.

"Wait," Luna said.

The humans still rejoiced in their victory.

Luna stood and slammed a silencing fist on a table. "Quiet!"

On the screens were A15 and his army of forty humans.

CHAPTER 4

AMBROSE

Ambrose broke the silence first. "That friend of yours is as strong as they come, isn't she?"

A15 nodded, his perplexed eyes glued to the screens.

"Might be as good as any time to find a way out of here," Ambrose said, while putting a hand on A15's shoulder.

A15 was still slightly nodding his head in silence.

Ambrose waited for a long time, then whispered, "Right you are." Then to the crowd, "All right. You two ugly bastards go to that side of the room and look for a way out. Well, you lot can figure it out. Scatter around the room and scan the perimeter while I see if I can get our fearless leader here out of his seizure."

"What are we looking for?" one human said.

"Anything with a handle, knob, pull, lock. Just don't speak to me unless you find it." He whispered, "Are you all right there, boss?"

"Yes, of course. Let's get out of here." A15 placed his spear against a control panel. His arms, which always looked tense, their muscles chiseling off his skin, were now relaxed. To the naked eye, he looked ten pounds lighter. To Ambrose, it appeared A15's soul had been sucked out of his body.

"That's the spirit! I hope you don't mind. I already put the goons to work."

A15 chuckled.

The control room looked as if people had left in a hurry. Papers stacked on the control board, cups with drinks left half empty, and rolling chairs untucked. A15 pushed one of the rolling chairs under a desk, took a stack of papers and placed them inside a drawer, and stared patiently out of the spired tower and at the primary school building.

Ambrose had seen this in a man before. A journal he had worked for was spearheaded by an animated man, confident, fearless. He assigned Ambrose to arduous tasks, which he took as challenges, to gain access to uncomfortable truths. The man had run his journal based on an integrity so pure, so determined, that nothing seemed to break him. One Monday morning, he was at the office before anyone. Ambrose had walked in early to finish his last edits on an interview, and this man, his name was Ted, was already in his office and came out holding a cup of coffee in one hand and waving a piece of paper in the other. "We have him," he said. "We bloody have him." And he went back into his office and slammed the door shut. Turned out he had evidence of a serious conspiracy involving local officials which would inevitably cause a stir in the town's governance, something about scientists accepting bribes from politicians to conduct experiments which resulted in their benefit. The politicians did so to gain favors with the underworld, who would force people to vote for them and secure them four more years in the comfy seat of power. It was a machine well-oiled by the blood and sweat of the working class, who knew no better than to follow orders in fear of losing their jobs, and with it, their identity. The newspaper was about to go into print when Ted came storming in, reeking of alcohol, head down, and put a stop on the print. He said nothing. The newspaper was rewritten and reedited, this time riddled with current events and advertisements. He never again walked in early. Never again did he flap a piece of paper passionately while smiling, as if he had just discovered Earth's eighth wonder. He walked head down to and from his office. Vodka replaced the smell of caffeine, and the newspaper didn't make it past that year. Ambrose now saw the same body language from A15, who almost trudged from one end of the room to the other, pretending to look for an exit.

"Anything, boss?"

"Nothing," A15 said, his eyes pointed at the ceiling. He whispered to himself, but close enough for Ambrose to hear. "What's the point? What's the point of getting out? In living? We're not needed. We're unnecessary. Of course, why didn't I see it before? She's an angel, half, but more than me, way more than me, a mere clone. I'm nothing but a sorry excuse of a life. Got trapped before I could even strike my weapon. My laughable weapon. Knife to a gunfight, and I was always right. Couldn't help 29, can't help the humans. What good am I? Not fit to lead, not fit to follow, an ant in a world of giants."

"I wonder if that glass is fragile enough to break," Ambrose said, looking out of the control room.

"Knife to a gunfight," A15 mumbled.

"Even if we did, it's a big drop to ground level. You two, if you find anything that passes as rope, let me know."

Two humans looked at each other and nodded.

Ambrose had left that newspaper company before it completely went into bankruptcy and he never saw Ted again. He often wondered what happened to him, if he should have stayed a little longer. Perhaps he might spark life into him with a new story or convince him there was still a way to deliver genuine news instead of the propaganda they had shifted to.

"Pull yourself together boss," Ambrose said to A15. "We need you."

A15 shook his head. "Right, right."

A hissing sound started.

"What the hell is that?" Ambrose said.

"Air conditioning?" a human said.

"I didn't notice it before. Keep looking, keep looking."

The hissing intensified and a slight cloud of green gas poured out of the ceiling vents.

Ambrose sniffed. "That's no air conditioning. Hurry, unless you want to be poisoned to death!"

The humans quickened their pace in panic, turning things over, pushing things aside, but the room was a box of four solid steel walls and a sealed door that merged seamlessly with them. There was no way out.

"Boss, what now?" Ambrose said.

The gas had formed clouds in the room, making it difficult to see.

A15 screamed. "Caught again, damn it. Caught again." He marched calmly toward his spear, grabbed it, then faced the glass in front of the controls. He struck it once, twice, the third time harder than was necessary to kill anyone. This was not a battle against a physical being, Ambrose saw, it was the perpetual war against a resurfacing trauma. He was exorcising his demons, domesticating his shadow.

The gas was now getting into their lungs. The room filled with poison and coughs.

"That's it. Let it out boss," Ambrose said. "Come on, lads! Ready your weapons, aim, and hit as hard as you've ever hit anything in your goddamn lives."

The humans did as told, pulling out axes, knives, swords, hatchets, hammers, sticks, bows, and striking the glass with everything they had. The glass flexed slightly.

"Don't give up," Ambrose said, coughing. "Hit that son of a gun with everything you've got."

A15 didn't stop to catch his breath. His attacks were relentless.

CHAPTER 5

LUNA

Green poison started pouring over the screen's image, covering most of the tragedy.

"No!" Luna cried, watching her only living childhood friend suffocating. "Stop this!"

A15 was desperately hitting the glass. The humans joined him. They took turns between attacking the glass and coughing. Some covered their faces, while others fainted.

Luna remembered A15 as always willing to help, saying "I want in" to every rebel plan of her childish mind. She now stood at the cliff of her plan's flaws, helplessly watching A15's hand slip from it, finger by finger, each one a step closer to his ending. She pushed a human out of her way and pulled on the Archive's door, the tendons in her shoulders almost snapping out of place, but it wouldn't yield to her strength. Defeated, she returned to the screen.

More gas poured in from the grilles on the walls, ceiling, and floor. Ambushed by poison gas, the humans viciously attacked a glass that merely bent on impact, mocking them of their frailty.

The picture on the screen converged into a thin, white, horizontal line, then died away into darkness.

CHAPTER 6

AMBROSE

A small crack formed in the middle of the glass.

"She's going to break!" Ambrose said, taking slow, shallow breaths.

The humans, seeing the product of their efforts, summoned strength from deep within them. Ambrose coughed and laughed, tears coming out of his eyes both from the poison and the spectacle of the human spirit.

"One last push. Let's show these angel bastards what humans are made of!" Ambrose said, as if yelling a war cry for one last push to victory.

The yell urged even A15, who took a few steps back, then galloped forward with gained momentum. He rushed like a knight with his spear forward and approached the glass with great speed. The spear hit the epicenter of the crack first, forming hairline fractures across the width of the glass. Then his body impacted it, shattering it into a million pieces.

"No!" Ambrose said, but by the time he ran forward and extended his hand, A15 had already jumped out of the spire and had made his final descent ten stories down.

CHAPTER 7

LUNA

Luna readied her stance to the Archive's opening door.

"Luna!" Ambrose said. "Luna, oh Luna."

"Ambrose. You are alive? I thought—"

"We made it, Luna. But A15..." He turned his gaze to his feet with a somber face. The other humans placed a fist on their chests.

Luna sheathed her knives. "What happened?" But from their faces, she knew. She prepared for impact.

"He went with honor, Luna," a human said.

Another squeezed forward, holding his spear. "We wouldn't be here without him."

Luna walked calmly toward him and grabbed A15's spear. Where there was once despair and anger, she found peace, or perhaps numbness, an absence of fear. "This ends here," she said, staring at the sharp ends of the spear. "No more games, no more cautioned plans."

Ambrose leveled his eyesight with her. "That's all fine and good. But, Luna. Where *is* everyone?"

Luna looked down and paced the room. "They knew we were coming. Someone is feeding them information, probably someone back in your Derinkuyu. I have my suspicions." She stopped and looked up. "Lucifer, Faith... the cowards set us up, leaving their henchmen to take care of us instead of getting their hands dirty, the same way they send their Watchers to Earth to take care of their business. Let's bring the dirt to their doorstep and bury them in it. I know where they are."

"Where?"

"The only other place they could be in all of Arvo. Follow me."

PART 2

CURRENT ARVO

CHAPTER 8

DANIEL

Daniel stared out through a window and nervously paced to the next one. When he saw nothing, he closed the blinds and made sure the front door was locked.

"No locks are going to stop her, you insolent bastard. We should have attacked together as I had planned. I do not know why I keep listening to you, traitor," Lucifer said.

"Traitor? Was my information not correct? You should thank me."

Faith stood up so fast, her chair creaked on the floorboards. "Thank you? Prisoners on our own planet, our own home? We should have killed you a long time ago."

Daniel turned to her. "Yes, thank me. We are alive, still, because of me and my foresight. I told you we should go to Earth. We are not safe here."

"And go where? To your underground hiding place? What are you so afraid of, anyway? She is nothing but a girl. I have faced her before," Lucifer said.

"And you still think she is just a girl, after all you have seen?" Daniel said. "No, the Seer knew. She is going to ruin everything if we do not think of a way to stop her."

Lucifer took a sip of his drink, leaning back in his chair.

"If all else fails," Daniel continued. "We still have her." He pointed at Istahar, tied to the fourth chair away from the table.

Istahar's eyes were red from sobbing and a piece of white cloth around her mouth, now drenched in her drool, kept her quiet. She tried to speak.

"Oh, what good was it to keep her, both of them? Tell me, Lucifer."

"Faith, you were curious about a child that I could not give you."

"Now it is my fault?"

"It is no one's fault. One thing leads to another, it is the law of life. It is written."

Faith scoffed.

"You may protest all you wish. There is no reason to despair when you realize that all is written. Let her come, child of Samyaza and Istahar, and whatever happens is the exact event that would have happened—should have happened." He opened his hand, and a spoon floated in the air and spun in vertices like a tornado. "Power is meaningless against His plan, the plan that binds us all. We think we are free, but we are not. The steel bars of our cage are simply so far away that no one can see them. It is not freedom, but the illusion of freedom." He pointed a finger at the sky. "His actions are not good, but the perception of it. He looks good while doing evil. My time is near. I earned my fate the moment I dared question Him. This I accepted a long time ago. I can see the cage, its walls closing in."

"What?" Faith cried. "Why did you not say anything? Why did you not try to—"

"To what? Alter my fate? Perhaps make the exact correct decision that would course correct my life? Who knows what the exact correct decision is? We can only take our shot at random and hope for the best. No. The moment I was enlightened, I was put on death row. That is when I understood. The game we are playing has no victors. No matter who wins, we all lose. I thought that if, perhaps, I played His game by His rules, and won, I might leave this universe deserving of the throne and a chance to restore order. But I see it now. He has sent His grandchildren to finish me before I prove my competence. It is all about perception. And when He is done with me, He will take care of my brothers."

Daniel stood idly and listened. A smirk made his ear rise a centimeter.

Faith slammed on the table. "Why would He care about perception? Why would He not end it all with the flick of a finger?"

"We are all judged. Even Him."

"So what? We throw our hands in the air and give up?"

"No, we do not give up. We give in. We play our part and go out on a blaze. It is the only thing we have."

Daniel inched toward the window, then spun around. "They are here."

PART 3

FIRST EARTH

CHAPTER 9

ZAQIEL

Lucifer's pride brought them together. It was sinful to believe one could carry the Ancestor's will by forcing it into existence. In time, they came to be known as the Rebel Watchers. Lucifer banished them to Earth, expecting them to perish during the next Earth reset.

"We are not prisoners of Earth, but His messengers. As nothing more than shadows, we will lurk in the dark like creatures of the night. Passive observers. Without killing, we will stop any interference to His plan. We are His Messengers," Samyaza, their leader, said, staring down from the foothills of a mountain in Turkey.

Zaqiel stood beside Samyaza and nodded. "We need something to distinguish us from other Watchers."

"A mark. On our skin. A mark which shall need to be renewed every time one wants to re-enter our settlement, to prove we have not deviated from the Path," Sarah said behind them, a radiant angel who, when assuming a human likeness, had taken the female form.

Zaqiel turned to Sarah. "And what mark shall that be?"

"444," Daniel said, standing alone, six feet away from the others. He had modeled his face from a vile ruler which had perished under the previous reset. Daniel gazed at the stars. He needed a mark, not to remind him of the Path, but to remind himself to whom he was accountable to. The four brothers. Three in Colonia and one in Arvo. If only he could figure out how to pin them against each other, destroy them from within, then he, Daniel, the true Archangel, might become ruler of this universe. It would take a long time to earn back Lucifer's trust and convince him he was at his service, that he would infiltrate the Rebel Watchers and his brothers' operations, and feed him the information he needed to succeed. And if the mark would hurt thrice, each line, each stinging, bloody line, would keep him in check. "Fate." He approached Zaqiel and placed a hand on his shoulder. He moved on to Sarah and did the same. "Will." And finally ended in front of Samyaza. "Hope." *Hate, Evil, and Hell*, he thought. "Three words to remind us of the reason for our sacrifice. The lands are quiet, vast. We will build a home in these lands, below the earth. A home which will survive the resets, so that we rest on the last day and emerge on the first as humanity's allies and the facilitators of His will."

Samyaza requested their approval. "Zaqiel? Sarah?" He waited for their nods. "Very well. So it shall be."

And so they dug out their home from the hollow earth, filling it with other Watchers who had come expecting barbarian earthlings, but finding most humans living in peace. In time, the Messengers began bringing their human targets with them, giving them a new chance at life. Sarah kept them fed with the perfect diet, trained in the ways of ancient combat, and safe from subsequent Watchers looking to finish the job. Zaqiel was always three steps ahead and kept a ledger of all Watchers who had become Messengers, all targets who had become their guests, and a vivid collection of all his dreams in written form. Samyaza organized the rescue missions and kept morale high in the city, which they named Derinkuyu, or "deep well", for it would always be an infinite source of water for dispirited souls.

One day, upon finding Zaqiel deep into his writing, Samyaza inquired about it.

"I am recording my dreams," Zaqiel said.

"May I?"

Zaqiel tore a page and handed it over to Samyaza.

Samyaza scanned the page; his eyes jumped from one sentence to another in disbelief. "How long have you known?"

"I was not sure at first. I believed them to be coincidences, fueled by fear or worry. But they happened too often to ignore."

"These are not mere dreams, they are visions. You know this. Half of them have come true, which means the rest has only not happened yet. Oh, my dear Zaqiel, your visions have blessed us."

"Blessed? I have seen friends get murdered in my dreams. It might happen today, tomorrow, or not for another century. There is no telling what the next moment will bring, not even with these... visions. I would very much rather not know at all."

"You must be at the initial stages of your awakening. Sarah might help you control it."

"Perhaps."

"Go spend time with her. I have faith in you and her. My dear Zaqiel, our seer."

"I apologize for interrupting your prayer. I know only humans should feel shame," Zaqiel said. "But I do not know who else to turn to. Samyaza suggested you might help."

Sarah knelt before an altar of candles, her head bowed to a stitched rug hanging from a large steel nail. The rug's design displayed a blue circle in the middle and a black bird hovering above it. Near the bottom, two silhouettes laid face up, and one towered over them. There were lines as corridors, beginning at the edges of the rug and shrinking into the circle in the middle. "I have been waiting for you. Say all and leave nothing in your mind."

"You knew?"

"I heard you speaking in your sleep. One of your dreams inspired this design." She motioned at the rug. "I find it peaceful."

"There are many more. Too many. None of them seem peaceful to me. It has been many suns and moons since I last slept, yet the visions find me in moments of weakness when I cannot bear to stay awake."

"Let us try to make sense of it. First, we must recreate the conditions in which the visions appear," Sarah said, her gentle voice just above a whisper. "Come, lay down."

Zaqiel stepped inside the cave, the altar now bright as a flashback. "I remember seeing this. I remember trying to wake up, closing my hands into a fist to see if pain would bring me back. But tried as I might, the vision forced me to see it through, paralyzed, terrified. It was the end of all things, the beginning of all things, and everything in between."

"It has not happened yet. Every action, every thought, every word, might alter the future, and thus, your vision."

The rocky floor was rough against his hands. He forced himself to lie still to stop from lacerating his arms and legs. His eyes trembled against his will to keep them shut. "Oh, please, hurry."

Sarah placed a hand over his eyes. "Now, sleep, so you can awaken."

In the next tick of time, his body dropped into another plane of existence. It had no pain, perceived no moisture from the cave, no drops falling into the echo of darkness. Two inches out of his reach were a series of events playing in loops, a collection of previews—alternatives of a near future. If he tried, he might guide his astral projection into one and extract from it its essence. When he approached one, ten more appeared. In a matter of seconds, the replaying futures overlapped. Sometimes their only differences were an out-of-place word, or an extra action performed or omitted. Thinking about the differences multiplied them a hundredfold.

"What do you see?" Sarah said, her voice an invader.

"An impossible number of choices. How can I see the future if the future will always change according to the present?"

"Try to focus. There must be one that is more likely than others, more significant. The details do not matter as much as the catastrophic repercussions."

"There! Two stand out among the rest."

"Tell me more about them."

"No. No."

"Tell me."

"One shows a gleam like an ocean under the sun, with its water sparkling blue. The other one displays a fire that burns through anything and everything, leaving only death in its wake."

"Good. Remember that feeling. Notice your body, your mind, the ground on which you stand. Those are the cues to look for to guide your vision on the right path. Powers are wild beasts. Without control, they run amok and cause more havoc than good. Harness it. This is your power. You control it, not the other way around. Now, follow my voice, and once you find it, you will awaken anew, and you will find your way back into the maze and reach the two main visions, the two main options for the future, always. The likely outcomes will appear more vividly each time you traverse the trappings of your mind. You have nothing to fear. Yes. Good. Follow my voice."

Zaqiel walked toward the echo, through the house of mirrors displaying distorted visions that had never happened. He followed the vibration, the explosions, and saw the broken image of a woman with a thousand faces waiting at the end. His body was heavy, as if he was moving in the wrong direction, and from the broken image of the woman appeared fingers, hands, and arms that pulled him out of the vision and back into Derinkuyu.

Over a long period, Zaqiel perfected his gift, and he no longer had to wait for his visions to come to him in his dreams; he only had to close his eyes and there they were. The house of mirrors had become only two large floor mirrors standing before him, and he had to choose the version of it he allowed others to see, while affecting the outcome by doing so. He carefully crafted his power of self-fulfilling prophecies, writing those which he deemed too terrible to say out loud.

One nightmarish vision involved a demon waiting in the shadows outside the door of Derinkuyu. The shadow schemed at night, eating animals alive, cackling with pride at his own treacherous nature. The vision repeated almost daily until Zaqiel could not focus on the second mirror—the horrible creature became the only outcome. One night, when Derinkuyu slept soundly in the desert lands of Turkey, he took a stroll through the corridors and pushed the rock covering the entrance. The wind had a nervous chill. He had seen this before. The door was always open, the creature was always standing outside, naked under the moonlight. But when he stepped outside, he was alone.

"What do you see?" a voice slithered in the dark.

Zaqiel listened for its source. "Who lurks in the shadows? Show yourself, you despicable creature!"

"You see too much. I cannot allow you to see me. I am only effective in the shadows. To appear harmless is a blessing I must keep. Yes, now, I will make you not see. Yes, not see."

There had been a third looking glass, a vision that went unnoticed in the house of mirrors. In the future that happened, the slithering creature jumped out of the dark at tremendous speed, with claws sharper than a sword, and gripped Zaqiel's head. It carved into Zaqiel's eye sockets and burrowed its way into the tiny muscles behind his eyes, and, once the claws had made it into his skull, it pulled and ripped his eyes out. "I will make sure you never see again," the creature said.

"Zaqiel?" Sarah said. "Is that you?"

"There, in the dark," Samyaza said.

Zaqiel knelt on the ground, blood dripping from the holes where his eyes used to be.

Samyaza scanned the area, hovering above, his search futile in the darkness. "Who did this to you?"

"No gift comes without a curse." Zaqiel cried and propped himself up with one leg that shook until he crumbled back to the ground. "It was my visions. First, it took my rest. Now they have rendered me blind."

<hr>

The wounds took months to heal, yet he never healed in full.

Stuck in a perpetual premonition, unsure of what was real or prophecy, he begged to not be called Zaqiel. He said he was no longer worthy of an angel's name. Without his sight, he became the only thing he could ever be. A looker of visions, a navigator of mirror images and possibilities—The Seer.

CHAPTER 10

DANIEL

An angel of the dark scavenged the carcasses of decaying animals. It growled viciously at the black vultures which had found the prey first. "Away with you, vermin!" it yelled, a trail of saliva dripping from his mouth. The creature crawled on the ground and approached the dead animal with a terrible hunger and feasted on the sun-beaten body. "How do you get to Hell? You lie," it said between swallows. "What do you do if they find out?" Its teeth devoured the flesh, tearing out the skin and crushing bones. "Kill everyone, of course." The creature scurried across the sand and rested its back against a boulder. "You have done well. Not long now. One more reset, maybe two. For my will. For my will." It cackled into the night. "All hail Daniel."

"I have a proposition," Daniel said at the table.

Samyaza motioned his head to hear the rest of it.

"I can return to Arvo," Daniel continued, "infiltrate Lucifer's ranks and pinpoint Watchers and their targets."

Sarah scoffed and stood from the stone she was leaning against. "You know he will never take you back."

"It will be difficult, yes. But perhaps I disagreed with you, the rebels, and had to stray away to be guided back into his light. Perhaps I will do anything to prove my loyalty."

The Seer raised his eyebrows, swallowed, then looked away.

Samyaza noticed. "What do you see?"

"Allow it. The vision is too far away to grasp, but the strategic position might be to our advantage someday."

CHAPTER 11
DANIEL

Until the first reset, there were only four Messengers under the Earth's crust. And in silence they waited for other Watchers to see what they saw, feel what they felt, to question, to hesitate at the kill's finishing move. The first Watcher to waver was a young male, age unknown, nameless, who, after seeing the human target holding the hand of a boy, dropped his knife in shock.

The target pushed the boy behind him. "What do you want? Take my wallet, I don't care, just let my son go."

"He would not send me to murder a target in front of his child," the Watcher cried. "He would never do such a thing."

Like a serpent dragging its body slowly at the sound of its prey, the rustling grass startled them, and from the ground, the figure rose and spoke. "Oh, but he would, and he has. It was wise to pause, Watcher, for you would be the one to live with the product of your actions. Burdens, they grow heavier the longer you carry them. It is best to not carry them at all."

"What are you?" the young Watcher said, squared against the talking shadow.

Taking advantage of this distraction, the target and his son fled the scene. The noise of their shoes over the wet streets made the Watcher flinch.

"Let them," the speaking shadow said. "We have more important matters. To begin with, waking you up to the truth."

The Watcher took a step back toward a streetlight and searched for the correct button on his bracelet.

The shadow disappeared and reappeared behind him. "You will not need this any longer." And in one sudden move, snatched the bracelet off the Watcher's wrist.

"How did you...?"

When he turned, the streetlight had uncovered a piece of the shadow's face, its demonic, terrible face full of patches of black hair and horns that bled out of its skin. The Watcher sank to his knees and swept the ground, looking for his knife.

The next downpour fell, this one bringing with it a slew of thunder and hail. "Do not bother, Watcher. Give in to the unknown." A cracking of glass turned the Watcher blind to the night. "It is the dark that makes light necessary. Without it, it is useless, as is the Ancestor without the Archangel that sent you."

All the Watcher discerned was a change in the blowing wind, and the shadow's legs kicked the knife further down the street.

"Come along now, child. You have so much to learn."

The Watcher crawled on the floor and patted the street in search of the knife. He looked around him at a sea of darkness. "Get away from me, creature!"

"There is only one path forward." The voice said, its slow, confident pace following closely behind. "A path which will be easier once you give in to it. Follow me into the light, the true light. One that will survive the absence of darkness, one that is self-sufficient, that does not require all of this Archangel nonsense. Follow me, and together we will reach the Ancestor before any of them. We will not need them. I am the true heir."

Hail crashed on his back, his body drenched, tired, afraid. The Watcher's resolve depleted. The only way to life was to survive this moment. Survival first, then escape. He stopped crawling. "If I do as you say, what will happen to me?"

"You need not to worry. I will introduce you to the Rebel Watchers, now called the Messengers, which I have infiltrated as an ally. Stay close to me," the creature told the Watcher. "I will teach you to lurk in the shadows until the time comes to step into the light." Satisfied with the target's silence, the creature said, "Messengers have names, and I shall name you Mark. Mark, I like it. It sounds human, like mine. I also like my name. Daniel. Something about it rings true, does it not?"

Daniel flew Mark to Derinkuyu's entrance and said the vow over the enchanted rock while drawing blood by pressing his overgrown fingernails into his skin. "With my blood's ink, I swear to carry the secret to my grave. For His will, we are His Messengers." He turned to Mark, who gazed at the branding burning on his forearm. "From now on, we do not speak of this to any human or Watcher. You are no longer of them or against them, you are somewhere in between. You and me, we stand as an army of two, for now. Repeat these words, my pupil. It will be your first lesson, to say those words and believe them, even if you lie. And once we are inside, you listen to me and only me. You understand? Good. You see, we fight a war inside a war, you and I. The brothers have their armies in the Universe, the Messengers will have theirs under Earth, but we,"—he laughed a sinister laugh— "we will have our army everywhere, hiding in plain sight. We will be both with them and against them, waiting for the perfect moment to turn and retrieve the spoils of war. For a weak mind, strength comes from numbers, but for a strong one, strength comes from patience. The strongest one is one who survives. And if we must crawl into the sewers, keeping our heads down and displaying weakness, so be it. Now go ahead, so that we can integrate you as a founding member. I will initiate a vote for your seat at the table and you will be my eyes and ears when I am away stroking Lucifer's ego or while I am kissing

Michael's feet and spoiling everybody else's plan in Colonia. All of them will believe they know everything, when all I will be doing is creating a bridge between them. I will facilitate their war at all costs. They do not want to face each other, because it is against the Ancestor's rules, but I will make it happen. I will destroy them without lifting a finger or getting a single bruise. That is my strength. Now speak the oath, Mark, and walk this lonely path with me. In time, they will all see my brilliance. They all underestimate me, my power. The universe will give me my due soon. I can feel it approaching. Be on the right side of history, Mark. Walk with me or fall. Speak the oath, but speak it even though you do not believe it within. Words are simply words, vibrations, sounds. They evoke meaning for other people. They do not have to evoke the same meaning for you. Remember this well, my student. Your tongue is nothing more than another weapon in your arsenal, the most powerful of them all. You can bend your reality at will. Intelligent beings have an inherent proclivity for trust, and your tongue can use that trust against them. But aim sharp and aim well, because once that trust shatters, there is no putting it back. Time is limited. We shall aspire for a plan that will take four Earth resets for maturity, at the most. Here, I will show you. Turn your forearm over. That is where the stamp will appear. Tattooed on your forearm will be the rules of this game as a reminder, you see. Four, four, four. Four Archangels to trick, four resets to do so, and, finally, four points of contact, three stepping stones—Arvo, Earth, Colonia—and the goal, the door to the Ancestor. Do you understand now? It is all calculated with deadly precision. Now, repeat the words, young Mark. You have a long, arduous life ahead of you, and so do I. Let us get you a seat at the table, so that I can be free to roam."

"I thought you were never coming back," Sarah said. "One can only hope."

Daniel chuckled, now in his humanoid form. "Of course I came back. I missed you too, Sarah. And I did not come alone. This is Mark. He comes to us straight from Lucifer's Watchers. He renounced his loyalty when he saw the cruelty of his ruler's intentions."

The Seer sat in silence.

Samyaza looked at Mark's 444 engraving on his skin and seemed pleased. "Mark, welcome."

"There is one other thing," Daniel said. "I once said I would be more useful in the field, traveling to and from Arvo. The longer I wait, the less of a chance I have of Lucifer trusting me."

"I agree," the Seer said, his artificial eyes pointing at a distant reality.

"And while I am gone, in my place, we can give my seat to Mark here to act as the fourth voice. I have taken him under my wing and will teach him everything he needs to know. I am confident he will do well."

"And you know this according to what?" Sarah said, her arms crossed.

"According to his mercy, his willingness to learn, and the oath. I created the oath so that only the pure at heart can speak it and activate it. Do you not trust me?"

"You know I do not," Sarah said.

"Enough of this. I will not allow it. We are together in this. Our group is small, yes, but we must trust ourselves and treat ourselves as —what is that human word?—family. It is the only way to grow and become what I know we can become, what we need to become if we are to be successful in carrying His will. Remember why we are here. The Ancestor wants humans to figure it out for themselves. He wants humans to live, thrive, survive, or perish, whatever it may, on their own, with no interruptions. We must have faith that they will do so. In the meantime, we live beneath the Earth and only come out when needed. We can not be Him, but we can imitate Him, live according to His example. We must show mercy, we must show trust, we must expect our brothers and sisters to figure it out. And so I accept Mark at the table in place for Daniel, so that Daniel can come and go to Arvo and let us know about future human targets, and perhaps, in time, influence Lucifer into reason."

Sarah dropped her arms. "Fine."

The Seer nodded.

Daniel's hair on his neck stood on end, and he rejoiced in silence.

During the Rebel Watchers' escape from Arvo, Daniel had stolen the blueprints to his bracelet. He produced them now in Derinkuyu.

"Come, come, boy." He meant Mark. "Everything is always less than what it may become. The Ancestor hid an encoded secret inside humans, you see. I know this. Nobody else knows this. I have been saving this knowledge for the precisely correct moment, and that moment is before us, now. In that same way, this bracelet has hidden power. See here?" He pointed at the blueprint. "This is not just a travel device between Earth and Arvo, but a teleportation device to anywhere in the universe, if you just remove its restrictions. I noticed when I saw Lucifer wearing one. Why would the ruler himself wear a bracelet? Then it occurred to me. Maybe it holds more power than what they are letting us know. I came across the blueprints the next day, and you ask me how? Do you not know by now that I am resourceful? The most resourceful being in the universe. Come, come closer." He opened the bracelet's cover after carefully removing a combination of screws, clips, and pressing on its sides. "See this? It is just a matter of shorting this point in the circuit to this one, diverting its power to the blocked interface. There."

The bracelet's light turned green.

Daniel jumped back and covered his mouth to keep his evil cackle from resonating through Derinkuyu's tunnels. "Now it accepts any coordinate in the universe, and the first place I shall visit is Colonia. It is not he who works the hardest the one to win, it is he who places the pieces in front of very particular obstacles, and gives them precisely the right pickaxe to break through."

Mark looked blankly. "Why must we come between anything or anyone? What is it we have to gain? Why cannot we just be good?"

"Good, you say? Why be good when one can be the perception of good? Being good is weak, being perceived as good is power. Oh, you will see. Everything will become crystal clear in time. It is a sin to be this clever."

With a press of a button, Daniel was standing on Colonia's soil, a mile away from the Compound. He grinned, straightened his body, and walked, almost dashed through the arid lands. He had once lived under Lucifer's shackles, fantasizing about dark things in secret, but was now free to move across the stars like antimatter and bring his theater of shadow to the universe. When he had overheard Samyaza's plan to escape during their mission on Earth, he wanted—needed—in. He knew he only had one chance to bring forth the players to the stage. He liked to dance with death, always one move away from being untrustworthy, one move away from being hung for treason by either party. It excited him. He walked back and forth across the tightrope of life and death, each iteration with higher confidence and a bigger smile on his face.

"Tell your precious leaders Daniel is here to see them," he said to the two guards at the Compound's door. "Tell them I have information that will take them to the Ancestor."

One guard talked to his earpiece, then motioned his head to the other guard, who pulled Daniel by the arm and dragged him inside the Compound.

"You will regret this," Daniel told the guard grabbing his arm. "There are kings, knights, rooks, then there are pawns. You are so insignificant that you are not in the game at all." He laughed maniacally. "When the darkness comes, you will be among the first ones to get swallowed whole by it. Mark my words," he said. "Mark my words."

They walked through a solid door that turned momentarily into a holographic curtain, then back to a solid door. "I have Daniel here."

"Leave," Gabriel said.

Michael was sitting with his back turned to Daniel.

Gabriel took a step forward. "What do you want? Are you not Lucifer's boy?"

"I belong to no one, but perhaps we can help each other."

Raphael, who was standing next to Gabriel, scoffed. "Do you expect us to trust a traitor? You said so yourself. Your allegiance is only to yourself."

"While I do not serve anyone, I also do not look for enemies. I simply want to be free. And as long as Lucifer is in control of Arvo, as long as he lives, I will never be truly free."

Raphael lowered his voice. "You are aware of the Ancestor's laws. We cannot fight each other. We are powerless against him."

"Not directly, no. But what if you got to the Ancestor before him? If you gain control of the throne, you may abolish the rules and Lucifer with them. He is taking the long road. I brought you a shortcut."

"You are speaking nonsense. I will have you thrown away and fed to the animals," Gabriel said.

"Let him speak," Michael said.

"Ah, the sensible brother speaks, at last. Oh, great Michael. The Ancestor has respect for your technological advances, and so he has tasked the brothers to repopulate Earth after each reset with your genetically engineered monkeys."

"I will listen, but my patience wears thin. Get to the point."

"I know for a fact that there is something else encoded in the human DNA, something that can replicate the Ancestor's powers. What if you used your genetic engineering to unlock this hidden secret? What if you created the perfect human, created in the Ancestor's image? What if you nurtured him, controlled him, then used him to open the door out of this universe and into the throne?"

Michael stood. "That is impossible. We would have found this hidden gene by now."

"Think of it," Daniel said, desperately. "Just think of it. What better place to hide such power than in plain sight? The Ancestor would not have locked His sons without an escape rope should things go awry. It is not like Him to leave His sons helplessly in the dark. The Ancestor always leaves a key. I remember the legend, before these two even existed, and it was just Lucifer and you, Michael. Remember? When Lucifer—"

"Enough!" Michael said, frowning.

Gabriel looked at Raphael.

"I have had enough of you. Gabriel, Raphael, see that you extract whatever information this traitor thinks he has. Make him prove it, then kill him. And if he cannot prove it...kill him, anyway."

Gabriel opened his hand and pulled Daniel to him like iron to a magnet. Raphael clenched a hand on Daniel's other arm. "Come, traitor, show us this hidden power," Gabriel said. "And then stay silent forever."

Daniel tried to loosen himself, but their grip was too strong. "That was not the agreement, Michael. You are the reasonable one. The only true heir to the throne. You are better than this. Now, I am glad to show you the hidden power, but I must live."

"And why is that?"

"Creating the perfected lineage will take trial and error. A long time. So much so that many resets will come to pass, and time will allow for only one try per each. When the Ancestor allows you to repopulate Earth, that is your only chance to try a lineage and observe it. But use caution: if you have failed, you must abolish it entirely. You must kill any flaws. Then, once you perfect the lineage, the gene will not awaken fully until it has passed down several generations. The gene must mutate on its own. It is an exercise of patience. You need me to keep Lucifer distracted. You need me to keep him away from the lineage for as long as necessary to create the perfect human. I may not be as powerful as you, or have such a large following. But I know things, that is my power. I find things which are lost and forgotten, and I dig them out and bring them forth into the light. You need eyes and ears in Earth and Arvo. Allow me the honor of being your informant." He tried to bow down, but Gabriel pulled him up.

"Stop this spectacle. You do not serve anyone but yourself."

"That is true. I have my motives, but you will benefit from them. My path does not intersect yours." *It supersedes it.*

"Take him," Michael said. And when they were about to step out the door, "But do not kill him."

Daniel almost burst out laughing but coughed instead.

A man wearing a white coat rustled against Daniel's skin on the way out. A dozen others sat on black swivel chairs and observed the subjects through microscope lenses. Black nitrile gloves protected their subjects from contamination, and tight fitting white masks covered half their faces. The laboratory was dimly lit, and the scientists looked like floating eyes that moved from one black desk station to another, grabbing syringes, beakers, slides, moving them around to another station, scribbling notes, and placing their clipboard notes on a different desk, where a different scientist grabbed the notes, made a gesture with their hand, as if studying them, then signed the piece of paper, and stored it in a drawer. They did all this without speaking a word. Everything that Daniel saw, he stored in his box of manipulative tools.

Gabriel placed a finger on his lips. "We forbid them to speak. We find it counterproductive. These are our scientists, and also our first genetically engineered subjects. We made them smart enough to replicate themselves, but weak enough to not survive direct sunlight. They do not need any kind of nourishment, other than essential electrolytes and proteins which are directly injected into their bodies by an embedded, permanent cannula."

As Gabriel said this, a scientist got up from his chair, stood up in a corner, pulled out a thin tube from a machine and injected it in an opening on his forearm. He closed his eyes. A yellow liquid entered his body, and after ten seconds, he removed the tube and walked back to his post.

"It is as simple as that," Gabriel continued, pleased. "We have devised an operation with a hundred percent efficiency."

"Which is why, you insolent traitor," Raphael said, "if there was something to be found, we would have found it already."

Daniel knew how his eyes changed when he smirked, how his face transformed into a fear-inducing mask. He found this mask useful before bending someone to his will. He smirked. "With all your advancements, all your productivity, your robotic minions working tirelessly day and night, and who work so much they do not know the difference between either, you are still looking in all the wrong places. You see, what you are looking for is not a specific gene, but data encoded using the DNA nucleotides themselves. It is not in one location, but scattered throughout the DNA chain. You need a sequencer to gather the fragments in a specific order and decode them back into their original format. I will show you." Daniel waited for Gabriel to loosen his grip and walked to the station where the scientist had stored the notes. The scientist was still sitting at the desk when Daniel breathed in his neck. Daniel bent his hand upwards slightly, enough to aim at the embedded cannula on the scientist's hand and pulled enough on the cannula without touching it until it broke off its bond from his vein.

"Out," Gabriel said.

The scientist rubbed his wrist, stood from the desk, and walked to the recharging station.

At the desk, a screen connected to an electron microscope displayed a high-resolution image of the slide, magnified to see the molecules. Daniel sat on the now unoccupied chair. "See? Here." He pointed at the screen, looking at the recharging station with the corner of his eye. "And here. These are all fragments. By themselves, meaningless, but reassemble them just right—"

The scientist coughed, his skin as pale as a blank paper.

"Compose yourself," Raphael said.

The scientist choked. Yellow serum dripped from his wrist and onto the floor. He tried to grab on to anything to keep from falling, but failed, pulled a metal tray and brought it to the ground with him, causing a tremendous racket. Raphael and Gabriel went to his aid, and while the laboratory stopped its productivity for the first time in two millennia, Daniel opened the drawer and snatched out a document and hid it inside his armor.

"Get back to work. All of you!" Raphael said with his hand on the scientist, who was breathing his last breaths.

"I do not know how, traitor, but I know it was you who did this," Gabriel said.

"Me? I have barely moved. I was under your watch. That is a fact. A fact Michael will consider if he hears of this."

Gabriel stood in a rage. "I will kill you, you insolent—"

"Here it is. The decoder and the locations to all the hidden fragments, in order." Daniel produced a small electronic device on the desk. "With a drop of human DNA and this decoder, you will have access to the most powerful secret ever devised by the Ancestor. Wield it wisely and carefully, my dear Archangels. If not, it may come back to haunt you one day." His devilish lips rose at the corners. "I will see myself out."

After testing the device, the brothers had no choice but to bite their lips, swallow their anger, release Daniel, and watch him vanish.

In a blink of a vengeful eye, Daniel was back at the forbidden land, Arvo, the purple planet with golden sand where Lucifer brainwashed his angels into becoming Watchers that scanned Earth and plucked out its most influential humans. Lucifer had been successful, until the first reset, to send his loyal assassins without resistance, until Daniel saw an opportunity, a way to create a home base away from home, and from it, devise a plan that would destroy everyone in its wake while he watched from his prized throne. Arvo was the next pit stop of this devilish plan. Daniel produced the genetic engineering documents from his armor and sneered.

Arvo already had the training grounds, the multilevel building to hold the angels in training, but Daniel knew it wasn't sustainable. *A weakness, an entry point.* Lucifer was desperate to get his hands on the brothers' genetic engineering program, a technology which the Ancestor himself had trusted in Michael to repopulate Earth after each reset. The Ancestor did not allow anyone else, not even Lucifer, to use this. Lucifer's lesson was to control his pride, to watch the humans from afar, to watch them thrive and destroy and become extinct without so much as lifting a finger. The rest were supposed to repopulate Earth and make sure their brother did not interrupt. Lucifer had failed before the first reset.

"I have word, you see," Daniel whimpered at the hands of Lucifer's Redeemers, his most powerful guard regimen. "Word that will interest him."

"We have instructions to eliminate you and your group of rebels on sight," the Redeemer said, a strong and wide man whose arms were as thick as Daniel's legs.

"The gift that I bring is more valuable than my betrayal. I come to you as a betrayer to the Rebels, and a friend to Arvo, if he will take me back. Here, you may study the report yourself and decide. Kill me right here in the open air if you are not pleased."

The Redeemer grabbed the file and pushed Daniel to the ground. After he flipped the second page, his eyebrows rose. He turned to Daniel.

Daniel gave him a simpering smile.

The Redeemer pushed Daniel two steps in front of him.

"I should send for your execution at once," Lucifer said. After a long pause, "No, treason like yours deserves something more personal. I shall put my hands around your neck and squeeze until your life-force escapes you, until your last exhale falls upon my face."

"You should. If I were you, I would. Yes, I would. But only. Only..."

Lucifer inched forward, but Faith stopped him by the hand.

"Let him have his last words," Faith said.

Lucifer relaxed. "You have two breaths. Make them count."

"It was Samyaza. He persuaded us all. You know his sermonical tongue when he orates. He can persuade anyone. I fell under his spell. We all did. But, you see, I am smarter than the rest. I broke free from it, in time, and I saw the error of my ways. And so I come to you." He knelt. "My master, my lord, the true Archangel, to beg for one more opportunity." He bowed to the floor. "Please have mercy."

Lucifer seemed unfazed. "You are of no value to me. I do not give second chances."

Faith turned to leave. "Oh, that is quite enough, darling. Dispose of him."

"Very well." Lucifer raised his hand, the palm facing Daniel.

"Wait," Daniel said. "I do not expect blind trust to be given to me. I expect to earn it. Perhaps this might begin the healing process." He nodded at the Redeemer standing beside him, who pretended not to notice. He turned to Lucifer. "Your pigs have their hands dirty, but it is not their doing which has soiled them." And at the Redeemer. "Go on."

"What is he talking about?"

The Redeemer handed over Daniel's papers.

"Your goons here wanted the glory for themselves. But no, it wasn't them. It was me who took this straight out of your brothers' hands without them noticing. I am at your service, lord of all lords. You will see, in time. This is only the beginning."

Lucifer grabbed the document and glanced at it, flipping pages, slowly at first, then vigorously. "This is—"

"It is," Daniel said, standing.

Faith turned back and looked over Lucifer's shoulder at the

papers. After a few seconds, she gasped and covered her mouth. "Is it?"

Lucifer closed the document and Faith grabbed Lucifer's free hand.

"Lord, you must trust me. Accept this as a small token. Their factory of humans—my life for many. Imagine, just imagine. Having as many Watchers as you want and controlling their inclinations, their talents, every cell, every neuron, tailored to your liking. No more losing your powerful angels. Send the disposable humans to Earth instead. It is a perfect system. Sustainable."

"I will never trust you, insolent, lesser angel," Lucifer said, and Faith gripped his hand harder. He turned to her. "But perhaps I can learn to tolerate you."

"That is all I ask, my lord. But I must be free. That is how I am most valuable, free to be everywhere at once. And I shall roam the stars gathering information for you, sir, and bring it to your doorstep. I shall be your eyes on Earth and your ears in Colonia, but my soul will forever be in Arvo."

"You will have nothing until I see the successful construction of this factory. You will breathe it, live in it, work in it like a dog. If I am to allow your freedom, you will be my slave on Earth and my personal jester in Colonia, juggling blades for my brothers' pleasure to distract them from my plans."

PART 4

CURRENT EARTH AND COLONIA

CHAPTER 12

ROBERT

What does it mean to be at peace? I've lived in constant motion, a life built on chaos—it's the only thing I've known. I crave it, the unknown. There's a romance in letting destiny rob me of my life and place me somewhere else, somewhere new where I can once again grow roots deep enough so that when I'm yanked from what was once dirt, I can be nostalgic about its rich soil. Destiny came for me that day. I felt it ripping my feet from the ground, breaking parts of me I would never see again, elevating me into its tumultuous wind. Life was a storm, and I would come pouring down in a different place. I knew beginnings all too well. Perhaps now I would get an ending to this start.

An immense dust storm came from the north, and a gigantic, spinning wheel with clouds of lightning that sounded like a roaring waterfall approached us. We stood at the top of a mountain looking up. The three creatures surrounded me, making sure I watched it all. Next to each of the creatures, three wheels formed on the ground.

"Come," the one who sent shivers down my spine said. He had dark brown hair and blue eyes that pierced into me like ice daggers.

I stepped with him into the circle embedded on the ground, and a new set of wheels with rims like diamonds reflecting the sun formed within it. The inner wheels spun out of the earth and turned like a gyroscope around us, and we floated toward the large wheel in the sky. The other two floated next to us inside wheels of their own.

I watched the mountains below turn into not more than specks of dust, and I wanted to speak, to break free and pound on the stone door that Luna had crossed. I had held her hand on the rooftop in fear of her floating away, yet it was I who had always been floating, waiting to be held, waiting for an external weight to keep me still. I wanted to fall back to Earth and beg to be let in and promise that I would never hesitate again. But I was paralyzed, and could only turn my head slightly, enough to witness the horror I was approaching.

The wheel in front of us now looked like a city, its machinery turning and whirring, almost inhaling and exhaling like the fiery belly of a metal dragon. And I could do nothing but look at it as it grew before me and opened its insides to us. The wheels turning around us gleamed and sucked us into the brilliant light coming from within the metal beast.

Once the door closed, the gyroscope stopped, and the circles compacted into the ground and disappeared. I fought with all my strength to escape but couldn't move. Anger rushed through my body. I thought of screaming threatening words, but the sounds never came.

The one with red hair turned to me and spoke without speaking. "We will not hurt you. We are only doing our duty."

And a rush of emotions came over me as if my brain had not produced them but someone had inserted them into my body, and I felt guilty. "I'm sorry," I said, but I didn't hear my voice nor had I moved my tongue. My shoulders dropped and my body calmed into complete stillness. They guided me through a corridor inside the giant wheel, which now resembled the interior of an aircraft. On either side of the corridors were steel chairs that emanated lights of various hues. Some chairs were empty, others had the sleeping bodies—or what looked like sleeping bodies—of humans of different eras. A few of them had clothes like mine, others had tunics or armor, and some had only a piece of cloth covering their lap. Their mouths were connected to black rubber masks with tubes up to the ceiling.

"Not too far along now," the red-haired man said. The blue-eyed one was leading in front, followed by the one with the blackest hair I have ever seen.

They took me along the corridor until and ascended stairs until we reached a top level that looked like a cockpit, with controllers and levers in the front and surrounded by glass windows from where one could stare out into space. They pushed me to a chair near one of the glass windows without touching me and sat me down.

"Be not afraid, this will all be over soon," the red-haired one said, and smiled. "My name is Raphael."

There was something calming about his voice, his harmless demeanor. It compelled me to follow his directions and try very hard to not be a bother to him. I knew everything I was feeling was the exact opposite to the thing I was really feeling underneath this cloud of emotions, but I couldn't shake the veil off. It was as if my body was on autopilot and all I could do was watch. So I watched.

Looking out the glass window, at Earth as Carl Sagan's pale blue dot, I thought about my childhood. My father got me used to getting a toy every time we left the house. It didn't matter if we went down the street or two towns over; I was getting a piece of plastic. By thirteen, I had a collection, which I dragged every weekend to my grandparents's house—the whole family gathered there every Sunday. When I opened my box of toys, my cousins dug their claws into it to pick their favorite. They never brought boxes of toys of their own, which I didn't see as odd until I was an adult. I never thought of us as of a higher economic class than them. To me, they were my cousins, my friends. We played until our stomachs grumbled. That usually meant hours had passed and my grandmother had something boiling on the stove. She cooked for over twenty people. I don't recall anyone ever saying thank you, or people helping her at all, though they must have, right? By sundown, each family left with their stomachs full and their energy depleted. One by one they went into the night, dialing down the house's volume, taking its spirit with it. When everyone else was gone, and the only ones remaining were my parents and grandparents and the generational jokes and pleasantries, and the silence that hides so easily in crowds was now dead center, I wondered what was it all for. I looked at the stars above, coming out, dimming slowly into existence. Most of them were still as the giant rocks on the mountainside by the house. But every so often, I saw one moving. I wondered if a being from a distant planet was passing the Earth on a regular trek across the cosmos, and never so much as batted an eye at us, an inferior race. Looking now through the glass windows aboard the spaceship, I wondered if a boy from Earth was looking up and seeing us moving, navigating the space of the universe. I wished to tell him it was all for nothing but to do it anyway.

At some point, the hypnotic line lights of the planets passing by put me to sleep. Red hollow clouds hovered across the room and endless meadows made of rosy fields stretched out to the horizon. A figure stood in the sunken valley at the center. From so far away, it appeared as a young oak tree at the onset of its long, weathered life. Driven by the urgency of the dream's end, I ran toward it. I always ran toward things and figured out if I had the legs for it later. I sprinted down the hill to uncover the mysteries of my subconscious. When I came closer, the oak tree's roots became her legs, its branches, her arms.

I don't know why, I surrendered in her embrace. Her eyes latched onto mine, and the connection was enough to pull me up. I knew then I would never fall down, not completely, as long as she breathed. My connection to the world, to the universe, and every living thing—Luna. My right hand curled in her left, my left hand fell on her right hip, her right hand behind my neck. We stared at each other for no other reason than because we could, because whether this moment was real, a higher power had allowed it. We had been separated before, but here no one dared to say a word in fear of a sound interrupting the moment.

My hands moved to her neck, my thumbs at her cheeks. I guided her face up to mine and kissed her. Assassin. Human. Angel. All of her. I gave in to the possession, my heart on the verge of exploding. My skin beamed with the blue aura of life and enveloped my body. When we kissed, the light crossed to her skin, and we were bound. We knelt on the fields and our aura sparked a fire over the meadow. The pinkish grass around us turned brown, then black.

I kissed her neck, and it electrocuted my lips. She pushed away, worried she might hurt me. I pulled her back to me, reassuring her I embraced the risk and welcomed the pain. The clouds had their fill of passion, and acid downpoured over us.

Then the sun disappeared, and a streak of moonlight illuminated her, and memories of events that I had never lived flashed across my mind. An ambush. Swords clashing. Death. The smell of blood. A wave of danger crashed over me. I wanted to run away, to escape certain death, but before I moved an inch, Luna appeared in front of me, covering her stomach. There was a growing red circle larger than her hands.

"No!" I said.

Her voice called out to me in a whisper. "Robert, please. Let me go. I need to die. It's in the prophecy. No matter what, I die."

I heard her words but rejected them. "You're the only connection I've ever felt to anyone and anything, ever. I will not let you go. Without you, I'm—"

Blackout. Thunder.

She was now on the ground with her eyes shut, motionless.

I hurried my hands to her body, hoping my aura would do something to her, as it had done to her bracelet on the bookstore's roof. I wanted to set her free from the prophecy's restraints.

Thunder. Darkness. Thunder. Darkness.

She lay still, mouthing soundless words. "Robert. Stop. Let me die."

The more the dream muted her voice, the more I strained to bring her back.

A force pulled my body back away from her, and in time, I could no longer reach her. The more I fought, the more the force pulled me farther away, away from the darkness and into the thunder.

My journey back to forced consciousness took me to this strange vessel floating in the black sea among the stars. After some time acting as the universe's spectator, I regained control of my body. Raphael was smiling, urging me to look at the front glass. It was then that I saw a yellow marble that slowly grew into a sphere.

"Colonia," Raphael's voice resonated in my mind. "Our home at the doorstep to the Ancestor. Is it not beautiful?"

It was like a sun I could stare directly into. Its light, somber and pale, yet powerful, mesmerized me. My destiny awaited in that jewel sitting on a dark cloth, waiting to be appraised.

The blue-eyed man stood, and the one with black hair took command of the ship.

"My son, our creation. Soon you will understand your purpose, your power. We created you in our image, and so in our Ancestor's image. Only you have the strength to open the door to him, but we shall give you the key, the knowledge of your lineage. May your path nurture your strength." He turned to the front glass when the spacecraft broke the atmosphere. His voice changed slightly, as if put off by the fire. "Let me begin by formally introducing myself. My name is Michael, the true Archangel. You have met Raphael. And he is Gabriel. We do not expect you to trust us blindly, but in time, you will see."

The craft hovered before landing softly over the golden terrain. I stepped out behind them, free, yet restrained, as though my only movements were the ones within their approval. In one moment, I wanted to incapacitate them and run away, but the thought evaporated, and a second, more powerful one, replaced it. In that second thought, all I wanted to do was bow my head and follow their orders. It brought me a great joy to do so.

"This way," Michael said as if there was another way.

I was not a guest here, that was obvious. Raphael and Gabriel pulled me forward by either arm. There was no escape.

We had landed close to a building which was protected by a tall concrete barrier the length of its perimeter. When we were in front of the barrier, Michael stood in front of a door and inserted his arm in a round slot by its side.

One thing about dreaming of being a writer was my proclivity of sinking in other people's works. I wanted to not only read their magnum opus but also their biographies. I wanted to know what made them tick, what path had led them there. To know they had endured insecurities and failures put me to sleep at night. If I juxtaposed my life over theirs and our failures stacked, perhaps the best for me was yet to come. I read even more when I inherited the bookstore. Everything, from fiction to nonfiction, memoirs to gardening, pharmacology to psychology. Learning how things worked and why became an obsession. In Jungian psychology, there was this thing called the Shadow. According to Jung, everyone possessed a Shadow, and it was of the greatest importance to find it within yourself and learn to control it. Most people went through life without this knowledge, being pushed to do horrible things by not controlling their Shadows, or living an uneventful life by not finding it within themselves.

The mechanism unlocked, and the door opened. And inside, the Shadow was on full display. It slithered on the ground, biting the legs of visitors and infecting them with its venom, its venom splattered on the walls from all the previous victims it had clawed into. It polluted the air and infiltrated one's lungs; if a person entered this place, it would mark them forever, for this was not a building, but a factory. A factory of humans.

. . .

Humans grouped into sets of fifteen were leaving one section of the building and entering another. There were groups of various ages: children, teenagers, and adults, fifteen boys and fifteen girls per group. On closer inspection, the males were all identical to one another, and so were the females.

"Take your shoes off, Robert," Gabriel said. He placed his laced black shoes on the concrete edge and walked over to the grass with his eyes closed. A child's grin overtook his face. "Let it sink into your skin."

Ahead on the concrete path stood the tallest skyscraper I had ever seen. The building must have been hundreds of stories high. Its weathered stone walls seemed to stretch out a mile in every direction. It looked like a pillar extracting life-force from Heaven itself.

I turned back to face the grass, bending at the waist to take my shoes off. The firm blades of grass poked at my feet, and a displaced rush of joy overcame me. My eyes closed on their own. A pure bliss that took me on a flashing journey. At once, it transported me to Europe, where I exiled myself after I quit college. I walked over the plains of Scotland and hiked over Scandinavian mountains. I hadn't thought of that period of my life in years, but for no apparent reason, it now consumed me whole. The energy of my twenties merged with the wisdom of my thirties and beyond. It was as if I had momentarily ascended into another plane of existence.

"Shall we?" Gabriel said. His voice brought me crashing back to wherever the hell I was.

After putting our shoes back on, we walked towards the giant skyscraper at the center of the compound.

"What is this place?"

"The Ancestor called upon us in the first reset," Michael said from behind us. He had been observing Gabriel and me with a strange patience, like a scientist observing a rat in a lab. "He gave us responsibilities. And in the process of repopulating Earth with its creatures, we learned to manipulate genes to our liking. Genes are the switches that bring forth your unique light. We flicked one of them and got an entirely different subspecies. It became our obsession to create a perfect human, one who modeled the Ancestor in every way possible." We were well underway toward the main building when he continued, "But on our way to perfection, we created mistakes. Control groups, if you will."

"Now the control groups live here, training, tending to the soil, keeping things running while we are away," Raphael said with a smile, and the atrocity of his words seemed to pass through me like a gentle breeze.

I got a feeling in the pit of my stomach that when they were done with me, there would be an infinite number of my copies plowing the land, sweeping the floors, providing maintenance for their mother ship. I wanted to question it, to call out the sins they were committing, but all my defensive energy drifted away and his words became reasonable. In a matter of seconds, I was almost nodding to the three men, as if this was normal and if I stepped into their shoes, I would have done the same thing.

We made it into the building. Inside, its quiet atmosphere and clean, white walls reminded me of a museum. Its shiny marble floors whined as we walked over it.

"The buildings have many floors. Each floor has a name and a purpose. This, for example, is the Cenotaph," Gabriel said.

"Who was it built for? For what war?"

Raphael jumped in with an answer. "The Great War, the *only* war, of course. Everything else is a distraction."

They led me to the second floor. There were elevators, but we took the stairs to the second-floor hallway. Several closed doors hung like vertical paintings on satin black walls that made the doors look like bloody slits in space. There were crystals at the top of each door, and one of them turned green. A row of children walked out of the room and passed right by us, never batting an eye. On their wrists, steel bracelets illuminated a green pulse.

"Now it's their turn to step on the grass," Gabriel said. "Here, it is mandatory for our children to play."

"Why?"

"Humans need to play. We learned that the hard way. They need their time in nature to become one with all things alive. Or else they lose their humanity and revert to barbaric creatures."

Gabriel opened a door on the far side of the hall and held it open for the rest of us. Fortunately for him, I had the urge to jump right into things that scared me. Whatever my preconceptions were, I did not expect this.

Plain blue walls adorned the room. It was what was in front and center which shocked me. In rows of six, glass cylinders filled the seven-hundred-square-foot room. Inside each cylinder, a torso floated in an aqueous solution, connected with cables to a central circuit board in the ceiling. The torsos looked bloated; their bellies distended —pregnant. Outside of the cylinders, a monitor displayed vitals in a way not too different from what I saw in Earth's hospitals. All the cylinders had a ramp at an angle at the bottom. All the ramps disappeared into a slit on the ground.

"Let us witness a miracle," Raphael said.

I couldn't say no.

A torso expelled what appeared to be a ball through the bottom. In seconds, a baby appeared on a tray, rolling slowly down the ramp and into the slit on the ground. I looked back up to the torso and watched it go from full to slim to full again.

"The miracle of life," Gabriel said, proud of it. "We get to experience it, and we have humans to thank for it."

Gabriel glanced at Michael, who stared at him with a stern look.

"Right," Gabriel said. "Let us continue."

If this was the introduction, I was afraid of what was waiting for us at the conclusion.

We walked back down to the Cenotaph, my legs shaky and my head spinning.

The row of children was now coming in. Their faces didn't look any better than before. Maybe they hadn't played enough. They went up the stairs right by us in silence, as if we weren't there.

Gabriel led us to an enormous wall on the first floor. The wall had the drawing of a maze with squares on it. As we approached it, the squares became plaques with pictures and names below each face. The lines connecting those plaques formed the maze.

"The lineage," Gabriel said, presenting it with one hand and placing the other one behind his back. He admired it.

I chose a starting point and followed it, looking for Michael, or a name I might recognize. The start of the line was in the center. A plaque of a man looked human, but that surprise wasn't as big as the name under the picture. *Jesus Christ, Nazareth, Israel.* My hands shook. I followed the line. It went through the centuries of history, passing through the Vikings and the stoics, shamans, and lost civilizations. My throat dried when I knew I was approaching the end of the maze. The last plaque was larger than the rest—there was no doubt. Embedded in a black stone plaque, the name read, "Robert Cohen, Williamsburg, Virginia."

CHAPTER 13

ROBERT

They took me away from the Cenotaph before I articulated any question. "All in time," was all that they said. I nodded like an idiot, like their words were my gospel, and meant it. That overwhelming feeling to please them came over me again, and again I failed to control it. One thing kept popping into my mind as we walked down the halls and stairs and out of the building: these beings not only looked human but lived as humans. They walked as we walked, talked as we talked; their buildings resembled our buildings. According to them, they had created me for a higher purpose. But if they breathed as humans, did they also err as humans?

We had made it to the compound's entrance. My general distrust for anything outside myself battled with my newfound inclination to obey. The one called Michael seemed distant, his face worried. He had stepped outside the building and now stood, waiting. Raphael motioned his head at Gabriel and headed toward Michael.

"I am aware it was a lot of new information," Gabriel said. "What you should be concerned with, for now, is that we have worked tirelessly for millennia to make you. You are of supreme importance to us, to the course of life itself. Every stone in the lineage's river was a learning lesson. With every iteration, we carefully modified the outcome. We removed unnecessary abilities, introduced new ones, mixed our own DNA with what was available in yours. Humans can unlock the Ancestor within them, if they could focus enough. We gave you a mind capable of such focus."

He waited for a response. "I wish I had my manuscript with me," I said, de-escalating the seriousness of this dreamlike reality.

Gabriel let out a chuckling exhale. "Allow us to show you how to focus. Once you see what you are capable of, everything will become clear. Nothing else will matter."

We approached the other two.

"He is ready," Gabriel said.

Michael stared at me. "Is he?"

A tingle that disconnected my mind from my body traveled through my arms and legs, then crawled back up my shoulders. "He is," I said. In the place in the back of my mind, where I was still myself, I knew I wasn't.

They walked me to a beach outside the building. Blue Field, they called it, a recreation of Earth's oceans made of synthetic sand and artificial salt water, and commanded me to stand before the waves. The sand crunched beneath my feet, and I obeyed their every request.

"This is where our humans swim," Gabriel said, his eyes intent on the water.

Michael waited by the side. He was growing more impatient by the second, as if this initiation was not only unnecessary, but ridiculous. Raphael approached him and whispered, and the two hung back in silence.

"An ascended human," Gabriel continued, "must not only swim, but walk on water, divide it in two and forge paths anew, if he must. Nothing stands in his way. Before you may open a portal, you must learn to control nature at your will. That which you think must also be. Therefore, the energy that emanates from your mind must also merge into the world and alchemize thought into existence."

Imagine and it will become real. I pictured the waves turning sideways and carrying water apart to either side, revealing a sand floor with rocks and crabs and sea urchins. I shook my head when nothing happened.

Gabriel stepped forward. "Try again. There must be no insecurity. If you can think it, believe it must be true."

I complied. This time, instead of straining, instead of imagining a translucent ghost arm coming out of my body and into the world, moving things for me like a construction crane, I simply closed my eyes and called out to my muse as if I was entering my dream world to extract a scene for a story. Reciting Homer's prayer to the Muse in my head—as written by Pressfield—I transported myself to a shadow copy of this reality.

O divine Poesy!

Goddess, daughter of Zeus,

Sustain for me this song of the various-minded man,

Who, after he had plundered the innermost citadel

Of hallowed Troy, was made to stray grievously

About the coasts of men,

The sport of their customs, good and bad,

While his heart, through all the seafaring,

Ached with an agony to redeem himself

And bring his company safe home.

Vain hope! For them! For his fellows he strove in vain.

By their own witlessness, they were cast aside.

To destroy for meat the oxen of the most exalted Sun,

Wherefore the sun god blotted out the day of their return.

Make this tale live for us in all its many bearings, O Muse!

There was a sea in front of me. I was barefoot, my toes digging into the abrasive sand. I felt the warmth of the sun and smelled the salt in the air evaporating from the water. Once I felt inside of the scene, I carried out my story. This wasn't an imagined thought, but me bending my reality at will. I was the master, and everything else, my playground. Another thought reigned king in the back of my head. If what they said was true, and I was who they said I was, then my only way out of here was to harness this potential into a weapon I could wield against them. It was the only way I might find her again. Luna. How does one find a person across the universe when finding one constrained to one planet seems impossible? No time to jump ahead. My engineer father always said: break large problems apart into the smallest viable tasks and ask yourself, "What's next?" What was next was to deliver to them the portal creator by displaying my so-called powers and, somewhere along the way, turn it against them.

I returned my attention to the sea coming apart in the middle, its two sides forming perpendicular walls as tall as the eyes could see. I approached it with a confidence I had never once felt in my life. Walking on the sea floor, I looked up to the sides. The walls seemed to stretch so high that one could swim straight into Heaven. Sea creatures ventured to the edge of the wall, then turned back to safety. Sharks, whales, and fish looking outward at the strange being who had broken their home in two. Gabriel clapped his hands behind me. For a moment, my struggle and the scattered manuscript of my life came together, forming a sculpture from its broken-off, blood and tears smeared pages, and converging into a future I could have never dreamed of. My headstrong stubbornness had paid off, and no one was here to see it. I marched to the other side of the ocean, making progress rapidly across the sand road, and contemplated on the great authors, questioning if this was what they felt when they crafted their masterpieces. Not writing, no, but creating a reality with each letter, each word; every sentence, a discovery of a new hidden power, unknown even to them. I reached the end of the path and turned around. The three Archangels looked at the ocean split in half. And from that moment forward, my life and my imagination would be one, and what I saw in my mind would not be the remnants of fantasies, but reality waiting to happen.

Michael floated toward me between the two ocean halves. He hovered freely, arms crossed, never looking at his sides. With a motion of the hand, the wave walls behind him came crashing down, covering the path. By the time he had arrived at my side, the ocean was an ocean again. We stood at the shore opposite to where we had started.

"Beautiful, is it not?" Michael said. "Humans regard their environment as something to contend with, when, in reality, it is all a life-force that emanates from the same source. Animals, humans, plants, planets, universes. It is one and the same. You hurt it, you hurt yourself. You master yourself, you master it. Homeostasis." He floated toward the ocean, hovering over the water, his body casting a pulsating shadow over it. His wings stretched, strong and controlled. He let himself drop slowly on the ocean's surface and coiled his wings. With an outstretched hand, he said, "Come."

I approached hesitantly, staring at silhouettes of gigantic sea creatures swimming beneath our feet. Water wobbled like hardened gelatin under every footstep. During moments of insecurity, the gelatin softened and converted back to water, and great whites and other opportunistic creatures sprinted to the top. There was no room for disbelief. In the middle of a sea full of hungry animals with sharpened teeth ready to devour, one false step meant death. Michael walked straight ahead without speaking, as if he was taking a meditative stroll through a park. I watched him, tried to imitate him, every once in a while turning my gaze to my feet and remembering where I was. The beasts followed us, swimming in pirouettes at our feet, hoping for one of us to fall through the thin layer that separated us. I knew how to handle people expecting me to fail. Faced with adversity and mockery, the trick was to use that energy as the fuel that extinguished them, their tiny existence shrinking into oblivion. I erected my stance, imagining a string pulling me up from my head. There were no animals, there was no ocean, there was only a goal ahead. I simply walked.

CHAPTER 14
ROBERT

The three men took me to a place outside and pointed at a concrete slab on the floor. Strange hieroglyphs and letters of an unknown language adorned the stage. I stepped on it and a slight smile escaped Michael's stern face. Gabriel turned to Raphael, an unconcealed smile forming across the two.

"Think of the sky, not as a door, but as an ocean you must part," Michael said. "There are no stars, no astral bodies in your way, only an open tunnel."

I stretched my hands at the sky, and the symbols at my feet illuminated in red, blue, and green, then rotated, merging its colors and forming yellow, orange, and purple hues around me. The lights embraced me in their warmth, and my smile mirrored theirs because I felt a part of something—my existence useful to someone.

The voices of two people resonated in my head. The first one came from my mother's mouth during my childhood. "You can't do it," she had said, taking the small plastic spoon from my hand and feeding me. It was my first memory, and the one that kept invading my thoughts throughout my life. Every time I faced a new challenge, there it was, echoing from the deepest chambers of my brain.

The second voice materialized from my subconscious. When I

smiled, and saw the three beings smiling with me, I heard the voice of Aleksandr Solzhenitsyn. I had never heard his voice, but I imaged its sound when I read The Gulag Archipelago. In all his wisdom, he had written, "The line separating good and evil passes not through states, nor between classes, nor between political parties either—but right through every human heart—and through all human hearts. This line shifts. Inside us, it oscillates with the years. And even within hearts overwhelmed by evil, one small bridgehead of good is retained." I saw that line cutting through me, escaping my body, and traversing Michael and his brothers' center, splitting them in half, one half building a human factory, playing with humans on Earth as if they were mice in a lab; the other taking me in and believing in me, giving me the spoon and encouraging me to try.

Electricity poured out of me and into the universe, causing a rift at the edge. A mixture of ecstasy and nostalgia clouded over me, its struggle turning into tears that blurred my vision. They had faith in me, and I delivered. But soon it would all be over, my purpose fulfilled, my place in the Master Plan done. All things come to an end, and so would I.

A surge of energy melted away the warmth of the lights dancing at my feet, the intensity of it enough to keep me from opening the portal. Standing in the valley of sand below was a demonic figure engulfed in flames, and it looked at me. I knew that look, that intent to kill.

PART 5

CURRENT COLONIA

"Are you a happy person?" the interviewer had said. After a long silence, "Pol, are you still with me? I think we lost him. Pol?"

"Entertained? Sure. Distracted? Most certainly. Happy? No. I'm not happy. But neither are you, nor your listeners. There is strength in not knowing your weakness. Confidence in not knowing you march gleefully toward slaughter. To be truly happy, you must first be free. And to be free, you must first be honest. And no one wants to be honest. Honesty builds a future while destroying the present as it is."

"Yeesh," said another voice in the phone call.

"All right. No, that's all right. So what you're saying is... you know what? I haven't had my cup of coffee yet. Can you explain to the listeners what you mean?"

"Well, it's simple, really. Just walk to your nearest supermarket, gas station, or simply look at the car next to you at a stoplight. They're either staring at a phone—distracted—or singing along to the radio— entertained. The ones bawling their eyes out or staring into the horizon. Those are the honest ones. Those are the ones on the verge of freedom, and ultimately, happiness. But the way from honesty to happiness is such a painful and lonely one, most turn back and rush to the embrace of comfort."

"And how about you, Pol? Why aren't you happy? What's stopping you from being honest?"

"My honesty is scattered all over my lyrics. I'm already honest, as honest as the world allows me to be."

"Ok, then. What was the next thing—"

"Freedom," said the other voice on the call.

"Right, right. What's stopping you from being free?"

"The answer to that question is the one thing I'm after."

"Well, ladies and gentlemen, you heard it here first on the Lowkey and Avery show. Pol will be on tour starting next month, tickets on sale next Saturday with pre-sale code: HAPPY, that's all caps. Go see him live, help him find freedom," Lowkey's voice deepened, "so that he can finally be happy," and back to his normal tone, "Great talking to you, Pol."

"Ok."

Click.

The conversation seemed a lifetime ago now, stepping foot with an angel named Sarah on the yellow lands of the planet Colonia. Life had been easy on Earth. Surely he had been happy. How could he not? Everyone else was struggling with things that for him were not even worthy of a thought. If Maslow's Hierarchy of Needs was correct, people lived their entire lives in the red, lower level, while he had dug his way out to the top with surprising ease. Yet nothing stopped the ever-expanding black hole in his soul. It was as if, for him, the hierarchy was upside down, and the more he achieved—the more he accrued—he was not climbing to the top, but digging himself deeper into a burning core full of lava and scolding heat; he thought he had been carving a tunnel to Heaven when his efforts were taking him to Hell.

"Are you ready?" Sarah said, snapping his mind back into his body.

"For what?"

"To execute your path, human."

"Do you think I am ready?"

"Fear not. All we need is our faith."

"It is like this, human," Sarah had said in Derinkuyu. "Fire can burn a city to the ground, turn settlements into ashes, laughter into pain, buildings into ruins. But it can also be the warmth with which a man survives a cold winter, the flame upon which a man discovers the dangers lurking in the night. It can bring as much sorrow as joy. What matters most is the vessel, the hand that wields it. That is why you must learn to turn the curse of your genes into a favor, the fractures of your past into openings in which you can plant seeds and grow an oasis. Every situation, every conflict, is only a chance to display your use of perception. Allow me to demonstrate." She dashed toward him with one arnis stick over her head. "Choose your move, human."

Pol clenched his hand into a fist, and fire formed around it. He swung his hand back and catapulted the fire toward Sarah, who ducked it, slid in front of him and struck his legs with the stick, taking him down with one blow.

"Wrong move," Sarah said. "Stop reacting, visualize the next move, and the next. Do not think you can do it, but believe it. Have faith." Sarah resumed her initial position. "Try again." She rushed toward Pol, rolling the stick over her head. Pol bent to protect his legs from the attack, but Sarah kicked the ground and used his shoulders as a step to jump over him. She appeared behind him, hitting the back of his knees and weakening his legs.

He fell to the ground, let out a frustrated scream, and turned to Sarah, his hands already on fire.

Sarah jumped back and straightened her relaxed body. "You are reacting again, letting your rage get the best of you." She closed her eyes. "Know you can win. Try again."

Pol wasn't listening. He swung bursts of fire at her, which she ducked with ease without looking. When he was right next to her, she kicked his chest with a spin.

He fell back, unable to breathe. Pol pushed his body up, trying to catch his breath.

"Relax," she said. "Be resourceful with your energy."

Instead of trying to force his breathing, he allowed it to come on its own.

"Good," Sarah said. "Perhaps we try again tomorrow."

"No. One more time."

Sarah grinned. "Very well. Are you ready?"

Inhale. Exhale. "Yes."

She gained speed toward him. This time, she rolled the stick from hand to hand, around her back and over her head again.

He closed his eyes and saw without seeing. He heard every swing of the stick, every change in the airwaves. Her footsteps were louder, the sound of the stick raising and lowering as she moved it around her body. A slight moment of silence told him she was gaining momentum to prepare for a strike, and when the air changed again, he felt the stick coming down. Pol stepped aside when a slight breeze landed on his arm. He sensed her missing her shot and trying to regain her balance. He grabbed the stick, and it went in flames, disintegrating from existence. Pol opened his eyes to Sarah with a look of shock on her face.

CHAPTER 16

SARAH

Sarah pulled on Pol's shirt and pushed him against a dune.

"What are they doing this far out in the desert?" Pol said.

Two patrolmen marched out, speaking into their bracelets.

"We are in position," one said. "Nothing but clear skies."

The second patrolman sat and leaned his rifle on his leg. "What are we looking for, anyway?"

"They said to stay vigilant and keep our eyes up." He kicked the other one's feet. "Stay vigilant. Keep your eyes up."

Sarah followed their gaze to the sky, then said, "No."

"What are you doing?" Pol hissed when she came off the sand wall.

"I am afraid our time together is coming to an end faster than I had anticipated. Let this be your final lesson. When the path calls, we do not hesitate. We answer."

She rushed out into the open, her hands outstretched in the desert air. "We are here. We have arrived."

The patrolman who had been sitting grabbed his rifle with his hands at the trigger and grip, perfectly positioned for a shot. He aimed at Pol first, who had made himself known following Sarah's display. The patrolman shot at Pol and took him down while the other approached Sarah.

"Are you—"

"I am. I am the one you are looking for," Sarah said. "Luna, daughter of angel and human."

The patrolman tossed a bracelet to the other. "Seize them before the other one wakes up."

He grabbed the bracelet. "What is so special about her? Why can't we kill her?"

Pol was waking up, and both Sarah and he were about to march out of the desert guided by the two patrolmen when a strange roaring noise filled the sky.

Sarah tried to release herself from the patrolman's grip. In front of her, the second man had Pol in a hammerlock. She threw her neck up. "No," she said, her eyes pointing at a falling meteorite and a second light rising to meet it. "It is too soon. We are not ready."

"Quiet," the patrolman said, his tense muscles almost bulging out of his black uniform.

Then, in a single motion, Sarah outstretched her arms and released herself from the man's grip, pushing him to the ground. She closed her hand in a fist and motioned it forward. A blue ray of light shot out of her palm, missed Pol's custodian by an inch, then disappeared into the sky. She crumbled to the ground in the aftermath, as if her life had left her body.

The man rose quickly with emasculated anger. He clamped his hands on Sarah's arm, his strength leaving red marks on her skin. "Get up."

Pol tried to escape but was too weak to break free. "Let her go," he howled.

Sarah looked at Pol, a light purple circle had formed around her eyes, and breathed. "Remember your faith. Everything you need is already in you."

Sarah's words transformed the patrolman's arms into the fences that trapped him in the orphanage as a child. He remembered watching helplessly from under a nun's embrace while his father walked away and everything the broken image took with it. He reached for the gate, as he did every morning with boyish hope, to stand on a bar and lean over the gate. The nuns found him there, neck stretched as far as it would go, just to see if his father was walking his way. He fantasized that the whole thing had been a mistake, that his father only needed a few days to get sober, that this was a temporary pain. Little did he know that if he would have stepped over the gate, he could have escaped. This time, he stepped over the bar; he kicked his leg over it; he escaped.

Pol saw it clearly before it happened. His body scorching to the touch, the patrolmen letting him go without him moving an inch, then him grabbing him by the neck, raising him up to the sky with one hand, melting the flesh on his neck until his jugular exploded. The other one, in shock, trembled a tranquilizer dart into the gun he forgot to reload. And Pol, letting the lifeless body fall limply from his hand, turned in his direction. With no rush, no hope, only certainty, Pol marched toward him. He had left Sarah unattended while he tried to shoot at Pol, who was coming in like an intense eclipsed sun, whose darkness he couldn't look at for more than a second without his irises burning.

The patrolman removed his glasses, his eyes fuming. He cried in pain, "What are you?"

"I am your Hell," Pol said, and with a flick of his finger created a flame under the patrolman's feet that climbed up to his head and consumed him. In seconds, his life ended with the sound of crackling flesh and despair.

Pol was used to Sarah's face getting rid of his possession. He walked toward her, knelt, and held her. She grimaced at his touch, his hands still endowed with fire.

"I can't turn it off," Pol said. He tried to release her, but she held on to him, the skin on her fingers opening up to the bone. "I can't stop it, you'll—"

"A monster with two heads, twins sprouted from the same

genetic seed. It is almost prophetic that only you can stop him." She coughed up an aqua blue liquid. "I fulfilled my purpose, now the Path calls to you. Whatever you do, you must keep the door closed. He is the key, but you, Pol, you are the lock. Whoever wants to open the portal must first go through you."

"What are you talking about?" Pol lifted her. Her radiance glimmered on her skin like sunlight on the ocean's surface. Her scorched skin was still so obviously angelical. It felt almost wrong for him to be holding her, a life so indispensable that it made her death feel as if there had been a shift in the cosmos. It had put a reaction in motion and His plan was underway. Her body became translucent, then it wasn't a body at all but a million drop-sized fireflies forming her shape, and the same way a gust of wind scatters a pile of dust, the swarm of lights flew to Heaven like the smoke of a burning bush, their flight untangling her shape, one by one, until there was nothing left but air.

CHAPTER 17

POL

Pol stood up, his towering body casting a shadow over the ground where Sarah was laying, now the emptiest patch of dirt in the universe. He opened his hands in front of him, cursing the fire running through them. Blame brewed within him, firing from the pits of his soul, arching for its target. It almost hit him, but he had learned from a young age to place blame on things outside of himself. *The door*, he thought. There, he found another being that blame could puncture with its venomous claw.

A cloud of smoke rose in the distance. Whatever Sarah had spent her last energy shooting at had crashed. But when he started toward it, another, more intense itch drew him back—a shudder, a magnetism, an instinct, as if two unstoppable forces were about to clash. Pol sensed him, his infectious energy. When he turned to it, it was as if he was standing before himself. Reality was only but a mirror between images. Pol marched to it, his feet melting the dirt beneath him, and with each step forming pellets of dirty glass. Pol didn't know why he hated this energy so much, why, in an instant, the answer to the question posed in every one of his songs lay a few miles before him. The skin around his knuckles was so stretched from clenching, bone might, at any moment, break free from it. There was only one outcome that was acceptable to him, only one way to honor Sarah and set free the boy standing on the fence of that orphanage. To incinerate this energy and scatter its ashes into the wind.

There was a figure atop a flat dune. The figure's energy vibrated in a celestial harmony. If Pol hadn't witnessed her death, he would have thought it was Sarah standing there, arms outstretched, piercing the veil of the universe. For a moment, Pol's flames rescinded slightly. Hope humanized him, gave him a reason to fight the fault of his genes into remission. A lot had blurred the line between what was possible and impossible. But when he was close enough that the distorted silhouette focused into a strange man and not Sarah, his hatred burned deeper, this time reaching into the darkest corners of his psyche. Above the man, a growing opening had formed in the sky. "Whatever you do, you must keep the door closed," Sarah had said. The curtains had opened, the crowd had cheered for his presence. Pol aimed calmly at his target as if he was repositioning his microphone. He concentrated the rage of his abandoned inner child into his hand as if he was pressing on the strings of a dissonant chord, and, together with his strumming hand, released the melody of his fury.

A tunnel of fire reached the man and bounced off an invisible layer surrounding him. The man startled. Even inside his force field, he had felt it. He tried to ignore it, pushing more blue light into the opening. Pol had made an impact. The man was rushing. It was all the confidence Pol needed to approach the man—the key, as Sarah had called him—and visualize him melting to the touch of scorching heat.

Pol had lived a life of hiding, of burying pieces of him and leaving them as breadcrumbs for listeners who dared dig them up. He had hid them so well, that even if the path led to him, no one ever saw it. His fans jumped to the beat, cried about what they thought the lyrics meant, applauded his talent. His voice and the way he chained chords across the body of his guitar hypnotized them. But even the most faithful of listeners could only reach as far as the surface allowed. Knowing that this was it, that he was at the end of life and there was no point in hiding any longer, Pol opened up like a shell cracking so the animal inside could break free. It was the destruction of musical instruments at the end of the last song of the tour. Going out with a bang in a definite finale, Pol exploded, his dormant volcano erupting to the surface and burning off what was left of his skin and turning it into molten lava. His eyes blackened. The flames consumed his hair and clothes. Eyebrows, small, ascending embers of fiery light. Long, searing black gauntlets covered his hands. He was not human any longer but a walking Hell that projected a bright red and yellow light in the shape of a six-foot ethereal being.

Pol turned to the blue light and raised his arm. He opened his hand and aimed through the gap between his fingers. In a single motion, he blasted a blazing fire toward the Key. The force field protecting him disintegrated. One by one, the lights revolving at his feet died out, and he stood there in the open air, unprotected. Pol smirked at the destruction he had created. The Key stopped aiming at the stars and acknowledged Pol for the first time. He looked at Pol as if he had recognized him somehow.

"No! Do not stop, human," a voice screamed desperately, although barely audible from the distance. "We are almost there."

Three shapes that had been flying close to the opening, too far for Pol's eyes to see, approached him.

"What is this?" one with long, yellow hair said.

"Looks human, yet..." the other said.

The one in the middle crossed his arms. "Kill it." He turned away and flew toward the Key.

PART 6

CURRENT COLONIA

ROBERT

When I looked at him, it was as if I remembered someone I had never met, as if two memories had finally found each other, completing the two sides of a story. Michael and the others descended upon him. I was paralyzed, surely by Michael's doing. He left Gabriel and Raphael to take care of him and returned.

"We shall continue," he said. "Pay no attention. Nothing but a minor mishap. Concentrate on the task at hand."

My arms rose to the sky. The weapon was aimed, and all that was left was for me to pull the trigger. But the burning man's fate sequestered my attention, as if his hurt was my own. Gabriel and Raphael evaded his napalm projectiles with sufficient ease. They constricted him without touching him, then sent him flying and pounded his body to the ground. They were toying with him. Occasionally, the being took shots at me, but either Raphael or Gabriel intercepted them.

I shot at the opening. When I turned to face it, Michael had his hand open, palm facing me.

"Focus," he said.

I obeyed, though every few seconds I turned my gaze to the pit encircled with fire that had formed at the bottom of the desert. The being appeared to have studied the brothers' weaknesses, played their strengths against them. When Gabriel was about to constrict him, he spiraled, and the attack fell on Raphael. The being then used this opportunity to come at Gabriel from behind, burning a side of his body. I heard Gabriel's painful screams from here.

Michael forced my gaze toward the opening. It was now almost large enough for a person to go through.

"More," Michael said. "We are close." He looked at his brothers for a second, then faced the opening.

I fought his hold on me, every time becoming easier to force myself out of it. My body was learning Michael's strength; it was learning how to match it and surpass it.

The being had scorched Gabriel, who was now crawling on the ground, screaming, "I know what you are. You are the damned son, the mistake. How could we have missed this?" His flesh was rotting away by multiple severe burns. In time, he fell over on his back. His jaw opened. "Michael," he said, his raspy voice numbed down by his burning tongue and traveling through the air with ease. "Help." He stretched his hand toward Michael like an infant begging to be held. "Help, brother." It was the last sentence he ever spoke.

Michael hovered by my side, forcing my eyes to the portal with his hands. "Almost there."

Raphael rushed toward the demonic figure, his attacks unplanned, unsophisticated. The burning creature evaded them with ease, standing tall, confident in its victory. The scorching monster swatted away invisible attacks and marched forward until he was a foot away from Raphael. "Get away from me, you genetic mistake, nature's error," Raphael screamed. But it spurred the creature on, and before Raphael could do anything else, it grabbed Raphael's neck and instantly chewed through it with its fingers, decapitating Raphael. Raphael's head rolled on the ground, and when it stopped, its eyes were pointing upward, looking at me.

The sight of it stopped me from opening the portal.

Michael grabbed my shoulder. "It is not complete, human."

I shook him off and stepped out of the concrete slab. The demon tossed Raphael's body to the side and advanced toward me.

More than running toward each other, it felt as if an inevitable force pulled us together. We both knew our purpose was to stop each other, but I got a sense that neither of us knew why. He unleashed his fire. I met it with blue energy, and they canceled on impact. We were evenly matched. Blue and red, Heaven and Hell.

Michael went up to the opening. He attempted to force himself through it, but it proved too small for his size. He pounded at it in frustration, screaming bursts of power that escaped his body, as if he had been saving his full strength for whatever came after his journey through the portal.

A dark gray weather system had formed above us. Clouds so dense that they darkened the world. Every clash between the creature and me sparked an earthquake over the planet that shook all living things walking on it. Our struggle resulted in a clinch, his fire burning through my skin, and my blue aura restoring it as it melted.

"What are you?" I said.

"I was once a man named Pol. Now, I am your nameless, eternal punishment. All my life, I have been searching for my purpose. Guided by suffering, my path has led me here. I am the only one that can stop you. Your life ends with me."

I attempted to release myself from the grapple, but his energy seemed to increase with my efforts. I leaned into the struggle, putting all of my strength into it. He was hurting, even if he wanted to hide it. My aura was a spigot of water putting down his fire, but more flames sprouted from his skin as an effect. The bigger my faith in myself, the stronger his response.

"I see it now," I said. "I felt it in the fire and the first time I saw you. We come from the same place, you and I. Our ancestors do. Can you sense it?"

Flame and aura crashed into a purple mix of energy. He stared at the amethyst-colored vapor as if a miracle hypnotized him. He then shook his head and clamped his arms on mine, almost crushing my bones. "You are opening a portal that should remain closed. I cannot allow it. The Path asks that I make sure of it, and when the Path calls, we don't hesitate, we answer."

"I am," I said, my teeth gritting against each other, oxygen barely reaching my lungs. "But it is not me who wants it to happen. It's him." I motioned my face toward Michael. "Michael, the archangel. Yes," I said, struggling to form a sentence. "It is my blade forming a scar on the universe, but it's his hand who wields it."

He looked over my shoulder at Michael, who was trying to expand the portal with his power and failing.

"Maybe we should use our combined strength to work together instead of fighting each other."

He remained silent. In his eyes, punishment times infinity.

"A full-force attack. He will never see it coming. I have faith that you'll make the right choice." I released my hold on his arms, and he pushed me out of the way and concentrated his entire power in an attack, his body slowly metamorphosing into a human, and his power escaping his body and shooting up into the sky.

"What is this?" Michael said when he turned to the bright sphere of fire coming his way. He laughed at it. "Do you really think you stand a chance, a human against an archangel?" He straightened his body and put a hand behind his back and an open hand forward. He closed his eyes, and I felt an evil I had never felt before. The sphere crashed in his hand, but instead of damaging him, it split in half, either side flying past him and exploding into the universe's emptiness.

Pol lay next to me, naked and powerless. Michael hovered over us, stronger than ever. It disarmed me. His power seemed to run as deep as an endless well, unbound by any constraint, real or imaginary. Michael landed in front of me. "What a disappointment. I was not planning on killing you after you opened the portal. I was to offer you a seat on the throne next to me. We could have done such great things."

Pol's naked body sizzled on the ground, his chest rising and falling slowly. He didn't have long. I was glad he wouldn't see his sacrifice made in vain.

Michael was about to take a step forward when a shape came flashing next to me and landed on Michael's face, sending him flying across the desert. Hunched forward with a hand closed in a fist was the image of Luna.

PART 7

CURRENT ARVO

CHAPTER 19

LUNA

"Stay here," was all Luna said when they were a few feet from Lucifer's front door.

Ambrose stepped forward. "But, Luna—"

"Do as I say. This fight is mine alone." She turned to Ambrose. "It has been all along, and I recognize it now. No one else needs to die fighting it. I was too afraid to fight alone, too afraid to fail. I'm not afraid of that anymore. Whatever happens, don't come in."

Luna walked to the front door and placed a hand on the doorknob. She readied a knife in the other hand, holding it over her shoulder with its blade pointed down. After turning the doorknob as slowly as she could, she pushed the door forward, peaking in through each revealing inch. The house looked neat, organized, clean—empty. She kept her guard up and scanned the interior. At the far edge of the large living room was a chair with a large black blanket over it. Something moved underneath. She gasped and ran toward it. When she uncovered the object, she found her mother. Her mother's eyes were open as wide as humanly possible. Her head was shaking, her tied hands and feet jerking. Her muffled voice screaming under a cloth, and her eyes shifted to something else over Luna's shoulder. When

Luna turned, the towering figure of Lucifer, the Archangel of death, stood behind her.

"I saw what you did to C16. Show me. I wish to see the great power that was carefully bred and raised to destroy me." Lucifer kicked Luna in the stomach and she fell on her back. Lucifer looked at the sky with arms outstretched. "Is this it? Is this your secret weapon?" He walked toward Luna, who had rolled to her knees and was trying to stand up. "Perhaps you require some assistance?" He raised a hand, and Luna hovered over the floor, grabbing at her neck and gasping for air. "Where is that power now that you need it? Has He abandoned you when you need Him the most?"

Her mother whimpered, her face drenched in sweat and tears with strands of her jet-black hair glued to her face. Luna turned her gaze to her and closed her hand on a fist. A spark of new energy allowed her to move her body slightly against Lucifer's control, and Lucifer noticed, laughing at the attempt.

"Do you even know what you are fighting for, child? If only you understood. If only your brain were capable of it," Lucifer said. "I could end you in this moment and wait for the Ancestor's next conspiracy against my life a few resets into the future. But curiosity has a grip on me." He released Luna, and she dropped to the tiled floor. He then raised the other hand and Luna's mother floated in the air, still tied to the chair. "In the end, how alike are we? What would you do to save your ancestor from certain death? What would you do to save Istahar?"

Luna paused at the sound of the name; It was the first time she had heard it.

Lucifer squeezed his hand, and Istahar gagged under the cloth covering her mouth, her hands motioning desperately under the tied rope. "All we want to do is to help, is it not? We want the best possible outcome, but the best possible outcome requires sacrifice." He squeezed harder.

"Something isn't right. Stop this. Please, stop this," Luna said without looking at her mother. She ignored Istahar's muffled noises that screamed she was fighting for her life. The ticking time bomb inside of her took precedence. "I don't know what will happen."

Lucifer laughed. "Show us your power, child. Stop holding back."

"Lucifer, end this," Faith said from behind a table. "End this, now."

"Dear Faith, do you not understand it? We are dead, either now or a million years from now. It is over for us. I want to see, to witness how a piece of the Ancestor manifests when nested inside a human body. I once believed that the earthling created in my brother's image could stop her. But, of course, they banded together—the Ancestor wrote it so. Again and again, no matter what I tried, an unbreakable wall stopped it. In my wisdom, I conclude I should only worry about the things I can control. I can control where I die and when—I choose here and now. Come, child, come out of your shell." He squeezed even harder, the chair under Istahar breaking into a million pieces, her limbs falling to her side and twisted together like a wrung towel.

Luna locked arms around herself. "No, no." She shook her head and knelt. She rocked her body back and forth. "No."

"Some auditory motivation, perhaps?" Lucifer flicked his finger, and Istahar's cloth disintegrated.

"Luna, listen to me," Istahar said the second her lips were free. "No matter what happens, I love you. We love you, not because of what you do, but because you exist. Nothing will ever change that—" Lucifer's constricting force tightened, and she let out a scream that resonated through the walls and ceilings of the house like a chant in a chapel "—There's no need to keep holding it all in, you understand? Don't worry about me. Don't worry about unleashing your power and killing me in the process. I already had a life. Stand up, my love. It's OK. You can release the pain. You don't have to hold on to it any longer."

"Inspiring speech," Lucifer said. "Unfortunately, it did not work." He swung his hand to the side, sending Istahar crashing through a wall.

Luna's gaze turned to Lucifer. Daniel was escaping through the back door, but before leaving, he turned and locked eyes with her. He wiped his forehead, swallowed, and hurried out. She paid no attention to Daniel and instead pushed Lucifer backward without touching him.

His feet slid over the floor for a few feet. He looked more excited than afraid. "What is this? Is this all—"

Luna sent him flying through three sets of walls, the entire building shaking and almost collapsing from the demolition. She swayed her hand and removed the debris, uncovering Lucifer underneath. Before he spoke, she raised his body again and sent him flying through an exterior wall. She stepped outside after him. Every time he tried to retaliate, she reacted quickly, sending him farther away from the house. Luna smashed his body against a bolder, and a stream of blood came flowing from his smiling mouth.

"I had not felt this alive since I fought the Ancestor. I can see Him in you," Lucifer said as he wiped his mouth. He spit on the ground and pushed a wind of energy toward Luna.

Luna mirrored his move, and they struggled evenly over the Arvonian desert.

Lucifer opened his hand wider, increasing the attack's power. Luna didn't know how to control it. She mimicked his every move and moved Lucifer backward inch by inch until he landed next to the boulder. She raised him against the boulder, his feet hovering above the ground. Luna's power wave clenched at his neck like gripping hands. Luna was shaking, tears coming out of her eyes.

Sometimes a memory invades the mind of people about to commit a heinous crime.

"I don't like the name Lucifer for you. It sounds... evil," Luna had told Lucifer once.

"I had no say in it. It is the name The Great Ancestor gave me," Lucifer said.

"I will call you something else from now on."

"What will you call me then?"

"Absalon."

"Absalon? What is the meaning of that word?"

"It is Hebrew. We learned it at school in case our mission took us to Israel. It means father is peace."

"Is that what I am to you? A father?"

Luna shook her head and pushed through the now corrupted memory, piercing it with the proof of who he really was, what he really was, Lucifer, and strengthened her grip by inching her fingertips toward each other. Lucifer grabbed at his neck as if trying to rip invisible hands away from his skin. He then extended his arms to his sides, lowered his gaze to meet hers, and laughed. Luna elevated him higher in the sky. At the new height, Lucifer's mocking laughter sent echoes that bounced off Arvo's mountains, filled its terrain with vibrating terror, and returned to Luna with such disdain, that it seemed to flow through her.

Lucifer lowered his body to the ground against Luna's power. To Luna, Lucifer's descent looked like a crucified demon falling back into the fire pit from where he had spawned. "I have seen enough," Lucifer said. "You show promise, undeveloped promise. Perhaps in another life, another version of you will be ready to be called upon. But for now"—he pointed a hand at Luna—"I am afraid my time is yet to come."

"Now!" a voice said from behind the boulder near where Lucifer had landed. Ambrose and a pack of humans rushed toward Lucifer and, while a couple held him by his legs, and two more by his arms, Ambrose locked a collar around Lucifer's neck, and another human cuffed Lucifer's hand with an interlocked pair of bracelets.

Luna released her hand, her body both at ease and in shock.

"You didn't really think we were going to leave you alone, did you?" Ambrose said, smiling. "You're one of us."

Lucifer wrestled the humans off his arms and legs.

"Oh, no you don't," Ambrose said and pushed a button on a controller, and it sent an electrical shock to Lucifer, rendering him powerless. The humans cheered and raised their weapons to the sky. They hugged each other, celebrating their part in this victory. "We might not be as strong as you," Ambrose said, "but boy are we resilient." He turned to the rock and waved his hand. "Boys, bring them out!"

Two humans had taken hold of Lucifer's Redeemers and stripped them of their weapons.

"We found these two clowns outside the house and took their little gadgets, forced them to teach us how to use them. Turns out the devices work for everyone."

Luna smiled. "You humans really are something. Barbaric, sure, but perhaps that isn't such a bad thing at all."

Istahar squirmed on the ground close to them. Luna looked at her, then at Lucifer.

"Go," Ambrose said. "We have him under control." He laughed and shook his controller at Luna.

Luna rushed toward Istahar. "Mother?"

"You did it," Istahar said.

"We did, together. All of us."

Istahar turned her gaze to the humans, who were toying with the controller, zapping Lucifer at random. She chuckled. "The human spirit is as courageous as it is playful." She took breaks of labored breath between sentences. "When I go—"

"Don't talk like that. There's still time. There must be a way to—"

"Listen to me, Luna. There's not much time left. I can feel it. When I go, I wish to be laid to rest next to your father. They buried the captured Rebel Watchers outside of Armas, outside the school where these monsters raised you. I wish I had the honor of raising you myself, to give you all the love that I had to give instead of watching idly as fate carved you. I wish I could have protected you more." She touched Luna's shoulder. "But I think you turned out to be a fine woman." She smiled. "You'll be OK."

"Why? Why must I always lose?"

Istahar smiled. "Oh, Luna, my dear. Life is suffering. You haven't lost, you simply lived."

"Sometimes being alive feels like dying." Luna wiped away the tears with her forearm. She jerked away, frowning at the half-moon. "There it is, the damn birthmark that started it all. I wish I had never seen it. I wish I had never been born."

Istahar blinked slowly, her whole face giving in to her last great surrender.

"Mom. Wake up. Please, Mom. What do I do now? I don't know what to do."

"Now you finish what you started. You go and give them Hell," Istahar whispered with a slight grin on her face. "Only when all of them are gone, will we ever have rest."

"How can one unarmed person with no army possibly make a difference?"

"You must never lose hope." Istahar coughed, blood splattering on Luna's clothes. "Go to Jophiel's house, a bright red house in the city. There, you will find what you're looking for." Her face shifted as if a glow of life had poured across it. "I'm so, so thrilled to have seen you, talked to you, hugged you, my baby. I love you so much, and so did your father. We are so sorry to have brought you into this world, into this life. It's almost...over. Just a little bit longer. We will be with you... always..."

"Mom? Mom? Mom, wake up. Mom!" Luna's world was a blur. "Mom!" She put her forehead to Istahar's and rocked her still body until Arvo's sun had set on the horizon.

Ambrose and the other humans waited for this ritual to complete without interrupting. When Luna stopped rocking Istahar's body, he approached.

Ambrose removed his hat and placed it on his chest. "Luna, I'm very sorry."

Luna stared at the ground and said nothing.

"What should we do now?" Ambrose said.

"Find Faith."

"Then what?"

"It's only proper for their life to end inside the school where they created so much pain. Help me take them there."

Once at the school, Luna placed Istahar's body against a wall, but it slid and crumbled to the ground. She propped her up, as if she was rearranging a doll. "You should leave."

"We won't leave you here alone, not until we know it's safe," Ambrose said.

Luna turned to Lucifer, who was on the floor with his arms tied behind his back. "He can't hurt anyone anymore, I'll make sure of it. Now go, barbarian." She let out an unconvincing smile, and Ambrose nodded an unconvincing response.

Ambrose hugged Luna as soon as she stood.

"Pleasure," he said while patting her back.

She remained still and nodded when Ambrose broke the hug.

"OK, you heard the lady. Time to go!"

One by one the humans pressed on their bracelets and left, and the life of the room left with them. Ambrose was the last one, who just as he was vanishing, straightened his stance, saluted Luna, and smiled.

CHAPTER 20

LUNA

Before nightfall, Luna carried Istahar's body to the rebel Watcher burial grounds, which were nothing more than a dune over decomposing corpses outside of Armas, the walled-off city she had trained in to become an assassin. Alone after sending the humans off to Earth, she dug a hole in the dirt next to the mound, her fingernails packed with sand. She dug until she hit a rock. She should have stopped, yet kept clawing desperately at the hard stone, her nails shaving off on the abrasive surface and bleeding at the edges. The pain helped ease the weight stomping over her soul. Once her fingertips were red and raw, the nails shattered to a million pieces over the rock, she stopped, picked up her mother's body and brought it to the hole. She placed the bloodstained body over the rocky bed. Luna placed one of her knives in her mother's hands and brought them close to her chest so that she could protect herself in the afterlife, and her bleeding hand over her mother's face so that both could be together for all eternity, blood with blood.

Luna stepped out of the hole, knelt over the dug out dirt, and pushed it into the hole. The dirt slid heavily into the grave, as if protesting the goodbye, the last snapshot of what she had embarked upon this cosmic adventure for. She was planting the root of what was her, her origin, the reason for her existence, and with it, her past, everything she had or could have been. She pushed more dirt in. Istahar's body was almost completely covered. Istahar's eyes poked out in the spaces between the dirt, open and aimed at Luna. Luna stopped and a throbbing, buzzing pain scattered through her body. She shook her head and pushed more dirt in, covering her mother in her entirety. After the grave was level with the rest of the ground, all hope for this to reveal itself as nothing more than a dream vanished. She climbed the dune next to her. Beneath her, somewhere, laid the bones of her father. With both her parents six feet underground, she no longer had the constraints that allowed her a life of controlled autonomy. Faced with true freedom, she found herself paralyzed. She turned her gaze up to the stars. One loop closes, another opens. Her aim locked into place. She knew what she had to do.

From the high vantage point, she looked into the city, its lights already gleaming under the sunset. One house stood out, a red elevation among dull, adobe-colored squares. *Red means blood.* But she wasn't scared, as fear had died when there was nothing left to lose.

Luna turned and studied the building standing in front of her in all its evil glory. She counted the floors up to the Archive, and recounted her teenage escapades with her friends, now nothing more than ghosts preserved in memories like bacteria in a jar, memories she promptly shook off her mind. Next to the building, a black spire towered beside, so tall it almost scratched the atmosphere. From this tower, scientists and archangels had observed her like a lab rat in a maze. Now she stood before it, the rat that got away, the one that had burrowed her way to the exit. Its surface, the shiny mask of evil. Its windows, the eyes to a soulless center. She stared back, an empty vessel, and wondered if she would ever be whole again.

Determined to illuminate it as a firefly of the night, she marched toward her dark history. She placed her hand on the building's cold concrete. She put her ear to the walls to see if the echoes of her friends still somehow resonated from within, if by some miracle, her mother survived in some cosmic way inside the atoms of this place.

Inside, Lucifer screamed, "Luna, you do not have to do this!"

Luna approached the voice and knelt in front of them. Them. The ones who had lit the wick of this restless dynamite.

"Luna, listen to us. We can change, and with it, we can change the universe. Together," Faith said. Their hands cuffed and their bodies powerless, useless, almost... human.

Luna placed a hand on their shoulders. "You had your chance."

And now the incendiary path had led to this. One last explosion. One last fire to burn her past and cleanse her path like holy water. On a wall, a torch spit shades of red and orange light on their faces. Luna snatched the torch and moved it over the explosives she had gathered from the Archive.

"You always wanted to be cremated, Lucifer," Luna said and lowered the torch. The wick burned with fire and the fire consumed the wick inch by inch. "Wish granted."

"Absalon, you may call me Absalon. Remember?" Lucifer said.

The fire separated into little wick lanes, ending at explosives scattered on the surrounding floor.

Luna stood up and stared at him with pity. "No. I'll call you by your name. Lucifer." And with that, she turned back toward the exit. Their screams were like tiny needles that stung rhythmically, tattooing this reality. Luna, the Watcher, the assassin, fulfilling what they had trained her to do—to kill, mercilessly.

Luna marched out of Armas, down the dune, and into the city. Behind her, explosives went off one by one, adding to the consuming flames. Soon enough, the building crumbled to its demise. Groups of in-training Watchers waited for her, perfectly still, shooting glances at their bracelets, eager for their next order.

"You don't need those anymore. You're free to choose. Free to live. Go," Luna said.

A girl that resembled Luna at that age looked at the boy next to her, puzzled.

A boy pushed another one lightly and ran off, laughing, and the girl looked at Luna.

Luna smiled. "Go. It's OK."

People were coming out of their houses following the explosions. They pointed, screamed, and squinted their eyes at the spectacle.

"We are under attack!" one said, a child curled in fear behind his leg.

Luna shook her head. "No, you have been liberated." She pointed at the children, who were now loose and playful in the sand. "They will need parents. Make sure they're taken care of." She stared him down into a nod and continued on her way to the red house.

"Wait! Who are you?" the man said.

She turned. "I'm Luna, daughter of Samyaza and Istahar. Half-angel, half-human. The unredeemed sin."

Jophiel's red house looked like a raw chunk of flesh, alive among bland sand-colored structures. The door was unlocked, and Luna walked into the guts of her future, or perhaps another detour into an untold past. The home appeared serene, as if their owners didn't leave in a rush, but simply vanished. There was a wooden square table with two plates set with metal cutlery. Luna grazed her fingers on the porcelain, on the wooden table, then sat on the chair. *She was here. I know it. I feel it.* The bookcase in front of her was at a slight angle away from the wall. Luna approached the bookcase, and, before pushing it back into alignment, felt a cold breeze coming from the wall. She pushed the bookcase away from the wall to reveal a doorknob. She half-wished the doorknob wouldn't turn all the way, because if it did, she'd had to open it. To someone who was born and raised in lies, the insatiable search for truth never ended; the more one learned, the more it felt incomplete. Nothing stopped the doorknob from rotating a full circle and the door pulled from its frame. Ignoring the dark heed of warning, she crossed the threshold of light into the shadow.

A steep staircase led her into a basement. The smell of sulfur urged her to cover her face. She recognized the smell. Blood. Pain.

The trapped tragedy didn't just hang in the air, it lived there, suspended in a perpetual memory of suffering. Luna pulled on the chain hanging over the center of the room and a jolt of imaginary electricity shot through her body. Now in the light, a bed filled with a large brown stain in the middle drew her in. Close to the bed, curled up on the floor, was a pillowcase wrapped in a bundle, hollow in the middle—incomplete, its insides taken away. *It was here, wasn't it?* she thought, *in this room is where it happened.* She turned away from the bed and toward the steps. *What are we here for?* She scanned the basement for something else of significance. When she absorbed all the drops of painful history she could carry, she made her way upstairs.

The reason Istahar had sent her to this house emerged when she took the last step out of the basement. In front of her, hanging on the wall near a window, was a sword, flickering in the sunlight, calling out to her as loud as her destiny. Her hands twitched, hungry for the sharp weapon. Luna stepped in front of it, mesmerized by its beauty, its ability to kill. She pulled it from the hanger. In the sword, she found her own familiar weight; it was her, and she was it. Next to where the sword had been, hung a leather strap with a scabbard fitted for the sword. She wrapped it around her torso and slid the sword into its sheath. The weight on her back strengthened her. Now, all the suffering she had been carrying concentrated on a single point, a single direction, a single aim. No matter how hard she tried to rehabilitate from her path, it beckoned her once more. Kill.

Luna found the ship in the exact place where she had learned how to fly it.

"Now, go," she said to the Arvonian who had taken her there. "Live your life in peace."

Of course, after listening to Stanley's life story, she knew the words carried no meaning. For him, a mere citizen, his daily life would remain unaffected. He was a farmer and a street merchant. He would plow the land and dry the sweat of his efforts from his fore-head, unaware of the Archangels and their plot to control fate. His land was his world, his children, his universe. He only used his vehicle to visit his farm and bring his produce to market. He was older now, but he had overheard Jophiel say disturbing words many years ago, and, seeing Luna entering his house, had followed her. Stanley was his name, and he offered her not only a ride, but his life story.

Stanley had worked the lands since he had memory. He didn't remember, however, how he learned the skills or when, only that his desire to work was in his blood, his family's blood, and those of his neighbors. It was his only desire. He also said he had a recurring nightmare, a cold room with dazzling lights overhead and two doors at his feet. He said he could sometimes, if he tried hard enough, look around the room and see glass incubators with babies resting inside them. Then he saw himself and realized he was a baby, too. The dream always ended the same way: at some point, the surrounding people would grab the incubators and roll each one through one of the two doors. He would always go through the door on the right, into the blinding light of wakefulness.

"Are you sure you know how to fly that thing?" Stanley said.

"I'll figure it out." She pressed a lever, and a ramp lowered from the spacecraft. The interior was so intact that she could easily project herself and Lucifer sitting at the controls. She was about to pull the lever from the inside to close the ramp when Stanley approached.

"Jophiel was a good person. We never had a real interaction, but I could tell. Here, take this. Jophiel paid me once with it, said to hang on to it, said it was more valuable than money, but I have no use for it."

Luna grabbed the folded paper from Stanley and pulled the lever, and, as the ramp finished its ascent, nodded.

She made her way to the flight deck and sat on the pilot's chair.

The takeoff sequence has three stages. First, power up the aircraft.

The aircraft hummed.

Wait until it has reached full power, then slightly pull on the yoke.

It levitated from the ground.

Now, push the craft forward.

It inched forward.

And pull on the yoke, ascending at an angle.

It shot up toward the sky, into the atmosphere, and away from Arvo until the only thing visible was the burning Watcher Development Center, and everything and everyone that ever was, until that too shrunk into a blob of purple nothingness.

The aircraft hovered in space. She had not prepared for everything going according to plan. Luna scanned the three glass windows in front of her, out into the expanding, silent sea of a million lightbulbs.

The screen in front of her displayed a blinking cursor, prompting her for directions. She was the crystal, and the ship the bracelet. She typed in *Colonia*. After a few moments, the machine beeped in rejection.

A fist to the screen, a kick to the floor. "Stupid machine! What do you want? Just take me there."

The paper Stanley had given her fell on her lap. She unfolded it to reveal a series of block letters and numbers. The machine kept buzzing and flashing in front of her. Luna placed the piece of paper next to the screen and typed in its contents. After the last number, the entire ship went dark. In the blackout, the only thing visible was a blinking cursor on the screen, and Luna gasped, waiting in terror for the cursor to type in the words *You've won!*, and turn this flight into another trap, another level in the Watcher Development Center, another descent into Hell. Instead, the ship hummed as if concentrating its energy for the ultimate blast. Metal handcuffs broke out of the armrests and wrapped around her wrists. Then, a mechanical arm descended from a hidden compartment in the ceiling. She tried to pull her hands out from the cuffs, but the fit was too tight. The arm unfurled its extremity and hovered it over Luna's head like a deconstructed hooded hair dryer. When her frustration was about to come out in loud bursts of anger, the domed extremity closed on Luna's face until the only thing uncovered were her eyes. A smoke hissed inside the dark helmet that enveloped her, and the screen flashed the numbers *10*...*9*...8. The numbers appeared doubled, blurry, jumping in and out of themselves, 7...6...*5*. She could barely keep her eyes open, *4*...*3*...*2*... She gave in. *1*.

It was like the throbbing of an irregular heartbeat, the release of an elastic band that was pulled back and was about to snap in two. It was with great force that she was thrusted into the universe, a sin slingshotted toward Goliath, and in her sedated mind, the only possible outcome was to end this forever.

CHAPTER 21

LUNA

Luna awakened with a pain to the left of her sternum that radiated toward her arm. She licked her chapped, bloody lips and forced her burning eyes open to see a blurry sphere in the glass.

"Prepare for landing," the machine said.

"Get this thing off of me!"

As if by command, the dome helmet separated into its layers and raised above Luna's head. Smoke still oozed from it, the chemical reaction that had roused her system awake. She pushed the helmet up and hunched under it to stand and touch the glass. "Where are we?"

The machine's voice echoed through the cabin. "As requested. Colonia. Prepare for landing."

"I never practiced landing."

"Automatic landing engaged."

She slumped in the pilot's seat. "How long before something goes wrong?"

"Fuel analysis... Adequate. Landing gear analysis... Functional. Ship Integrity analysis—"

"OK, OK, I get it. Do your thing. I'll enjoy the view while it lasts."

The ship reached Colonia's orbit and rotated to its descent. During the spin-fall, a flash filled the cabin with blinding light from the sun that was shortly replaced by the colossal Colonia, now in plain view, then the view turned to light again. The ship was close enough to the planet that Luna distinguished clouds and weather systems above the oceans. A relentless vibration took her out of the hypnotic view. An all-consuming flame covered the glass, and the cabin fell into the shadow of a red darkness.

Luna craned her neck to one side, then another, looking for an inch of clear glass and, finding none, gripped the chair's armrests.

"All normal," the machine said. "Worry not."

She closed her eyes. "You should know I don't react well when others try to take control of my life."

"Rest assured, I am programmed to—"

"Shut up, you're not helping. Just hurry."

The ship vibrated and shrieked in pain from the atmospheric pressure. Luna sat, free-falling, with her back facing the planet. In front of her, nothing but the safety of dark matter fading away. The lights died off, leaving the cabin at the mercy of red, dim emergency lights.

"We are on our final descent. Rest assured—"

Luna gripped the armrests even tighter, her scrunched-up face wrinkled and tense. "Shut...up..."

"My apologies."

Waaaaah. Waaaaah. Sounded the distress signal. *Waaaaah.* The siren was deafening.

The machine whispered, "Permission to speak."

"Yes," Luna said. "What is it now?"

"Incoming projectile approaching rapidly. Impact imminent."

Luna opened her eyes. The flames had subsided. The clear view of golden Colonia filled the glass, and in a corner, a small but growing fireball.

"Complex maneuver ahead," the machine said. "Autopilot disengaged."

Luna turned to the ceiling as if the machine's mouth was open above her. "What?"

Silence.

"Ugh." She sat at the flight deck with eyes glued to the fireball and lowered her gaze to the controls. Letters and symbols of unknown origin labeled each one. "That one lowers the landing gear," she said, scanning with trembling fingers for something to tell her "I am the answer." The search ended with her punching the control board. The fireball was close to impact. If only there was more time, she could figure this out, the same way she thought she could figure everything out when she was a kid. But she had now grown to the reality of adult helplessness, one where death seemed to follow her. Why would this time be any different? She closed her eyes and tried to replicate what she had achieved in Arvo by accident, to freeze time, or at least slow it long enough. But miracles belonged to the Origin book, and outside its pages, her life story was told by someone else's words. When she opened her eyes, the fireball was now a missile, its metal body shining in Colonia's sunlight. Luna closed her eyes, her lips rising slightly at the corners. If her shoulders could speak, they would say, "I tried."

The next sound was the sound of a crash, an aerial explosion that shook the ship in its aftermath. Still, the vibration of the ship's path remained. When Luna opened her eyes again, the missile had vanished, and Colonia's soil was visible again.

"Autopilot engaged. Landing sequence initiated."

"No," Luna said. "I think I remember now how he did it."

Luna grabbed the lever with her right hand and hovered her left hand over the landing controls. When the ground was close enough, she pulled slightly on the lever and the ship slowed down, straightening over the ground. A memory of Lucifer landing the ship in Arvo, now as distant as a fading dream, shot through her like an invisible bullet. She wiped her eyes and pressed the last button on the landing routine. The landing gear dropped; she felt its vibration under her seat, its whirring an applause of a successful trip. Then the ship lowered to its graceful descent. She could have sat there and waited in silence for the universe to resolve itself or perish altogether —the ruminations of someone with nothing left to fight for. Then she saw the sword, its hilt and an inch of blade peeking out of its scabbard. She heard the voice of her mother speaking words she had never spoken. "Inaction is a form of action, Luna," Istahar's voice said. "You could sit here in the comfort and safety of this old hunk of metal, but this is not what you were made for, now is it? You're a fighter, Luna. Go. Fight."

CHAPTER 22

LUNA

Michael pushed himself off the ground, massaged his jaw, and spit blood at his side. "Is this the honor that you humans write about at length in your literature? Very well." He stood up, shook dirt off his clothes, and raised a finger. "You had one chance." He smirked, and in a moment, he had traveled thirty feet and was now right in front of Luna. All the hair on her body stood on end, as if she was in the presence of a demonic apparition. He punched her stomach with such intensity that Luna's sight filled with grainy black speckles, and she fell forehead-first on the ground. "You are not worthy." He turned around and walked toward the portal. "Robert, my patience is running out."

As soon as Luna caught her breath, she rose and sent a kinetic air wave that traveled close to the speed of light toward Michael.

Michael turned and absorbed the attack, concentrating all its energy into a single, compacted sphere. "You have learned a few tricks, but you are going to need a lot more than that."

"I already killed one of you."

"My brother Lucifer? His affection for you made him weak." Michael released the compacted sphere toward Luna.

She tried to mimic Michael and held her hands forward to absorb the impact, but instead of stopping it, it sent her sliding back and slamming into the side of a mountain.

"Oh, poor girl. Face it, you are out-powered a million to one," Michael said, holding Luna down with ease.

Luna dug for more. She pushed out against this the same way she had pushed back against every other danger in her life, with unproven bravery and brute force. Her efforts were meaningless against Michael's greatness, which he released with such poise, such ease that the mere image of him throwing his hand open in front of her and hiding the other hand behind his back discouraged her. It was the smirk on his face, the disrespect he had for everything that was her, that urged her on. Her anger clouded her mind and convinced her to throw her knife while rushing at him. Michael knocked the knife off its path, and it landed blade-first on the dirt.

Michael laughed. "Barbaric. Your human blood boils with stupidity. What an embarrassment."

She came at him again, raising large rocks from either side and sending them flying at Michael while picking up her knife from the ground and throwing it at him. He was always a few steps ahead. For each of her attacks, he countered with a sharper, more effective strategy. It was as if he controlled not only physical objects in their environment but time and space as well. His presence existed in all dimensions at once. He disappeared and reappeared next to her or far away.

"Robert," Luna said. "I've seen your power. Maybe the two of us together. Maybe we can—"

"He-he has full control over me. I can't move."

"I can't do this alone," Luna said.

Robert's eyes turned to hers.

"Enough of these games. Now, you,"—Michael picked up Luna from the floor without laying a finger on her, and turned to Robert—"will do as you are told. You will carry out what I have been patiently waiting for. You will carry out your destiny—my will. Bow to your god."

"Let her go!" Robert said, and his body radiated in a bright blue pigment.

"You are powerless against me, you simple, barbaric monkey," Michael said, and with his free hand turned Robert off, powering him down as if he held a cosmic light switch. "Do as I say, or the girl dies."

Luna choked under Michael's diabolical grasp. She levitated with her limbs stretched out as if held in place by invisible chains, two anchored by Hell, and two by Heaven. *The girl will forever exist somewhere in between, casting a shadow over Hell by blocking Heaven's light,* the Seer's writings had read, *She is not of us, nor of them. She belongs to the dimensions.* Another shift birthed within her, a pain she didn't want to run away from, the burden of purpose.

Robert faced the edge of the universe and focused his energy into a single point. He unfolded his hands, spread out his fingers, and the blue light radiated once more, concentrating on his hands. He closed his eyes at the sight of Michael's smirk. Then, his energy shot against the fabric of space, drilling into it with astonishing powers. Dark matter and astral bodies alike seemed to shudder from the vibration— the universe wept.

"Oh, great Ancestor," Michael said, his voice shattering the cosmos, soaring above the opening portal. "How eager am I to see you again. I come bearing gifts, new powers I have been training, perfecting. And I owe it all to you and the time you allowed us to discover them. Thank you. But now, you must perish. Your time is over."

Robert divided the universe in two, and from the horizon came a blinding door that opened before them.

Michael closed his hand in a fist, crushing Luna's bones and throwing her to the ground like crumpled paper. She felt it but didn't scream. It didn't hurt any longer. Nothing mattered to her, not her past or what could happen in an uncertain future. It was all about this moment. And, rather than fighting it, she gave in to the moment, to the celestial light brewing inside of her, the dreaming light of a sunrise, the healing power of letting go. For the first time in her life, there was an assurance in her soul that screamed, *You are enough! You are enough! You are enough!*

From her back, her bones pushed through her skin. Wings extended out. Then more appeared, multiplying into hundreds of wings that seemed to extend to the horizon. She understood the message. She had already fought for the humans and must now fight for the angels. Her body straightened into place, her bones snapping back to their correct position. The wings broke the sword's scabbard and the scabbard fell to the ground. She grabbed the sword from the scabbard and flew toward Robert, who was still opening the portal to completion. "Robert!" Luna said, almost flying through him. She pushed his hands toward the sword's hilt and away from the portal. "For our people." And she aimed at Michael, her wings fluttering and whistling at the end of the world. The only sound. The last action by the last angel.

Michael, mesmerized by the portal, had begun his way to it. "What is this?" he said when Luna curled up behind him, wrapping him with her arms, legs, and wings. She rendered him immobile. "Get away from me, half-bred sin. We should have killed you when we had the chance!"

"Robert. Now!"

PART 8

CURRENT COLONIA

CHAPTER 23

ROBERT

The blade in my hands mirrored my unrecognizable face against the light of the portal.

"What are you waiting for? I can't hold on much longer," Luna said. "Robert!"

The gurgling croak of a raven resonated above me, but looking up, there was nothing but a sky that shivered with the fear of its demise. Then, the raven's grating sound emerged in front of me, and its phantom flight crashed on my chest with thunderous energy. It riddled my body with a sudden rage. I gripped the rigid hilt in my hands and a torrential war cry bellowed out from my throat.

Luna had forced Michael to the ground, though his efforts were gaining strength against her hold. I marched toward them with a vengeful disposition. I flourished the sword with each step. Each breath I savored, each spin of the sword propelled me forward—I had missed carrying a weight I had never known. Clouds accumulated above me, crashing and sending roaring electricity to my body. When I was next to them, I grabbed Michael by the shoulder and thrust the sword back to gain momentum. I hesitated, and Luna rose her eyes to meet mine. The clash of timelines stopped me in my tracks.

"What are you doing, Robert? Do it!"

The echoes of my forefathers argued. *Avenge a generational wound while cutting opening another. One Giant dies, another one is born.*

"Robert!"

I saw her hands slipping, and, with no time for trepidation, I howled and lunged the sword into Michael's heart, through his flesh, bones, and skin, and into Luna.

Michael's body sparked in consuming blue flames. His arms unfurled, skinny, and spikes came out of his elbows, and his face became hideous, almost demonic, with fangs for teeth and black marbles for eyes. His human likeness vanished. A pair of wings broke out from its back, ripping out of his skin. Then more appeared, extending as far as the eyes could see. And the creature burned down to its bones, disappearing into the cosmos, shrieking a soundless shriek.

Luna's body inched forward, held in place by the sword buried in her heart. I embraced her. "No." I touched her face, focusing my energy on her, as if I could recreate once more the life that once possessed her, like pouring the edited soul and voice back into a second draft. But nothing happened.

She forced a smile. "Don't be sad. It was written, human. It was always written." She convulsed, her words coming out in short bursts of unintelligible cries. Her wings had dropped and now fell graciously on the ground. "It was—always—from when we were kids, remember? I told you."

"What?" I said.

"That our moment would come."

In a painless rendition, she left. The only human I had ever felt anything resembling a connection with took her last breath in my arms. A sudden burst of air came out from my mouth and hers, a duality of smoke that intertwined in front of us and dissipated out into the universe, and in a final exhale I felt as light as any human should. I found peace.

I rested her body on Colonia's soil, removed the sword from her insides, and placed it in her hands. I had never seen her so calm. She had never been still. Mark's voice pushed me out of this moment. "Do not ever wallow in the hardships," Mark had said. "Life is the in-between, the spaces formed from the hollow of a sad moment and the euphoria of a happy one."

A breeze blowing in intervals throughout my body called to me. The portal I had opened hummed in the air above us and beckoned my will toward it. *I did this.*

My mother had envisioned it once when I was little, and I had come to her for comfort.

"The teacher said I couldn't read," I had said. "She said it, and all the kids laughed."

She held me close. "You will do great things," she had said. "Mi niño, no llores. All the bullies, the rejections, everything. If you are patient, you'll find the reason for your pain. There's always a reason." Then, when I was calm and falling asleep, she read to me from the Bible. John 10:9 "I am the door: by me if any man enter in, he shall be saved, and shall go in and out, and find pasture."

I stood in front of the blinding portal—the door—on my way to salvation.

CHAPTER 24

ROBERT

obert's eyesight adjusted to the blinding light as if being plunged into it from a deep darkness and was seeing for the first time.

A lonely figure sat on a wooden throne. The room was bare, gray, lifeless. He wore a crown that appeared heavy, yet he made it look easy, as if he had nothing but a feather sitting over his head. His eyes were exhausted, the exhaustion that only comes from extreme conscientiousness.

"My sons. I erred in believing they could settle their differences," He said.

My legs trembled with the immensity of his voice, and I stood there with everything to say, but no air to say it. Then I shook my head, and my voice came out before my thoughts stopped it. "I'm here on behalf of humanity to take back what you took from us."

"Free will took it, not me."

"Bullshit," I said, stepping forward. "You're responsible for creating the Archangels and setting them loose."

His face grimaced in mourning of the sons he had sent off and would never see again. And in only a few seconds, his face was stoic again. "I will restore the simulation to its last incarnation. But in everything, there must be balance. You must act with extreme caution. Change one thing, change everything. In order to return things as they were, you must lose the knowledge of what might have been."

"What about Luna? Will I remember her?"

"Not her, or me, or any of the events that occurred during or after your acquaintance. Stay in this simulation and keep her dead but alive in your memory, or lose everything and wake up in a reality untouched by my sons, a reality where humans will be on their own, as it should have been."

"Simulation...Is any of this real?"

"It matters not. Digital renditions of the archetypes cannot tell the difference. It is real to you. It is real to all of you, as it is real to me. You think, therefore, you exist. The parameters of your existence do not make a difference unless you are aware of them. In the end, all we have is bits of information."

I looked around. The wooden throne was nothing more than a chair. The heavenly realm was nothing more than a room in a house. The crown in His head was nothing more than a headdress to keep his overgrown hair away from His face. He was not here by choice. Someone or something had abandoned Him. Lost, like all of us. I felt compassion, and a deep sadness overcame me. "Why do you do this?"

"Every living thing needs a purpose."

I let out the accumulated waves of grief I had pushed down into the empty spaces of my soul, and I wept. I figured it out, the impossible equation of my life. *This isn't about me, it never was.* There were things so far outside my understanding that explaining them to me would be as absurd as a conversation between a man and an insect. I let go of my desires, of my goals and ambitions, and aimed to give Him purpose, to make Him feel seen, heard...alive, as I would have hoped for when I was living in the streets. I knelt before him and bowed. "Thank you," I said. "Do unto me your will, Father."

"So it shall be." The wooden chair creaked from the Ancestor's elated rising. He raised his arms, closed his eyes, and filled his lungs.

And everything went dark.
Then light.
Dark.
Light.

I'd never smelled this smell or felt these sheets. I woke up in an unknown house. A buzz on the nightstand. I turned. *Whose phone is that? Where am I?*

I opened my hand. When the phone didn't come flying to me, I picked it up and answered.

"Hello?"

"Robert? Are you up?"

"Who is this? "

"Always with the jokes. Listen, if things keep going well, this might be the weekend. *The* weekend. Do you understand what I'm saying?"

Before the phone woke from a black screen to a name, Laura, I glimpsed at my reflection. Clean shaven, healthy, no darkened bags under my eyes. *This isn't like me.*

"Your novel just might hit the bestseller list."

"Novel? I don't understand. I have written no novels."

She sighed, then continued, "We need to celebrate, even if you don't get it. Where in god's name are you?"

I looked around the room. I wasn't at ground level. *Hardwood floors this high?, not USA.* I stood up, slid a curtain to the side, and looked out the window. Daylight.

"Looks like Bergen."

"Norway?" She almost sounded excited.

"I can see the fish market from here." I also saw cruise ships of various sizes and people sitting in the bars in front of the docks. It looked like early evening, yet I knew better than to trust the Norwegian's midnight Sun to tell me the time. I put the phone in front of me again. 10:30 p.m. displayed across the screen.

"Jesus, this is going to cost me an arm and a leg, isn't it? But hell, that's what excellent agents are for. I'll figure it out. Just sit tight."

Sounds of keys jiggling, zippers zipping, clothes thumping over the bed. She was packing.

"Wait."

The muted sound of a bag landing on a mattress came through my speakerphone. "Yes?"

"What's it called?"

"What?"

"The novel."

She sighed, thinking I was being sarcastic. "444." Click.

I unlocked the phone. And with my thumb still hovering above the screen, I locked it again. *Dream or second chance, I might as well enjoy it while it lasts.* I found a hotel key. Radisson. The layout of the city sprung into my mind. The eateries, the bars, the buses, the tourists, and the locals downstairs.

I ordered the first drink on the menu as an excuse to be among humans, to breathe among humans; to feel alive. I placed my beer on a table and pulled out a chair, away from groups but close enough to still hear their chatter. The beer was too bitter for my taste, but it was a small price to pay to earn my seat at the table. I looked at people who were about to take off and others who had just landed, taking pictures, looking at menus, eating, laughing, with their luggage sitting safely between their feet. I let the beer get warm, mesmerized by the normality of it all. The simplicity of life, if you just let it happen. *Bestseller.* Either I wasn't as big as Laura had built me up to feel, or the book had not broken in Europe yet. I enjoyed the air of confidence it provided me, while giving me the relaxing tinge of anonymity.

It was two in the morning, and the bars were closing for the night.

Unknown among family, I drank alone until another lost soul stopped in front of me.

"Another loner, huh?"

Between the sun dying off and his beard, I could barely make up his face.

"It's a dying breed." Was the first thing I muttered.

He chuckled.

"Is it ok if I sit here? Usually, I prefer to be alone, but today, for whatever reason, I feel like I could use a friend."

"Go ahead."

"I noticed your accent. American? What brings you to Norway?"

"You know, I'm not sure."

"I get it. Half of us feel lost and the others are so busy looking, we don't even know how lost we are. You can do worse than Norway to find lost things. I can tell you that much." He scanned the tables close to us, then turned to me. "Are you a hiker?" His voice sounded familiar, but I couldn't place his accent. It sounded like all the English accents of the world merged into one.

"I can walk."

That made him laugh. It got chilly in Bergen at night, and he had a black beanie that covered half his face with black, long hair coming out the sides, and a bushy beard that moved up and down when he talked. "Have you done the Ulriken steps yet?"

"Doesn't ring a bell."

"Then it's decided. I'll meet you there in the morning, 7:00 sharp, before the heat comes out. I don't know what you're looking for, but if you don't find it when we reach the top, you might as well give it up. You will not find it anywhere."

"I—"

"It's not a question," he said, laughing, pushed the chair back, got up, and disappeared up the cobblestone hill leading to Bergenhus.

What did I get myself into?

. . .

That thought came over me again when I showed up, following my phone's GPS to make sure I got off the right bus stop. What was I doing there?

The man waited for me in front of an open chain-link fence that led to a gravel road. Uphill. Always uphill.

His squinted eyes looked like a grin. "You made it. I thought you would not show up."

"That makes two of us."

A few minutes after, walking over the gravel road that seemed to go on forever, I felt my heart thumping in my chest. I wished it would be over soon. The more we walked, the more we would have to walk to come back down. The embarrassment of an old lady rushing past me prompted me to say anything to distract him. "So what do you do?"

"Said the American. Such an American thing to ask. What do I do? I live. That's what I do."

"How do you make your money, I mean?"

"Ah. I need very little. All I want is to travel the world and make friends with strangers. Europe is good for that. You can hop on and off of trains and busses."

"How do you pay for tickets?"

"I'm a world class entertainer, and I'm cheap. People are glad to dispose of their loose change into my hat for what they get from me. It's surprising how little you need if you're brutally honest with yourself. Ah, we're here."

Finally, I thought. "That was fun."

He laughed again. So much joy. It was almost infuriating. "You're a funny guy. Just a little ahead, now."

"What?"

"The Ulriken steps."

"Do you mean it hasn't started yet?"

He said no, and to not think about the steps ahead as much as the one I was walking over. To turn around every once in a while, enjoy the view, then carry on ahead. It was an inverse world where Heaven seemed connected to Earth, and people were more afraid of what was above them than what was below.

So, I walked one step at a time, like he had said. For a while, at least. Until the old heart thumped again, and I saw spots. I sat over a rock beside the steps. "You know what? You go on ahead, I'll wait for you here."

"Drink some water."

I did.

He looked down at Bergen for a few minutes, then said, "Ok, let's go."

I sprung up without thinking and walked beside him, a little routine we repeated every few hundred steps.

After an hour, I pushed my body over the last step. The view was spectacular.

"Quite something, huh? I bet you don't feel so lost anymore."

"I don't know what I'm feeling."

I had a 365 degree view of the city and beyond. I saw the cruise ships coming and going. He told me some of them headed to Flåm and a visit to the fjords. Everything looked so familiar. I took a moment to see, really see, the Earth expanding before me, and I looked up at the sky with the fear that a meteor was hiding just beyond a cluster of clouds.

At the top of the walkway, a thousand, three hundred and thirty-three steps later, was a small restaurant with baked snacks, drinks, and an a la carte menu.

"Order something. I need some water on my face. Back in a second," the bearded man said, and went to the restrooms. I walked with my chest puffed into the restaurant, looking for some kind of reward.

The bearded man reminded me of someone. But I don't think I ever knew someone who exuded so much lust for life.

A line had formed in front of the cashier, made up with the sweaty champions that stuck to the steep path. Six people stood before me, and through the holes of the line I saw flashes of the cashier, picking out baked goods with a pair of tongs, giving out menus, and taking payments. She moved with ease, almost floated with the grace of someone who had mastered life. Someone who unfolded its ultimate secret: just live. Her smile was so bright, I could almost see it through the dark souls doubtlessly living inside the people in front of me.

I was the next customer, behind a newlywed couple who snuggled side by side. They must have been six feet tall a piece. When they finally finished paying for their feast, I saw her in all her glory.

"How can I help you?" she said, a smile stamped on her face.

I froze. How? But why was I surprised? Had any of our encounters been normal? Or made any sense? It was her; I was sure of it.

"I'll have one of those," I pointed at the pastry, "and a water, please."

"Sure." She picked out the pastry and placed it in a folded napkin. "Water's over there." She pointed to a fridge next to me, and I confirmed it. The half moon birthmark on her forearm.

Just as I was about to say something, she turned her face to the kitchen behind her.

"Hey, Mom! We're running out of pastries."

An older lady leaned into view, with the biggest smile to ever fill a face. "More pastries? You got it, dear," the lady said, and the smile grew even wider. "My love." Then her eyes met mine. "Isn't she beautiful?"

"What?" I said and caught the pastry just as it slid out of its napkin.

"My daughter."

"Mom!" She apologized for her mother and handed me the receipt. Our fingers grazed for only a moment in the transaction, and I saw in her eyes the entire universe as we had traced it in another life.

I told her it wasn't a problem. *Change one thing, change everything.*

Before I turned around, the old lady waved at me with slanted eyes, a bobbing head, and a smile someone can only muster when they are exactly where they should be. It was a good wave, a genuine one. I waved back, though I don't know if my face was as inviting as hers. In the grand scheme of things, I knew what it meant. *Hello and goodbye.*

I searched for a table as if it mattered and sat facing her. Luna. She didn't remember me, of course. Then again, did anything really happen? It seemed I had turned into an author: a professional imagineer of things. Maybe I had also concocted this fallacy, this nice little heaven for myself. But why would I be the only one to remember everything? Not Heaven. Hell.

The bearded man came walking into the restaurant and gave a smiling nod when he saw me. He had his beanie in his hands, his hair wet and combed back, and his beard tied neatly in a knot. I saw more of his face than I had seen until now.

It couldn't be.

"Pol?"

His eyes now covered most of his visible face.

In shock, he said, "Do you know me?"

"It was bound to happen," Pol set his beanie on the table, turned his neck to the door, and back at me. "You're the first one to recognize me out here. Don't make a scene, please?"

"Scene?"

"I don't want people to ask for autographs and all that. I like to come here." He turned his neck at the door again. "I don't want to stop coming here."

After he turned his head to face the door a third time, I knew it. It wasn't the door he was observing, but the woman behind the counter. Luna.

"Do you like her," I said, "that woman?" My eyes shifted between Luna and him.

"Yes," he lowered his head and scratched his hair. "I'm embarrassed to say. I do. It's my favorite part of the day."

"You mean you walk those steps every day to be here?"

"It's worth it for her."

"Didn't we see a funicular coming up?"

"We did."

"You don't have to walk, then."

"I like to. It makes me feel...worthy."

The words were painful as they came out of my mouth. But she wasn't Luna. At least not my version of her. And this wasn't life as I had known it. In this reality, I was nothing but a guest. An intruder. "Why don't you go talk to her?"

It took some convincing for him to walk up to the empty counter, beanie in hand.

I left just as she greeted him. I couldn't bear it.

Sometimes I wished my ending had been a dream, or that I had never woken up at all, and instead drifted away into eternal darkness. That humans could control how much life to experience— nothing more, nothing less—and, knowing the highest high, could make a clean break at the vertex. But I did wake up. Sometime, somewhere. Here, but not here. A parallel universe. One where I might be everything I wanted to be, but had to shed everything else.

I stopped five hundred steps down the path of Ulriken and looked down at the city radiating with life. The mountain air had cooled off my lungs, and my heart soothed down into the background. Somehow, I couldn't shake off the feeling that Norway was my home, that my blood was rooted in its history; that I was where I was supposed to be. People were passing me by, some walking up, some making their way down. I continued my slow descent back to humanity. One life for many. So it is, so it would always be.

I had grabbed a loose tree branch from the ground and used it as a walking stick. Then my phone vibrated, and I was already at the end of the path.

"Robert? Where the hell have you been? Have you seen it yet?"

"Seen it?" I stopped and planted the tree branch into the soil with such force, I expected blood to ooze from the dirt.

"Stop playing games. Listen, you're going to want to be sitting down for this. Are you ready?"

My eyes shot at the view. I don't think I had ever stood so straight in my life. "I can handle it."

"Your novel just hit bestseller."

THE END

Thank you for reading the 444 saga. If you enjoyed it and would like to help support me, the best thing you can do is leave a review on Amazon.

Feel free to leave a review on Goodreads, YouTube, or your personal blog—reviews help other readers determine if a book is to their liking, and authors, especially independent authors, rely on such word of mouth to get their books in front of new readers.

You can also join my email mailing list at https://relvingonzalez. com/subscribe/, where I give free books just for joining. The list receives weekly updates on my next books, as well as recommendations of other authors you might like. You'll also receive some free short works and a behind-the-curtains peek at my writing process and daily life.

"No glorious plan ever existed without a cautionary measure," a voice said, its confidence shattering in the silence of an empty universe. "From the fire, I arise to take what is rightfully mine. If a throne would not be given to me, I will create my own. If He does not deem me worthy of a universe, I shall take one, not by force, but by my cunning mind. I will repopulate the worlds. Not only Earth, no, but every world that can harbor life. I will leave no planet empty. Every creature will bow down to my name; my name, and my power. The Ancestor's Will is no more. He has moved on and left my ashes to burn here eternally alone. But from the ashes, the only true Archangel has risen. A shadow, once cast, always follows the light, and as long as there is light, I will exist. Lucifer is my name. I will do alone what could not be done with an army of angels and humans. By my will, and not His, I will repair the fabric of destiny and bring order to the chaos." Lucifer's body formed from the ashes, stronger and more powerful than ever. He rose in his full Archangel form, with wings proudly outstretched, his long hair pouring down on his shoulders, and his tall body appeared to tower above the firmament itself.

"But you are not alone," a voice said.

When Lucifer turned around, a knife stabbed him in the heart. It was unmistakeably Luna's knife, its decorative hilt sticking out of his chest. When he turned his gaze up, he said, "It cannot be. You? Insolent—rat—" He fell to his knees, landed on the ground on his back.

"It was always written for me to put all these things in motion. The Seer almost found me out and turned me in once, but I took away his sight. Oh, how dark those days were. But He shepherded me back into His Path. My faith was strong, and He delivered. It was also written for the knife to be buried in that spot, waiting for me. I dirtied my hands digging it out, but I was used to the dirt. It has been a tiresome, long life."

Lucifer gagged on his own blood and looked up to make sure it hadn't been a mirage. Towering over him, coming in and out in front of the sun, was Daniel.

"Finally, I can rest." Daniel sobbed. "Thank you, Lord. I hope I have brought you joy. I hope I have done your Will justice." He pulled the knife from Lucifer and stabbed himself several times in the stomach. Blood came splashing out of his mouth, and he fell next to Lucifer. He stared at the sky and saw a spectre of the brightest light. "I can see it now, Lord. Your light is so beautiful, so majestic. Forgive me for my sins. I am only but a weak angel. But I did my best for you. Against my nature, against my instincts and temptations, I did not kill him or her—sun and moon—as you had requested. Power beckoned me. Oh, it did. It took me down dark alleys, but your light always guided me back, and I carried your will even when it was such a heavy burden. Oh, my kind Ancestor, how beautiful and eternal is your light. I am eager to meet you." He grabbed the knife and slid it across his neck and laughed, with bouts of blood coming out of the corners of his mouth. He stretched his hands to the sky, and the spectre of light grabbed him from the soil and lifted him up, embraced him, and, together as one, faded away.

THE VOID BEYOND THE WALLS

A PREVIEW

CHAPTER 1

A deer's cry shrilled near a hill behind our house. I was afraid to follow the vocalization disturbing the untroubled night. As I paced in my room, something urged me to put on my shoes. I had to check if it was human. When I came close, it tried to run away, but crumbled to the ground. Its back was warm, that I do remember, and also the blood. I gathered what I could find in my mother's medicine cabinet and rushed back to the forest.

"No running inside the house," Mother said, bending at the waist and looking into the oven.

The body was gone, and below the penumbrae of the trees, a trail of blood tracked its way deeper into the woods. I took a step forward but lost to trepidation, and in minutes I was back facing the house, and saw the window in front of the kitchen sink.

"What's wrong?" Mother meant the tears in my eyes as I walked into the house.

"Nothing."

With the bathroom door locked, I emptied my pockets on the countertop. The bottles rattled on their way to the medicine cabinet, and I turned each flask around so that the labels pointed forward, and the jars lined in ascending order; just the way Father liked them. I sat very still near the open window in my bedroom and closed my eyes. The wind changed when he was near, and all the creatures in the grass and dirt silenced and bowed to his arrival.

Every morning before brushing my teeth, I would rush into the shores of the woods with a heart ballooned with hope only to find a family of trees harboring nothing more than lonely soil on their feet. I yelled all kinds of names into the leafy ocean in hopes of a rescue boat. Other times, even a shipwreck would have done. On those occasions, the water was not on the horizon, but overflowing my eyes. I headed down the path, as far as I dared, deaf to my ears, deaf to the morning, deaf to the house, and I hoped that maybe when I came back, it would have turned itself into a home, that this path led to the same place, but different.

It was my disguise to pick apples from the trees and offer them as a tribute during breakfast. That seemed to please him. He would smirk and press hard on my shoulder, and I knew I had done well. The echo of my offering would not last until the evening, though, and that was when things usually got rough.

People that grew up blind in darkness could not recognize when it had spilled over beyond the length of their limbs. Over time, it splattered on the floorboards and flooded the other rooms of the dwelling. A girlfriend I had in middle school once went with us on a family outing and asked me what was wrong with my father. After watching him frowning at nothing at all, staring at the ground for minutes at a time outside a store where my mother was shopping, pulling my mother out of the store, and hurrying us up the stairs to the movie theater to a showing that would not start for another hour, she said, "It looks like something terrible happened to him." But I didn't know. My father, it seemed to me, appeared one day on this Earth out of nowhere, like a thunderstorm on a sunny day forecast. I didn't get many life lessons or family history from him, only glimpses that I rather not know. He would throw these gems out into the air only when it was just the two of us in the car, but by the time I caught them, they had turned into charcoal, disintegrating and rotten.

"Do you know what your grandma used to do when I was a kid?" he said. "She would lie in bed, motionless, for minutes at a time, and I stood there calling her name and rocking her still body. And just when I had given up, and imagined my life without my mother, she would open her eyes and laugh."

Then, he would speak about his work as if the two belonged to the same conversation.

"You know, Son. Sponge painting can hide minor flaws and imperfections on a wall, but it's all about the technique. The trick is to dab the sponge into the corners of the imperfection and work outward."

He did not like awkward silences, and he filled them up with snapshots of his life, like what he said one time while turning the corner of Oliver and Sunset Lane.

"Once, while I was living with my aunt," he said, "a group of Mexican kids beat me into a pulp and left me laying on the ground for hours until my aunt came back from work."

Over the years, these facts popped up and created a Picasso image of my father. It was the rugged terrain on which I poured the slab of my life, and it went like this.

My body punished me for not looking after my mind and letting my dragons feast whenever they fancied my flesh. It didn't matter what I ate, my intestines exploded every morning on my way to school. It was good that old Ms. Ruth lived right next to it and let me use her bathroom. The things I did to that toilet, I wouldn't wish upon my worst enemy, Duncan.

A classroom was a hostile environment where kids grew at all sorts of disproportionate rates. Some of them still brought action figures to class in third grade, while others rolled up their already short sleeves to show whatever could pass as muscle. It was possible to imagine some of these kids holding a cigar on a ledge, blowing smoke into the open air while looking at some distant memory of their youth. By then, the girls flocked in groups and gravitated toward some of the boys. The boys noticed, too. It was hard to tell what came first, the girls or the balls. These boys were fearless. They had no shame because they had no predator. I wondered about life without a predator; it was all I did when Duncan locked me in a dark locker. I learned that while our seats were next to each other, all the kids sat in different classrooms, intertwining across different realities.

"I missed you today, dear," Ruth said over the school fence.

"Oh, hi, Ms. Ruth. I skipped breakfast today."

"Dean, let's go!" my dad said from the car.

"Bye, Ms. Ruth."

"What did I tell you about talking to that woman? What the hell happened to you?"

The dampened sound of the unsealed car door numbed my hands. I never got it on the first try. "I fell."

"Inside a trash can? How many times do I have to tell you to make sure the door closes right?" He leaned over me, reaching for the door, reeking of alcohol. My father unlatched the door and, with a powerful pull, closed it tight like it was nothing. It shook the car and the contents of my stomach with it. "Can you believe this guy? Come on, let's move it!"—he honked several times—"This country, I tell ya. No one knows how to coexist; everyone is trapped in their little world. No regards to the fellow man. Come on!"—he honked again—"Enough of this." He slammed on the reverse and drove the car straight into a steel pole. "I'm such a spaz. I'm such a spaz. I'm such a spaz."

I put on a face my friend Michael showed me at lunchtime; it was really funny.

"What is that? What are you doing?"

I remained on guard until the beast inside my father retreated. The storm cleared, and my father laughed.

"All right, kid. Let's go home."

I was late for class the next morning, but I swear I didn't want to be. Duncan, the bastard, had put me in a locker again. "And I better not hear you moving in there," he said.

I enjoyed collecting things; I always have. Dissected butterflies and boxes of trading cards filled the shelves of my walls. It drove Mother crazy. She liked things spotless. My mother begged me to clean my room until one day I came home, and it was already neat, the cards stowed away, and the butterflies were somewhere in the city dumpster. When Hurricane Duncan hit, I started carrying a small pocket lantern. Once inside the day's locker, I turned on the lantern and looked around. Being in a locker made me feel good. I didn't enjoy thinking unless I was forced, and I thought a lot in those lockers. When I finished thinking, I grabbed a small item from it to take home, just to remind myself of the real good thinking I did. The janitor opened the locker when the halls were silent enough for him to hear my breathing. By the end of the school year, I had collected one item from every locker. It was quite a collection, which I hid from my mother's clean hands.

Love is knowing what another person might be willing to do for you and never asking such a thing from them.

We were in the middle of the forest, my father and I, and the first flakes of snow had already fallen.

"Again," Father said.

"I can't do it."

"I said, again."

The axe fell heavily on the thick stump, but it didn't make a dent.

"I don't think it will crack," I said. My skinny arms were shaking.

"You need a better grip. Give me those." He took away my gloves.

"But I'll get frostbite."

"Stop whining and go again."

Flesh to wood, I grabbed the axe, and descended my arms in a fury.

"Again."

"Oh my god, what happened?" Mother said as soon as the screen door opened.

"We have firewood, that's what happened," my father said, threw a pile of wood in the fireplace, and opened a can of beer.

"Let me take care of that." Mother put my hands under the running water in the sink, and I watched the tiny Red Sea as it swirled and flushed down the pipes. I imagined it clean and purified of my blood and flowing clear to another house, and my blood floating stagnant in a dark chamber among the secret blood of the world. She knelt with a roll of paper towels to wipe the floor, but a few of the drops had set in and tainted the cherry hardwood. Regardless, she tried a combination of chemicals, but failed to undo the damage. Days later, she came in with a new rug, placed it over the trail of stains, and cooked dinner.

"Again," I said in the schoolyard. A crowd surrounded Duncan and me as he punched the steel locker door with all his strength. His bloody knuckles were turning purple. The tears had exploded from his eyes and now flowed freely for everyone to see.

"Again," I said. I had grown three feet high and bulked out to the sides.

It was a disappointment when I opened my eyes and saw my mother sitting in the corner of my bed.

"Dean, it's time." She meant to go to school, and all the other good parts of a weekday. "Eggs are on the table."

"I'm not hungry," I said and held on to my growling stomach.

———

As a child, I was the only boy in the neighborhood without a television set lighting up the living room. Father said that no son of his would grow up carrying around a melting brain, skipping along to the sounds of June's promise while the world blew itself to bits. He used to get all philosophical like that sometimes, and then he put on his daily play edited with effects of breaking glass and fists to the wall. Mom looked through the faux wood blinds at his car snaking in. She gauged his alcohol level as he fought with the car's door handle and made haste to decide on the best place to put me. Sometimes, we would take our seats at the dinner table and play our parts of a normal family. He cursed both mortals and gods, trying to force us to meet his frustration level. After the fight became a monologue, he stumbled his way to the bed. Mom ran after him to take off his shoes and rub his brilliantine oiled hair until he fell asleep, letting out the victory scream with a sigh of relief. Other times she would hide me away in our secret place, a hole in a sidewall of my closet with a rug door that hung from an anchor. He came into my room looking for me, and my mom swore I was sleeping over at a friend's house. He hit her until he couldn't discern her still body from my bedposts, and I looked through the porosity of the fiber in the rug until it was safe to emerge again, trying not to reveal my whereabouts from an onset of excessive shivers.

Once during recess, some schoolboys and I formed a circle in the yard, some standing, others sitting on the steel structures scattered around the playground.

One boy, the tallest one, was breaking a twig into smaller pieces and throwing them at the ground one by one.

"Sometimes he's just rude," he said, "and won't buy me any toys."

"I know what you mean. I got a stupid book for my birthday this year," one boy said.

"Bummer For Ya!"

At that moment, I realized that something connected most people together. They were like clothespins hanging tight to an invisible thread that spanned timelines and state lines, weaving together the human experience in one cohesive pattern. I looked at this pattern from the outside and nodded my head in confusion, watching the rest of the boys as they yelled in unison.

"They turn my TV off at 10:00 p.m. at my house!"

The other boys all turned around to this small freckled one who, mostly, kept to himself. The shock came from both the sentence and the vessel speaking it.

"Sneak out of the bed after they fall asleep and turn it on again. That's what I do!"

The next morning, the small, freckled boy was quieter than usual. At lunch time he sought the group with a tear in his eye.

"Hey!"

All the boys stopped laughing and lowered their field of vision to listen to what the small boy had to say.

"You forgot to tell me to lower the volume before I turned on the TV again!"

They roared with laughter, and the wave infected me as well. And the thought of the thread came over me again. This time I realized that if there was a thread, at least I was still hanging on to it, even if by a small, lost strand of it. This filled me up for the rest of the week.

———

My understanding of my parents' life before me is so convoluted and twisted that I usually make a story up, or just brush it off with the bristles of omission. I know my mother didn't have an easy upbringing.

It had been pouring, and there was nothing to do. School had been out, plays cancelled, the television blown. My young mother let her hair fall down where it may, unspoiled of its nature, uncured. A gunshot came about, loud and piercing, and vibrated up to the steps of her loft. Seconds later, another shot, and a thud. She remained seated, as history had taught her to not show herself until called for. Then the sirens arrived, and a herd of officers opened the door.

A uniformed youngster, Lucas, spoke first, "Oh God," he stowed away his gun. "Dad, over here!"

The old captain pulled himself up and started climbing up the stairs. "How many times have I told you? When we're on duty, it's captain!" On the last step, he saw my mother sitting still on the edge of her bed. "What's your name?"— silence—"All right, Lucas. Bring her down."

"Dad—"

"Just do it," he turned it into a whisper. "I have enough shit to deal with already."

The scanner hawked and beeped. "10-35. Two victims."

Meanwhile, Lucas held my mother's hand, careful not to break a bone. She was frail. Maybe it was the frailty, or her big, blue marble eyes, but he loved her from that moment until his death. He loved both of them. Mary, my mother, then later John, my father, as Mom spread her wounded wings and flew into his perverted nest.

She'd met my father at a state fair. Lucas had insisted my mother had to get out of that house, away from the phantoms, and plant a goalpost somewhere in the future. Anything to look forward to. At the fair, my father stood leaning against a steel rail outside the circus tent. Lucas waved and nodded and pulled Mom towards him. Lucas introduced them. She always told this story with great hesitancy, with a plain fear of getting the facts too polished.

For years, my parents were married with no children. The neighbors spoke of this in secret, but shot their laser eyes publicly, as to say without saying that there must be something wrong with them. One time, one of many, Father arrived at their doorstep with the stench of alcohol. Mom was with child nine months later. Lucas knew the child was not the result of a love-struck romance, as that same night Father had left his house in a haste. Mom withdrew more so than before. She did not submit her famous pie recipe for the neighborhood competition that year. She set her eyes and goals into the care of her boy, Dean.

They had inherited the house of her childhood, which in time proved too painful to live in. Mom convinced Father she wanted to move. We moved to a cabin just outside the city, at Father's request, to not move so far away from his job.

A few years later, Mom could tell from the shaking sheets of zinc and how dark it had become at the cusp of the afternoon hours, that this evening would have to end without her usual post dinner walk through the forest. And there had to be a forest, since she waved the unfinished, long streets and dim light posts of the city away years ago, around the time she woke up with a purple eye that layers of Naked Cream Dust could not cover.

The trees Mom had marked always led her to a stream she had discovered in one of her walks. "He'll be OK for a few hours," she had whispered to herself the day before, only to open the door to a sleeping husband that stank of a failed attempt of sobriety, and thus another broken promise, and a son inside a hole in his closet wall, covered with a thick veil of wool knitted patterns. The desk had an open hardcover book, which she closed. *Texas Wildflowers* was the title.

Mom set a basket full of wet clothes on the bed and bounced her knuckles off the wall in a musical pattern. She spoke first, "You mustn't leave the book sitting in the open like that. You did well."

"Is he gone?"

"The next best thing. Sleeping."

"Did you find any?"

She reached into her pocket, unfurling her hand to reveal a handful of golden, wrinkled berries.

"Now?"

"No, he must eat them."

"When, then? Tonight?"

"Tonight."

"Wake me up if I'm sleeping."

"I will."

But my father did not wake at all until the next morning, not even for his midnight snacking raid. Mother had the berries hidden in the cookie jar at the edge of the top kitchen cabinet, away from his Viking eyes.

"What time is it?" Father said.

"10:00 a.m."

"Is the boy still sleeping?"

"I think so. I'll get him." She stopped him from getting up.

The lack of light had my circadian rhythm in disarray. My eyes opened to my mother sitting on my bed, and the room was dark as if the cabin sat covered whole under a twenty-foot wool veil.

"Is it time?" The wind forced tree branches to sway and scratch the log walls of the cabin.

A timer went off back in the kitchen.

"Come."

Mother set the table with three plates and cutlery on the side of the porcelain, wrapped in a fabric napkin. Father made his presence known by disheveling my hair and landing on his seat like a missile in reverse. He had a newspaper in his hand, which he swatted open, and read in silence. I looked at my mother, who turned back to get the pancakes out of the pan and onto the plates. A confused boy could not move on with the next thought while sitting on a lingering curiosity. Were they in the pancakes? Ground in the coffee, maybe? Mom crossed eyes with mine across the table and directed my stare to the top of the kitchen cabinets, where a red can peaked down on us. Mom smiled. I chuckled in relief, ready to enjoy the pancakes.

"Enough!" Father slammed his fist on the table with a ferocity, the wave of which the spoons and forks could not escape.

"He didn't mean to, John."

Father engaged once more with the compelling news article at hand, unbeknownst to his boy's attention on the assortment of construction tools his father had assembled on the kitchen counter to prepare for a day of honest work. Some tools were sharp, others blunt, but he could take his pick of either type, and forever end this horror, or at least exchange it for a lesser one.

The morning went uneventfully outside of my mind. Father's truck tracks were still visible in the mud in front of the house as the first sprinkles of the storm had landed. He ended his work journal early that day when the newscasters relegated the governor's stay at home order. His time away, though, was enough for Mother and I to spend quality time together scheming of ways to get the berries inside the belly of the beast. We decided that ground in his dinner and drink were the best of ways. I had opted for the mortar and pestle instead of the grinder. I had mentioned something about enjoying the process, but Mom did not make a fuss about it.

Their hugs never lasted long, but that day she pulled away quicker than usual. She scrunched her nose, focusing on his good spirits and on the rose in his hands.

"I got you this."

"Thank you." She inhaled the fantasy. "Food is almost ready."

A storm brewed in full strength, as they said it would. Our family sat at the dinner table, as Mother and I had planned. Father chewed merrily on the chicken with berry sauce, now his favorite dish. My shoulders felt light for the first time. After dinner, Mother pulled me aside and unveiled the golden berry dust had not made it into the sauce but lay scattered outside the kitchen window. My shoulders tensed at the thin veil of change, the promise of second chances, the tracks of the tires of his pickup truck, the forest, the ever damming forest, and the peaks of buildings sneaking on the horizon.

Most of the kids at school had divorced parents. I had parents that stuck together for dinners like that. My stomach churned in terror in the anticipation of something setting things off.

Until something did.

"Don't worry, kid, I'll take care of it," Lucas Jackson said.

Lucas Jackson had become a family friend and local Texas Ranger sheriff. He patted a white blanket on my shoulder. The lights of ambulances and police cars, blue, red, and white, blinked in harmony all around me. I must have been twelve. They explained to me that someone had entered our house and killed both my parents, though at the time I couldn't make sense of it. The doors of the ambulance hung wide open, and I sat, legs dangling in the air, on the hard carcass of the patient compartment. They rolled out two bodies on stretchers, covered in blue bags, and tightened to the bed with a trio of red strings.

"You'll be OK, kid," Lucas said.

A nurse ran towards me with a wet towel that turned red as she cleaned my hands.

Through the years, that night has revealed to me piece by piece, like flinders of a splinted two by four, pricking my feet whenever I become ever so close to normalcy. I remember my father getting home with the mist of alcohol in his breath. I could smell it from my room. That night, fear creeped in with the alcohol. The wall became my bed, and after the usual struggle, the night became silent. Even more so than usual. I couldn't hear my mother sobbing on the other side of the wall. It was dead silent. I built enough courage to grow out of my hide. I crawled out of the hole, legs first. My father was kneeling down, searching for signs of life on my mother's lifeless body. I grabbed the black little league bat with white stripes my dad got me as a birthday gift years before. He turned around for long enough to make the son out of the figure that swung him to death.

The news never reported it, and the town never talked of it. Lucas forced his wife to take me into their home. At their home, the Jacksons treated me at arm's length, leaving enough distance for a quick getaway should it become necessary. In the outside world, parents pulled their children closer, and whispers became the new town dialect. Uplifting quotes said that life is what you make of it. In reality, your life is also what life makes of you. The way the world reacted to you shaped the way you reacted towards it. It became an infinite tennis court, swinging the ball back and forth harder and harder, until one becomes more aggressive than the other, pushing the other into submission, ending its life, and saving its own. One morning, I woke up in the Jackson's guest bedroom to a book neatly placed on the nightstand. The meditations of Marcus Aurelius guided me back into the light, or at least into my version of light, as bright as it was possible.

By eighteen, I had inherited my father's construction business. It survived in dire straits until I was old enough to manage it. I rebuilt it completely, destroying its crumbling infrastructure and putting it back together, hammering it down to what I knew was right. I fired the dead weight and hired the helium filled brains of the young and restless. Business blossomed to greater heights over the next few years. The awards and projects poured in, like the perfect foundation of a thousand story skyscraper, inching every second higher towards the sky.

The town soon forgave and forgot, and I became the local hero. It's funny how that goes. The company boomed out of what they criticized in the state papers. We hired only townsfolk and talked plainly to our clients, explaining the what and the why. My guys were never knocking on doors holding a tablet and vomiting sales pitches, or instructed to request an in-house estimate that allowed them to find the potential client's demographics and place the quote on either side of the pricing sliding scale. They sat comfortably at our office and waited for customers to seek them out. While others compartmentalized, awarding only one menial job per pair of hands, snatching all power and replacing it with a neatly packed paycheck, we integrated, and one man did the job of five, empowering their path to become as wide as they wanted it to become. We were structuring artisans. We knew everything from the nails to the elevations, from the current of the waters, to the flow of electrons. Our waitlist spanned months. We brought in sacks of coins until one day we didn't.

I had asked Lucas for a cadaver dog. He, of course, obliged, no questions asked. Back when my father was still alive, sometimes, when he got home sober, he would bring me candy he would carry in his work briefcase. After a while, I came to crave it so much that I would look inside the briefcase in his car before scanning his level of sobriety. Sometimes I would find a couple of Texan bars. Other times I would find the silver end of a belt as it struck my face for being an inquisitive brat. There was this one time when the briefcase was full of papers. No candy bars. But in the corners of the papers, there were various heart-shaped drawings with the words "John and Lucas" in them. I never opened the briefcase again. But my father found out, and he became much more violent, and Lucas much more giving.

While I managed my father's corporation, I took the German Shepard, Glory, with me on my business trips. Every trip was a chance to come that much closer to perfection. Until one day, the bodies were not detectable to the dog's olfactory acuteness. Through the layers of drywall, their desperation released in an eternal sigh. It was I who alleviated their burden. Only I could expedite their peace.

***

A scorpion and a frog converged at the boundary of a treacherous stream. Desperation overcame the scorpion, who asked to ride along the frog's back to the other side.

The frog hesitated and asked, "How can I be so sure you won't sting me?"

"Because if I do, we both drown."

Halfway across the water, the scorpion stung the frog.

"Why?" the frog asked, sinking to its death along with the scorpion.

To which the scorpion replied, "It's my nature."

I considered this prologue often in daydreams that others would think as nightmares. Where a person would lie frightened and immobile in night terrors, trying futile attempts at opening their eyes, I would force myself back to sleep just to see them through.

Men possess an unspoken darkness, a dark place far away in the distance after the forest from which they come and go when they let loose and find their way again. My permanent property is in the purlieu of that forest. I am the divider of souls. A decider. A threshold back from madness. I am what lost souls must get through to install themselves back into society.

My mother had been an insightful one. She used to tell me a story of when I was a baby. Mother had felt like staying home that day, but my father insisted on driving to our grandparents' house to show me off to them. She begrudgingly packed my things and set them inside the car's trunk.

"You haven't installed the car seat, John," my mother pointed out.

"Why didn't you remind me earlier? Forget about it. There's no time now. Just bring him in front of you."

Mother said she gave him the look of a thousand deaths.

"Come on. Don't be like that. It's only five blocks."

Mother said she insisted still, but persuasive as my father's fists were, she assented.

I got a pretty good knock on the head a few minutes later, at the intersection of Javalin and 649. My father saw blinking yellow lights as bright green, and his volition to save two seconds would be the thunder that shattered all mirrors, the birds that flocked from left to right, the indoor ceremony of opening umbrellas, the shoes on the table, or so have explained the doctors. The sky became my leaning ladder, and if I wanted to walk, I would have to do so underneath it.

Apart from being unconscious for thirty seconds during that car crash when I was a baby and my head hitting the dashboard of our sedan, the routine beatings from my alcoholic daddy following a frustrating day trying to save his company and my uncle's games involving a red blindfold and wandering hands when my parents got rid of me for a weekend, my childhood was somewhere between the American standard and the American dream. I remember cartoons of a sort that overstayed their welcome into my teenage years right around when the bullying began. I also recalled the disappointed faces of interested female counterparts when I did not make a move when others would. The stages of life often trapped me, either a previous one or one that lay undiscovered for light years ahead.

The entelechy of a tadpole was to develop into a frog. This was who I became because that was who I was. It was not a trait I flaunted, but something I must haul away with every step, dragging it across state lines and continents. Wherever I went, there it was. I was neither vengeful nor vigilant. I did not hunger for it with the stinging power thirst of a Roman senator, nor was I an Athenian claiming the approval of my public by applause, but I must carry the weight that I was given either way.

My mother used to fold a piece of paper if she held it in her hands for more than a few seconds, stacking and flattening its creases until it would not fold any longer. The house was full of thick, square papers I picked up, guided by the rays of half-light coming through the kitchen windows. It was in her nature. The monsters lived in the anxious swaying of the body or an involuntary wagging of the legs. It kept the plates towered, and the cutlery ordered, the lawn green, and the cars clean. It was there, right in the middle of compulsion and phobia, where the nature of men lived. Killing was in my nature.